A HUNGER LIKE NO OTHER
is also available as an eBook.

PRAISE FOR
IF YOU DARE

"Filled with heated passion and wonderful repartee from one of romance's fastest rising stars!"

—*Romantic Times* Magazine (Top Pick)

"A classic romantic adventure that will leave you breathless!"

—*New York Times* bestselling author Julia Quinn

"Kresley Cole's voice is powerful and gripping, and *If You Dare* is her steamiest yet!"

—*New York Times* bestselling author Linda Lael Miller

"*If You Dare* is a tale that sizzles, generating heat that will scorch the reader. Kresley Cole has a definite talent for creating exciting stories and characters who will keep you on the edge of your seat."

—readertoreader.com

PRAISE FOR
THE CAPTAIN OF ALL PLEASURES

"Kresley Cole captures the danger and passion of the high seas in this electrifying debut."

> —*New York Times* bestselling author Joan Johnston

"In her truly winning debut novel, the very talented Kresley Cole takes readers on the adventures of a lifetime. . . ."

> —*New York Times* bestselling author Susan Wiggs

"*The Captain of All Pleasures* is an exciting, sensuous story that will thrill you at every turn of the page."

> —readertoreader.com

"Fast-paced action, heady sexual tension, steamy passion. . . . Exhilarating energy emanates from the pages of this very smart and sassy debut."

> —*Romantic Times* Magazine
> (Reviewers' Choice Award Winner)

"In *The Captain of All Pleasures*, author Kresley Cole has created a spitfire for a heroine and a hero who is a temperamental, passionate hunk. . . . There are many steamy scenes for those who enjoy passion in their read, and those who hunt for a book that mixes action and sensuality will not go away unhappy."

> —America Online

ACCLAIM FOR
THE PRICE OF PLEASURE

"A splendid read! The sexual tension grips you from beginning to end."

—*New York Times* bestselling author Virginia Henley

"Sexy and original! Sensual island heat that is not to be missed."

—*New York Times* bestselling author Heather Graham

"Savor this marvelous, unforgettable, highly romantic novel by a fresh voice in the genre."

—*Romantic Times* Magazine (Top Pick)

"What a fabulous read! Ms. Cole has created a cast of characters that are fun and believable, and the plot to complement them. For a steamy read on the beach, I highly recommend this book."

—Scribes World (Reviewers' Choice Award Winner)

Books by Kresley Cole

The Sutherland Series
The Captain of All Pleasures
The Price of Pleasure

The MacCarrick Brothers Series
If You Dare
If You Desire
If You Deceive

The Immortals After Dark Series
A Hunger Like No Other
No Rest for the Wicked
Wicked Deeds on a Winter's Nifght
Dark Deeds at Night's Edge
Dark Desires After Dusk
Kiss of a Demon King
Pleasure of a Dark Prince
Demon from the Dark

The Sutherland Series
Playing Easy to Get
Deep Kiss of Winter

A HUNGER LIKE NO OTHER

KRESLEY COLE

SIMON &
SCHUSTER

London · New York · Sydney · Toronto

A CBS COMPANY

First published in Great Britain by Simon & Schuster, 2011
A division of Simon & Schuster UK Ltd
A CBS COMPANY

1 3 5 7 9 10 8 6 4 2

Simon & Schuster UK Ltd
1st Floor
222 Gray's Inn Road
London WC1X 8HB

www.simonandschuster.co.uk

Simon & Schuster Australia
Sydney

A CIP catalogue record for this book
is available from the British Library

ISBN: 978-1-84983-557-2

Printed in the UK by CPI Cox & Wyman, Reading, Berkshire RG1 8EX

For Richard,
my real, live Viking.

Acknowledgments

Many, many thanks to Beth Kendrick, who rightfully dubbed us primal scream buddies. Without you and a telephone, there would be no word count. Thank you to the wonderful Sally Fairchild for all her much appreciated continued support. And my heartfelt thanks to Pocket Books own Megan McKeever, who is, at this very moment, most likely plucking me out of some book-related crisis.

Prologue

Sometimes the fire that licks the skin from his bones dies down.

It is *his* fire. In a recess of his mind still capable of rational thought, he believes this. His fire because he's fed it for centuries with his destroyed body and decaying mind.

Long ago—and who knows how much time has toiled past—the Vampire Horde trapped him in these catacombs deep beneath Paris. He stands chained against a rock, pinned at two places on each limb and once around his neck. Before him—an opening into hell that spews fire.

Here he waits and suffers, offered to a column of fire that may weaken but is never-ending—never-ending, just like his life. His existence is to burn to death repeatedly, only to have his dogged immortality revive him again.

Detailed fantasies of retribution have gotten him this far; nursing the rage in his heart is all he has.

Until her.

Over the centuries, he has sometimes heard uncanny new things in the streets above, occasionally smelled Paris changing seasons. But now he has scented her, his mate, the one woman made for him alone.

The one woman he'd searched for without cease for a thousand years—up until the day of his capture.

The flames have ebbed. At this moment, she lingers somewhere above. It is enough. One arm strains against its bonds until the thick metal cuts into his skin. Blood drips, then pours. Every muscle in his weakened body works in concert, striving to do what he's never been able to for an eternity before. For her, he can do this. He must. . . . His yell turns to a choking cough as he rips two bonds free.

He doesn't have time to disbelieve what he's accomplished. She is so close, he can almost feel her. *Need her.* Another arm wrenches free.

With both hands he clenches the metal biting into his neck, vaguely remembering the day the thick, long pin was hammered into place. He knows its two ends are embedded at least three feet down. His strength is waning, but nothing will stop him when she's so close. In a rush of rock and dust, the metal comes loose, the recoil making him fling it across the cavernous space.

He yanks at the bond wrapped tight around his thigh. He wrests it and the one at his ankle free, then begins on the last two holding his other leg. Already envisioning his escape, not even glancing down, he pulls. Nothing. Brows drawn in confusion, he tries again. Straining, groaning with desperation. Nothing.

Her scent is fading—*there is no time.* He pitilessly regards his trapped leg. Imagining how he can bury himself in her and forget the pain, he reaches above his knee with shaking hands. Yearning for that oblivion within her, he attempts to crack the bone. His weakness ensures that this takes half a dozen tries.

His claws slice his skin and muscle, but the nerve running the length of his femur is taut as a piano wire. When he even nears it, unimaginable pain stabs up its length and explodes in his upper body, making his vision go black.

Too weak. Bleeding too freely. The fire will build again soon. The vampires return periodically. Will he lose her just when he's found her?

"*Never,*" he grates. He surrenders himself to the beast inside him, the beast that will take its freedom with its teeth, drink water from the gutters, and scavenge refuse to survive. He sees the frenzied amputation as though watching a misery from a distance.

Crawling from his torture, abandoning his leg, he pulls himself through the shadows of the dank catacombs until he spies a passageway. Ever watchful for his enemies, he creeps through the bones littering the floor to reach it. He has no idea how far it is to escape, but he finds his way—and the strength—by following her scent. He regrets the pain he will give her. She will be so connected to him, she'll feel his suffering and horror as her own.

It can't be helped. He is escaping. Doing his part. Can she save him from his memories when his skin still burns?

He finally inches his way to the surface, then into a darkened alley. But her scent has faltered.

Fate has given her to him when he needs her most, and God help him—*and this city*—if he can't find her. His brutality had been legendary, and he will unleash it without measure for her.

He fights to sit up against a wall. Clawing tracks into the brick street, he struggles to calm his ragged breaths so he can scent her once more.

Need her. Bury myself in her. Waited so long. . . .

Her scent is gone.

His eyes go wet and he shudders violently at the loss. An anguished roar makes the city tremble.

In all of us, even in good men, there is a lawless wild-beast nature, which peers out in sleep.

—Socrates (469–399 BCE)

1

One week later . . .

On an island in the Seine, against the nighttime backdrop of an ageless cathedral, the denizens of Paris came out to play. Emmaline Troy wound around fire-eaters, pickpockets, and *chanteurs de rue*. She meandered through the tribes of black-clad Goths who swarmed Notre Dame like it was the Gothic mother ship calling them home. And still she attracted attention.

The human males she passed turned their heads slowly to regard her, frowns in place, sensing something, but unsure. Probably some genetic memory from long ago that signaled her as their wildest fantasy or their darkest nightmare.

Emma was neither.

She was a co-ed—a recent Tulane grad—alone in Paris and hungry. Weary from another failed search for blood, she sank onto a rustic bench beneath a chestnut tree, eyes riveted to a waitress drawing espresso at a café. If only blood poured so easily, Emma thought. Yes, if it came warm and rich from a bottomless tap, then her stomach wouldn't be clenched in hunger at the mere idea.

Starving in Paris. And friendless. Was there ever such a predicament?

Couples strolling hand in hand along the gravel walk seemed to mock her loneliness. Was it just her, or did lovers look more adoringly at each other in this city? Especially in the springtime. *Die, bastards.*

She sighed. It wasn't their fault that they were bastards who should die.

She'd been spurred to enter this fray by the prospect of her echoing hotel room and the idea that she might find another blood pusher in the City of Light. Her former hookup had gone south—literally—fleeing Paris for Ibiza. He'd given little explanation for abandoning his job, saying only that with the "arrival of the risen king," some "serious epic shit" was brewing in "gay Paree." Whatever that meant.

As a vampire, she was a member of the Lore, that stratum of beings who'd convinced humans they existed only in imagination. Yet though the Lore was thick here, Emma had been unable to replace her pusher. Any creatures she could scout out to ask fled her solely because she was a vampire. They scurried without knowing that she wasn't even a full-blooded one, nor that Emma was a wuss who'd never bitten another living being. As her fierce adoptive aunts loved to tell everyone, "Emma cries her pink tears if she dusts a moth's wings."

Emma had accomplished nothing during this trip that she'd insisted on taking. Her quest to uncover information about her deceased parents—her Valkyrie mother and her unknown vampire father—was a failure. A failure that would culminate in a call to her aunts to get them to retrieve her. Because she couldn't feed herself. Pitiful. She sighed. She'd be razzed about this for another seventy years—

She heard a crash, and before she even had time to feel

bad for the waitress getting docked, another crash and then another followed. She tilted her head in curiosity—just as a table umbrella across the walk shot fifteen feet up to be batted high in the sky, fluttering all the way to the Seine. A cruise boat honked and Gallic curses erupted.

Half-lit by the walk's torchlights, a towering man turned over café tables, artists' easels, and book stands selling century-old pornography. Tourists screamed and fled in the wake of destruction. Emma shot to her feet with a gasp, looping her satchel over her shoulder.

He was cutting a path directly to her, his black trench coat trailing behind him. His size and his unnaturally fluid movements made her wonder if he could possibly be human. His hair was thick and long, concealing half his face, and several days' growth of beard shadowed his jaw.

He pointed a shaking hand at her. "*You,*" he growled.

She jerked glances over both of her shoulders looking for the unfortunate *you* he was addressing. Her. Holy shite, this madman had settled on her.

He turned his palm up and beckoned her to come to him—as if he was confident she would.

"Uh, I-I don't know you," she squeaked, trying to back up, but her legs immediately met the bench.

He continued stalking her, ignoring the tables between them, tossing them aside like toys instead of varying his direct pursuit of her. Furious intent burned in his pale blue eyes. She could sense his rage more sharply as he neared, unsettling her, because her kind were considered the predators in the night—never the prey. And because, at heart, she was a coward.

"*Come.*" He bit out the word as though with difficulty and motioned for her again.

Eyes wide, she shook her head, then leapt backward over the bench, twisting in the air. She landed facing away from him and began speeding down the quay. She was weak, more than two days without blood, but terror made her quick as she crossed the Archevêché Bridge to exit the island.

Three . . . four blocks covered. She chanced a look behind her. Didn't see him. Had she lost him—? Sudden glaring music from her purse made her cry out.

Who in the hell had programmed the Crazy Frog ring tone into her cell phone? Her eyes narrowed. Aunt Regin. The world's most immature immortal, who looked like a siren and behaved like a frat pledge.

Cell phones in their coven were for dire emergency only. Ringers would disturb their hunting in the back alleys of New Orleans, and even a vibration would be enough to trigger a twitching ear in a low creature.

She flipped it open. Speak of the devil: Regin the Radiant.

"Little busy right now," Emma snapped, taking another peek over her shoulder.

"Drop your things. Don't take time to pack. Annika wants you at the executive airport immediately. *You're in danger.*"

"Duh."

Click. That wasn't a warning—that was narration.

She'd ask the details once she was on the plane. As if she'd needed a reason to return home. Just the mention of danger and she would scamper back to her coven, to her Valkyrie aunts who would kill anything that threatened her and keep malice at bay.

As she tried to remember her way to the airport where she'd landed, the rain started to fall, warm and light at first—

April lovers still laughing as they ran under awnings—but swiftly turning to pounding cold. She came to a crowded avenue, feeling safer as she wound through traffic. She dodged cars with their wipers and horns going full-force. She didn't see her pursuer.

With only the satchel slung around her neck, she traveled quickly, miles passing beneath her feet before she spied an open park and then the airfield just beyond it. She could see the diffused air around the jet engines as they warmed, could see the shades on every window already drawn tight. Almost there.

Emma convinced herself she'd lost him, because she *was* fast. She was also adept at convincing herself of things that might not be—good at pretending. She could pretend she took classes at night by choice, and that blushing didn't make her thirsty—

A vicious growl sounded. Her eyes widened, but she didn't turn back, just sprinted across the field. She felt claws sink into her ankle a second before she was dragged to the muddy ground and thrown onto her back. A hand covered her mouth, though she'd been trained not to scream.

"Never run from one such as me." Her attacker didn't sound human. "You will no' get away. *And we like it.*" His voice was guttural like a beast's, breaking, yet his accent was . . . Scottish?

As she peered up at him through the rain, he examined her with eyes that were golden in color one moment, then flickering that eerie blue the next. No, not human.

Up close, she could see his features were even, masculine. A strong chin and jaw complemented the chiseled planes. He was beautiful, so much so that she thought he had to be a fallen angel. Possible. How could *she* rule out anything?

The hand that had been covering her mouth roughly grasped her chin. He narrowed his eyes, focusing on her lips—on her barely noticeable fangs. "*No,*" he choked out. "No' possible. . . ." He yanked her head side to side, running his face down her neck, smelling her, then growled in fury, "*Goddamn you.*"

When his eyes turned blue sharply, she cried out, her breath seeming to leave her body.

"Can you trace?" he grated as though speech was difficult. "Answer me!"

She shook her head, uncomprehending. Tracing was how vampires teleported, disappearing and reappearing in thin air. *Then he knows I'm a vampire?*

"*Can you?*"

"N-no." She'd never been strong or skilled enough. "Please." She blinked against the rain, pleading with her eyes. "You have the wrong woman."

"Think I'd know you. Make sure, if you insist." He raised a hand—to touch her? Strike her? She fought, hissing desperately.

A callused palm grasped the back of her neck, his other hand clenching her wrists as he bent down to her neck. Her body jerked from the feel of his tongue against her skin. His mouth was hot in the chill, wet air, making her shudder until her muscles knotted. He groaned while kissing her, his hand squeezing her wrists hard. Below her skirt, drops of rain tracked down her thighs, shocking her with cold.

"Don't do this! *Please* . . ." When her last word ended with a whimper, he seemed to come out of a trance, his brows drawing together as his eyes met hers, but he didn't release her hands.

He flicked his claw down her blouse and sliced it and the

flimsy bra beneath open, then slowly brushed the halves past her breasts. She struggled, but it was useless against his strength. He studied her with a greedy gaze as rain splattered down, stinging her naked breasts. She was shivering uncontrollably.

His pain was so sharp it nauseated her. He could take her or he could tear open her unprotected belly and kill her. . . .

Instead he ripped open his own shirt, then placed his huge palms against her back to draw her to his chest. He groaned when their skin touched, and electricity seemed to flash through her. Lightning split the sky.

He rumbled foreign words against her ear. She felt they were . . . *tender* words, making her think she'd lost her mind. She went limp, her arms hanging while he shuddered against her, his lips so hot in the pouring rain as he ran them down her neck, across her face, even brushing them over her eyelids. There he knelt, clutching her; there she lay, boneless and dazed, as she watched the lightning slash above them.

His hand cradled the back of her head as he moved her to face him.

He seemed torn as he watched her with some fierce emotion—she'd never been looked at so . . . consumingly. Confusion overwhelmed her. Would he attack or let her go? *Let me go. . . .*

A tear slipped down her face, warmth streaking down amidst the drops of rain.

The look disappeared. *"Blood for tears?"* he roared, clearly revolted by her pink tears. He turned away as if he couldn't stand to look upon her, then blindly swatted at her shirt to close it. "Take me to your home, vampire."

"I-I don't live here," she said in a strangled tone, staggered by what had just occurred, and by the fact that he knew what she was.

"Take me to where you stay," he ordered, finally facing her as he stood before her.

"No," she amazed herself by saying.

He, too, looked surprised. "Because you doona want me to stop? Good. I'll take you here on the grass on your hands and knees"—he lifted her easily until she was kneeling—"till well after the sun rises."

He must have seen her resignation because he hauled her to her feet and pushed at her to get her moving. "Who stays with you?"

My husband, she wanted to snap. *The linebacker who's going to kick your ass.* Yet she couldn't lie, even now, and never would have had the nerve to provoke him anyway. "I am alone."

"Your man lets you travel by yourself?" he asked over the downpour. His voice was beginning to sound human again. When she didn't answer, he said with a sneer, "You've a careless male for yourself. His loss."

She stumbled in a pothole and he gently steadied her, then seemed angry with himself that he'd helped her. But when he led them in front of a car a moment later, he threw her out of the way, leaping back at the sound of the horn. He swiped at the side of the car, claws crumpling the metal like tinfoil, sending it skidding. When it finally stopped, the engine block dropped to the street with a thud. The driver threw open the door, dived for the street, then darted away.

Mouth open in shock, she frantically scrambled backward, realizing her captor looked as though he'd . . . *never seen a car.*

He crossed to her, looming over her. In a low, deadly tone, he grated, "I only hope you run from me again."

He snatched her hand and again lifted her to her feet. "How much farther?"

With a limp finger, she pointed out the Crillon on Place de la Concorde.

He gave her a look of pure hatred. "Your kind always had money." His tone was scathing. "Nothing's changed." He knew she was a vampire. Did he know who or what her aunts were? He must—otherwise how could Regin have known to warn her about him? How could he know her coven was well-off?

After ten minutes of her being dragged across avenues, they pushed past the doorman of the hotel, garnering stares as they entered the palatial lobby. At least the lights were dimmed. She pulled her soaked jacket over her ruined blouse and kept her head down, thankful that she'd braided her hair over her ears.

He released the vise-grip on her arm in front of these people. He must know that she wouldn't attract attention. *Never scream, never draw the attention of humans.* They were always more dangerous in the end than any of the thousands of creatures of the Lore.

When he draped his heavy arm across her shoulders as if they were together, she glanced up at him from under a wet lock of hair. Though he walked with his broad shoulders back, like he owned this place, he was examining everything as if it was new to him. The phone ringing made him tense. The revolving doors had done the same. Though he hid it well, she could tell he was unfamiliar with the elevator and hesitated to enter. Inside the lift, his size and his energy made the generous space seem cramped.

The short walk down the hall to her room was the longest of her life, as she devised and rejected plan after plan of escape. She hesitated outside the door, taking her time retrieving the key card from the inch-deep puddle in the bottom of her purse.

"Key," he demanded.

With a deep exhalation, she handed it to him. When his eyes narrowed, she thought he was about to demand "key" again, but he studied the door lever and gave it back to her. "You do it."

With a shaking hand, she slid it in. The mechanized buzz and then the click of the lock were like knells to her.

Once inside her room, he checked every inch of it as though to make sure she was in fact alone. He searched under the brocade-covered bed, then tore back the heavy silk drapes to reveal one of the best views in Paris. He moved like an animal, with aggression at every turn, though she'd noticed he favored one leg.

When he slowly limped to her in the hallway, her eyes widened and she eased backward. Still he continued toward her, studying her, weighing . . . before his gaze settled on her lips.

"I've waited a long time for you."

He continued to behave as if he knew her. She would *never* forget a man like him.

"I need you. No matter what you are. And I'll wait no longer."

At his baffling words, her body inexplicably softened, relaxing. Her claws curled as if to clutch him to her, and her fangs receded to ready for his kiss. Frantic, she rapped her nails against the wall behind her and tapped her tongue against her left fang. Her defenses remained dormant. She was terrified of him. Why wasn't her body?

He placed his hands against the wall on either side of her face. Unhurriedly, he leaned in, brushing his mouth against hers. He groaned from the small contact and pressed harder, flicking her lips with his tongue. She froze, not knowing what to do.

Against her mouth, he growled, "Kiss me back, witch, while I decide if I should spare your life."

With a cry, she moved her lips against his. When he stilled completely as if to force her to do all the work, she slanted her head and brushed his lips lightly again.

"Kiss me like you want to live."

She did. Not because she wanted to live overmuch, but because she thought he would make sure her death was slow and torturing. *No pain. Never pain.*

When she darted her tongue against his as he had done to her, he groaned and took over, cupping her neck and head so he could hold her as though for the taking. His tongue stroked hers desperately, and she was shocked to find it was . . . not unpleasant. How many times had she dreamed about her first kiss, even knowing she would never receive one? But she was. Now.

She didn't even know his name.

When she began shivering again, he stopped and broke away. "You're cold."

She was freezing. Being low on blood did that to her. Being tackled into the wet earth and soaked through hadn't helped. But she feared that wasn't why she shivered. "Y-yes."

He raked his gaze over her, then gave her a disgusted look. "And filthy. Mud all over you."

"But you . . ." She trailed off under his lethal glare.

He found the bathroom, yanked her inside, then tilted his head at the fixtures. "Clean yourself."

"P-privacy?" she croaked.

Amusement. "You have none." He leaned his shoulder against the wall and crossed his muscled arms, as if awaiting a show. "Now, undress for me and let me see what's mine."

Mine? Bewildered, she was about to protest again, but he jerked his head up as though he'd heard something, then bolted out of the room. She slammed the bathroom door, locking herself in—another laughable gesture—then turned on the shower.

She sank down on the floor, head in her hands, and wondered how she would get away from this lunatic. The Crillon boasted foot-thick walls between the rooms—a rock band had stayed next door to her and she'd never heard them. Of course, she didn't envision calling for anyone—*never scream for a human's help*—but she was contemplating digging her way out through the bathroom wall.

Soundproof walls, ten floors up. The luxurious room that had been a haven, protecting her from the sun and nosy humans, was now a gilded cage. She was trapped by some being, and Freya only knew what.

How could she get away when she had no one to help her?

Lachlain heard a scarcely squeaking wheel, smelled meat, and limped for the room's door. In the hallway, an old man pushing a cart yelped with fright at the sight of him, then stared wordlessly as Lachlain snatched two covered plates from the cart.

Lachlain kicked the door closed. Found steaks and devoured them. Then pounded a hole in the wall at a sharp memory.

Flexing his now bleeding fingers, he sat on the edge of the strange bed, in a strange place and time. He was weary and his leg pained him after running the vampire down. He pulled up his stolen pants and inspected his regenerating leg. The flesh was sunken and wasted.

He tried to push away memories of that loss. But what other recent memories did he have? Only those of being burned to death repeatedly. *For what he now knew had been a hundred and fifty years.* . . .

He shuddered, sweating, and retched between his knees, but kept himself from vomiting the food he needed so badly. Instead, he ripped his claws through a table by the bed, just preventing himself from destroying everything in sight.

In the last week since his escape, he would be doing well, focusing on his hunt for her and his recovery, seeming to acclimate; then something would put him in a rage. He'd broken into a manor to steal clothes—then destroyed everything inside. Anything he didn't recognize and understand, destroyed.

Tonight, he'd been weak, thinking unclearly, his leg still regenerating, and still he'd gone to his knees when he'd finally picked up her scent once more.

But instead of the mate he'd expected, he'd found a *vampire*. A small, fragile female vampire. He hadn't heard of a female being alive in centuries. The males must have been secretive about them, cloistering them all these years. Apparently the Horde hadn't killed off all of their own women, as the Lore told.

And Christ help him, his instincts still said this pale-haired, ethereal creature was . . . his.

The Instinct screamed inside him to touch her, to claim her. He'd waited for so long. . . .

He put his head in his hands, trying not to lash out again—to get the beast back in its cage. But how could fate rob him once more? For more than a thousand years, he'd searched for her.

And he'd found her in what he despised with a hatred so virulent he couldn't control it.

A vampire. The way she existed disgusted him. Her weakness disgusted him. Her pale body was too small, too thin, and looked like she'd break with her first stiff fucking.

He'd waited a millennium for a helpless parasite.

He heard the squeaking wheel, going much faster past his door, but his hunger was sated for the first time since the ordeal began. With food like tonight's, he would shake off any physical trace of the torture. But his mind . . .

He'd been with the female for an hour. Yet it had been an hour during which he'd only had to push the beast back twice. Which was a considerable improvement, since his entire existence was of constant bleakness interrupted only by sharp rages. Everyone said a Lykae's mate could soothe his any woe—if she really was his, she had her bloody work cut out for her.

She couldn't be. He must be delusional. He seized on that idea. The last thing he'd regretted before they forced him to the fire was that he'd never found her. Perhaps this was a damaged mind playing tricks. Of course, that was it. He'd always pictured his mate as a buxom redheaded lass with wolven blood who could handle his lusts, who would revel in the raw ferocity with him—not this fearful wisp of a *vampire*. Damaged mind. Of course.

He limped to the door to the bathing chamber and found it locked. He shook his head as he broke the knob easily, then entered a room so thick with steam he could hardly spy her balled up against the opposite wall. He lifted her up by her arms, scowling to find her still wet and dirty.

"You've no' cleaned yourself?" When she only stared down at the ground, he demanded, "Why?"

She shrugged miserably.

He glanced at the cascade of water within a glass chamber, opened the door, and ran his hand under it. Now, this he could use. He set her away, then stripped.

Her eyes widened, focused on his cock, and she covered her mouth. You'd think she'd never seen one. He let her look her fill, even leaned back against the wall, crossing his arms over his chest while she stared.

Under her rapt gaze he grew hard, his length distending—his body, at least, must think she was his—until she gasped and lowered her gaze. His wasted leg caught her attention, seeming to startle her even more. That alone embarrassed him, and he stepped into the water to break her stare.

He closed his eyes with pleasure as the water ran over him, noticing that it did nothing to quell his erection. He sensed her tense as though to run, and opened his eyes. If he'd been stronger, he would've hoped she would try it. "Looking at the door like that? I'll catch you before you make it from this room."

She turned back, saw he'd grown harder, and seemed to choke on a cry.

"Take off your clothes, vampire."

"I-I will not!"

"Do you want to come in here with them on?"

"Preferable to being naked with you!"

He felt relaxed under the water, even magnanimous after

the excellent food. "Then let's make a bargain. You grant me a boon and I'll return one."

She looked up at him from under a curl freed from her tight braids. "What do you mean?"

He put his hands on each side of the door and leaned forward out of the water. "I want you in here, unclothed. What do you want of me?"

"Nothing of value equal to that," she whispered.

"You'll be with me indefinitely. Until I decide to let you go. Do you no' want to contact your . . . people?" He spat the word. "I'm sure you have much value to them, being so rare." In fact, keeping her from her vampire kin would just be the beginning of his revenge. He knew they'd find the idea of her being fucked repeatedly by a Lykae as revolting as his clan would find it. She nibbled her red bottom lip with one tiny fang, and his anger flared again. "I doona have to grant you anything! I could just take you in here and then in the bed."

"A-and you won't if I agree to be in there with you?"

"Come willingly and I will no'," he lied.

"What will you . . . do?"

"I want to put my hands on you. Learn you. And I'll want your hands on me."

In a voice so soft he could scarcely hear her, she asked, "Will you hurt me?"

"Touch you. No' hurt you."

Her delicate blond brows drew together as she weighed this. Then, as though in great pain, she bent down to her boots, unfastening them with a buzzing sound. She stood and grasped the edges of her jacket and ruined blouse, but she seemed unable to proceed. She shook wildly and her blue eyes were stark. But she was agreeing—in a flash of insight, he knew she wasn't agreeing because of any reason he could fathom. Her eyes seemed so expressive, yet he couldn't read her.

When he loomed closer, she peeled the wet jacket and blouse away, then the shredded undergarment beneath them, hastily draping a thin arm over her breasts. Shy? When he'd seen the orgies of blood the vampires reveled in?

"Please. I-I don't know who you think I am, but—"

"I think"—before she could blink, he'd ripped her skirt clean from her body and tossed it to the ground—"that I should at least know your name before I set to touchin' you."

She shook harder if possible, her arm tightening over her breasts.

He studied her, his gaze drinking her in. Her skin was perfect alabaster covered only by her strange pantalettes, the black silk that was like a V on her body. The front was transparent jet lace and teased against the blond curls between her legs. He remembered his two fleeting tastes of her skin in the howling rain and unnatural lightning, and his cock pulsed, the head growing slick with anticipation. Other men would find her exquisite. The vampires would. Human males would kill for her.

Her trembling body was too small, but her eyes . . . wide and blue like the daytime sky she would never witness.

"M-my name is Emmaline."

"*Emmaline*," he growled, slowly reaching forward one claw to slice away the silk.

2

She'd been a fool to agree to this, Emma decided when the remains of her underwear fluttered to her ankles.

Why should she trust him? She shouldn't, but what choice did she have? She had to call Annika, her foster mother. She would be frantic when the pilot reported Emma had never shown up.

But was that really the reason she'd agreed to this? She feared it wasn't so selfless a reason. Throughout her life, men had asked things of her—things her hidden vampire nature made impossible. Not this male. He knew what she was, and he wasn't asking the impossible, he was *demanding* . . .

A shower.

And yet . . .

He held out his hand. Not aggressively or impatiently, but accompanied by a slow perusal of her wholly naked body with eyes that were intense but now warm and golden. He gave a sharp groan that she knew was involuntary. As if he found her beautiful.

His size was still terrifying, his leg sickening, but with a deep breath, and more courage than she'd conjured in her entire life, she slipped her hand into his.

Just when she fully grasped that she was completely

naked in a shower with a six-and-a-half-foot crazed male of indeterminate species, he pulled her under the water with him, turning her back to him.

He took her left hand and placed it against the marble. The other he placed against the glass. Her mind was racing. What would he do to her? She couldn't be more unprepared for a situation like this. A sexual situation. He could do anything he wanted. She couldn't stop him.

She drew her head back in surprise when, all business, he began running soap down her back, over her backside, his palms big on her. She was embarrassed that this stranger saw her like this, but she was also intrigued by *his* body. She strove not to peek at his huge erection as he bent and moved, but it was . . . eye-catching. She tried not to notice that the hair on his arms, legs, and chest was golden-tipped, or that his skin, but for that of his leg, was tan.

He bent down to wash her legs front and back, and scrubbed the grass and mud from her knees. When he rubbed toward her upper thighs, she shoved her legs together. He gave a frustrated growl, then stood to draw her back against his chest, until she could feel him prodding her. He started the same leisurely exploration of her front, one arm bent by her side, his hand clasping her shoulder.

Suddenly his callused palm cupped her breast. She would fight, or scream—

"Your skin's so damn soft," he murmured in her ear. "Soft as the silk you wore."

She shivered. One compliment, and Emma—who'd never suspected she was *easy*—relaxed somewhat. When he ran his thumb slowly over her nipple and back, she sucked in a breath, glad he couldn't see her eyelids briefly slide closed. How could anything feel that good?

"Put your foot there." He motioned to the narrow bench along the shower's back wall.

And spread her thighs? "Um, I don't—"

He lifted her knee and placed it there himself. When she began to move it, he snapped, "Doona dare. Now, lean your head back against me."

Then both his hands were back on her breasts, now rubbing with friction since the soap had washed away. She bit her lip as her nipples hardened almost painfully. She should be terrified. Was she so desperate for touch—any touch—that she would submit to this?

His fingers inched lower. "Keep your legs open to me."

She'd just been about to shove them together again. She'd never been touched there. Or anywhere else, for that matter.

She'd never even held a man's hand.

Swallowing nervously, she watched as his hand trailed down to her sex. "B-but you said—"

"That I would no' fuck you. Trust me, you'll know when I'm about to."

She gasped at the first touch, involuntarily jerking in his capturing arms, staggered by the intensity of feeling. Two fingers caressed her sensitive flesh, stroking and teasing her, and it was all the more pleasurable because he was . . . gentle. Slow and gentle. When he felt her wetness, he rumbled foreign words and brushed his mouth over her neck as if pleased with her.

He tried to dip his finger inside her, but her body clenched against the unfamiliar touch.

"Tight as a fist," he rasped. "You have to relax."

She wondered if she should tell him that all the relaxing in the world wasn't changing that.

He reached for her from the back. When he began working his middle finger into her sex from behind, she gasped and rocked to her toes as if to get away. But his other hand bent her forward slightly, then trailed down to stroke her from the front. She heard panting, and was startled to realize it was her own.

This stranger was petting her body—inside her body—and she was aroused.

Did the air charge with electricity? For her? *Please let it be for me. . . .*

He shook more and more as he touched her. She sensed that he barely held onto his control. . . . She should be wary, afraid. But his fingers were so slow on her, the one inside her hot. So much unfamiliar pleasure. The urge to moan arose.

She had never moaned with pleasure before. Never in her life had she been moved to. . . .

Her claws curled like they never had, and as she panted, she imagined sinking them into his backside as he thrust into her. What was happening to her?

"Now, there's a good lass," he growled in her ear, just before he turned her and lifted her in his arms. "Put your legs around my waist."

Her eyes had been heavy-lidded with lust, but now they widened in panic again. "Y-you said you wouldn't."

"Changed my mind when I felt you wet and needing." She *did* want him—as she was supposed to.

He frowned, uncomprehending when she struggled. Even in his weakened state, quelling her fight took little more effort than holding a wildcat.

He pressed her against the wall, pinning her there, and set his mouth to sucking her throbbing little nipples. He closed his eyes with pleasure, groaning as his tongue swirled around them. When he opened his eyes again, he found hers squeezed shut, her balled fists resting on his shoulders.

He set her on her feet again and stroked between her legs. She'd gone tight again. If he tried to fuck her like this, he'd tear her—but he didn't care. For all he'd done just to get this far, only to find a vampire, he wouldn't be stopped now. "Relax," he bit out. Just the opposite happened—she began that useless shaking again.

Need to be inside her. Haze. She would make him wait longer for the mindlessness he craved? *Torturing me just as her kindred did.* He bellowed with rage, his hands shooting out on each side of her head to crush the marble behind her.

Her eyes went stark once more. Why couldn't she have been of his kind? If she had, she would have been clawing him to fill her, *begging.* She would have fed him into her body and sighed with relief when he rocked into her. The mental image of this creature doing that made him groan in misery at his loss. He wanted her willing. But he'd take what fate had given.

"I'm going tae be inside you tonight. Best relax."

She gazed up at him with her brows drawn as though with despair. "You said you wouldn't hurt me. You p-promised."

Did the witch think that promise would be enough to save her? He gripped his cock, dragged her leg up to his hip. . . .

"But you said," she whispered, devastated that she'd believed him. She hated being lied to, especially since she could never lie back. "You said. . . ."

He stilled. With a deep growl, he released her leg and hit

the wall again. Her eyes widened when he grabbed her and turned her around. Right when she was about to scratch him, bite him, he pulled her into his arms again, her back against his chest. He shoved her hand to his erection, inhaling sharply at the first touch. His voice gone guttural, he said, "Stroke me."

Glad for the reprieve, she tentatively held him, in no way able to fit her palm around him. When she didn't begin at once, he bucked his hips. She finally ran her hand over him in long strokes, looking away.

"Harder." She tightened her fingers, face hot with embarrassment. Was it so apparent that she had no idea what she was doing?

As if reading her mind, he rasped, "That's it, lass." He was kneading her breast, his mouth against her neck, broken sounds coming from his chest. She could feel his muscles tensing. His arm tightened around her until she didn't think she could breathe. His other hand dipped down to cup her sex.

He growled, *"Going tae come."* Then, with a raw groan that drew her gaze back to the sight, his seed came, pumping out into the shower. *"Ah, God, yes."* He pawed her breast, but she scarcely felt it, her eyes widening as it continued on and on.

When he'd finished, she realized she was dazedly continuing to stroke him. He stayed her hand as he shuddered, the muscles of his torso rippling.

She was losing her mind. She should be appalled, yet she recognized her body was aching. For him? For the firm hand he'd removed from between her legs?

He pushed her back against the unmarred wall under the showerhead. Leaning his chest against her, he placed his

chin on her head and his palms by her face to box her in.
"Touch me."

"Wh-where?" Was that her voice sounding so . . . husky?

"Doona care."

She began rubbing his back, and as she did so he kissed
the top of her head, absently, as if he didn't realize he was
being kind to her.

His shoulders were broad and, like the rest of him, hard
and thick with muscle. Seemingly of their own accord, her
hands glided over him more sensually than she would have
liked. Each movement brushed her achy nipples against the
ridges of his torso. The golden hair on his chest tickled her
lips, and despite herself, she imagined kissing that tanned
skin. Her sex still throbbed for the semi-erect penis pressed
high against her belly, yearned for it even though she'd seen
how huge it had grown.

Just when she thought he was about to fall asleep, he
murmured in her ear, "I can scent you're still aroused.
Deeply so."

She sucked in a breath. What exactly *was* he? "Y-you say
these things just to shock me." She thought he spoke so
bluntly because he'd quickly determined how uncomfortable
it made her—and she resented him for it.

"Ask me to make you come."

She tensed. She might be a coward, without accomplishment or talent. But right now she felt fiercely proud.
"Never."

"Your loss. Now, take down the braids. You'll keep your
hair loose."

"I don't want to—"

When he reached down to do it himself, she unraveled
them, trying to keep her pointed ears covered.

His breath left him with a sharp exhalation. "Let me see them."

She said nothing as he brushed her hair back.

"They're like the fey's." He ran the backs of his fingers against the sharp tip at the top and she shivered. By his watchful gaze, she knew he was noting her reaction. "Is that a trait of female vampires?"

She'd never seen a full-blooded vampire, male or female. She shrugged.

"Interesting."

He rinsed her hair, studying her face with an inscrutable expression. When finished, he ordered, "Turn this water off," then drew her from the stall. Taking a towel, he dried her completely. He even pinned her still—by hugging an arm around her waist—to run the cloth slowly between her legs. Her eyes grew wider as he continued to inspect her as if she were a prospective purchase. He palmed the curves of her bottom, then brought his hand down hard on each side, making sounds of . . . approval?

He must have noticed her bewildered expression, because he said, "You doona like me learning you?"

"Of course not!"

"I'll allow you to do the same." He placed her palm flat on his chest, dragging it down, a challenging look in his eyes.

"I'll pass," she squeaked, jerking her hand back.

Before she could even cry out, he swooped her up in his arms and carried her to the bed, roughly tossing her there.

She scrambled up, dashing for her dresser full of clothes. In a flash, he was behind her, peering over her shoulder, pressing into her with his entire body, his penis hardening against her. He picked out a revealing red lace nightgown, pulling it out with one finger under the straps.

"Red. To remind me of what you are."

Red was her favorite color. She wanted to be reminded, too.

"Raise your arms."

Enough! "I—can—dress—myself," she snapped.

He yanked her around to face him, and his tone went deadly. "Doona displease me, vampire. You canna imagine how many years of rage I've got pent up, ready to be tapped." She glanced past him, and her jaw slackened when she saw the distinct claw marks that had rent the bedside table. *He's a madman.*

She helplessly raised her arms. Her aunts would have told him— Her brows drew together. Her aunts wouldn't have told him anything, because they'd already have killed him for what he'd done. Frightened Emma raised her arms. She was disgusted with herself. Emma the Timid.

When he smoothed the gown over her, he insolently brushed her nipples, which were hard as if seeking his touch. He stood back to rake his gaze over her from her toes up to the gown's high slit at the leg, finally resting on the lace bodice. "I like you in silk." His voice was a deep rumble, his gaze as strong as a touch, and even after everything that had happened, she responded.

He gave her a cruel smirk. He knew it.

Her face flushed and she turned away.

"Now, get in the bed."

"I'm not *sleeping* with you."

"We're going to do something in that bed. I'm weary and thought we'd sleep, but if you have other ideas . . ."

Emma had always wondered what it would be like to sleep with someone.

She had never experienced it, never felt another's skin against her own for more than the briefest moment. When he'd tucked her against his body in a spooning position, she'd been shocked by how warm he was. Her body, which had paled and cooled with hunger, grew warm as well. She had to admit this unfamiliar closeness was . . . remarkable. The hair on his legs tickled her, and his firm lips pressed against her neck as he slept. She could even feel his strong heartbeat against her back.

She finally understood the appeal of this. And knowing what she did now, she wondered how anyone could *not* want a bedmate. He was answering so many questions she'd had, proving so many of her secret dreams.

And yet he could readily kill her.

At first, he'd squeezed her to his chest so hard it was everything she could do not to cry out. She didn't think he held her so tightly to hurt her—he could have just hit her if that was his intention—so she was confused by his obvious need to clasp her to him.

Now he slept at last, his breaths growing even and slow. She called up her meager reserve of courage, and little by little, over what seemed to be an hour, she eased his arms open.

If only she could trace, she could escape so easily—but then she never would have been taken by him in the first place. Annika had taught Emma about tracing, the Horde's means of travel. She'd warned that vampires could teleport to any place they'd been to previously. The stronger ones could even teleport others, and only a fierce struggle might prevent it. Annika had wanted Emma to learn how. Emma had tried her hardest, failed, and been discouraged. She'd stopped paying attention. . . .

When Emma was finally able to duck from under his arms, she rose in cautious degrees. Free of the bed, she glanced back at him, and again was struck by how handsome he was. She was saddened that he had to be like this. Saddened that she couldn't learn more about herself—and even about him.

Just as she turned, his big hands snared her around the waist. He flung her back into the bed, then joined her once more.

He's playing with me.

"You canna escape me." He pressed her back, then levered himself up beside her. "You only provoke my anger." Even as his eyes flickered, they appeared unseeing. He behaved as if he was still dreaming, like a sleepwalker.

"I-I don't want to anger you," she said with a shaky breath. "I just want to go—"

"Do you know how many vampires I've killed?" he murmured, either ignoring or not hearing her words.

"No," she whispered. She wondered if he truly saw her.

"I've killed thousands. I hunted them for sport, stalking their lairs." He ran the back of his dark claw across her neck. "And with one swipe of my claws I severed their heads—before they even woke." His lips brushed over her neck where he'd trailed his claw, making her shudder. "I could kill you as easily as taking a breath." His voice was a low rumble like a lover's might be, gentling her, so inconsistent with his cruel words and actions.

"Are you going to k-kill me?"

He smoothed a strand of hair from her lip. "I have no' decided. I've never hesitated a second before you." He was shaking from holding his position above her. "When I wake from this haze—when this madness clears, if I still believe you are what you are . . . who knows?"

"What I am?"

He took her by the wrist and forced her hand to his naked shaft. "You feel me hard. Know that the only reason I'm no' inside you right now is because I'm weak. No' because of any concern for you."

Briefly closing her eyes with embarrassment, she tugged at her hand until he finally let it go. "You would hurt me that way?"

"Without a second thought." His lips curled. His gaze seemed intent on her face, but his eyes were still vacant. "And that's just the beginning of the things I'll do to you, vampire."

3

The next morning Lachlain lay beside her, sleep barely shaken off, as content as he'd been in hundreds of years.

Of course, he'd been in hell for nearly two hundred of those, and now he was clean and fed, and toward morning he'd slept like the dead with none of the grueling nightmares of the last week.

She'd lain tense and still for most of the night. It was as if she suspected any movement on her part might make him want to come again. She'd have been right. Courtesy of her soft hand, he'd ejaculated hard, shockingly so. She'd eased the heavy ache in his ballocks, but he'd still wanted to be inside her.

All night he'd squeezed her to him. He couldn't seem to stop himself. He'd never slept the night with a female before—that experience was reserved for a mate—but apparently he liked it. A lot. He recalled speaking to her, but not what he'd said. He remembered her reaction, though. She'd looked hopeless, as if she'd finally realized her situation.

She'd attempted escape one last time, and again he'd enjoyed letting her think she was about to succeed before he dragged her back and tucked her into his side. She went limp, then passed out. He didn't know if she'd fainted or not. Didn't particularly care.

He supposed it could be worse. If he was going to possess a vampire, she might as well be a beautiful one. She was a hated foe, a *blood drinker,* but beautiful. He wondered if he could put meat on her bones. Was that possible for a vampire? Drowsily, he reached forward to touch her hair. Last night when it had dried, he'd found it curled wildly and was a lighter blond than he'd thought it. Now he marveled at the glossy locks shining in the sun. Lovely, even for a vampire—

Sun.

Mother of Christ. He leapt from the bed, yanking the curtains closed, then rushed back to her, turning her in his arms.

She was scarcely breathing, unable to speak, pink tears of blood tracking from her dazed eyes. Her skin burned as though with fever. He rushed her into the bath, fiddling with the unfamiliar dial until the water streamed out icy cold, then put them both under it. After several minutes, she coughed, breathed deep, then went limp again. He gathered her closer to his chest with the crook of his arm, then frowned. He didn't care if she'd burned. *He* had burned. Because of her kindred. He merely wanted to keep her alive until he determined with certainty that she wasn't his mate.

The evidence that she wasn't kept mounting. If she had truly been his, he never would have thought, *Now you know how it feels.* Not when his life's purpose had always been to find her so he could protect her and keep her from harm. He was sick—his mind was playing tricks on him. It had to be....

He kept them in the water until she cooled, then plucked the sodden silk from her body to dry her tender skin. Before he returned her to the bed, he dressed the vampire in another gown—this one an even deeper red. As if he needed to be reminded of what she was.

He drew on his own battered clothes, then prowled the

suite, wondering what in the hell he was going to do with her. It wasn't long before her breathing returned to normal, her cheeks pinkening again. Typical vampire resilience. He'd always cursed it, and hated her anew for demonstrating it.

With disgust, he turned from her, his gaze landing on the television set. He studied it, trying to determine how to turn it on. He shook his head at the simplicity of modern devices and cleverly deduced how by selecting a button labeled "on."

Over the past week, it had seemed to him that every inhabitant of every residence on the outskirts of Paris had convened in front of one of these boxes at the close of each day. With his keen sight and hearing, Lachlain had been able to watch from outside. He would drag stolen food up a tree, then lean back to be stunned by the different information inherent in each one. And now he had his own to listen to. After a few moments of button pressing, he managed to discover a static place that only reported news, and it was in English—her language, and one of his, though he was more than a century out of date with it.

As he rummaged through her things, he listened to the unfamiliar speech patterns and the new vocabulary, learning them quickly. Lykae had that talent—the ability to blend, to pick up new languages, dialects, and current words. It was a survival mechanism. The Instinct commanded, *Blend. Learn everything. No detail to be missed. Or die.*

He studied her belongings. Back to the silk drawer, of course. The underclothing of this time was smaller and therefore preferable to yore. He imagined her in each elaborate scrap of silk, imagined biting them off her, though a couple of pieces baffled him. When he realized where the string was supposed to go and pictured her thus, he groaned, nearly coming in his trews.

Then to the closet to examine her strange clothes, so many of them red in color, so many of them lacking in coverage. The vampire would not be leaving this room in some of them.

He emptied the satchel she'd had with her last night onto the floor, noticing the leather was ruined. In the wet pile was a silver contraption with numbers like the numbers on the—he frowned—*telephone*. He shook it, and when water sloshed out, he tossed it over his shoulder.

A smaller leather case contained a hardened card that was a "Louisiana Driver's License."

Vampires in Louisiana? Unheard of.

The card had her name as Emmaline Troy. He paused for a moment, thinking back to all the years he'd prayed for just a name, a mere hint of how to find his mate. He frowned, trying to recall if he'd told the vampire his own name the crazed night before. . . .

Her height was listed as five foot four, her weight as one hundred and five pounds—not even sopping wet could she achieve that—and her eyes as blue. Blue was too tame a word for their color.

There was a small likeness of her smiling shyly with her hair braided to cover her ears. The likeness itself was amazing, but puzzling. It was like a daguerreotype, but this one had *color*. He had so bloody much to learn.

Her birth date was listed as 1982, which he knew was false. Physiologically she wasn't older than her early twenties, frozen forever when she was strongest and most able to survive the future, but chronologically, she would be older. Most vampires had come into existence centuries ago.

And why in the hell would the leeches be in Louisiana? Had they taken over more than just Europe? And if so, what had happened to his clan?

The thought of his clan made him glance up at the vampire, sleeping still as a corpse. If she was supposed to be his mate, she would be his queen and would rule over Lachlain's kind. Impossible. The clan would rip her to shreds at the first opportunity. The Lykae and vampires were natural-born enemies—had been since the first nebulous chaos of the Lore.

Blood adversaries. That's why he was impatiently returning his attention to her things—to study an enemy. Not because he was itching with curiosity about the female.

He opened a thin blue passport book and found another likeness with another smile that looked coaxed, then a "medic alert" card listing her medical condition as "sun allergy and extreme photosensitivity."

As he pondered whether the card was a jest, he pulled out a "credit card." He'd seen advertisements for those on the television—he'd probably learned as much from the advertisements as he did from the grim person who sat and divulged news—and he knew they purchased everything.

Lachlain needed everything. He was starting his life over, but his most pressing needs were clothing and transportation away from here. As weak as he was, he didn't want to remain in a place where the vampires knew she stayed. And until he could sort through everything, he would be forced to take the creature with him. He supposed he needed to figure out a way to keep it alive during their travels.

All those years spent devising ways to kill them, and now he had to figure out how to protect one?

Knowing she would most likely sleep until sunset—and couldn't escape during the day in any case—he left her to make his way downstairs.

The questioning glances he was sure to receive would be met with an arrogant glare. If he showed his ignorance of the times, he would cover it with a gaze so direct that most people would think they'd misunderstood him. Humans always cowered under that look.

Audacity made kings. And it was time to reclaim his crown.

Though he continually found his thoughts returning to his new prize, Lachlain was able to garner much information during his foray. The first lesson he learned was that whatever kind of card she owned—this black "American Express"—denoted extreme wealth. Not surprising, since the vampires had always been rich.

The second? A concierge in a lavish hotel like this could make your life very easy—if he thought you were a rich, but occasionally confused, eccentric. Who'd had his luggage stolen. Though initially, there had been some hesitation on the man's part. He'd asked if "Mr. Troy" could provide any identification whatsoever.

Lachlain had inched forward in his seat, staring him down for long moments, his expression balanced between anger at the question and embarrassment for the man for asking. *"No."* The answer was casually threatening, succinct, subject-ending.

The man had jumped at the word as he might at an unexpected gun report. Then he'd swallowed and hesitated no more, even at the most bizarre demands. He hadn't even raised an eyebrow when Lachlain wanted sunset and sunrise charts—or when he wanted to study them as he devoured a twenty-ounce steak.

Within hours, the man had arranged for fine clothing to fit Lachlain's large frame, transportation, cash, and maps, and had secured reservations for lodging in the coming nights. He supplied every basic essential Lachlain might have needed.

Lachlain had been pleased by what the man considered "essential." One hundred and fifty years ago, humans, with their aversion to bathing, had been an embarrassment to the Lore, who were almost to a species fastidious. Even the ghouls dumped themselves in water more often than nineteenth-century humans. Yet now, cleanliness and the tools requisite to achieve it were *essential* for them.

If he could get used to the speed with which this time moved, he might begin to enjoy its benefits.

Toward the end of the day, when he'd finally finished all his tasks, he realized he hadn't lost control or had to fight a rage once in the several hours he'd been away. The Lykae were prone to fits of temper—in fact, they spent many years of their lives learning to control it. Couple that tendency with what he'd been through, and he was shocked that he'd felt only a flare or two of anger. To quiet each one, he'd pictured the vampire sleeping up in his room, in what was now his bed. It was in his possession, to do with as he pleased. The knowledge of that alone helped brace him against his memories.

In fact, now that his mind had cleared somewhat, he wanted to question her. Impatient to return, he considered the elevator. Certainly they'd existed when he'd last walked above ground, though back then they'd been an amenity for the indolent rich. They weren't now, and using it was expected. He rode it to his floor.

Inside the room, he removed his new jacket, then crossed to the bed to wait for sundown. He studied her at leisure, this creature he'd been deluded enough to mistake as his.

Brushing aside her thick blond curls, he studied her fine-boned face, the high cheekbones and delicately pointed chin. He traced a finger over her pointed ear and it twitched under his touch.

He'd never seen a being like her, and her fey appearance sharply separated her from the seething, towering male vampires with their red eyes. The ones he would exterminate one by one.

And soon he'd be strong enough to do it.

Frowning, he lifted the hand that rested on her chest. Examining it closely, he could barely see a smattering of scars across the back. The web of fine white lines looked like a burn scar, but it didn't extend to her fingers or past her wrist. She'd been burned as though someone had seized her fingers and held only the back of her hand to a fire—or to the sunlight. And she'd been burned young, before she'd been frozen into her immortality. Typical vampire punishment, no doubt. Vile species.

Before the fury engulfed him again, he allowed his gaze to settle on other parts of her, then dragged the cover from her. She didn't protest, still soundly asleep.

No, she was not what he had normally been attracted to, but the nightgown he dragged up past her navel and down to her waist revealed those small but plump and perfect breasts that had fit in his hands, and her hard nipples that had aroused him so last night.

The back of one finger trailed across her tiny waist, then over the bunched silk and down to her blond sex. He had to admit he liked that and wanted to taste her there.

He was a sick bastard to contemplate these thoughts about a vampire, to find one so attractive. But then, shouldn't he be allowed some latitude? He hadn't seen a Lykae female in nearly two centuries. That was the only reason why his mouth watered to kiss her.

He knew it was nearing sunset. She'd wake soon. Why not wake her with the pleasure she'd forfeited the night before?

When he spread her silky white thighs and settled between them, she moaned softly, though she still slept. Last night, she might have decided her fear or pride was stronger than her desire, but her body had wept for release. She'd *needed* to come.

With that thought in his mind, he didn't even attempt to start slowly, but fell upon her, ravenous. At his first taste, he groaned from the intense pleasure. He licked madly at her wetness, grinding his hips into the sheets. How could she feel so good to him? How could he be experiencing this much pleasure—as if she was truly the one he'd waited for?

When her thighs tightened around him, he took her with his stiffened tongue, then suckled her small flesh. A glance up revealed that her nipples had hardened into tight points and her breaths came hectic. Her arms fell over her head.

He knew she was close even though she slept. A weird charge came into the air, making him uneasy, making his hackles rise. The taste of her made him forget. He savored her as she grew wetter and wetter against his mouth.

He felt her tense, wakening. "*Come for me,*" he growled against her flesh.

She drew her knees to her chest, resting her feet on his shoulders. Interesting, but he was game if—

She kicked him hard enough to send him across the room.

A stab of pain told him she'd torn muscles in his shoulder. A red haze covered his sight and confused his mind. He roared as he charged her, throwing her to the bed and pinning her down. He freed his trews and gripped himself, about to shove into her, crazed with his rage and lust, ignoring the Instinct's warnings: *Her mind won't bend—she'll break. You'll destroy what you've been given.* . . .

He saw her fangs as she gasped with fear, and wanted to hurt her. A vampire *given* to him? Bound to him for eternity? More torture. More hatred.

The vampires had won again.

He bellowed with fury, and she shrieked. The sound shattered the glass lamp and the television and splintered the door to the balcony. His eardrums nearly burst and he leapt back, clamping his hands over his ears to block out the sound. What the bloody hell was that?

A scream so high-pitched he didn't know if humans could hear it.

She shot from the bed, and as she yanked her gown into place, she gave him a look of . . . betrayal? Resignation? She flew to the balcony, ducking through the thick curtains.

Dark now, no danger. Let her go. He slammed his head and fists against the wall, mad with lust. With hate. Memories of fire and torture stabbed him. *The feel of the bone finally giving way under his shaking hands.* . . .

If he was cursed to carry those memories, to have that burden, it was little better than still being there, trapped in fire. He'd rather die.

Maybe fucking her regularly, taking his pain out on her, was what he was supposed to do. Of course. He felt himself calming at the thought. Yes, he'd been given a vampire solely for his pleasure, for his revenge.

He stalked to the balcony, assessing his shoulder, and tore the curtain aside.

His breath left him.

4

The vampire stood scarcely balanced on the balcony railing, her hair and gown whipping in the wind. He swallowed hard. "Come down from there." Why had his chest tightened with such alarm?

She whirled to face him—somehow keeping her balance. She looked hurt, her luminous eyes filled with pain. He resisted the recognition taking hold in his disordered mind.

She whispered, "Why are you doing this to me?"

Because I've wanted what's mine. Because I need you and I hate you. "Come down now," he ordered.

She shook her head slowly.

"You canna die from this. From sun, or losing your head, but no' from a fall." He made his tone casual, though he was uncertain. They were how many floors up? If she was weak . . . "And I'll easily follow you down to bring you back here."

She glanced over her shoulder down at the street. "No, I might die in my condition."

For some reason he believed her, and his alarm spiked. "Your condition? Because of the sun? Damn you, tell me!"

She turned toward the street and put one foot off the railing.

"Wait!" He tensed to spring for her, not understanding how she could possibly still be balanced. *Won't bend. She's broken.* "I will no' do that again. No' until you want me to." The wind was picking up, plastering the silk to her body. "When you woke . . . that was meant to give, no' to take."

She put the foot back and faced him. "And when I refused your *gift?*" she cried. "What was that?"

If she died . . . The fear for her brought him his first true clarity since before the fire. Twelve hundred years he'd waited. For . . . *her.*

For whatever reason, the world had given a vampire to him, and he'd pushed her to this? *Destroy what you've been given.* He was devastated by what she was—but he didn't want her dead. Or ruined.

It enraged him even to contemplate the hell he'd just been through, much less to talk about it, but he had to try anything. *Have to get rid of this feeling—this dread.* "Understand that I've been . . . locked away for one hundred and fifty years. Without comfort, without a woman. I'd only just escaped a week before I found you and I have no' . . . acclimated well."

"Why do you act as if you know me?"

"I've been disoriented. Confused. I know we've never met."

"Who are you?"

Just minutes before, he'd been about to claim her—without even telling her his name. "I am Lachlain, head of the Lykae clan."

He could hear her heart speed up with fear. "Y-you're a werewolf? You must let me go."

She looked otherworldly, with her hair streaming about and her skin so pale. She was not of his kind, and he had no idea how to be with her. "I will. After the next full moon. I vow it."

"I want to go now."

"I need you . . . to get to my home," he said, adding lie to truth. "And I will no' hurt you again." Possibly another lie.

She laughed bitterly. "You were going to force me just then, and I almost died this morning. Of *sun*." She whispered the word. "Do you know what that's like? The pain?"

He had a bloody good idea.

Her expression suddenly grew horrified, as if she was recalling a nightmare. "I haven't felt the sun on my skin"—she swayed on the rail—"since I was three years old."

Inching closer, mouth gone dry, he said, "I doona ken how to care for you, but you will tell me. And this will no' happen again."

"I don't want your attentions. You . . . you *frighten* me."

Of course he frightened her—his rages left even him shaken. "I understand. Now, come down. I know you doona want to die."

She glanced over her shoulder at the waxing moon rising, giving him her flawless profile. A gust pushed her hair across her neck. In all his years, he'd never seen such a preternatural scene as her pale skin against her blood-red gown with the moon glowing behind her.

She didn't answer, only exhaled wearily, swaying.

"Look at me." She didn't—she glanced down. "Look at me!"

She seemed to wake up, her brows drawing together, her eyes bleak. "I just want to go home," she said in a small voice.

"You will. I vow you'll go home." *To your new home.* "Just help me get to mine."

"If I help you, you swear you'll release me?"

Never. "Aye."

"You won't hurt me?"

"No, I will no' hurt you."

"Can you make that promise? You can't seem to . . . control yourself."

"Every hour I gain control." Because of her? "And know that I doona *want* to hurt you." That, at least, was now true. He thought.

"You won't do those . . . th-things to me again?"

"I will no' unless you want me to." He held out his hand to her. "Do we have an agreement?"

She didn't take it, but after several agonizing moments, she did come down with a bizarre movement. She *stepped* down as if she were strolling and had stepped from a curb without breaking stride.

He gave her shoulders a shake. "Doona ever do that again." He had an odd urge to squeeze the vampire to his chest, and set her away.

She looked down. "I won't. Unless it's a better alternative."

He glowered at that. "Do we have an agreement?"

When she nodded, he wondered if it was only the position he'd forced upon her that had made her agree, or was it more? He'd thought he might have seen *compassion* in her eyes for just a brief moment when he'd admitted his imprisonment.

"Then we leave tonight for Scotland."

Her lips parted. "I can't *go* to Scotland! I was going to *direct* you. Or at least, MapQuest was," she added in a mumble. "How would you plan to get there without burning me alive?" She was clearly panicked. "I-I can't travel easily. No commercial planes. No trains. *The sun* . . ."

"I've secured a car. We'll drive there." He was pleased by how casual he sounded, since a week ago he hadn't known what a bloody car was. "And stop well before sunrise each day. A man downstairs mapped it out for me."

"You know how to drive? You acted as though you'd never even seen a car—"

"No, I doona know how to drive, but I'm guessing you do."

"I've only driven short jaunts from home."

"Ever been to the Highlands?"

"Uh, no—"

"Ever want to?"

"Who doesn't—?"

"Then, vampire, you'll be going with me."

Emma lifted an unsteady hand to her hair and pulled a hank in front of her face. She stared in horror.

Streaked. By the *sun*.

He'd left her to shower and dress, and alone in the bathroom, she gaped at the vivid evidence of how close she'd come to dying. Dropping her hair, she slid off her nightgown and twisted in the mirror to assess her skin.

It was unharmed now, pale and healed—unlike the last time. She glanced at the back of her hand, growing nauseated. Thank Freya, the memory of her burn was mercifully hazy as usual.

Though she couldn't recollect specifics, she'd learned her lesson well, avoiding the sun for nearly sixty-seven years, yet near dawn she'd passed out before she could either escape this Lachlain or beg him to shut the curtains.

Shivering, Emma turned on the shower and stepped in, avoiding the broken marble. She still sensed his presence from the night before. She could almost feel his hands skimming over her wet skin, his finger pressing full inside her, his powerful body shuddering and tensing as she'd stroked him.

When she turned in the shower, the water sprayed her sensitive breasts, making her nipples hard— In a flash, the memory of waking under his mouth hit her.

She'd struck out at him with such violence because she'd been confused and frightened. Yet she'd also been nearer to orgasm than she had in her entire life. She was a weak woman, because for the briefest second the temptation to lie there docile and let her knees fall open to accept his fierce kiss had been nearly overwhelming. Even now she found herself wet.

For him. She was bewildered by her response. She wondered how she would react to him if he *wasn't* debating killing her.

At least now she knew why he was so savage. Besides clearly having *issues*, he was a Lykae, considered a ruthless menace by even the lowliest in the Lore. She recalled what her aunts had taught her about them.

Each Lykae housed a wolflike "beast" inside, like a possession. This rendered them immortal and made them crave and appreciate the elementals: food, touch, sex. But, as she'd seen tonight and the night before, it also could make a Lykae unable to control its ferocity, a ferocity their kind *willingly* unleashed during sex, reveling in scratching, biting, and marking flesh in a frenzy. Which had always sounded hellish to Emma—a being cursed with fragility and a deep-seated fear of pain.

How such a handsome façade could mask an ungovernable animal was beyond her understanding. He was a beast in the form of a fantasy. His body, except for the incongruous leg injury, was nothing short of . . . divine. His hair was thick and straight, a rich, dark brown that she imagined would look golden in the sun. She'd noted that sometime today he'd had it trimmed, and his face was now cleanly shaved to reveal his perfect features. On the surface *divine*, beneath . . . a beast.

How could she be *drawn to* a being that she needed to be *running from*?

Her arousal was involuntary, shaming in a way, and she was glad when the weight of her exhaustion stifled it. She was flagging by the minute, and the idea of driving to Scotland enervated her even more.

As she slumped against the shower wall, she wondered how Annika was holding up right now. Probably shrieking with worry and fury, ensuring that their hometown of New Orleans got flailed with lightning and that every car alarm in three parishes went off.

Emma also wondered if she really would've jumped. Yes, she thought with a start—if this Lachlain had been the same insane, howling animal of before, if his eyes hadn't slowly warmed to golden, she would've taken her chances.

And she wondered how he'd hurt his leg and where he'd been "locked away" for so long and by whom—

Immediately she shook her head as if to dislodge the questions.

She didn't want to know. Didn't need to know.

Annika had once told her that vampires were cold and dispassionate, able to use their powerful logic as no other in the Lore because they could disregard any detail outside of their goal as incidental.

Emma had a job to do. Period. And when she completed it, she would be awarded her freedom. She just had to keep her eye on the ball. *Never played baseball, freak. Oh, yeah.*

Didn't matter. Finish the task—*get to go on as usual.*

As she lathered and rinsed her hair, she mused over her typical week prior to the misbegotten trip. Monday through Friday she did research for her coven and trained before watching a late movie with the more night-owlish of her aunts. Friday and Saturday the witches came over with their Xbox and blenders full of pastel drinks. Sunday night she rode horses with the good demons who often loitered around the manor. If she could tweak just a couple of little aspects about her existence, life could be damn near perfect.

She frowned at her thoughts. As a natural-born vampire, she couldn't lie to others. If an untruth arose in her thoughts and the impulse to use it fired in her mind, she would become violently ill. No, Emma couldn't lie to others, but she'd always had a talent for lying to herself. A couple of little tweaks? In truth, there was a yawning loneliness in her life—and a fear about her nature that rode her constantly. . . .

As far as she knew, she was like no one else in existence—she truly belonged nowhere—and though her Valkyrie aunts loved her, she felt loneliness as sharply as a blade driven into her heart every day.

She'd figured if she could determine how her parents had lived together and had been able to have her, then maybe she could find others like herself. Perhaps then she could finally feel a *connection* to something else. And if she could discover more about her vampire half, she might allay her fear that one day she would become like them.

No one should have to worry each day that she might turn into a killer. . . .

If she'd assumed he would give her privacy because he'd learned a lesson, she'd have been wrong. He walked right in and opened the shower stall door. She jumped, startled, fumbling not to drop the conditioner bottle before catching it on the pad of her forefinger.

She saw his fists clench and open, and that finger went limp. The bottle thudded.

One hit . . . The image of the shredded bedside table flashed in her mind, then the memory of the car he'd batted like a crumpled piece of paper. Chunks of marble that hadn't been pulverized still littered the shower floor. Fool. She'd been a fool to think he wouldn't hurt her. Of all the things she *should* fear, she feared pain the most. And now a *Lykae* clenched his fists in anger. At her.

She turned into the corner, giving him her side to try to shield her nudity. And because if he hit, she could sink down and draw her knees to her chest. But with some foreign curse, he stalked off.

After showering, she returned to the bedroom to find almost all of her belongings gone. Had he taken them to the car he'd secured? If so, ten euros said that he'd tossed her laptop *under* everything else. She supposed it didn't matter anyway, since she'd uncovered nothing about her parents to go into said computer. Just because she could navigate Tulane's research library did not mean she could crack the Lore in a foreign country—oh, and in the hours between sundown and sunup.

She'd accomplished nothing on this trip. But for her abduction, of course.

Why should she even be surprised?

She exhaled wearily and trudged to the items he *had* left her—one outfit laid out on the bed. Of course he'd chosen the tiniest, most sheer lingerie she'd brought with her. The thought of him handling her underclothes, deliberately choosing them for her, made her blush for the thousandth time since she'd met him. She must have wasted a gallon of blood blushing because of him.

He'd also picked out long pants and a turtleneck and a sweater and a jacket. Did he want her to be buried in clothes?

At that moment, he appeared again. She leapt backward, clearing the length of the mattress to stand at the headboard. Even with her keen hearing, she hadn't heard a hint of his approach.

He raised his eyebrows at the quick movement. "That frightened of me?"

She clutched her towel. *I'm that frightened of my own shadow, much less an overgrown Lykae!* But his voice hadn't been cruel, and she gathered the courage to study him from beneath her lashes. His eyes were that warm golden color and he was wearing new clothes. He looked like a mid-thirties millionaire. Or more aptly, a physique-model playing one.

The bastard was a remarkably handsome man. And he obviously knew it, which nettled. "You've attacked me twice. You've given me no reason not to be frightened."

He was getting irritated again. "That was before I gave you my word that I would no' hurt you." Then, seeming to get his temper under control, he said, "Everything is ready. I have a rented car waiting and I've settled the bill for this room."

She could just imagine that bill. Even though he'd annihilated the antique bedside table in this room, it wouldn't add up to the cost of her stay. "But I've been here for weeks. I can pay for my own—"

"You did pay. Now, come down from the bed."

When he held out his hand to her, she crossed to the opposite side and stepped down, feeling dizzy and fearing the worst—the utter abuse of her credit card. "And I suppose I paid for your new clothes?" she dared to ask with the bed between them. Emma knew fine things—all Valkyrie did—since they'd inherited Freya's acquisitiveness—and the cut of his clothes reeked of money.

He wore a dark leather car coat that was hand-stitched and flat-front trousers, camel in color and lean in fit. Under the opened jacket, a black thin cashmere shirt molded to him like a second skin. Between the edges of his coat, she could see the rigid outlines of his chest. His clothing said, *I'm rich, and I might be a little dangerous.*

Women would adore him.

"Aye. The man downstairs has many resources and our card has no limits." His tone dared her to say something.

Our card? Her Centurion AmEx with instructions that some purchases might seem *off* and that the owner would be traveling, so do not hinder in any way. A safeguard had now turned into a financial weapon in his hands.

Like all in the coven, she had a yearly allowance for clothes and entertainment and it was very generous, but she'd been saving up, thinking of buying something major that would be all her own—an antique or her own horse or anything that she wouldn't have to share with her aunts. No longer.

Among her other trials with him, the Lykae appeared determined to break her bank.

"You didn't leave me any way to cover my ears," she said, glancing down, avoiding his eyes as usual.

Her comment made him scowl again at her clothing. She wanted to hide something *he* found attractive, and yet her garments were so revealing to others? Her black trews scarcely came up over her hipbones and hugged the curves of her arse. Her red shirt, though high-collared, had strange, asymmetrical seams that drew the eye to the swell of her breasts. When she moved, flashes of her flat midriff came into view. He'd chosen those clothes to cover her—not advertise her. He'd buy her new ones at the first opportunity, spending lavishly of the vampire's money. He intended to find out how much he could *possibly* spend.

"I just need a scarf or a way to fasten my braids. Or people will see them—"

"You'll leave your hair down."

"B-but the humans—"

"Will no' dare do anything when I am there." When he found himself crossing to her, she took several steps back. Terrified of him.

Lachlain had little memory of the field and even the rest of the night before was hazy, but he knew he'd been . . . less than gentle. Then tonight he'd leapt onto her, pinning her to the bed about to shove into her, even while knowing he would hurt her. He'd seen her in the shower warily noting his clenched fists. She was right—she had no reason not to.

On the balcony, he'd discovered pain within her. That's what she had in her eyes. He had it, too, and he was too damaged to help her. Too full of hate to *want* to help her.

"Then can I at least call my family?" she asked. "Like you promised?"

He frowned. He'd said "contact her family," as in a letter. He'd seen the man downstairs use the telephone. On the television, he'd seen it as well. He'd never thought she could have called another country. "Be quick about it. We have to make good time tonight."

"Why? Are we going very far?" Her voice grew panicked. "Because you said an hour before sunrise—"

"Are you nervous about this?"

"Of course I am!"

"Doona be. I will protect you," he said simply, annoyed that she relaxed not a whit. "Make your call." He turned the corner into their room's foyer, strode down the hall to the door, opened and closed it.

But he never left.

5

"Do you have any idea how dead you are?" Regin asked. "Annika is freaking out. She's making berserkers look like candy-stripers right now."

"I know she's worried!" Emma said, clenching the phone in both hands. "I-is she there?"

"Nope. There was an emergency she had to take care of. Em, why in the hell weren't you on the plane? Or answering your cell phone?"

"The cell phone's toast. Got wet in the rain—"

"And why weren't you on the plane?" Regin snapped.

"I've decided to stay, okay? I came here for a reason and I'm not finished yet." Not a lie.

"You couldn't answer any of our messages? Any of the messages the manager tried to deliver to your room today?"

"There could've been knocking, I don't know. Go figure—daytime and I was asleep?"

"Annika's sending a search party for you," Regin said. "They're at the airport right now."

"Well, call and tell them to make a U-ee, because I won't be here."

"Don't you even wanna know what you're in danger from?"

Emma glanced over at the bedside table. "I quite know, thank you."

"You spotted a vampire?" Regin shrieked. "Did he approach you?"

"A *what?*" she shrieked back.

"What did you think I meant about danger? Vampires have been following Valkyrie all over the world—even *here.* Vampires in *Louisiana,* if you can wrap your mind around that. But wait, the insanity builds: Ivo the Cruel, number-two man to the vampire king, was on *Bourbon Street.*"

"So close to home?" Annika had moved their coven to New Orleans years before to get away from the Vampire Horde's kingdom in Russia.

"Yeah, and Lothaire was with him, too. You might not have heard of him—he's an elder in the Horde, kind of does his own thing, but creepy-creepy. I'm thinking he and Ivo weren't in the Quarter for a Hand Grenade and a Lucky Dog. Annika has been out searching for them. We don't know their intentions, why they don't just kill as per usual, but if they found out what you are . . ."

Emma thought back to her nightly forays around Paris. Had she been followed by members of the Horde? Could she even tell a vampire from a human? If her aunts had taught her that the Lykae were monsters, they'd told her every day of her life how vicious the Horde was.

The vampires had captured Furie, the Valkyrie queen, more than fifty years ago and no one could find her. There were rumors they'd chained her to the bottom of the ocean, dooming her to an eternity of drowning only to have her immortality surge her to life again and again.

They'd wiped out Regin's entire race of beings—Regin was the last of the Radiant Ones—which made for a conflicted relationship between her and Emma, to say the least. Emma knew Regin loved her, but she was hard on her. Her own foster mother, Annika, made a hobby of killing vampires, because as she often said, "The only good leech is a *dead* leech."

And now the vampires might discover Emma. For seventy years, that had been Annika's worst fear—ever since Emma had first tried to nip her with her baby fangs in public. . . .

"Annika thinks these are signs that the Accession has begun," Regin said, knowing that would strike fear in Emma. "And yet you're away from the safety of the coven?"

The Accession. A chill crept through her.

Bringing prosperity and power to the victors, the Accession wasn't an Armageddon type of war—it wasn't as if the strongest factions of the Lore met on neutral turf after an invitation to "rumble." About a decade into it, events began to come into play, as if fate was seeding future, deadly conflicts, involving all the players at a startling rate. Like windmill vanes on a rusted spoke, it began creaking, creeping to life, only to gain momentum and soar with speed every five hundred years.

Some said it was a kind of cosmic checks-and-balances system for an ever-growing population of immortals, forcing them to kill each other off.

In the end, the faction that lost the fewest of their kind won.

But the Valkyrie could not increase their numbers like the Horde and the Lykae, and the last time the Valkyrie had dominated through an Accession was two millennia ago. The Horde had won it ever since. This one would be Emma's first. Damn it, Annika had promised Emma that she could stay under her bed through the thick of it!

Regin's voice was smug when she said, "So, I suppose you'll be wanting that ride home now."

Can't lie, can't lie. "No. Not yet. I met someone. I met a . . . man. And I'm staying with him."

"A man?" Regin gasped. "Oooh, you want to bite him, don't you? Or have you already? Oh, Freya, I knew this would happen."

"What do you mean, you knew this would happen?" The coven had forbidden Emma to drink straight from a living source because they didn't want her to accidentally kill. Plus they believed blood was mystically alive when inside a being, its powers—and side effects—dying when outside. It had never been a problem for Emma. In New Orleans, they had delivery from a Lore-owned blood-bank setup, the number on speed dial like Domino's.

"Em, this was law. You knew better than to get dental with somebody."

"But I—"

"Hey, Lucia," Regin called out, not even bothering to mute the phone. "Pay up, suckah, Emma got dental with some dude—"

"No, I didn't!" Emma said in a rush. "I've never gotten dental!" How many Valkyrie were home to hear Regin? "You placed bets about me?" She strove not to sound as dismayed as she was by this. Was Regin the only one who thought Emma would behave as other vampires would? That she would slip up—or revert to her true vampire nature? Or did they all share Emma's fear that she might turn killer?

"If not to drink him, then what would *you* want with a man? Huh?"

Her voice quavering with anger, Emma said, "What any woman wants! I'm no different from you—"

"You want to, like, sleep with him?"

Why did she sound *that* disbelieving? "Maybe I do!"

Regin sucked in a breath. "Who are you and what have you done with my niece's body? Come on, Em! You've never even had a *date* and all of a sudden you're meeting a 'man' and thinking about lifting tail? You, sweet seventy and never been kissed? Don't you think it's a little more likely that you want to drink him?"

"No, it's not like that," she insisted. The vampires in the Horde sublimated the sexual urge. Blood lust and the need to kill ruled them. And for all these years, Emma had not been a sexual person. She'd never been in a sexual situation.

Until last night.

She felt a glimmer of hope. She'd been aroused by Lachlain. She'd felt regular lust—*not* blood lust. And she'd been so *close*. Even tonight, she'd been to the edge with him. Could she use him to answer this question once and for all? She bit her lip, thinking of the possibility.

"Have you gotten yourself into trouble?" Regin asked. Emma could *hear* her narrowing her eyes. "Is someone there right now?"

"No, I'm alone in my room. Is this really so hard to believe?"

"Okay, I'll play. Who is he? How did you meet?"

This could get tricky. "He was a stranger. I met him outside of Notre Dame among the vendor stands."

"And? Want to not be the secretive vamp you always are and spill the details? *If* this is true. . . ."

"As if I can lie! All right, you want to know? I think he's . . . he's wildly handsome!" With emphasis on *wild*. "He knows what I am and we're leaving Paris together."

"Great Freya, you're serious. What's he like?"

"He's strong. Said he'd protect me." Great kisser. Intermittently insane. With a broad chest she'd wanted to lick like ice cream.

In a scoffing tone, Regin asked, "Strong enough to take down a vampire?"

"You have *no* idea." Getting out of town with a powerful Lykae—the natural-born enemy of the vampires—was sounding more and more like a bingo idea. But then she frowned. If Lachlain hadn't been the danger they'd warned her of, then what was his agenda? What did he want with her? Why didn't he simply kill the vampire he'd captured?

A suspicion tickled her mind, but she mentally scratched it away. *He can't even drive a car—obviously he needs help. And I'm from the Lore. . . .*

"When are you leaving Paris?"

"Tonight. Right now, actually."

"That's good, at least. Tell me where you're going."

"So Annika can come drag me home by my ear?" And fight Lachlain to the death? "Nope. Tell her I'll be home week after next at the latest, and that if she tries to find me, I'll know she doesn't trust that I am more than capable of taking care of myself—"

Regin snorted, then laughed outright.

"I *can* take care of myself." Her tone hurt, she asked, "Why is that funny?"

Shrieking laughter.

"Piss off, Regin! You know what? I'll send you a postcard!"

She slammed the phone down, then snatched up her boots. Stomping into the first one, she muttered angrily, "I will *so* go." Another boot shoved on. "And I won't be catching any Stockholm syndrome."

When the phone rang seconds later, she yanked it back up. "What?"

"Alrighty then, have it your way—you're officially on your own," Regin said, then sniffled as if she'd cried from laughing so hard. "Now, if you come across a leech, no offense, remember your training."

"None taken. And would that be the sword training where you fly past my defenses and swat me on the ass, chirping, 'Dead!'? Another swat. 'Dead!'? Yeah, I'll get right on that."

"No, that would be the training where you sprint like hell whenever you hear that I'm looking for you to train."

Once she'd hung up the telephone again, Lachlain strode around the corner without even acting like he hadn't listened.

She jumped again, then her brows drew together. "You eavesdropped, didn't you?"

"Aye," he answered without compunction.

"Learn anything new?" she asked in a nervous tone.

Not really. "Your accent's odd and you speak too quickly," he answered honestly. Then he smirked. "But I did hear that you think me 'wildly handsome.' " He wondered why he'd felt a flush of pleasure at that. As if he cared what she thought.

She glanced away, but not before he saw her face flush. He thought he heard her mutter, *Emphasis on the wild.*

"Why did you no' tell your family what I am?"

"I would never want to worry them unduly."

"And knowing you are with a Lykae would worry them?" he asked, as though he didn't know how violently they would react to the news.

"Of course it would. They've told me about you. About what you are."

He crossed his arms over his chest. "And what am I?"

For the first time since he'd taken her, she purposely met his gaze. "Deep down, you're a monster."

6

Emma wears her fear like a flag.

That's what her aunts said about her, not cruelly, just with baffled shakes of their heads. Compared to them, she feared so much—and she was the first to admit it.

They were courageous, fierce, and each of them had a purpose in life—some to guard indestructible weapons that could never fall into the wrong hands. Some watched over a bloodline of a particularly strong or noble human family. They were considered guardian angels.

Emma? Well, Emma had undertaken the epic endeavor of . . . college. At *Tulane*. She hadn't even ventured outside of her hometown to earn her identity of Emma the Co-ed, possessor of a B.A. in pop culture.

She remembered one time when she was young, playing at night in her sandbox. Out of the corner of her eye, she'd seen the yellow glow of a troop of ghouls as they descended on the manor.

She'd fled inside, bursting through the door, screaming, "Run!"

Her aunts had all shared glances. Annika had appeared embarrassed, her stunningly beautiful face displaying a frown. "Emma, sweetling, what precisely do you mean by *run?* We don't *run* from anything. We're the creatures they run from, remember?"

How surprised they'd been when Emma had wanted this trip abroad. How shocked they would be that her finger was very decidedly pushing the lobby button of the elevator to take her to the Lykae waiting for her. After she'd called him a monster to his face, his eyes had flickered, then he'd stormed out of the room, ordering her to meet him at the car downstairs.

The car downstairs. Holy shite, was she really going to do this? As she descended, she did a quick mental tally of the pros and cons of cooperating and leaving with him.

Pros. She could possibly use him to finally understand more about herself and her nature, and he would kill any other vampire in sight, thereby protecting her from them.

Cons. He'd never told her whether he ultimately planned to kill her or not. The Lykae might protect her from the vampires, but who would have her back against him?

Her aunts might never run—but Emma excelled at it. Until she got into the car with him, she thought, she still had a chance. . . .

When she exited the elevator, she spotted him through the lobby as he waited in the drive. His gaze was already locked on her. She took a steadying breath, glad for once that she and Regin had bickered—it always fired her up, sometimes enough to make Emma throw down her pompoms and toe the sideline.

He was standing beside a black sedan, a black . . . *Mercedes?* She raised an eyebrow. He'd rented what looked like a 500 series that was going to cost her a fortune to drop off in a different country. *Werewolf couldn't find an S6?*

Yes, he was a Lykae, but seeing him like this, she realized

that no one would ever know he was of a different species. When he casually leaned back against the door and crossed his arms over his chest, he appeared human, just taller, stronger, with some kind of inexplicable pull.

Although he appeared relaxed, his eyes were watchful, and the streetlamps lit an expression that was intent and never wavering from her face. She suppressed the urge to glance behind her for the woman he was truly devouring with his eyes.

Was this whole scary situation worth it just so she could experience that look? Just so she could have the knowledge of what it was like to have a man like that look at her as if she were the only woman in the world?

All her life she'd lived in the shadow of her aunts, who were so stunningly lovely that eddas were written about them. Though Emma's mother was dead, Emma was still overwhelmed by universal tales of her fabled beauty.

Emma was scrawny, pale, and . . . befanged.

Yet a man this handsome was giving her a look that could smelt metal. If he hadn't terrified her and attacked her—if he could be the gentle lover who'd cupped her breast and rumbled in her ear that her skin was soft—would she leave with him? Her eyes met his. This male had touched her and made her feel things she hadn't before, things she'd envied others. Merely nestling her face against his naked chest had been a new experience that she would never trade for anything.

Feeling bolder, she allowed her gaze to flicker over his body before slowly inching back up to his face. He wasn't smirking or scowling, but looked as if he was thinking the same thoughts she was.

She found herself drawn to him, her mind and thoughts

shutting down, like she was disconnected from reality. As her heels clicked across the lobby's marble floor toward him, her body seemed to come alive. He stood fully, visibly tensing.

Her breasts seemed fuller. Her ears were uncovered in public, with only her long, freed hair to conceal them. She felt as though she'd gone out without a bra—she felt a little . . . naughty. When the sudden urge came to taste her lips, she did. He clenched his hands in response.

She wanted one thing from him, and if he could give it to her, shouldn't she risk the rest? She'd risked the shower with him for the same reason, and he hadn't hurt her then. No, in the end, he had kept his promise—

The spell was broken when a Ferrari, reeking of burned clutch, screeched to a stop behind the Mercedes. Two European starlets with perfect bodies clad in tight dresses spilled out. Perplexing, but Emma grew dismayed knowing he would appraise them just as he had her. The leggy blondes with bubble breasts spotted him and stopped in their stiletto-toed tracks, finally recovering enough to giggle loudly in a bid for his attention.

When it wasn't forthcoming, they pouted, and one "dropped" her lipstick to roll by his feet. Emma gaped as the woman bent down before him, then checked for his reaction.

Between her and Lachlain, she was the only one watching the scene—he'd never taken his gaze from her. But she had the impression that he was well aware of their antics. His eyes bored into hers as if saying, *I'm looking at what I want.* She shivered.

Having been completely ignored, the two finally gave up and shot Emma venomous looks as they passed. As if he was hers? As if she was keeping him from them? She was a prisoner—more or less! "You can have him, kitties," she hissed for their ears only. They blanched before scuttling away. She might be a coward against Lore creatures, but with humans she could hold her own in the tabby arena.

Now, how would she fare traveling with a wolf?

Lachlain had watched as Emmaline glided through the lobby, moving too gracefully to truly look human. He'd been struck by how wealthy and coolly composed she appeared—like an aristocrat. One would never imagine her timorous nature, because she seemed to have donned a cloak of confidence.

Then she'd changed.

He didn't know what caused it, but her gaze turned heated. She gave the impression that she needed a man—and he'd responded. *Everything in him* responded. But others had, too. Though she seemed unconscious of it, her sensual walk and movements lured every male gaze to her. In mid-conversation, they turned and stared, enthralled. Even the women did. Lachlain pinpointed each of their focuses. The women stared at her clothing and shiny hair; the men ogled her breasts, lips, and eyes, their hearts and breaths speeding up at her mesmerizing beauty.

Did each of those fools think he'd be the one to give her what she desired? Fury fired in him. She'd told him with a steady gaze that deep down he was a monster. She'd been partly correct, and right now that beast wanted to kill every male that dared look at her when he had not claimed her. This was a vulnerable time, and the Instinct was screaming at him to get her away—

Realization hit him. Female vampires had always been

born beautiful—as a defensive and predatory tool. They manipulated with it and used it to kill. This one was at work even now, doing what she'd been born to do. And he'd been reacting just as she'd known he would.

When she stood before him, he cast her a black look. She frowned at his expression, visibly swallowed, then said, "I'm going to go with you. And I won't try to run or escape." Her voice was silky and seductive, a voice made for wicked murmurs in bed. "I'll help you, but I'm asking you not to hurt me."

"I told you I'd protect you."

"You told me the night before that you might kill me."

His scowl deepened.

"Just please, um, could you try *not* to?" She looked up at him with those blue eyes that appeared so guileless.

She thought to use her wiles to handle him? To gentle the beast inside him? *He* couldn't even control it—

An odd, chill wind blew, batting a curl against her cheek. Her eyes narrowed. A second later, they widened and her hands flew to his chest. He glanced down and saw her shell-pink claws go from curling to straight—like little daggers.

She'd perceived a threat. His eyes scanned the area; he was feeling something, too. But it was fleeting, and his senses weren't as keen as they normally were. Not yet. In any case, a menace of some sort near her wasn't surprising. As a vampire she had many blood enemies—a fact he'd once applauded. Now he would have to fight them because he would destroy anything that sought to hurt her.

Instead of telling her that, he removed her hands from his chest with an expression of distaste. "I'll bet you're better off with me than alone out here."

She nodded, *agreeing*. "Then can we go?"

When he gave her a tight nod, and drew away from her to go to the passenger side of the car, the valet opened the driver's door and helped her in. Lachlain cringed at not having assisted her, then grew angered over his chagrin.

After a brief grappling with the door handle, he joined her, sinking into the plush seat. The interior was luxurious—even he would know that—though it was strange that the accents in the car looked like wood but didn't smell organic.

She peeked at the back seating of the car, no doubt noticing the cache of magazines he'd had the concierge amass for him, but without even a questioning glance she faced forward. "I can get to London"—she pushed a button that said *OnStar*—"but after that I'll need help."

He nodded, watching as she hurriedly adjusted her seat far forward before strapping a harness over her front.

At his look, she explained, "It's a seat belt. For safety," then reached down to move a lever to D.

So help him, if that stood for "drive" and that was all it took to engage this machine, he was going to fall out. When she glanced at his *seat belt*, he raised his eyebrows and said simply, "Immortal."

He knew he'd irritated her. She moved her foot to the longer of two pedals on the floor, stomping it, and the car surged forward into traffic. She glanced at him, no doubt hoping to have startled him. Not possible—he could already tell he was going to love cars.

Her tone defensive, she said, "I'm immortal, too, usually, but if I get in a wreck and get knocked out till morning, that sun allergy card my aunts make me cart around won't do jack. Okay?"

"I understood fifty percent of that," he observed calmly.

"I can't afford this car," she retorted, clenching the steering wheel as she directed the vehicle around other cars.

Why this concern about money? Who would dare withhold funds from her? The vampires had always been wealthy and had just begun investing in seep oil when he was imprisoned. Obviously, the market had grown. Not surprising, since everything their king, Demestriu, touched turned to gold. Or died.

Thinking of Demestriu made rage flare, nearly choking him. Pain radiated through his leg, and he clenched his hand on the handle above his head, crushing it.

She gasped, then locked her gaze straight ahead, murmuring to herself, "How much can a handle cost? Really."

Her unnecessary worry over something that would have no bearing on their life irritated him. His wealth—their wealth—was in his, *their* home. They need only get to it.

Their home. He was returning to Kinevane, his ancestral estate in the Highlands, with his woman. Finally. And if she weren't a vampire, he might feel pleased about that fact.

Instead of slighted.

He wondered how the clan would react to the incredible insult of her presence.

7

"How fast are we going?"

"Eighty kilometers an hour," Emma answered in an offhanded tone.

"How long is a kilometer?"

She'd known he was going to ask that. Sad but true—she didn't know. She was just matching the dial on her speedo to the kilometer-an-hour limit posted on the signs.

Many of his questions over the last half hour were making her feel stupid, and for some reason she felt it vital that he didn't think that.

The questions accompanied the stockpile of news magazines he'd acquired, no doubt from "the man downstairs" who'd mapped out this journey. Emma had seen Lachlain flying through them, realizing he was reading them that quickly because he would ask her for definitions every few pages. Acronyms seemed to stump him, and though she'd nailed NASA and DEA and PDA, she came up short on MP3.

After he'd read the magazines cover to cover, he took up the car manual and the questions resumed. As if she could define "a transmission."

Even with her limited assistance, she could *feel* him learning, could perceive how intelligent he was. And his questions indicated that he was deducing much, reasoning out his own answers as he soaked up knowledge in a way she'd never imagined was possible.

The rental car's copy of French traffic rules followed the manual, but he skimmed it, then tossed it away as if unimpressed. At her look, he explained, "Some things doona change. You still put on the parking brake on a hill, horse carriage or no."

His arrogance, his easy dismissal of things he should be awed by, rankled. A car would terrify her if she'd never been in one until she was an adult. Not Lachlain. On the road, he was too pleased with himself. Too comfortable in the leather seats, too curious about his window and air controls, flicking them on and off, up and down, and mauling the German technology with his huge paws. If he'd been locked away for so long, then shouldn't he be discombobulated?

Shouldn't he still be shaken? She believed nothing could shake his colossal arrogance—

Great, he's found the control for the moon roof. Her patience was ragged. Open . . . close. Open . . . close. Open . . .

Every minute closer to dawn found her more tense. She'd always been so cautious before. This trip to Europe had been her first real independence and only allowed because her aunts had provided so many safeguards. Yet Emma had managed to run out of blood, get kidnapped, and be forced out into the world with no precaution against the sun other than a *car trunk*, heading for who knew where. . . .

And still all this might be safer than *not* going with him. Something had been back at the hotel—possibly vampires.

Just after they'd gotten into the car, she'd thought about telling him that her life might be in danger. Two reasons prevented her. For one, she didn't think she could stand it if he shrugged and gave her an "I should care about this why?" look. And secondly, she'd have to explain what she was.

The Valkyrie were enemies of the Lykae as well, and she'd be damned if she allowed herself to be used as ammunition against her family. In fact, she didn't want Lachlain to discover anything about her to use against her. Luckily, she didn't think she'd revealed any weaknesses in her conversation with Regin—weaknesses like her critical need for blood. She could just imagine him saying, "I could find you some blood"—he would clap and rub his hands together— "right after shower time!" Besides, she could make it the three days it would take to get to Scotland. Surely.

She closed her eyes briefly. *But the hunger* . . . She'd *never* been tempted to drink from another, but with no alternative in sight, even Lachlain was starting to look good. She knew exactly where she would tap that neck. She would dig her claws into his back to hold on to him for a little reverse-mainline. . . .

"You drive well."

She coughed, startled, wondering if he'd caught her staring and rubbing her tongue against her fang. Then she frowned at his comment. "Um, how would you know?"

"You seem confident enough. Enough to take your eyes from your path."

Busted . . . "For your information, I'm not a particularly good driver." Her friends complained of her indecisiveness and her habit of letting everyone in front of her to the point of standstill.

"If you're no' a particularly good driver, then what *do* you do well?"

She gazed down the highway for many moments, contemplating an answer. Being good at something was relative, wasn't it? She liked to sing, but her voice couldn't compare to the pipes on a siren. She played piano, but twelve-fingered demons schooled her. She said honestly, "I'd be lying if I said I did anything particularly well."

"And you canna lie."

"No, I can't." She hated that. Why couldn't vampires have evolved until they could lie without pain? Humans had. Now they merely flushed and felt uncomfortable.

A few more go-rounds with the moon roof control followed. Then he drew some slips of paper from his jacket pocket. "Who is Regin? And Lucia, and Nïx?"

She glanced over, her jaw dropping. "You collected my private messages from the front desk?"

"And your *dry-cleaned* clothing," he replied in a bored tone. "Which sounds like an oxymoron to me."

"Of course you did," she said sharply. "Why wouldn't you?" *Privacy? You have none*, he'd sneered. He'd eaves-dropped on her speaking with Regin—as though it were his right.

"Who are they?" he demanded again. "They all order you to call except for this one message from Nïx. It makes no sense."

Nïx was her befuddled aunt, the oldest of all Valkyrie—or the proto-Valkyrie, as she liked to be called. She had su-permodel good looks but saw the future more clearly than she did the present. Emma could only imagine what Nuck-ing Futs Nïx had said. "Let me see it." She snatched the mis-sive, placing it flat against the steering wheel, then took a quick glance at the road before reading:

Knock, knock . . .
—Who's there?

Emma . . .
—Emma who? Emma who? Emma who? Emma who?

Nïx had told Emma before she'd left for Europe that on this trip she would "do that which you were born to do."

Apparently, Emma was born to get kidnapped by a deranged Lykae. Her fate sucked.

This message was Nïx's way of reminding Emma of her prediction. She alone knew how badly Emma wanted to earn a real identity, to have a page in the Valkyrie's revered Book of Warriors.

"What does it mean?" he asked when she wadded it up and dropped it at her feet.

Emma was furious he'd seen that message, furious he'd seen anything that might give him insight into her life. The way Lachlain observed and learned, he'd have Emma pinned before they made the Chunnel.

"Lucia calls you 'Em.' Is that your nickname with your family?"

That was it. Enough. Too much delving, too many questions. "Listen, uh, Mr. Lachlain. I got myself into a . . . situation. With you. And to get out of it, I have agreed to drive you to Scotland." Hunger was making her irritable. Irritability was making her heedless of consequences, and that occasionally passed for bravery. "I have *not* agreed to be your friend, or . . . or share your bed, or reward your invasion of my privacy with more information about myself."

"I will answer questions if you will."

"I don't have questions for you. Do I know why you were *locked away*—and, hello, vague much?—for fifteen decades? No, and honestly, I don't want to know. Where you appeared from last night? Don't wanna know."

"You're no' curious why all this has happened?"

"I will try to forget 'all this' when I leave you in Scotland, so why would I want to know more? My m.o. has always been to keep my head low and not ask too many questions. It's served me well so far."

"So you expect us to sit in this closed compartment the entire way in silence."

"Of course not."

She clicked on the radio.

Lachlain finally gave up fighting not to stare and openly studied her, finding it disturbingly pleasing. He told himself it was only because he lacked something else to occupy his mind. He'd run out of reading material and was only half listening to this radio.

The music was just as bizarre and inexplicable as everything else in this time, but he'd found a few songs that irritated him less than the others. When he'd voiced the ones he preferred, she'd appeared shocked, then mumbled, "Werewolves like the blues. Who knew?"

She must have felt his gaze because she peeked over at him with that shy look, nibbling her lip before glancing away. He scowled to find that one look from this vampire made his heart speed up, like those laughable humans' had.

Recalling the way the men reacted to her and knowing how rare she was among vampires, Lachlain realized that she must be wed. He'd been uncaring before. He'd said, "His loss," in reference to any husband, and he'd meant it, because a marriage wouldn't have stopped him. But now he wondered if she loved another.

In the Lykae world, if she was his mate, then he was hers as well. But she wasn't Lykae. It was possible that she could hate him forever—that he would have to keep her imprisoned forever—especially after he meted out his revenge.

He planned to exterminate every one of those leeches, which meant the people who'd given her life.

Again he questioned fate, questioned his instincts. There was no way they could be together.

Even as he thought this, his hand itched to touch her hair. Even as he thought this, he wondered what her smile would be like. He was like a randy lad, ogling her thighs encased in tight trews, eyes slowly following the raised clothing seam that ran between her legs.

He shifted positions again. He'd never been this desperate to tup. What he wouldn't give to toss her on the back bench in this car and take her thoroughly with his mouth, readying her, then pin her knees to her shoulders to receive him. Damn it, it was what he was supposed to do.

Thinking of taking her, he was reminded of last night when he'd touched her inside. He shook his head, remembering her tightness. She had been long without a man. He would split her in two at the first full moon. If he wasn't regularly fucking her before then. . . .

She hissed in a breath when an oncoming car's light beam was stronger than the one before it. She rubbed her eyes, then blinked them several times.

She looked tired and he wondered if she was hungry, but doubted it. The vampires he'd tortured could go weeks without blood, feeding only so often—like a snake.

But to be certain, he asked, "Are you hungry?" When she didn't answer, he said, "Are you or are you no'?"

"It's none of your concern."

Unfortunately, it was. Providing for her needs was his

duty. And what if she *needed* to kill? For Lachlain's kind, finding one's mate was an imperative. For the ghouls, propagating by contagion was an imperative. Would her vampire nature crave killing so badly that she wouldn't be able to control it? And what would he do? Facilitate her? Protect her while she dragged down some unsuspecting human? Another . . . *man?*

Christ, he couldn't do this. "How do you drink?"

She mumbled, "Liquid goes into my mouth, whereby I swallow it."

"When was the last time?" he snapped.

As though he'd dragged the answer from her, she sighed, "Monday, if you must know," then peeked over, clearly noting his reaction.

"Just Monday you did it?" His voice conveyed a disgust that he didn't bother to hide.

She frowned at him, but then another bright light caught her eyes. She winced and the vehicle swerved before she righted it. "I need to concentrate on staying on the road."

If she didn't want to discuss it, he wouldn't press. Not tonight.

Having escaped the congestion of the Paris streets, they'd picked up speed on the smooth autoway, and as Lachlain watched the fields pass, the feeling was akin to running. The pure enjoyment of the experience dimmed the rage that always simmered deep inside him. He would be able to run soon. Because he was free and healing.

He deserved just one night of this, one night without having to think about blood and aggression and death. He wondered if that was even possible with a vampire seated next to him.

A vampire disguised as an angel.

Tomorrow. Tomorrow he would have to demand the answers he dreaded knowing.

Val Hall Manor
Just outside of New Orleans

"Is Myst back?" Annika shrieked as she ran through the doorway. "Or Daniela?" She clutched the thick door, sagging against it as she scanned the darkness outside. The light of the gas lamps made the oaks quaver in shadow. She turned to find Regin and Lucia in the great room just off the entry hall, painting each other's toenails while watching *Survivor*. "Have they returned?"

Regin arched an eyebrow. "We thought they were with you."

"Nïx?"

"Hibernating in her room."

"Nïx! Get down here!" Annika screamed to her sister as she slammed the door and bolted it behind her.

To Regin and Lucia, she said, "Is Emma back yet?" She put her hands to her knees, still gasping for breath.

They shared a glance. "She's, uh, she's not coming back right now."

"*What?*" Annika shrieked, even though at this moment she was grateful Emma wasn't here.

"She met some hottie over there—"

Annika held up her hand. "Got to get out of here."

Lucia frowned. "I don't understand 'got to.' Sounds like you want us to leave?"

"There's a plane about to crash, isn't there?" Regin asked,

her confusion genuine, her amber eyes curious. "That is *so* gonna hurt."

Lucia's brows knit. "I might run from a crashing plane—"

"Go . . . something's coming . . ." They didn't understand—the idea of fleeing so foreign. "*Now* . . ." She'd sprinted all the way from the city.

"We're safest here," Regin argued, her attention back to her toenails. "The inscription will keep anyone out." She looked up sharply, and then a sheepish smile spread over her features. "But, I, uh, I might not have renewed the inscription spell with the witches."

Lucia said, "I thought we were on auto-renewal. They charge our credit—"

"By Freya, I mean now!" Annika yelled, finally able to stand upright.

Taking their half-mother's name in vain? Eyes wide, the two scrambled up, lunging for their weapons—

The front door burst in.

A *horned* vampire stood in the doorway, eyes red and scanning Regin's and Lucia's faces intently. This was the one Annika had been unable to defeat. Only her knowledge of the maze of streets downtown had saved her. Now it was in their home.

"What is *that*, Annika?" Regin asked as she slipped a dagger from her arm sheath. "A turned *demon*?"

"Not possible," Lucia said. "That's supposed to be a true myth."

"Has to be." Annika had barely fought him off, and she killed vampires routinely. "Never seen one so powerful." The only reason she'd come back was to see if any of the older Valkyrie were here. The older ones could vanquish him. Regin and Lucia were among the youngest.

"Is he one of Ivo's minions?"

"Yes. Saw Ivo giving orders to this one. They're searching for someone—"

Two more vampires traced behind him just as Lucia readied the bow that was like an extension of her.

"Just go," Annika hissed. "Both of you—"

Ivo appeared directly after, his red eyes ablaze, his head completely shaven. All the runnels and reliefs of his scalp stood out as distinctly as his facial features.

"Hello, Ivo."

"Valkyrie," he sighed to Annika as he dropped onto their settee and rudely kicked his boots up on their table.

"You still have all the arrogance of a king. Though you aren't one." Annika regarded him gravely. "Can never be one."

Regin tilted her head at him. "Just a wittle wapdog. Demestriu's wittle bitch man."

When Lucia tried to bite back a snicker, Annika rapped Regin on the back of her head.

"What? What'd I say?"

"Enjoy your taunts," Ivo said pleasantly. "They'll be your last." To the demon, he said, "She isn't here."

"Who?" Annika demanded.

An amused glance. "The one I seek."

Out of the corner of her eye, Annika spied a flickering shape. Lothaire, an ancient foe of theirs as well, had traced into the shadows of the room, behind Ivo's seat. Everything about Lothaire was chilling, from his white hair, to his eyes that were more pink than red, to his expressionless face.

Tension stole through her; they were even more outnumbered. But Lothaire put his finger to his lips. *He doesn't want Ivo to know he's here?*

Ivo jerked his head around to see what had caught her interest, but Lothaire had traced away. Ivo seemed to shake himself, then ordered the demon, "Kill these three."

At his command, the other two sprang for Regin and Lucia. The demon vampire traced behind Annika *before his image faded in front.* As she whirled, his hand shot out for her neck, but she dodged, striking out fast as a blur to splinter his forearm. Another hit cracked his cheekbone and shattered his nose. While he roared, spraying blood, she kicked him between his legs hard enough to break his tailbone and send him crashing to the ceiling.

Yet fast and strong as if fresh to the fight, he snatched her neck. She twisted to get free, but he hurled her into the fireplace, propelling her headfirst so hard that the first layer of bricks turned to powder from the blow. Her head recoiled and she fell, unable to move as the second layer dropped like a flood onto her back. Unmoving but still seeing through the dust. . . . *Lightning. Beautiful lightning.* She couldn't think.

Regin scrambled from the vampire she'd been fighting to stand protectively over Annika. Lucia sped to her side, finally garnering room for a shot. Regin panted, "Lucia, the big one. As many arrows as you can. I'll pry his head off."

Lucia gave a quick nod and strung four arrows with supernatural speed. The legendary archer, invincible if she could just get room . . . Lucia unleashed her arrows that would tear through flesh and bone, then drill *through* the brick walls after.

The sound of her bowstring was as beautiful as the lightning—

Ivo laughed from his seat. The demon's muscles went rigid. He brushed three arrows aside, and *caught* the fourth.

And Annika knew they were going to die.

8

Lachlain directed Emma to the lavish hotel just outside London that the concierge had arranged, then observed every detail as she checked in. She seemed very put out at having to ask him for her credit card, and even more when he retrieved it from the hotel clerk. But she hadn't said a word about the expense.

He didn't believe this was because she trusted him to repay her. He thought she'd wanted to quit driving, at any cost. The journey obviously had been hard on her.

He should be driving, taking on the burden of seeing them to Kinevane, but he'd been forced to have her do it. Because of his inability, she was exhausted and the lights had hurt her sensitive eyes again and again.

When she requested two rooms, he slapped down a hand on the counter, not bothering to retract his dark claws. "One."

He'd realized she wouldn't make a scene around humans—few in the Lore would—and she didn't argue now. But while the bellman showed them up, she pinched her forehead and said under her breath, "This wasn't part of the deal."

She must still be unnerved about the night before. It had only been twenty-four hours ago when she'd gazed at him with a bleak expression and whispered, *"You frighten me."*

He frowned to find his hand reaching out to stroke her hair, and jerked it back.

While he tipped the bellman, she staggered past him into the spacious suite. When he closed the door, she'd already fallen forward half on the bed, nearly asleep.

He'd known she was tired, had reasoned driving was draining, but how could she be this bad off? Immortals were usually powerful, near inexhaustible. Was this the condition she spoke of? If she'd drunk Monday, and she had no discernible injuries, then what was it?

Was it the shock of what he'd done to her? Perhaps she was as fragile inside as her appearance suggested. . . .

He tugged her jacket off by the collar—easy to do, since her arms were limp—and found her neck and shoulders were knotted. Surely driving did that. Not sitting next to him for hours.

When he felt her skin was chilled, he ran water in the bath, then returned to roll her over and pull off her shirt.

She weakly slapped at his hands, but he ignored her protests. "I've drawn you a bath. It's no' good to sleep like this."

"Let me do it myself, then." When he removed her boot, her eyes opened fully to meet his. "Please, I don't want you to see me unclothed."

"Why?" he asked as he stretched out beside her. He picked up the end of a curl to run it along the side of her chin as he gazed down into her eyes. The skin beneath her lashes was pale like the rest of her face, so pale it matched the whites of her eyes, with only the fringe of thick lashes sweeping between them. Fascinating to him.

And looking down into them felt oddly *familiar*.

* * *

"Why?" She frowned. "Because I'm shy about things like that."

"I'll leave your undergarments on."

She did want a bath, desperately. It was the only thing that could possibly warm her.

When she closed her eyes and shivered, he made the decision for her. Before she could even finish sputtering a protest, he'd stripped her to her underwear, then *himself* completely, and clasped her in his arms. He dropped them into the steaming oversize bathtub with her between his legs.

In the warm water, his injured leg brushed her arm, and she stiffened. He was naked and aroused, and her underwear was no true barrier since he'd unerringly chosen a thong. He laid one heavy hand on her shoulder. A second later, she felt a finger from his other hand tracing the thong she wore. *"This pleases me,"* he growled.

Just as she tensed to leap from the water, he brushed her hair over one shoulder, put both hands on her neck, then pressed down with his thumbs.

To her morbid embarrassment, she moaned, loud.

"Relax, creature." Against her efforts, he pulled her back into him. When she lay fully on his erection, he hissed and shuddered, his reaction flooding her with heat. But she shot back up, fearing he would want to have sex with her. It didn't take an anatomist to make a case that they wouldn't fit like that.

"Easy," he said, continuing to work out the knots in her shoulders with an expert touch. As he drew her to him once more, the only struggle she could manage was internal, and she was glad no one could see that stumbling, pitiful attempt. Finally he forced her to relax against him completely, body gone limp.

What no one knew about Emma was that she loved to be touched. *Adored* it. Even the more because it was utterly rare.

While her family was affectionate in a spartan way, they wanted to toughen her up. Only one of her aunts, Daniela the Ice Maiden, seemed to understand her yearning, because she herself *couldn't* touch or have her freezing skin touched without extreme pain. She understood it, but for some reason Daniela didn't miss it, didn't feel the same need, while Emma thought she'd slowly die without it.

Creatures from the Lore who would be acceptable lovers for her, like good demons, were scarce in N.O.L.A., and most of those had been hanging around the manor since she'd been young. She saw them as nothing more than big brothers. With horns.

The infrequent demons who *were* strangers didn't exactly line up to come calling at the coven. Even they found Val Hall, their fog-enshrouded home in the bayou, terrifying, with the shrieks echoing within and the constant lightning hovering.

A few years ago, Emma had finally grasped that she would be alone when yet another cute, perfectly doable human male in one of her night classes had asked her out—for *coffee* the next *afternoon*. Emma loathed Starbucks for its very existence.

She'd realized then that she could never be with a man who was of her own kind, and could never be with most who weren't. Sooner or later they would discover what she was. The reasons she hadn't found someone in her life—*A matinee . . . ? Dinner and drinks . . . ? A picnic . . . ?*—weren't changing, ergo . . .

Later she'd "accidentally" bumped into the human just to know what she was missing. Warm touch, appealing masculine scent. She'd realized she was missing *a lot*.

And it had hurt.

Now Emma had a cruel but divinely handsome Lykae who couldn't seem to keep his hands off her. She feared she'd be a sponge for his touch even as she hated him.

She feared he could make her a beggar for it.

"What if I fall asleep?" she asked, her voice soft, her lightly drawling accent more pronounced.

"Fall asleep. Doona care," Lachlain said, as he kneaded her neck and her slim shoulders.

She moaned again and her head sank back against his chest. She sounded as if she'd never been touched like this. The utter surrender wasn't sexual, but he thought she'd give anything for him to continue. She seemed *starved* for it.

He remembered days in his clan. Everyone roughhoused, men always found an excuse to touch their women, and if you did something well, you received literally a hundred slaps on the back. Lachlain had spent most hours with his family with a child perched on his shoulders and two bairns dragging on his legs.

He pictured Emma as a timid little girl growing up in Helvita, the vampire stronghold in Russia. Though gilded with gold, Helvita was damp and dark—he should know, since he'd spent time enough in the dungeon. In fact, she might have been there when he was imprisoned, if she hadn't already journeyed to New Orleans.

The vampires who lived there were as cold as their home. They would not touch her with affection—he'd never seen a vampire display affection. If she needed it like this, how had she gone without it?

He'd suspected she'd been long without a man, but now Lachlain knew that if she had had someone, the man didn't touch her nearly enough and she was well rid of him. He re-called how when they'd been in the shower, her tightness and her reactions had made him wonder if she'd *ever* had a man. But now, as then, he thought it unlikely she was virgin, since not many immortals made it through centuries ab-staining. She was just small and, as she'd said, shy.

Remembering her tight sheath made his cock go painfully hard for it. He lifted her into his lap, turning her side to his chest. She stiffened, no doubt from his shaft throbbing under her arse.

Urges wracked him. She was wearing the silk that was lit-tle more than a string, and the sight of it was even better than his imaginings. He opened his mouth to simply inform her that he was about to stroke his fingers between her legs and then settle her down on his shaft. But before he could, her delicate hands lighted upon his chest, their paleness standing out against his skin. She waited a moment as if testing the waters. When he did nothing about her hands, she rested her face against him, settling in to sleep.

He drew back his head and frowned down at her, bewil-dered by this. Was this . . . did she trust him? Trust him not to take her while she slept? Damn it, why would she do that?

With a foul curse, he lifted her from the water. Her hands were still against his chest, clutching a little. He toweled her off, then laid her on the bed, her blond hair fanning out, the ends damp. The exquisite scent of it swept him up. Shaking, he peeled her wicked undergarments from her. He inwardly groaned at her body, about to spread her legs and set upon it with a vengeance.

Barely awake, she murmured, "Can I sleep in one of your shirts?"

He stood back, clenching his fists, brows drawn. Why would she want to be dressed in his clothing? Why did he want it as well? He ached, he needed to be inside her so badly, and yet he was stalking to his bag. At this rate, he'd be returning to the shower and bringing himself release. How else could he make it through the day with her?

He dressed her in one of his new undershirts though it swallowed her, then put her under the cover. Just as he'd drawn it up to her chin, she woke and sat up. She squinted at him, turned to regard the window, then gathered the cover and the pillow and bedded down on the floor, tucking herself into the side of the bed.

Out of the path of the window.

When he scooped her up, she whispered, "No. I need to be down there. I like it down there."

Of course she did. Vampires craved low places, sleeping in shadowed corners and under beds. As a Lykae, he'd always known exactly where to find them to sever their heads before they even woke.

Anger flared again. "No longer." She slept with him from now on, and he would never even entertain the idea of accepting that unnatural custom of his enemy. "I will no' let the sun get you again, but you'll break yourself of this."

"Why do you care?" she asked so softly he barely heard her.

Because you've been out of my bed for far too long.

Annika's broken body lay trapped in the bricks. Helpless, she could do nothing but watch when the vampire brushed away Lucia's arrows as though they were flies.

Annika shared Lucia's obvious disbelief. Cursed long ago to feel unfathomable pain if she missed a target, Lucia suddenly shrieked, dropping her bow as she fell. She lay writhing, her fingers curled, screaming until she'd shattered every window and light in the manor.

In the distance, a *Lykae* howled, a deep, guttural sound of rage.

Darkness, except for the lightning now thrashing the earth and a flickering gas lamp outside.

Ivo's red eyes were ablaze in the lamplight, his expression amused. Lothaire secretly appeared in the background once more but did nothing. Lucia still screamed. The Lykae roared in answer—nearing them? Regin alone against three. "Leave us, Regin," Annika bit out.

Then . . . a shadow moved inside. White teeth and fangs. Pale blue eyes glowed in the darkness. It crept over to Lucia's twitching form. Annika could do nothing. So helpless. In the scant lulls between bolts, he looked human. In the silver flashes, he was a beast, a man with the shadow of a beast.

Annika wanted her strength as she never had, wanted to kill it *so slowly*. The beast pawed at Lucia's face. Annika couldn't bear to—

It was trying to brush away Lucia's tears? He lifted her, then crossed to a corner, tucking her behind a table.

Why wasn't it ripping her throat out?

It reared up with a terrible fury and launched itself at the vampires, fighting beside a shocked, but quickly adapting Regin until the two vampire followers were decapitated. Ivo and the horned one traced away, *fleeing*. Enigmatic Lothaire merely nodded, then dissappeared.

The Lykae sprang for Lucia, then crouched beside her as she stared up in awe and horror. When Annika closed her eyes and opened them once more, it had disappeared, leaving Lucia shaking.

"What the fuck?" Regin cried, circling around as though shell-shocked.

Just then Kaderin the Coldhearted arrived, jogging up the glass-covered porch. Ever blessed to feel no raw emotions, she chided gently, "Language, Regin." Then she entered the war zone, and even she raised an eyebrow as she leisurely drew her swords from the thin sheaths at her back.

"Annika!" Regin cried, digging through brick. Annika strained to answer but couldn't. She'd never felt so helpless, never been beaten so badly.

"What has happened here?" Kaderin demanded, searching for a kill yet holding her swords so loosely, her wrists fluid as she swirled them in tight circles. When Lucia crawled out from behind the table, Kaderin backed her way to her.

"Vampires attacked. And you just missed the Lykae on top of all this," Regin sputtered, digging frantically. "The fucking monster mash—*Annika?*"

Annika managed to work a hand out of the rubble. Regin gripped it, hauling her free.

Dimly, Annika spied Nïx perched on the rail of the stairs above. She called down in a petulant tone, "How inconsiderate not to wake me when we are entertaining."

Emma woke precisely at sundown, frowning as she recalled the details of the morning. Hazily, she remembered Lachlain's big, warm hands kneading the stiffness from her muscles, making her moan as he'd rubbed her neck and back.

Perhaps Lachlain wasn't the insanely brutish animal she thought him. She'd known he wanted to make love to her—she'd felt how badly—yet he'd refrained. Then later, she'd sensed him returning from the shower and climbing in bed with her. His skin had still been damp and so warm as he'd tucked her bottom into his lap and placed her head on his outstretched arm. She'd felt his erection growing behind her. He'd grated a foreign word as though he cursed it, but he'd never acted on his desire.

She'd been distinctly aware that he'd lain between her and the window, and as he drew her to his chest, she'd felt . . . protected.

Just when she thought she had him figured out, he did something to surprise her.

She opened her eyes and sat up, then blinked as if the scene couldn't be right. If he noticed she'd woken, he didn't indicate it, just continued sitting in the corner in the dark, watching her with glowing eyes. Disbelieving her night vision, she reached for the bedside lamp. It lay crushed beside the bed.

She'd seen correctly. The room was . . . destroyed.

What had happened? What could make him do this?

"Get dressed. We leave in twenty minutes." He rose wearily, nearly stumbling as his leg seemed to give out, then limped to the door.

"But, Lachlain . . ."

The door closed behind him.

She stared, bewildered, at the claw marks in the walls, the floor, the furniture. Everything was rent to pieces.

She looked down. Well, not everything. Her belongings sat behind the savaged chair as though he'd hidden them away, knowing what was about to come. The blanket he'd strung up over the curtains sometime last night still hung where it added another safeguard against the sun. And the bed? Claw marks, mattress foam, and feathers surrounded her like a pod.

She was untouched.

9

If Lachlain didn't want to tell her why he'd huffed and puffed and torn their hotel room to bits, then fine by her. After she'd thrown on a skirt, shirt, and boots and very purposely tied a folded scarf over her ears, she dug her iPod out of her luggage and strapped it on her arm.

Her aunt Myst called it the EIP, or "Emma's iPod Pacifier," because whenever Emma got irritated or angry, she listened to music in order to "avoid conflict." As if this were a bad thing.

And if the EIP wasn't made for a time like this. . . .

Emma was pissed. Just when she'd decided this Lykae might be okay, that he'd finally begun leaning the right way in the *sane-or-not* conundrum, he had to go all big bad wolf on her. *But this little piggy can compartmentalize*, Emma thought, and Lachlain was cruising toward getting squared away in her mind forever.

His personality changed like rapid fire, from the soul-searing embrace in the rain when he'd pressed his naked chest against hers, to the howling attacks, to the gentle would-be lover in the bathtub last night. He kept her wary—an unfortunate and fatiguing state that she already tended to—and that frustrated her.

And now this. He'd left her with this ravaged room and no explanation. She could've looked like that chair.

She blew a curl out of her eyes, and found a wisp of upholstery filler had attached itself to her hair. As she swatted at it, she realized she was as angry at herself as she was with him.

Her first night with him, he'd allowed sun to burn her skin, and now, today, he'd used those claws—which had shredded the side of a *car*—in a frenzy while she'd slept unaware.

Why had she overprotected herself all her life, put forth the exhausting *effort* to do so, then thrown caution out the window regarding him? Why had her family taken pains to keep her safe, moving the coven to Lore-rich New Orleans to hide her, cloaking the manor in darkness only to have her die now—

Cloaking the manor . . . ? Why had they done that? She never rose before sunset, never remained awake past sunrise. Her room was shuttered and she slept under the bed. So why did she have memories of running through their darkened home during the day?

Her gaze was drawn to the back of her hand, her trembling immediate. For the first time since she'd been frozen into her immortality, the memory of her "lesson" erupted in her mind with a perfect clarity. . . .

A witch was babysitting. Emma was in the woman's arms when she heard Annika returning to the manor after a week's absence and struggled until she freed herself. Screaming Annika's name, Emma ran for her.

Regin had heard her and tackled her into the shadows right before Emma ran headlong for the sun shining in from the just-opened door.

Regin squeezed her to her chest with shaking arms and whispered, "What'd you do that for?" With another squeeze, she mumbled, "Boneheaded little leech."

By this time everyone had come downstairs. The witch apologized abjectly, saying, "Emma hissed and snapped and scared me till I dropped her."

Annika scolded Emma between her shudders, until Furie's voice sounded from outside the circle. The crowd parted to let her pass. Furie was, just as her name said, part Fury. And she was frightening.

"Put the child's hand in it."

Annika's face had paled even more than natural. "She is not like us. She's delicate—"

"She hissed and fought to get what she wanted," Furie interrupted. "I'd say she's exactly like us. And like us, the pain will teach her."

Furie's twin, Cara, said, "She's right." They always took each other's sides. "This isn't the first time there's been a close call. Her hand now or her face—or, worse, her life—later. It doesn't matter how dark we keep the manor if you can't keep her inside."

"I won't do it," Annika said. "I . . . can't do it."

Regin dragged Emma along, though she resisted. "Then I will."

As Annika stood by, her face perfectly stoic, like marble but for incongruous tears running down, Regin forced Emma's hand into the shaft of sunlight. She shrieked in pain, screaming for her Annika, crying "why" again and again until her skin caught fire.

When Emma woke, Furie was peering down at her with lavender eyes, tilting her head, as if confused by Emma's reaction. "Child, you must realize that every day the entire earth is saturated in something that will kill you, and only if you're wary will you elude it. Do not forget this lesson, for it will be repeated to bring you much greater pain next time."

Emma fell to her knees, then to her hands as she gasped for breath. The fine scarring on the back of her hand itched. No wonder she was a coward. No wonder . . . no wonder . . . no wonder . . .

Emma believed that they had saved her life, but they'd compromised it at the same time. That lesser evil they'd chosen shaped every day of her life. She stood, then stumbled to the bathroom, splashing water on her face. She clutched the counter. *Get it together, Em.*

By the time Lachlain returned for her bag, her emotions had fired into roiling anger, and she directed it to the deserving target. She made a show of brushing upholstery stuffing from her luggage with jerky, exaggerated movements, glaring at him. His brows drew together.

She followed him to the car, stifling hisses, wanting to punt the back of his knee. He turned and opened the door for her.

Once they were ensconced inside and she'd started the car, he said, "Did you . . . hear?"

"Did I hear when you flipped out like a ninja?" she snapped. At his blank look, she answered, "No. I didn't." And she didn't ask him to elaborate. She believed he wanted her to, felt that he was willing her to. When he wouldn't look away, she said, "Not taking that ball back in my court."

"You will no' address this?"

She gripped the steering wheel.

"You are angry? I dinna expect this reaction."

She faced him, her rein on her temper and her innate fear of him no match for such a close call with death. "I'm angry because you only gave me an inch-wide margin of error with your lethal claws. Maybe next time I won't get an inch. When I sleep I am utterly vulnerable—*I have no defenses*. You forced me into that situation and I resent it."

He stared at her for long moments, then exhaled and said something she'd never expected. "You are right. Since it happens when I sleep, I will no' sleep near you again."

The memory of his damp body so warm against hers flashed in her mind. She regretted giving that up, a realization that made her even angrier.

He sat stiffly in his seat, his body tense, as she dialed up her "Angry Female Rock" playlist.

"What is that?" he asked, as though he couldn't help himself.

"Plays music."

He pointed at the radio. "*That* plays music."

"Plays *my* music."

He raised his eyebrows. "You *compose?*"

"I *program*," she said, plugging in the earbuds—and shutting him out—with infinite satisfaction.

A couple of hours into the drive, Lachlain directed her to an exit for the town of Shrewsbury.

"What do you need here?" she asked as she unplugged her earbuds and took the exit.

As if uncomfortable to admit it, he said, "I have no' eaten today."

"Figured you didn't break for lunch," she answered, surprising herself with her snarky tone. "What do you want? Fast food or something?"

"I've seen those places. Smelled them. They have nothing that will make me stronger."

"This isn't exactly my area of expertise."

"Aye, I know. I'll let you know when I scent someplace,"

he said, directing them along the main thoroughfare to an outside market with shops and restaurants. "There should be something near here."

She spotted an underground parking garage—she loved those, loved anything underground—and drove inside. Once they parked, she said, "Will you get it to go? Because it's cold." And because vampires could be lurking anywhere while she waited outside the restaurant. As long as she was putting up with his Lykae b.s., she might as well get a little vampire protection.

"You *will* be coming in with me."

She gave him a blank look. "What purpose would that serve?"

"You stay with me," he insisted as he opened her door and stood in front of her. She noted with unease that he was looking over his shoulder and scanning the street, eyes narrowed.

When he took her arm and steered her, she cried, "But I don't go inside restaurants."

"You do tonight."

"Oh, no, no," she said, beseeching him with her eyes. "Don't make me go in there. I'll wait right outside—I promise."

"I'm no' leaving you alone. And you need to get used to this."

She dragged her feet—a useless gesture against his strength. "No, I don't! I never have to go into restaurants! No need to get used to it!"

He stopped, facing her. "Why are you afraid?"

She glanced away, not answering the question.

"Fine. You go in."

"No, wait! I know no one will notice me, but I . . . I can't help feeling like everyone would watch me and see that I don't eat."

He raised his eyebrows. "No one will notice you? Only males between seven years old and death." And *still* he pulled her along.

"This is cruel, what you're doing. And I won't forget it."

He glanced back and had to see the alarm in her eyes. "You have nothing to worry about. Can you no' just trust me?" At her glare, he added, "On this."

"Is it your *intent* to make me miserable?"

"You need to stretch yourself."

When she parted her lips to argue, he cut her off, his voice like iron. "Fifteen minutes inside. If you're still uncomfortable, we'll leave."

She knew she was going either way, knew he was merely giving her the illusion of choice. "I'll go if I get to pick the restaurant," she said, making a bid for some control.

"Deal," he answered. "But I get one veto."

The minute they emerged onto the public walk, amid all those humans, she wrested her hand from his, her shoulders shot back, and her chin jutted up.

"Does that keep people away?" he asked. "That arrogance you don whenever you go about?"

She squinted up at him. "Oh, if only it worked on everyone. . . ." Actually, it did on everyone *but* him. Her aunt Myst had taught her to do this. Myst kept people so busy thinking she was a snobby, heartless bitch with the morals of an alley cat that they never got around to thinking she might be a two-thousand-year-old pagan immortal.

Emma glanced at the walk and found several restaurant choices. With an inward evil grin, she pointed out the sushi place.

He surreptitiously scented the air, then glowered at her. "Vetoed. Choose again."

"Fine." She pointed out another restaurant that had an upscale club attached to it. She could almost tell herself it was a bar. She'd been to a few of those. After all, she lived in New Orleans, the world's leading manufacturer of hangovers.

He obviously wanted to reject her choice again, but when she raised her eyebrows, he scowled and grabbed her hand once more, dragging her along.

Inside, the host greeted them warmly, then strode over to assist her with her jacket. But something occurred behind her, something that had the host returning to his podium, paler, and left Lachlain alone at her back.

She could sense him tensing. *"Where's the rest of your blouse?"* he snapped under his breath.

The back was completely cut out and only a bow-tied string held it together. She hadn't thought she'd be removing her jacket, and if she did, she'd thought her back would be glued to taupe leather right now.

She looked over her shoulder with an innocent expression. "Why, I don't know! You should send me outside to wait."

Lachlain glanced at the door, clearly debating leaving, and she couldn't help her smug expression. He narrowed his eyes, then rasped in her ear, "All the better to feel their gazes on you," while the back of his claw traced up her back.

10

"Is your blouse Azzedine Alaia?" the girl showing them to their table asked Emma.

She answered, "No, you could say it's *very* authentic vintage."

Lachlain didn't care what it was; she'd never wear that damned unfinished shirt in public again.

The bow that swayed low across her slim back as she glided along was like a magnet for the gazes of every male in this place. Lachlain knew they were imagining untying it. Because he himself was. More than one man elbowed a friend and murmured that she was "hot," earning a killing look from Lachlain.

It wasn't only the men who openly stared at her as they passed. The women looked at her clothes with envy and remarked to each other that she dressed "cool."

Then more than a few of them eyed him with blatant invitation.

In the past, he might have enjoyed the attention, possibly accepted an invitation or two. Now he found their interest vaguely insulting. As if he'd choose any of them over the creature he followed so closely!

Ah, but he liked that the vampire noted their looks as well.

At the table, Emma paused, as if to make a last show of resistance, but he seized her elbow and assisted her into the booth.

When the girl left, Emma sat with her back stiff, arms over her chest, refusing to look at him. A waiter walked by with a sizzling plate of food and she rolled her eyes.

"Could you eat it?" he asked. "If you had to?" He'd begun to wonder if it was possible, and now prayed it was.

"Yes."

In an incredulous tone, he asked, "Why do you no'?"

She faced him with an arched eyebrow. "Can you drink blood?"

"Point taken," he said evenly, though he was disappointed. Lachlain loved food, loved the ritual of sharing meals. When he wasn't starving he savored it, and like all Lykae, he never failed to appreciate it. Now it hit him that he would never share a meal with her, never drink wine with her. What would she do at functions within the clan—?

He stopped himself. What was he thinking? He would never hurt them by bringing her to their gatherings.

She finally leaned back, clearly resigned to sitting there, giving a polite expression to the boy who briefly appeared to pour them water.

She tilted her head at the glass, as if wondering what would be the best course of action with it, then exhaled a long, wearied breath.

"Why are you always so tired?"

"Why do you ask so many questions?"

So she got braver in public? As if these humans would stop him from doing anything he wanted. "If you drank as recently as Monday and you haven't a mark on your body—

I would've seen it—then what is the condition you spoke of?"

She drummed her nails on the table. "And that would be yet another question."

Her answer sounded distant as a thought arose, a thought so abhorrent he fought it. He closed his eyes, gritting his teeth, and shook his head slowly as it hit him.

Oh, Christ, no. Was she with child? No, it couldn't be. The rumors had it that vampire women were infertile. Of course, the rumors had it that there weren't supposed to *be* any female vampires left whatsoever. But here she was.

What else could it be?

Not one, but two vampires under his care, in his home, delivered like a blight among his people. And some leech was going to want them back.

All the tension he'd felt during his long, crazed day came back redoubled. "Are you with—"

The waiter appeared just then, and Lachlain rushed through ordering, having never glanced at the menus he shoved into the man's hands, sending him away.

She gaped. "I can't believe you ordered me food!"

He waved her statement away, asking, "You're with bairn, are you no'?"

She tensed when the boy returned to refill her water glass, then frowned at Lachlain. "You switched our glasses?" she whispered when they were alone again. "I never saw you!"

"Aye, and I'll do the plates as well," he explained quickly. "But—"

"So I just pretend to eat?" she asked. "Then eat a lot for me. Okay? Because I *would* have a good appetite—"

"Are—you—with—bairn?"

She sucked in a breath as though scandalized, then said in

a rush. "No! I haven't ev— Um, I haven't even a boyfriend."

"Boyfriend? You mean lover?"

She blushed. "I *refuse* to speak with you about my love life."

Relief flooded him. The day for him turned just like that. "So you doona have one." He liked the small sound of frustration she made—especially since it came instead of a denial. No current lover, no vampire bairn. Only him and her. And when he claimed her, he would do it so hard and so long that she wouldn't be able to recall another before him.

"Didn't I just refuse to talk to you about this? Do you have a *talent* for ignoring my wishes?" To herself, she mumbled, "I swear, sometimes I feel like I'm getting punk'd."

"You want a lover though, do you no'? Your little body's greedy for one."

Her lips parted in shocked silence. "Y-you speak so bluntly just to provoke me. You like embarrassing me." She gave him a measuring look that gave him the feeling she was making mental tallies of every time.

"I could satisfy you." Reaching under the table, he snaked his hand up under her long skirt, touching her inner thigh, making her jump back in her seat. He found it amusing about her that she could be surprised, even shocked, so easily when most immortals developed a blasé attitude about everything. He supposed she was right—he did enjoy embarrassing her.

"Remove your hand," she said between gritted teeth.

When he rubbed his hand higher, circling his thumb over her soft skin, instant heat shot through him and he grew hard for her for the hundredth time this night. Her eyes darted around the room.

"Do you want a lover? I ken you canna lie, so if you tell me you doona, I'll remove my hand."

"Stop this. . . . " She was blushing furiously. An immortal who blushed at every turn. Incredible.

"Do you want a man in your bed?" he murmured, his thumb stroking higher until he found the silk she wore. He hissed in a breath.

"Fine!" she said in a strangled tone. "I'll tell you. I do want one. But it'll never be you."

"Why no' me?"

"I-I've heard about your kind. I know that you get mindless and savage, scratching and biting like animals—"

"What's wrong with that?" When she made that frustrated sound again, he said, "It's the females that scratch and do most of the *biting* as well. Should no' be so new for you, vampire."

At that, her face grew cold. "The next man I take into my bed will accept me for what I am and won't look at me with disgust just for the way I'm forced to survive. I want a man who goes out of his way to make me comfortable and content instead of the opposite. Which means you've disqualified yourself from the competition from night one."

She didn't understand, he thought as he slowly drew his hand away. Fate had settled them like this. He was stuck with her. Which meant there'd be no other *competitors* for either of them ever again.

Once Lachlain had stopped groping her under the table and the food arrived, he started his slow, sensuous love affair with his meal. He clearly relished every bite, so much that it almost made her want to eat as well instead of only pretending to.

At the end, Emma had to admit that their dinner filled

with shifting plates and food flying—from Emma's clumsy silverware activity—wasn't *unpleasant*.

After the waiter cleared their plates, Emma saw the woman at the table next to them excuse herself after her meal. That's what human women did. When finished eating, they drew their purses into their laps and patted them, then went to the bathroom to reapply lipstick and check their teeth. As long as she was pretending . . .

But Emma didn't have a purse. Her purse had been ruined when she'd been thrown to the muddy ground by this Lykae across from her. She frowned, but still moved to stand. "I'm going to the ladies' room," she murmured.

"No." He reached for her legs, which made her jerk them back under the table.

"Pardon?"

"Why would you do that? I know you doona have those needs."

She sputtered with embarrassment. "Y-you don't know anything about me! And I'd like to keep it that way."

He leaned back, hands behind his head, expression casual, as if they weren't discussing something so personal. "Do you? Have those needs?"

Her face flamed. She didn't. And as far as she knew, other vampires didn't either. Valkyrie didn't, because they didn't, well, *eat*.

"Your blushing answered me. So you doona." Did *nothing* embarrass him?

She was alarmed to see he was getting that analytical look, the one that made her feel like an insect pinned by the wings beneath a microscope.

"How else are you different from human females? I know your tears are pink. Do you sweat?"

Of course she could. "Not for ninety minutes a week, as my country's surgeon general recommends." Good, she'd lost him. But not for long. . . .

"Is it pink as well?"

"No! The tears are an anomaly. Okay? I am just like other women but for those things you crudely pointed out."

"No, you're no'. I watch the advertisements on the television. During the day, they're all about women. You doona shave, but your skin is smooth where they are. I went through your belongings and found that you doona carry the supplies with you as they do."

Her eyes widened as it hit her—what he meant. She stiffened, about to leap from the booth, when he stretched his leg out and dropped his heavy boot beside her, trapping her.

"There were rumors that vampire females grew infertile. Once a vampire male finds his Bride he does no' stray, so your species was depopulating. Is that no' why Demestriu tried to kill all of the females within the Horde?"

She'd never known this. She lowered her gaze, staring at the table as it appeared to wobble. The waiter had made a valiant effort to tidy up after her, but there were still crumbs. Crumbs from her. Because she was a freak who couldn't handle silverware and apparently couldn't have children either.

She'd never had a monthly cycle because she was infertile?

"Is that true?" he repeated.

She murmured, "Who knows what Demestriu was thinking?"

His voice less stern, he said, "So you are no' wholly like them."

"I guess not." She pushed her shoulders back. "But I still have a hairstyle I want to check and tales of a date gone bad that I want to recount, so I *will* be going to the restroom now."

"Come directly back to me." He bit out the order.

She dared a glare at him, then hurried away.

The restaurant shared its facilities with the bar, so she had to wind around men loitering throughout. It was like a video game maze fraught with opponents—any of whom could be vampires—but a time-out from humiliation seemed worth the risk.

Inside the sanctuary of the ladies' room, she crossed to the wall of sinks to wash her hands. She stared into the mirror, shocked anew at how pale she'd grown. Her cheekbones were sharp in her face from the weight she'd so rapidly lost. She was simply too young and too weak in general not to suffer immediate consequences from thirst. Hell, she was a walking homage to vulnerability.

She'd known she was weak. Had accepted it. And she'd accepted the fact that she couldn't even defend herself with a weapon. She could scarcely wield a sword, her archery was laughable—as evidenced by everyone laughing at her when she practiced—and her fighting? Well, she didn't exactly have the madskills going on.

Yet she hadn't known she could never have children. . . .

When Emma returned, and Lachlain stood and helped her to her seat, she noticed that while she'd been gone, he'd dug his claws into the table. Nothing like the hotel, merely five precise, deep indentations haloing the visible heat from his palm that was just receding.

He sank into the booth once more, his brows drawn as though deep in thought. He looked like he was about to say something, then seemed to think better of it. She'd be damned if she'd fill this groaning silence.

When her attention remained on the marks, he placed his hand atop them. He clearly didn't like that she stared, no doubt thinking she harkened back to the days—or, rather, this evening—of his destruction.

She wondered what had happened to make him do this. He'd probably spotted that club-kid girl with the sheer blouse and visible nipple piercings and felt the call of the wild.

Or was it possible that he regretted his humiliating questions? So much that he would react by absently digging into the table? She shook her head.

He wouldn't regret humiliating her—not when he so obviously enjoyed it.

"What do we know?" Annika asked. She took a deep breath, wincing as her healing ribs screamed in protest, and glanced over the Valkyrie who were present. Lucia, Regin, Kaderin, and others, waiting to act, waiting for the direction Annika would have to give.

Nïx was conspicuously absent, having likely wandered onto the neighbor's property again. Regin was on the computer, accessing the coven's database, researching Ivo and any other vampire sightings. Her brilliant face illuminated the shatterproof screen more than it did her.

"Hmm. That would be only two measly things for certain," said Regin. "Ivo the Cruel is seeking someone among all the Valkyrie. And he still hasn't found *her*, whoever she is, because the encounters haven't stopped. Our sisters in the New Zealand coven write that they're 'chockablock' with vampires. What does chockablock mean? No. Really."

Annika ignored the last. She was still furious with Regin for abetting Emma. Because of her, Emma was now running around Europe with a—what had Regin called him?—a *hottie*. On top of this, Regin had had the nerve to accuse Annika of "smothering." It wasn't as if Annika didn't want Em to meet a man, but she was still so young and they knew nothing about this male other than the fact that he was strong enough to take down a vampire. Regin had actually thought to make Annika feel better by saying, "Dude, I could tell—Emma wants him in the worst way. . . ." Annika inwardly shook herself, focusing on the situation at hand. "We have to determine Ivo's purpose."

Kaderin said, "Myst just escaped his dungeon five years ago. He could want her back."

"All this to recapture her?" Annika asked. Myst the Coveted, considered the most beautiful Valkyrie, had been under his power. She'd escaped when the vampire rebels took his castle. That situation always enraged Annika. *Indiscretions* between Myst and Wroth, a rebel general, had occurred.

Until two days ago, Annika had believed Myst had put that vampire and the entire disgusting situation behind her. Yet everyone had heard Myst's heart speed up at the mere mention of vampires in the New World. She'd checked her flame-red hair again and again before joining a group setting out *to hunt them*.

No, Myst hadn't moved on from the general. Had Ivo been unable to forget his stunning captive?

"Could be Emma," Regin offered.

Annika shot her a sharp glare. "He doesn't even know of her existence."

"That we are aware of."

Annika pinched her forehead. "Where the hell is Nïx?" This wasn't a time for conjecture—they needed Nïx's foresight. "Check Emma's credit card again. Any new purchases?"

Regin logged into the coven's card accounts, and within minutes she had Emma's statement pulled up. "These records are lagging over a day behind. But there were some clothing purchases—how much trouble can she be in if she's clothes shopping? And here's a *restaurant* bill from the Crillon. Tightwad better be paying her back."

"What would Ivo want with Emma anyway?" Lucia asked. As she did whenever she mulled possibilities, she plucked at the string on her bow. "She may be the last female vampire, but she's not full-blooded."

"If we think logically, the odds point to Myst," Kaderin said.

Annika had to agree. Considering Myst's heart-stopping beauty, how could Ivo not want her back?

"And one other thing that tips the scales in Myst's favor?" Kaderin added. "She hasn't returned from her hunt and she hasn't called."

Settled then. For now. "Try to keep tabs on Emma's movements. We'll begin searching for Myst."

Regin peered around her at all the damage in the manor. "Should I renew the inscription with the witches?"

"Mystical protection can be cracked, as we well know. Only one guardianship is foolproof." Annika exhaled wearily. "We will bring in the ancient scourge." And be forced to pay the wraiths in the currency they desired.

Regin sighed. "Well, damn, and here I was getting attached to my hair."

11

Gloaming arrived in the countryside of southern Scotland, casting a last light over their inn. As Emma slept, Lachlain sat in bed next to her, drinking yet another cup of coffee.

The majority of his day had been full, by design, so he wouldn't sleep. Now he relaxed next to her, clad in nothing but comfortable *jeans* that came broken-in like boots might be. He read one of the few contemporary novels from the inn's library and half-listened to the news. He might even have been content—if he had taken her last night. And if he was confident he was about to again.

There'd been no chance of that, even if she hadn't been shaking with emotion the entire drive after his blunt questioning debacle at the restaurant. He'd thought he could anger her into a response, get her nettled as she'd been just that evening over the state of the room. Instead, she'd tilted her head and given him an expression so stark it had torn at him.

By the time they'd reached the inn last night, Emma had been out of her head with fatigue and hadn't even protested when he'd stripped her to her underwear and put them in the bath. Of course, he'd found himself fighting unbearable lust once again. Yet instead of punishing her for it, when she'd gone soft in his arms he'd petted her once more, staring at the ceiling in confusion.

After the bath, he'd dried her, dressed her in one of her gowns—the chit hadn't asked for his shirt again—then placed her in bed. She'd looked up at him solemnly and voiced her concern that he might "wig out" again. When he'd assured her he wouldn't sleep, she'd regarded the floor with longing, actually reaching down to touch it, then passed out.

Now he glanced at the folds in the curtains, and saw no light beneath each one. The last two nights she'd woken precisely at sundown. There was no yawning or shaking off sleep—she'd simply opened her eyes, rising in a floating way, instantly awake as if she'd been brought back to life. Lachlain had to admit he found this foreign trait . . . eerie. Of course, he'd never seen this before—in the past, any vampire asleep in his presence never woke again.

At any moment now, her eyes would open, and he put aside the book to watch.

The sun set. Minutes passed. She still didn't rise.

"Get up," he said, shaking her shoulder. When she didn't respond, he shook her harder. They needed to get on the road. He thought they could make Kinevane tonight and he was anxious to see his home.

She burrowed down farther in the covers. "Let . . . me . . . sleep."

"If you doona get out of bed, I'm going to rip off your clothes and join you there."

When there was no reaction even to that, he grew alarmed and felt her forehead—her skin was like ice.

He drew her up and her head lolled. "What's wrong with you? Tell me!"

"Leave me alone. Need another hour."

He laid her back down. "If you're sick, you need to drink."

After a moment, she cracked open her eyes.

Realization hit and his body tensed. "This is from hunger?" he roared.

She blinked up at him.

"You told me you ate Monday—how often do you need to?"

When she didn't answer, he shook her shoulders.

"Every day. Okay?"

He dropped her shoulders just before his fists clenched. She'd been *hungry*? His mate had suffered from fucking *hunger* while under his protection. He had no idea what he was doing. . . .

Goddamn it, he couldn't care for her. Not only had he starved her for two additional days—obviously he'd kept her from hunting—but she needed to find a victim to drink *every* night. Each night they would go through this.

Did she kill each time as other vampires did? "Why did you no' tell me?"

Her eyelids were drifting closed again. "So you could make another 'bargain'?"

Could he allow her to take from him? Among his clan, being drunk by a vampire was reviled, considered a filthy act. Even if it was done against his will, a Lykae would suffer abject shame. But what choice did he have? He exhaled and said with a heavy heart, "You will drink from me for now on." No vampire had ever bitten him. Demestriu had debated it, arguing with his elders over the decision. For some reason, in the end he'd decided against it, preferring to torture Lachlain instead.

"Can't drink from you," she murmured. "Not straight from a source."

"What? I thought your kind took pleasure from that."

"Never done it."

Impossible. "You've no' drunk another? Never killed?"

She cast him an anguished expression. His question had hurt her?

"*Of course not.*"

She wasn't a predator? There were rumors of a small faction of rebel vampires who didn't kill—of course, he'd dismissed the tales immediately. What had they been called? *Forbearers?* Could she be one? But then he frowned. "So where would you get blood?"

"Blood bank," she murmured.

Was that a joke? "What the hell is that? Is there one nearby?"

She shook her head.

"Then you've got to take from me. Because I just signed on to be your breakfast."

She looked too weak to take his neck, so he sliced his finger with a claw. She turned her face away. "Put it in a glass. *Please.*"

"Do you fear I'll turn you into a Lykae?" He would never attempt that grueling ritual on her. "Or do you think you'll turn me?" Surely she didn't believe that. The only way to become a vampire was to die while one's blood was in your body. Only humans believed one could be turned from a vampire's bite, while those in the Lore knew one had a better chance of turning by biting the vampire.

"It's not that. A glass . . ."

He didn't understand what the difference was. Then his eyes narrowed. Did she find the thought of drinking from *him* objectionable? Galling. She had no idea what he was sacrificing for her. He snapped, "Take it, now," then dripped the blood across her lips.

She resisted for longer than he would've if he'd been starved. Finally she dabbed the tip of her tongue at her lip, then licked there. Her eyes turned *silver*. To his shock, he went instantly hard.

Her small fangs shot longer. She had sunk them into his arm before he could blink.

With the first draw, her eyelids fluttered closed and she moaned; he went dizzy with sexual pleasure, feeling on the verge of coming. Stunned, groaning, he reached out and yanked her gown down, exposing her breasts, covering one with his palm. He squeezed harder than he'd meant to, but when he stopped she raised her chest into his hand, her hips undulating, never hesitating her sucking.

With another groan he leaned down, opening his grasp to hold her breast so he could take her nipple with his mouth. Licking desperately, his tongue swirled around the throbbing peak. When he drew it between his lips and sucked, he felt her tongue flicking against his skin at the same time.

The pleasure he derived was indescribable, and her every draw intensified it. She clung to his arm so sweetly, holding it between her breasts. As if he'd ever take it away. Her nipple was so hard between his lips.

He placed his hand on her thigh, rubbing upward, but she withdrew her fangs and flung herself away, rolling to her side. He sat on his haunches in shock, trying to compose himself, baffled by his reaction.

"Emmaline," he said in a broken voice as he took her shoulder and turned her to her back. His eyes widened as her wee fangs grew smaller. Her eyes turned blue once more, and she rolled them with apparent ecstasy, falling back, her pale arms over her head. As she stretched and writhed, her nipples puckered tighter. Then she gazed up at him with her full, red lips curling. The lass had a smile such as he'd never known—

Euphoria, that's what he was seeing as her skin pinkened. His erection was growing unbearable—*watching* her skin warm was incredibly erotic. Every detail of this sordid act with her was erotic. Her face grew softer, her body fuller—God help him—*curvier*. If possible, her hair shone more.

He vowed she would drink him—only him—from then on.

And, sweet Christ, she needed it every night.

She rose to her knees before him, leaning forward, seeming hungry for something else entirely. Her uncovered breasts were plump and luscious, as if begging his palms to cup them.

"*Lachlain,*" she purred his name as he'd waited to hear for a millennium.

He shuddered and his cock pulsed. "Emma," he growled, lunging for her.

The back of her hand connected with his face. Caught off guard, he flew across the room.

The second time he attempted to rise, he realized she'd dislocated his jaw.

12

Never taking his eyes from her, Lachlain punched himself in the face in the direction opposite of how she'd hit him. She heard his jaw pop into place as he loomed closer, his expression menacing.

With no shirt on to disguise how strong he was, every sculpted muscle in his chest and torso was visible as it tensed. He looked bigger without clothes on? How exactly did that happen? Yet for some reason she was unafraid. Emma the Lamb was scanning him for something else to dislocate. Vampires were evil. She was a vampire.

And she was *on fire* with his delicious blood.

He was on top of her before she had time to react, pinning her arms above her head and shoving his knee between her legs. She hissed at him, struggling, making a better showing than before, but she was still no match for him.

"You're strong from my blood," he said as he wedged his hips between her legs.

"I'm stronger just for drinking," she snapped, which was true, but she also suspected his immortal blood, taken straight from his body, was seriously high octane. "I was hungry for anything."

He gave her a patronizing look. "Admit it. You like the way I taste."

She'd tasted power, tasted *him*, and lusted for more. "Go to hell."

He adjusted his position on her, his chest rubbing over her naked breasts. When he rested against her, she felt his erection hard as steel between them. "Why did you hit me?"

She raised her head aggressively—the only movement she could manage. "For everything you've done to me. For endangering me and for every time you've ignored my wishes." Her voice was different, throatier. She sounded like she should be on the cigarettes-and-curlers end of a sex line.

The list of reasons was endless, from ripping off the Band-Aid that had covered her traumatic memories, to making her go *mindless* with lust while drinking, to slicing through a thousand dollars' worth of hand-painted Jillian Sherry underwear his *first night*. She settled on, "For every time I've wanted to strike you and couldn't."

He studied her, clearly not knowing what to make of her. Then the hands that had been pinning her hard cupped over the top of her head. Wolflike. "Fair enough."

Her lips parted in surprise.

"Do you feel better for it?"

"Yes," she answered honestly. If only for a moment, she'd felt powerful for the first time in her life, surging with power. And the next time he forced her into a restaurant, or went rock star on their hotel room, or woke her by kissing down there, she'd smack him again.

As if he read her mind, he warned, "But doona hit me again."

"Then *doona* break your promises." At his frown, she said, "You vowed that you wouldn't touch me. But you . . . you touched my breasts."

"I vowed that I would no' touch you unless you wanted

me to." He leaned up to run the backs of his fingers down her side. She had to battle the urge to flex and stretch into his touch like a cat.

"Tell me right now that you dinna want me to."

She looked away, distressed by how attractive she found him, by how she had nearly keened when she'd lost the warmth of his hand covering her entire breast. The feel of his hot mouth sucking her nipple . . . Between them his erection was rigid, straining against her, coaxing her body to grow wet for it. "Make a note now that I will not in the future."

His lips curled wickedly, and her breath hitched at the sight. "Then all you have to do next time is remove your wee fangs from my arm for long enough to tell me no. Long enough for one single word."

She pulled her gown into place, yearning to hit him again. The bastard knew that tonight she could no more have taken her fangs from him than she could have stopped breathing. "You assume I'll drink from you again?"

With a sexy smirk and a rumbling voice, he said, "I'll have to insist."

She turned her face away as the full import of her actions hit her. She'd actually taken *living* blood. She was officially a leech. And drinking directly from him was like coming home, like something had shifted into place. She feared she could never go back to cold, plastic sleeves. Just what kind of schwag blood had she been drinking before him?

"Why had you no' ever before?"

Because it was forbidden. Yet she'd done just what her aunts had feared of her. . . .

And his blood was a drug she could grow addicted to. She

could become addicted to *him*. He could have that power over her.

No! If he tried to entice her to drink again, she wouldn't be starving and she would have more control to deny herself.

In theory?

"Get off me, you brute." When he didn't let her up, she raised her hand again, but he caught her wrist.

"Doona strike me again, Emmaline. Mates never hit each other."

"What do you mean by 'mate'?" she asked slowly, the fear she'd ignored returning, making her tone grow desperate. "Like . . . like Australian for 'buddy'?"

When he seemed to be deciding if he should tell her something, warning bells blasted. "You don't mean like a Lykae mate?" The idea had occurred to her briefly, but she'd easily pushed it away. Because it was ludicrous.

"And what would you know about that?" He was getting angry again.

She remembered Lucia warning her never to walk between a Lykae and his mate. And if another male accosted his female or tried to separate them—*get the hell away*. They were as bad as a vampire with his Bride, if not worse. "I know you have only one, and that you never separate." She knew if the other was hurt or was in danger, the beast rose up, and reason was lost. She'd seen him lose reason—and never wanted to see it again.

"What's so wrong with that?"

"You can't mean . . . You do want to separate from me? Right?"

"What if I dinna want to?"

"*Oh, God.*" She scrambled from him until he let her go.

He crooked his arm behind his head and leaned back. "Would it be that terrible to be with me?"

She feared he was acting deceptively casual. "Of course it would! Besides the fact that you can't seem to make up your mind whether to be nice to me or to hate me, and besides the fact that we are . . . different, you're a bully, you're out of control, and you don't care about how I feel whatsoever, and you *do* break your promises and we're on the cusp of the Accession and—"

"Now, doona hold back how you feel, lass," he interrupted. When she glared at him, he smirked. "It pleases me that you've obviously given us a lot of thought. Working out all the angles."

She clenched her fists in frustration. "Tell me I'm not your mate, then."

"You're no'. You're a *vampire*, remember? Think about it. My clan would want to rip you to bits on sight."

She tilted her head, studying him, trying to determine the truth.

"Granted, with all your new curves"—he raked his gaze over her, then shook his head in that way men did, as if he was a goner—"I would no' mind keeping you around as my mistress, but nothing so serious as my one mate."

Why did that comment cut to the bone? "You wouldn't lie about this?"

"Rest easy. I want you, but no' for that." He rose. "Now, unless you want to finish this evening properly with me bending you over the bed, you need to get dressed."

With a gasp, she immediately turned on her heel for the bathroom, then locked the door behind her. She pressed her back and palms against it, body quivering, his blood still affecting her.

She frowned. The paint on the door was glossy and cool, smooth but for the left middle panel. Paint had bubbled there. *Fascinating*.

When she ran the shower and tested the temperature, the water felt incredible on her hand, tickling her palm. Naked in the water was even better—it was as if she could perceive each tiny drop sluicing down her body. Running her fingers through her wet hair felt lovely. She realized she had energy again.

Clearly, Lachlain's blood was a cocktail full of Ritalin and Prozac. She should be awash in regret over her transgression and unnerved about the future, yet she couldn't seem to muster either. She assured herself it was the pharmaceutical aspects of his blood that brought about this sense of well-being—not the unfamiliar feeling of connection she'd delighted in as she drank.

After the shower, she dried off, making a note to commend the inn for the impossibly soft towels. As she wrapped one around her, it grazed over her nipples. She shivered and flushed, remembering his mouth so hot over her breast.

Shaking her head hard as if to dislodge the memory, she padded in front of the mirror, reaching her forearm forward to wipe the condensation from the cool glass.

I want you, but no' for that, he'd said, and now as she peered at herself she wondered *why* he wanted her. She tried to imagine how he saw her.

She thought she might be . . . she might be *pretty*, now that her color was back and any curves she'd had to begin with had returned—as he'd so rudely pointed out. But it was all relative, wasn't it? She might be pretty, until she stood next to any female in her family. They were fatales, temptresses. By comparison, Emma was . . . cute.

But they weren't here, and if Lachlain thought she was attractive when she wore conservative clothing and braids in her hair, what would he think when she dressed as she usually did?

She felt nearly liberated, now that he'd convinced her she wasn't his mate, even as part of her wished she was so beautiful he would regret that fact. . . .

She chose her favorite short skirt and strappy heels, and once she'd dried her hair, she left it free again, curling down. If the wind blew it back and someone did see her ears, she didn't doubt Lachlain would think of something to say or do. In fact, he seemed to like that they pointed. Feeling bold, she even wore *earrings*.

When she exited downstairs to meet him at the car, he gaped at her appearance. She knew she looked as shocked as he did.

Because Lachlain was driving.

He shot out of the car to rush around and toss her in. She supposed she must have flashed a glimpse of her panties in the melee because he growled low, before glancing around to see if anyone else had seen.

When he returned, he slammed his door shut, rocking the car. "What game do you play at, lass?"

She stared at him, speechless.

"You dress like this, when I can barely keep my hands from you now?"

She shook her head. "Lachlain, this is how I usually dress. And you scoff at the idea of me as your mate, so I should be safe."

"But I'm still a male. Who's been long without a woman."

Her heart sank. That's why he found her attractive—because he'd been so long without. He'd probably find a perfumed rock appealing at this point. "Then let me go. If you can drive, then you have no need for me and you can set about finding a woman who's interested in you that way."

"You agreed to stay with me till the next full moon."

"I'll only be cramping your style. And I'm sure there are lots of females out there who would like to be with you."

"And you doona count yourself among that number? Even after tonight?"

She nibbled her lip, recalling how she'd licked his tan, smooth skin as she'd taken his exquisite blood, and briefly lost her train of thought. "I just don't understand why you want me to stay," she finally managed to say. "You needed a driver. You no longer do."

"No, I can drive, but I want two other things from you."

She sighed and moved to sit with her back against the car door. When she crossed her legs, he stared at them as though enthralled. She snapped her fingers in front of him. "Let's hear them."

With a growl, he tore his gaze away and met her eyes. "I want you to go to Kinevane so I can settle our debt and reward you for your help. It was hard on you to drive, and now I ken your hunger made it worse than I thought."

"Reward me how?" She was suspicious and didn't bother hiding it.

"Money or gold. Or gems. I've been collecting jewels my entire life."

He emphasized the last words, catching her eyes, but she didn't know why.

"You can have your pick."

She raised her eyebrows. "You'd give me some antique jewelry, like out of a gold-filled treasure chest?"

"Aye, exactly." He nodded in all seriousness. "Priceless jewels. As many as you can wear."

"And they'd be *mine?*" Would she finally *own* something irreplaceable? "So I'd have mementos from my jaunt with a real-live, *certifiable*"—she cast him a too-pleasant smile when she said the word, but he didn't get it—"Lykae?" She doubted her aunts could top that escapade.

"Aye, *yours*. Though I doubt you'd classify them as 'mementos.'"

She shook her head. "This is all a moot point. If you've been gone for a hundred and fifty years, then you won't have a castle with a treasure, no matter how cool it sounds."

"What do you mean?"

"Lachlain, have you ever heard of a Wal-Mart? No? Something like that is probably on top of your castle right now."

He frowned, then said, "No, no' possible. Kinevane is the source of our kind and is protected from the outside. No threat has ever penetrated its walls. Even the vampires canna find it." His tone held more than a hint of smugness. "Nothing is *atop* it now, I promise you."

Her eyes narrowed. "Say you're correct and I get to make my score. Males who give jewelry expect sex."

"That's the second thing." His voice went low and he cupped the side of her face. "I'll be getting you into my bed."

Emma's witty retort? A dropped jaw.

"I-I can't believe you just put that out on the table," she eventually sputtered, ducking away from his hand until he dropped it. "Obviously, now that I know your agenda, I'm not continuing on with you."

"I see." He gave her a solemn expression. "You must have a verra real fear that I can succeed."

She shot him an impatient glare. "Hey, there are your hands—let me play right into them."

After a moment, the corners of his lips quirked at her comment. "But it's true. If you're confident I will no' succeed, then my 'agenda' is nothing more than an idle musing."

"So the game becomes, who gets what they want first."

"I suppose you could say that. Do you think you can reach your goal before I start enjoying you?"

She stifled a gasp and crossed her arms over her chest. For all he'd put her through, he owed her recompense. She'd earned every piece of jewelry she would separate him from! "You know what? I'm going to agree to continue. Mainly because I know you won't let me out of my promise anyway. But I'm also going to clean out your stash. And don't say I didn't warn you."

He leaned forward, far too close for comfort, putting his face directly beside hers to say in a low voice, "And I'm going to have your legs wrapped around me and your cries in my ear before the week is out. Count yourself warned as well."

She jerked away from him, her cheeks heating as she groped for a reply. "Then . . . then let's see your prowess with driving!"

He drew away from her slowly, only taking his eyes from her face for a last look at her legs, then put the car in gear. As he pulled out onto the street, she prepared herself to be amused, strapping her seat belt in place, waiting for him to screw up.

But—of course—he drove perfectly.

He was always analyzing everything she did—why would she think he hadn't been watching her drive? "When did you learn how?" Her question was sharp.

"Practiced in the parking lot when you showered. Doona worry, I could see the entrance at all times."

"I'd told you I would not leave."

"That's no' why I was watching. You look annoyed about this. If you want to drive . . . ?"

"It usually takes people longer to learn."

"It usually takes *humans* longer to learn." He patted her knee, making the gesture patronizing. "Remember, I'm preternaturally strong and intelligent."

He slid his hand higher and got it slapped away. "And preternaturally arrogant."

When Lachlain had seen her tonight outside the hotel, looking curvy in a sinfully short skirt, with her hair shining and full, his heart had hammered in his chest for her. He'd seen her sexy little shoes and imagined the heels digging into his back when she wrapped her legs around him. Her eyes were bright, her skin glowing.

He was stunned to realize that even the moon had never held his gaze so completely.

And she was staying with him by choice, lured by jewelry. *Which was already hers.*

He'd spent his entire life acquiring the pieces in anticipation of giving them to her, never having imagined a mate quite like her.

As Lachlain drove down the roadway, he felt optimistic for the first time since his capture some fifteen decades ago. No matter what had happened, he'd escaped his enemies and could go about building his life again. With Emmaline—who wasn't the killer he'd thought her. Who was unique among all the many vampires he'd encountered in his long life.

She was unique among all the females he'd ever seen.

He couldn't decide if she was fey or a siren in appearance. Her wrists, finely wrought hands, and collarbone appeared fragile, the pale column of her neck so delicate. Her face was ethereal, exquisite. In other places, especially now that she'd fed, she was all woman with her generous, sensitive breasts and soft hips.

And she had an arse that made him hiss "mercy" under his breath.

He glanced down at his arm, smirking slowly at her wee fang marks, disbelieving his reaction to her bite. Knowing his beliefs and aware of how sick others would find it, he reasoned he must be depraved—because he'd reveled in it.

It was as if she'd opened up a new sexual venue that he had never imagined. As if all there'd ever been was straight fucking, and then out of the blue, Emma had said, *What if I lick and suck your shaft into my mouth*. He shuddered, his erection pulsing.

Though it should be a mark of shame to be hidden, he found he liked to look at her bite because it reminded him of this foreign, secret pleasure—and that she'd never drunk from another. Only to him had she delivered that dark kiss.

He wondered who had taught her not to. Her family? Were they truly Forbearers, different from the rest of the vampires, forced to live in Louisiana because they were split from the Horde? He didn't see answers forthcoming. She was the most tight-lipped female he'd ever encountered, and after his blunt questioning debacle in the restaurant, he planned to refrain for a while.

But he was her first and would be her only, and that made him proud. He fantasized about the next time she would drink. He'd get her to take from his neck, freeing both of his hands so he could pull aside her lacy undergarments and finger her wetness. Once she was ready for him, he'd work her down his length. . . .

He stifled another shudder, then turned to ask her for the tenth time if she was thirsty yet, but he saw her curled up in the seat, looking soft and relaxed under his coat. He'd spread it over her, partly because he thought it would make her more comfortable and partly because it made *him* more comfortable not to see flashes of her thighs. She leaned her head against the window, staring out with that thing attached to her ears, and didn't seem to realize that she sang softly. He didn't want to interrupt her. Her voice was beautiful, lulling.

She'd said she did nothing well, which meant she didn't believe she sang well, since she couldn't have lied. He wondered why she wasn't more confident in herself. She was lovely, her mind was sharp, and deep down she had fire. No, not *too* deep down. She had, after all, dislocated his jaw—at the first opportunity.

Perhaps her vampire family had found her too sensitive or introspective and had been cruel to her. That thought made fury fire in him, made him relish the idea of killing anyone who'd treated her ill.

Lachlain was aware of what was happening. He was siding with her, beginning to consider all things in terms of *them*. Somehow the bonding with his mate had begun with a bite.

How much longer till we get there? Emma was tempted to whine.

Now that she had some energy again, she was getting restless in the car. At least, she told herself that was why she'd begun squirming in the seat. *Not* because she'd melted under his coat, still warm from his body and surrounding her with his delicious scent.

She stretched, pulling out her earbuds, which apparently in Lykae was code for "Interrogate me," because the questions, they came a-calling.

"Earlier you said you've never killed, never drunk another. Did you mean you've never taken a man's neck even during sex? Accidentally bitten him, even in abandon?"

She exhaled, pinching her forehead, disappointed in him. She'd been almost *comfortable* around him this night, but here came the sexual questions, the innuendo. "Where did this come from?"

"Nothing to do while driving but think. Have you?"

"No, Lachlain. Happy? Never went dental with anybody's arm but your own." When he immediately parted his lip for another question, she snapped, "Anybody's *anything*."

He relaxed a little in the seat. "Wanted to be sure."

"Why?" she asked, exasperated.

"Like being your first."

Was he for real? Was it possible he was asking these questions not to embarrass her, but because he was being a . . . a male?

"Does blood always make you react the way you did tonight—or was it taking from me that made you so wanton?"

Nope. Just to embarrass her. "Why is this important?"

"I want to know whether, if you were drinking blood from a glass—in front of others—you would behave as you did."

"You just couldn't let me go a few hours without tormenting me?"

"No' tormenting you. I need to know."

Emma was really beginning to hate speaking with him. Then she frowned. What was he getting at? When would she drink in front of others? She did at home, but that was from a mug or a margarita glass at a party. Not in a bed, partially undressed while a male licked her breast. Her heart sped up, anxiety erupting. Lachlain would never take her among his friends and family as she drank blood like wine, so why was he asking?

Was he making sordid plans that included her? She was struck once again by how little she truly knew about him. "I've heard about Lykae appetites and, uh, your openness with your sexuality"—she swallowed—"but I wouldn't want to be that way in front of others."

He frowned at her briefly, then a muscle ticked in his cheek. Immediately she sensed his building anger. "I meant in a social situation where others drank. I would *never* even contemplate the other."

She flushed. Now *her* mind was in the gutter, cruising past his mind's station there. "Lachlain, I'm no more affected than you would be from a glass of water."

He met her eyes, giving her a look so primal it made her shiver. "Emma, I doona know what you've been doing in the past, but know that when I take a woman into my bed, I will never *share* her."

13

"You doona seem to care that we had to stop tonight," Lachlain said over his shoulder as he triple-checked the blankets he'd strung over the hotel window.

After midnight, the skies had opened up, rain pouring, making their journey slow going. He'd said Kinevane was perhaps two hours away. Emma had known dawn was in three.

She tilted her head, aware that he was deeply disappointed. "I was game to go on," she reminded him. She had been, shocking herself. Emma didn't usually *que sera, sera* in matters solar.

After a final inspection of the blanket barrier, he allowed himself to sink down into the room's plush chair. In a bid to keep from staring at him, Emma sat on the edge of the bed, remote in hand, and began to scan the movie channels.

"You ken I would no' risk continuing." When he'd said he wouldn't let her be burned again, Emma supposed he'd meant it.

Still, she didn't understand how he'd prevented himself from rolling the dice with this one drive tonight. If she had been kept away from her home for one hundred and fifty years and she was within two hours' driving distance, she would have dragged the unwitting vampire along.

Lachlain had refused, instead finding them an inn, not of the caliber they'd enjoyed, he said, but he'd "sensed it was secure." He'd felt comfortable enough to get two adjoining rooms because he planned to sleep, and as he'd promised, he wouldn't do it around her. A quick calculation told her he'd gone nearly forty hours without.

Even so, he seemed uncomfortable having to divulge his need to sleep. In fact, it was only because his attention had wandered as he'd peered around them with narrowed eyes—which he'd been doing with increasing frequency—that he'd spoken of it. He'd absently admitted that he would have just gone without, but his injury was not healing as it should.

Injury, meaning his leg. The one that looked like a human's leg just after a six-*year*-long cast came off. The injury that she found herself thinking about, imagining scenarios for.

He had to have lost it. Her bite on his arm, which she'd caught him peering down at with an almost affectionate expression—an expression that she might prize even over a rare hug—was rapidly healing. Yet he continued to limp. He must be completely regenerating it.

She glanced up at him, realizing that as she'd been contemplating his leg, he'd clearly been doing the same to hers, staring at her thighs, getting that . . . that *wolfish* look in his eyes. She pinched the hem of her skirt, endeavoring to hop up and wiggle it down. His gaze was glued to her actions, a low, barely audible growl rumbling from him for long seconds. The sound made her shiver, irrationally made her want to exaggerate her movements so he'd enjoy them more.

When sane Emma blushed at her thoughts and tugged the corner of the cover over her, he gave her a brows-drawn expression of deep disappointment.

She looked away, picking up the remote once more as she cast about for a handle on this bizarre situation. She didn't need to be in a hotel room with this Lykae when both of them were lucid and when she was getting in the habit of falling asleep against his naked body in a bathtub each night. She cleared her throat and faced him. "I'm going to watch a movie. So I guess I'll see you at sunset."

"You're kicking me out of your room?"

"That about sums it up."

He shook his head—her desires ignored without even a thought. "I'll stay with you until dawn."

"I like spending time by myself, and for the last three days, you've allowed me none. Would it kill you to leave the room?"

He appeared confused, as if her wanting to be away from him was sheer craziness. "You will no' share this . . . movie with me?"

The way he'd phrased his question almost made her grin.

"Then after, you could finally drink again."

The urge to smile faded at his sexy, gravelly words, but she didn't look away, too fascinated by the heated way he studied her face.

He continued to ask her to drink, reinforcing her belief that he'd enjoyed it as much as she had. Though it had baffled her, she'd felt his erection—hard to miss, that—and had seen the desire in his eyes. Desire just like she saw right now. . . .

The moment was broken by the sound of some woman screaming her way to ecstasy. Emma gasped, and swung her head around to the TV. She'd been inadvertently pressing the remote and had somehow wound up on Cinemax. This late at night, Cinemax meant Skinemax.

Her face was hot with embarrassment as she frantically worked the remote, but even the regular channels seemed to delight in showing *Unfaithful* or *Eyes Wide Shut*. Finally, she landed on something without sex—

Oh, shite. *An American Werewolf in Paris.*

In full gory attack scene.

Before she could change it, he shot to his feet. "Is this how . . . is this how humans see us?" He sounded aghast.

She thought about other werewolf movies—*Dog Soldiers*, *The Beast Within*, *The Howling*, the oh-so-subtly-titled *The Beast Must Die*—and nodded. He was going to see these things sooner or later and he would learn the truth. "Yes, they do."

"Do they see all the Lore like this?"

"No, um, not really."

"Why?"

She bit her lip. "Well, I've heard the Lykae never concern themselves with PR, while the vampires and the witches, for instance, throw money at it."

"PR?"

"Public relations."

"And this *PR* works for them?" he asked, still watching with a sickened look on his face.

"Let's put it this way—witches are viewed as *powerless* Wiccans. Vampires are seen as sexy . . . *myths*."

"My God," he murmured, sinking onto the bed with a long exhalation.

His reaction was so strong, she wanted to delve. But delving meant being subject to the same. Just then, she didn't care. "So the werewolf appearance there . . . it was *all* wrong."

He rubbed his bad leg, looking weary. "Damn it, Emma,

can you no' just ask me what I look like when I change?"

She tilted her head at him. His leg clearly hurt him, and she hated to see *anything* suffering. Apparently even crude and rude Lykae, because to take his mind from his pain, she asked, "So, Lachlain, what do you look like when you change?"

His expression was surprised, and then he seemed not to know how to answer. Finally, he said, "Have you ever seen a phantom mask a human?"

"Of course I have," she answered. She did live in the most Lore-rich city in the world.

"You know how you can still see the human, but the phantom is clear, too? That's what it's like. You still see me, but you see something stronger, wilder, with me."

She turned toward him on the bed, lay on her front, and bent her elbows to prop her chin up, ready to hear more.

When she waved him on, he leaned back against the headboard, stretching his long legs in front of him. "Ask me."

She rolled her eyes. "Very well. Do you grow fangs?" When he nodded, she said, "And fur?"

He raised his eyebrows. "Christ, no."

She had many befurred friends and took offense at his tone, but decided to let it go. "I know your eyes turn blue."

He nodded. "And my body gets bigger, while the shape of my face changes, becomes more . . . lupine."

She grimaced. "Snout?"

He actually chuckled at that. "No. No' like you're thinking."

"Then it doesn't sound that different from you now."

"But it is." He grew serious. "We call it *saorachadh ainmhidh bho a cliabhan* . . . letting the beast out of its cage."

"Would it scare me?"

"Even older, powerful vampires cower."

She bit her lip, contemplating all he'd said. Try as she might, she couldn't imagine him as anything other than *hot*.

He ran a hand over his mouth. "It's getting late. Do you no' want to drink again before dawn?"

Embarrassed by how badly she wanted to, she shrugged and studied her finger tracing the bedcover's paisley design.

"We're both thinking about it. We both want to."

She murmured, "I might, but I don't want what comes with it."

"What if I vowed no' to touch you?"

"But what if . . ." She trailed off, her face heating. "What if I forget . . . *myself?*" If he kissed her and stroked her as he had before, she had no doubt she'd soon be begging for him to bend her over the bed, as he'd put it.

"It would no' matter because I'd put my hands on this cover and I would no' move them."

She frowned at his hands, then nibbled her lip. "Put them behind your back."

He clearly didn't like that. "I would put my hands"—he glanced around, then spread his arms over the top of the headboard, palms down—"here, and I would no' move them. No matter what occurs."

"You promise?"

"Aye. I vow it."

She could try to convince herself that mere hunger compelled her to walk on her knees over to him. But it was so much more than that. She needed to experience the sensuality of the act, the warmth, the taste of his skin beneath her tongue, the feel of his heartbeat speeding up as though she'd *pleasured* him by drawing greedily.

When she knelt before him, he leaned his head away, exposing his neck, beckoning her.

She saw he was already hard and grew nervous. "Hands stay put?"

"Aye."

Unable to stop herself, she eased forward, took his shirt with her fists, and sank her fangs into his skin. Rich warmth and pleasure exploded within her, and she moaned against him. She felt his groan reverberating beneath her lips. When she almost toppled over from the rush of sensation, he bit out, "*Straddle . . . me.*"

Never taking her lips away, she did, gladly, better able to relax and revel in the taste and feeling. Though he never removed his hands from the headboard, he thrust his hips up against her. Then, with another groan, he seemed to make an effort to stop.

But she liked the sounds he'd made, liked that she could *feel* them, and wanted to hear more. So she lowered herself fully to his lap, uncaring that her skirt was slipping up her thighs. The heat that met her made her ache. Thoughts grew dim. *So hard. . . .* Gone nearly mindless, she rubbed against him to ease it.

14

"*Release me from my vow, Emmaline.*"

She didn't respond, wouldn't release him, and damn it, it had begun to matter to him if he broke his word to her. Her only answer was spreading her knees wider over him, then slowly, sensuously rubbing his length between her legs, with only his trews and her silk between them. "Ah, God, yes, Emma," he grated, shuddering with need, disbelieving that she was doing this to him.

He would use this against her, he thought hazily. If his blood on her tongue made her lose control like this, he would force her to drink him until she surrendered everything. . . .

Force a vampire to drink him . . . what was happening to him?

She put her hands on the headboard between his and held on as she ground against him, making his head fall back. The scent of her hair, flowing just before him, the feel of her bite, and her own obvious pleasure were sending him over the edge. "You're going tae make me come like this. If you doona stop . . ."

She didn't. She continued grinding against him as if she *couldn't* stop. The frustration was like nothing he'd ever known. To not be able to touch her, or put his mouth to her flesh . . . She brushed her breasts against his chest and back again. The headboard began to crack under his hands.

The throbbing pressure built up inside him, had been building all night from her first taking. Now his breaths grew ragged as she moved faster, riding his length. Just when he perceived she'd stopped drinking, she whispered in his ear, "I could drink you forever."

You will. . . .

"Taste so *good*," she said, moaning the last.

"You drive me mad," he grated, then threw his head back and yelled out as he came hotly under her movements, forced by the firm bucking of her hips against him. The wood beneath his hands disintegrated to splinters and dust.

When he finally finished shuddering, he clenched his ragged fists beside her legs. She fell against his chest, clinging to him, her small body quivering.

"Emma, look at me."

She faced him, her silvery eyes mesmerizing. He knew her, she felt familiar, and yet he knew he'd never seen anything like the stunning creature she was. She tilted her head, regarding him with an unsure expression.

"I want to touch you. I want to bring you to come."

She glanced at his torn hands with raised eyebrows.

"Then I'll kiss you. Pull your undergarments aside and kneel up right here."

She shook her head slowly.

"Why?"

She whispered, "Because these things keep escalating."

"I dinna break my vow now." Hands still clenched, he lowered his voice to say, "I ache, I want to pleasure you so much."

He saw her eyes grow soft just before she put her forehead

to his. As if she couldn't help herself, she leaned in to lick and tease at his lips. Her hair fell forward, brushing his neck. Her exquisite scent washed over him, and he felt himself growing hard again.

Between her kisses, he rasped, "Why can this no' go further?"

"This isn't me," she murmured. "I'm not like this. I barely even know you."

Sheer frustration welled in him at her ridiculous assertions, said between tonguing his lips. He believed they were sentiments she felt she *ought* to be saying. "Yet you've taken my blood directly from my body? That's as intimate an act as two can have."

In an instant, she stiffened and drew back. "That's true and regrettable. But I couldn't share myself so completely with someone I don't trust." She rose and then curled up in the chair. "Someone who's been so unkind. . . ."

"Emma, I—"

"You know you have been. And just three nights ago, you frightened me more than I've ever been in my entire life. Yet now you want something from me?" She was trembling. "Just leave. Please? For once?"

He growled in frustration, but he did limp to the door. At the hallway adjoining the rooms, he turned and said, "You've bought yourself a few hours. The next time you drink, you're mine and we both know it." The door slammed behind him.

Emma lay in her nest on the floor, tossing in her blankets. When had her clothing become so textured? She seemed to feel every line of thread against her sensitive breasts and belly.

And she wore silk.

Just thinking about what she'd done to him made her hips undulate as if she could still feel him beneath her. She'd made him . . . have an orgasm, by *riding* him.

Her face burned hot. Was she becoming Emma the Wanton?

And she'd almost experienced one, too. When she'd bathed, she'd found herself wetter than she'd ever been. She was beginning to suspect that blood lust for her wasn't the craving to drink, it was sexual lust *because* of drinking.

He was right—the next time she took from him, he could make her his, because tonight, she'd temporarily lost her mind, forgetting why she couldn't sleep with him. Though she'd desperately wanted to convince herself otherwise, she wasn't the type of person who could give it up without some kind of bond or commitment.

She didn't think of herself as old-fashioned about sex—there was, after all, a reason for her familiarity with Skinemax—and she had a very healthy attitude about the whole subject, for all that she'd never had an orgasm. But she knew deep down that she would need something lasting—and that it could never be with him.

Besides the fact that he was a crude and menacing Lykae who delighted in her discomfort, she couldn't imagine taking him among her friends. She couldn't see him watching movies at the manor, eating the popcorn she always made just so she could smell it and throw it at anyone who stood in front of the screen. He wouldn't fit in with her family because they would be sickened at the very sight of "an animal" touching her. And because they would always be plotting to kill him and such.

Not to mention that in addition to all of their differences, he had another female out there who had some cosmic destiny to be his.

Emma was up for a little healthy competition, but against a Lykae's mate . . . ?

Well. Now she was just being silly—

He knocked on the adjoining door, opening it without a decent pause, but luckily she'd cut out all that lolling and petting her breasts business.

His hair was wet from a recent shower, and he leaned against the doorway in jeans that rode just a little below his waist and just a little loose—as they *should*. He wore no shirt and she noticed one of his palms had a knot of cloth around it. She swallowed. Injured from when he'd cracked her headboard as he came.

He crossed his arms over that muscled chest. Her appreciation for it bordered on idolatry. She would *so* give him another amen. . . .

"Tell me one thing about you that I doona know," he demanded.

When able to force her gaze to his face, she debated, then finally said, "I went to college and got a degree in popular culture."

He appeared impressed, but of course he hadn't been around this time long enough to know that most people thought pop culture was a do-you-want-fries-with-that degree. He nodded, turning toward his room, and because he didn't expect her to, she said, "Tell me one thing."

When he faced her again, he did appear surprised she'd asked. His voice gravelly, he answered, "I think you're the most beautiful creature I've ever seen."

She was certain he heard her gasp before he closed the door.

He'd called her *beautiful!*

Before, she'd only felt a sad resignation, but now she was giddy. Oh, she was in a bad way. Her emotions were like a crazy compass dial, spinning wildly—

She narrowed her eyes, realizing what this was. Stockholm syndrome. Surely. Identifying with your bullying captor? Check. Forming an attachment to him? Check.

But in all fairness to herself, how many captors—actively acquiring—were six-and-a-half-foot-tall gods with delicious, sun-darkened skin, the coolest accent, and the warmest, hardest body she'd ever dreamed of? All this *and* the predilection to wrap that body around her? All this *and* he thought she was beautiful.

Not to mention the fact that he couldn't seem to give her enough of his luscious blood.

Was she becoming this Lykae's Patty Hearst?

Didn't matter. The bottom line was that she wasn't his mate, so even if he did seduce her and they had a little some-something going on, she'd be merely idling time until he found his true one. And if she got herself nailed and bailed by a man like Lachlain, she thought she might turn into one of those blubbery, weepy females. Which was not an option.

She was relieved she wasn't this mate of his. She *was*. If she had been his mate, it would have been like a life sentence. He would never let her go, she'd be browbeaten and miserable with him, and if she escaped he would come for her until her aunts finally killed him.

Her coven would delight in it. If they found out he'd kissed her and touched her intimately, they would unleash hell on him and his kind. As far as she knew, she was the only one of her coven ever to be touched by a Lykae.

And her mother had been the only one to fully succumb to a vampire.

Emma woke at sunset, sensing something.

She scanned the darkened room, popping up her head, peeking over the side of the bed, but saw nothing. She told herself it *was* nothing, even as she hastily dressed and packed, then rushed to Lachlain's room.

She found him still clad only in those jeans, with no blanket to cover him because he'd used his to secure her window. Right before her eyes, he began shuddering as though in the grip of a nightmare. He rumbled words in Gaelic, and his skin grew slick with sweat. All the muscles in his body tensed as if he was in great pain.

"Lachlain?" she whispered. Without thought, she hurried to him, reaching out to run her fingers down his cheek and through his thick hair, trying to soothe him.

He did still. "Emmaline," he murmured, without waking. Was she in his dreams?

She herself had had a doozy of a dream, the most realistic one she'd ever experienced.

She absently stroked his forehead as she recalled it. It seemed to be from Lachlain's point of view—she could see things that he saw, smell scents he smelled, feel as though with his fingers.

He was in a shop under a tent. Jewels were spread before him, and a beautiful woman with long, coffee-colored hair streaked from the sun and sparkling green eyes was by his side.

He selected a pounded-gold and sapphire necklace and purchased it from the shopkeeper. By the design of the jewelry and the currency he used, Emma knew this was long ago.

The woman sighed and said, "More gifts."

"Aye." Lachlain was irritated with her because he knew what she was about to say.

The woman, whose name Emma somehow knew was Cassandra, said, "Nine hundred years you've waited. I've waited almost as long. Do you no' think that we—"

"No," Lachlain interrupted sharply. *How many times will she broach this?* he thought.

Cassandra might not believe, but he did.

"I'd accept a night with you."

"I doona see you as more than an old friend. Know that that can end." His ire was growing. "And you are of the clan and will meet her. Do you possibly think that I would put her in that uncomfortable position?"

Emma shook her head at the bizarre dream, still thrown by how authentic it had felt. He only had to mention jewelry and she was dreaming up wonky scenarios.

She glanced down and saw with a blush that she'd begun stroking his chest. She didn't stop, just marveled at how gorgeous his body was, marveled that he wanted to make love to her with it—

His hand shot to her neck, tightening before she could scream.

When he opened his eyes, they were completely blue.

15

Emmaline was touching him gently, murmuring his name. More of the nightmare—she would never do that, would never seek to comfort him. He saw nothing but a red haze, felt nothing but fire melting away his skin. He'd sensed his enemy for three days and now it was *near his mate.* He attacked.

When the haze cleared, he couldn't comprehend what he saw. Emma's neck was clenched in his tightening grasp, her claws embedded in his arms as she gasped and fought for her life. Before he could even react he saw a vessel in her right eye burst.

He yelled and released her, lunging away from her.

She fell to her knees, struggling for air, coughing. He rushed to her to try to help, but she flinched, shoving her hand out to ward him off.

"Ah, God, Emma, I dinna mean . . . I'd sensed something . . . I thought you were a vampire."

She coughed, then rasped, "I—*am.* . . ."

"No, I thought there was . . . another, one of the ones that imprisoned me." The bite, the blood, must've triggered the nightmares in full fury. "I thought you were him."

"*Who?*" she bit out.

"Demestriu," he finally grated. Against her weak

protests, he drew her in his arms. "I never wanted to hurt you." He shuddered. "Emma, it was an accident."

But his words had no effect. She shook in his arms, still afraid.

She didn't trust him—never had—and he'd just reminded her why.

Out of the corner of her eye, Emma saw him take one hand from the steering wheel, reaching out once more to touch her. As he had each time before, he closed it to a fist and brought it back.

She sighed, leaning her face against the cool glass, staring out, seeing nothing.

Her emotions were so torn over what had happened, she didn't know how to react.

She wasn't angry with him over this particular incident. She'd been stupid enough to touch a Lykae in midnightmare and had paid the price. But she regretted that her throat hurt and that she couldn't take a pill to ease it. And she regretted what she'd learned about him.

She had wondered if it was possible that the Horde had imprisoned him, but she'd dismissed the idea because prisoners simply didn't *escape* the Horde. She'd never heard of a single instance. Even her aunt Myst, who'd actually seen the inside of a Horde stronghold, hadn't escaped until rebels had taken the castle—and until a rebel general had freed her in order to make love to her.

Having ruled out the Horde, Emma had figured that since he was the Lykae leader, this was political, possibly some kind of coup by his own kind.

Yet it had been Demestriu, the most evil and powerful of all vampires, who'd imprisoned him. And if the rumors were true about Furie, if the tales of her torture at the bottom of the sea were correct, then what had he done to Lachlain? Had Demestriu ordered him drowned as well? Chained him in the earth and buried him alive?

For one hundred and fifty years they'd tortured him until he'd escaped the inescapable.

And she feared he'd somehow *lost his leg* to do it.

She couldn't imagine the pain—endless pain that he'd experienced for so long only to culminate in that . . . ?

What had happened tonight wasn't his fault. Though judging by his bleak expression he certainly thought so. Yet now, knowing what she did, she resented him for keeping her with him. What in the hell had he been thinking? After what he'd been through, Emma now knew that the incident tonight had been inevitable. Eventually he would have exploded in rage at her, and might do it again.

She wouldn't allow this to happen again. She might not survive it. And if she did, she didn't want to have to tell people she had bruises circling her throat and a starburst of blood radiating from her pupil because she'd run into a sodding door. Why had he kept her with him?

To take out his pain on her.

He'd treated her like a vicious vampire. Disdained her as one for days. If he didn't watch out, she'd begin to behave like one to protect herself.

They'd make Kinevane tonight, and at sunset tomorrow she'd be gone.

Emma leaned against the window and had that thing in her ears, though she didn't sing as she had last night.

He wanted to remove it and talk to her, apologize to her. He was fiercely ashamed of his actions, had never been more ashamed, but he thought if he took it away from her, she would break. Since he'd seized her, he'd terrified and hurt her, and he sensed she was at her limit, barely coping with the events of the last four days.

The streetlamps shone down from overhead, illuminating her face—and the bruises on her pale throat, making him wince again.

If he hadn't come to his senses when he did, he could have . . . he could have killed her. And because he didn't understand why he'd done it, he couldn't ensure it would never happen again. He couldn't guarantee her safety around him—

A bell pinged, startling him.

She leaned over to look, nodding at the fuel gauge that was now lit red. She pointed out the next exit, still without saying a word. He knew she was silent because it *hurt her to speak.*

He was distracted, restless in the car that now seemed far too small for him, clenching the steering wheel. Yes, he'd been through hell, but goddamn it, how could he have *choked* his mate in any state of mind? When all he'd wanted to do was find her?

When she'd been his salvation?

It didn't matter that he hadn't claimed her—if he hadn't found her and been near her, been eased by her soft words and gentle touches, right now he'd be in a back alley, irretrievably mad.

In return, he'd made her life into a hell.

Off the exit, he spotted the sign for a gas station. He turned into the dirt lot, parking in front of the fuel pump she indicated. Just as he shut off the ignition, she pulled the things from her ears. He opened his mouth to speak, but be-

fore he could say anything, she gazed upward, sighed, and
held her hand flat out—which meant he was to give her the
credit card. He did, then followed her outside to learn how
to fuel the car.

While they waited, he said, "I want to speak with you
about what happened."

She waved her hand. "Forgotten." Her voice was hoarse,
belying the ridiculous statement. Under the harsh, unnatural lights of the station, her right eye appeared awash with
red. She had to be furious again—why hide it?

"Why will you no' confront me? Rail at me? I give you
free leave to scream at me."

In a low tone, she said, "Are you asking me why I *avoid
conflict?*"

"Aye. Precisely," he said, then, seeing the glare on her
face, wished he hadn't.

"I am sick of everyone accusing me of that! Now someone who doesn't even know me has thrown that my way."
Her scratchy voice was rising with anger. "The better question would be, why *wouldn't* I want to avoid conflict, because you'd be avoiding it too if . . ." She trailed off and
looked away.

He placed his hand on her shoulder. "If what, Emma?"

When she finally faced him, her eyes were anguished. "If
you always lost."

His brows drew together.

"Lose enough times, and guess what that makes you?"

"No—"

"When have I won a conflict with you?" She shrugged
from under his hand. "When you kidnapped me? When you
got me to agree to this insanity? When you got me to drink
from you? You were imprisoned by vampires, Lachlain, and

had just escaped them when you took me. Why in the hell would you keep me with you? You hate vampires—have shown me more disgust in less than a week than I've encountered in my entire life. Yet you kept me with you." She gave a bitter laugh. "How you must have loved your little revenges. Did you get off making me nauseated with humiliation? Get a perverse thrill by insulting me one second then shoving your hand up my skirt the next? And at every opportunity to let me go, you demanded I stay, knowing the entire time that I was in danger. From you."

He could deny nothing. He ran his hand over his face as everything she said sank in. His feelings for her had become clearer to him, just as hers had reached a boiling point with him. He wanted to admit to her that she was his mate—that he hadn't kept her with him solely to hurt her. He knew he couldn't tell her now.

"Like everyone else, you walk right over me and never even look back to see how I fared," she said, her voice cracking at the end, making regret cut at him. "Whoa, better shut myself up before I get too upset. Don't want to offend you with my repulsive tears!"

"No, Emma, wait—"

She slammed her car door shut, seeming surprised by her strength, then stalked away over the dirt lot. He let her go, though he moved to keep her in sight.

He saw her sink down on a bench beside the station building and put her forehead in her hand, sitting like that for many moments. Just as he finished refueling, a strange chill wind blew, bringing a mist of rain with it and brushing a flower against her knee. She plucked the spent flower, smelled it, then wadded it up in frustration.

He realized she'd never seen one blooming in the sun.

His chest tightened with some unfamiliar feeling, so strong it shook him.

The problems between them weren't because he'd been given the wrong mate. They were because *he* couldn't adapt—

Three vampires appeared out of nowhere just beside her.

To take her away from him forever.

In an instant, he knew he should let her go to her family and free her from his hatred and pain. Earlier, as he'd tightened his hand around her throat, she'd stared up at him, begging him. She'd believed he was going to kill her. He could have so easily.

The bruises on her neck stood out like an accusation in the harsh lights.

But she gaped at them, as if shocked they'd just appeared when this was the way they traveled.

The scene hit him as *wrong*. He leapt over the top of the car for her and they turned. The largest one was . . . a *demon*? Yet all of their eyes were solid red. A demon turned vampire?

"Stay back, Lykae, or we'll kill you," one of the vampires grated.

As Lachlain charged for her, the oddest thing happened.

Crying his name, she sprinted for him.

16

Before he could reach her, one tackled Emma to the ground, the impact wrenching her breath away. Lachlain bellowed with rage. If he couldn't reach her . . . if she couldn't fight hard enough . . . the vampire could easily trace her. The two others appeared between him and Emma, baring their fangs. When she dug at the earth to escape, the beast rose up inside Lachlain and he let it free. He'd never wanted her to see it. . . .

Power surged through his body with the turning. *Outrage. Protect.*

The smaller vampire hissed, "She's his mate!" just before Lachlain attacked, slashing at him. He ripped and bit his body to pieces as he warded off blows from the other.

The mist turned to hard, stinging rain with lightning clattering all around. Lachlain twisted the vampire's neck with his fingers until he'd separated it, then faced off against the demon. It was strong, but coming off injuries. Lachlain's claws were drawn to the wounds unerringly, just as the demon aimed for his leg. From the corner of his eye, Lachlain saw Emma wrestle to get free of the third. She rolled to her back beneath him, then soundly knocked her forehead against her attacker.

The fiend howled in pain and slashed down her chest,

leaving deep furrows that gushed blood into the mud. Lachlain roared and leapt for the demon between them. One slash of his claws rent the demon's head from his body, sending both pieces flying in different directions.

The last vampire, crouched over Emma, stared up at him in horror, frozen, seeming too shocked to trace. As Lachlain swung for the killing blow, he saw Emma had squeezed her eyes shut.

Rid of the third, Lachlain fell to his knees beside her. She opened her eyes as if she couldn't help it, blinking up at him, stricken by his appearance, more shocked by him than her wound or the attack. As he grappled for control, he comprehended that she was struggling to speak, choking on her blood and the pouring rain. All the while still edging away from him. She'd run to him before, but after witnessing what he was, she fought him.

Against her weak resistance, he scooped her into his arms. He shook his head hard, breathing in deeply. "I will no' hurt you." His voice was low, broken, and, he knew, unrecognizable.

With a shaking hand, he tore open what was left of her shirt, and as the rain washed away the blood and mud, he could see the damage that had savaged her delicate skin down to the bone. He clutched her to him and roared, *needing* to kill them again. She whimpered at the sound and, amid the rain, pink tears tracked from her eyes.

That alone was enough to give him the strength to take control.

When he reached the car, he threw open the back door to lay her down on the seat, gently pulling her long hair out of the doorway before shutting her in. He rushed into the driver's seat, then raced down slippery roads for Kinevane, glancing back every few seconds. Dread settled over him when half an hour had passed and she still showed no signs of regeneration. Her wounds continued to bleed freely with none of the closure he should already be seeing.

Never slowing, he bit his wrist open and thrust it back to her lips. "Drink, Emma!"

She turned her face away. He put it against her once more, but she refused, clenching her jaw shut. She could die if she didn't drink.

He'd been so busy hating what she was that he hadn't worried about how she saw him.

He pulled to the side of the road, reaching back to dig his fingers into her mouth and part her teeth. When he dripped blood into her mouth, she couldn't stop herself from latching onto him, closing her eyes and drinking deeply. She stopped bleeding at once. When she passed out, he sped off again.

The drive to Kinevane was a new kind of hell for him. He ran his other arm over his forehead, sweating, not knowing if more would attack or where they'd come from. He didn't know if she was strong enough to sustain this wound. How had she known to run *from them*?

He'd almost lost her four days after finding her. . . .

No, he'd almost *given* her away, allowed them to take her to Helvita—which he'd never been able to find. He'd scoured Russia for it, perhaps had just gotten close when they'd ambushed him last time.

So close to losing her. . . . Now he knew he would do anything to keep her.

He could work past his pain and torturing memories because he'd seen tonight how different she was from the others. Her appearance, her movements, everything was different. Her nature wasn't about aggression and killing like the others'. Blood for her—and now for Lachlain—was about life.

Her wounds had begun healing immediately when she drank from him. He could sustain her.

Which was the least he could do, since she'd finally made his life worth living.

Emma woke to the sound of bellowing and cracked open her eyes.

The headlights illuminated Lachlain shoving his shoulder into a massive gate, against the crest in the center. The raised seal was made up of two halves, one wolf on each side facing each other. The wolves were depicted as they might be in antiquity, showing the heads and forepaws, fangs and claws bared, ears forward. Great, Lykae-land. Not in Kansas anymore. . . .

Lachlain was not making a dent in the metal, even with his strength. Mystically protected? Of course. Thank Freya he'd known better than to try to drive the car through.

She watched through heavy-lidded eyes as he prowled in the drizzle, raking his hand through his wet hair as he studied the gate. *"How the fuck do I get in?"* Once more he attempted to power it open, and once more a gut-wrenching bellow reverberated as if down a valley.

Should she tell him about the intercom? *Could* she physically? Just as she was debating it, the gate was opened by someone unseen.

Lachlain rushed back into the car. "We're here, Emma!"

Though the heater ran full blast, and the seat warmer as well, she shivered in her damp clothes with a cold like she'd never known. When the gate clanged shut behind them, she rested her eyes, at last feeling safe. At least from more vampire attacks.

She was dimly aware that they drove and drove over a property that must be miles long. Finally Lachlain parked, and leapt out of the car to throw open the back door and draw her out. He held her close to his chest, hurrying into an entranceway that blazed with light, hurting her eyes. He bounded up the stairs, giving orders to some young man following in his wake.

"Bandages, Harmann. And hot water."

"Aye, my liege." He snapped his fingers, and Emma heard someone running to obey the command.

"Is my brother here?"

"No, he's overseas. He . . . we thought you were dead. When you didn't return and the searches came up empty—"

"I need tae speak with him as soon as possible. Doona tell the elders of my return yet."

Emma coughed, an ugly, rattling sound, and she realized she'd never fathomed what pain was. She willed herself not to look down at her chest.

"Who is she?" the young man asked.

Lachlain drew her in closer to him. "She's *her*," he answered, as if that made any sense. To her, he said, "You're safe, Emma. You're goin' tae be fine."

"But she's . . . not a Lykae," the man said.

"She's a vampire."

A strangled sound. "A-are you certain? Of her?"

"I've never been surer of anything in my life."

Her thoughts grew hazy, and blackness beckoned.

Lachlain carried her to his room, laying her in his ancient bed, the first woman he'd ever brought to it.

Harmann followed, then set about starting a fire. Lachlain might feel uneasy with the fireplace at his back, but knew Emma needed the warmth.

A maid swiftly returned with hot water, cloth, and bandages, and another two carried in their bags from the car. Then with pensive expressions, the maids left with Harmann so Lachlain could care for her.

Emma was still weak, in and out of consciousness as he stripped her damp clothing from her and bathed her wounds. Though she was visibly healing now, her fragile, soft skin was still ravaged between her breasts down to her ribs. His hands shook as he washed her.

"That hurts," she rasped, flinching when Lachlain inspected her wounds a last time before bandaging her.

Relief washed over him. She could speak once more. "I wish I could take the pain for you," he grated. His own wounds were deep, yet he felt nothing. The idea of *her* suffering made his hands unsteady when he began rolling the bandage around her chest. "Emma, what made you run from them?"

Not opening her eyes, she murmured, "*Scared.*"

"Why were you afraid?"

A small movement, as though she'd tried to shrug and failed. "Never seen a vampire."

He finished the binding and forced himself to tie it tight, wincing when she did. "I doona understand. You *are* a vampire."

Her eyes opened, but they were unfocused. "Call Annika. Number on medic card. Let her come get me." She grabbed his wrist, gritting the words. "Please let me go home . . . I want to go home. . . ." then passed out.

As he tucked the blanket around her, he ground his teeth

with frustration, not comprehending why her own kind would hurt her so. Not understanding why she would say she'd never seen a vampire.

She wanted him to call her family. Of course, he would never let her go back to them, but why not let them know that? Why not find out answers? He dug through her luggage, found the number for this Annika, then called for Harmann.

Minutes later, he was standing beside the bed, holding a telephone *with no cord*, ringing *the United States*.

A woman answered, "Emma! Is that you?"

"I have Emma with me."

"Who is this?"

"I am Lachlain. Who are you?"

"I'm the foster mother who's going to annihilate you if you don't send her home right now."

"Never going to happen. She stays with me from now on."

Something sounded like it exploded in the background, yet her voice was calm. "Scottish accent. Tell me you are not Lykae."

"I am their king."

"I hadn't thought you would commit an outright act of aggression against us. If you wanted to rekindle a war, you've succeeded."

Rekindle? The Lykae and the vampires *were* at war.

"Know this. If you don't free her, I will find your family, and I will sharpen my claws and *peel* them. Do you understand me?"

No. No, he didn't at all.

"You can't imagine the fury I will unleash on you and your kind if you hurt her. She is innocent of any crimes against you. *I* am not," she screamed.

He heard another woman in the background say softly, "Annika, ask him to speak with Emma."

Before she could ask, he answered, "She sleeps."

This Annika said, "It's *night* there—"

From the background again: "Reason with him. Who could be monster enough to hurt little Emma?"

He had been.

"If you hate us, then bring the fight here, but that creature has never hurt any living thing. Send her home to her coven."

Coven? "Why is she afraid of vampires—?"

"Did you let them get near her?" she shrieked, forcing him to hold the phone away from his ear. She sounded more furious that the vampires had gotten near Emma than she was about him having her.

The one with the reasonable voice said, "Ask him if he means her harm."

"Do you?"

"No. Never." He could now say this with confidence. "But you said, 'let them get near her'? You *are* them."

"What are you saying?"

"Are you split from the Horde? There was rumor of a faction—"

"You think I'm a vampire?"

With that shriek, he removed the phone from his ear more quickly. "If no', then what are you?"

"Valkyrie, you ignorant dog."

"Valkyrie," he repeated dumbly as his breath left him. His weak leg gave way and he sank onto the bed. His hand found Emma's hip and squeezed.

Now it made perfect sense. Her fey appearance, her glass-shattering screams. "Emma is part . . . that's why her ears . . ." Christ, she was part shield maiden?

He heard the phone being passed. The reasonable one said, "I am Lucia, her aunt—"

"Her father's a vampire?" he asked, cutting her off. "Who is he?"

"We don't know anything about him. Her mother never told us before she died. They attacked?"

"Aye."

"How many?"

"Three."

"They will report back. Unless you killed them all?" she asked with a hopeful note in her voice.

"O' course I did," he snapped.

He heard her exhale as though relieved. "Was she . . . hurt?"

He hesitated. "She was"—immediate and numerous shrieks in the background—"but she's healing."

The phone was passed yet again. Someone said, "Don't let Regin have it!"

"This is Regin, and you must be the 'man' she was with. She told me you promised to protect her. Way to go there, Ace—"

He heard something like a scuffle, then slaps, then Lucia had the phone. "We are the only family she knows and this is the first time she's traveled away from the protection of her coven. She's very gentle in nature, wary, and she will be frightened away from us. We beseech you to treat her with kindness."

"I will," he said, and he meant it. He knew he would never hurt her again. The memory of her eye bursting red just before him, and of her running *to* him for his protection, were forever seared into his mind. "Why would the vampires attack like that? Do you think her father seeks her?"

"I don't know. They've been hunting Valkyrie everywhere. We've kept Emma hidden from them. She'd never even seen one. Or a Lykae, for that matter." She added almost to herself, "Em must be terrified of you. . . ."

Terrified of him. Of course she was.

"If they have some agenda that includes Emma, they won't stop searching for her. She must return home where she can be safe."

"I can keep her safe."

Annika had the phone again. "You failed to do so."

"She's alive and they're dead."

"What's *your* agenda? You say you won't harm her, yet you're rushing into war with us?"

"I want no war with you."

"Then what do you want with *her?*"

"She's my mate." He heard her retch in response, and his hackles rose.

"So help me Freya"—she retched again—"if you have lain one of your filthy animal hands on her—"

"How do I care for her?" he asked, struggling to control his anger.

"You send her back to where she belongs so we can help her heal from you."

"I said no. Now, do you want me to protect her in your absence?"

He heard murmuring in the background, then Lucia spoke, "She has to be protected from the sun. She's only seventy and is incredibly vulnerable to it."

Seventy? Another squeeze of her hip. Christ almighty. The way he'd treated her . . .

"Like I said, she's never seen a Lykae and will be frightened of you. Be gentle with her, if you have any conscience.

She must drink every day, but never straight from a living source—"

"Why?" he interrupted.

Quiet. Then Annika asked, "You've already made her do it, haven't you?"

He said nothing.

Her voice was deadly. "What else have you forced her to do? She was innocent before you took her. Is she now?"

Innocent.

The things he'd said to her . . . the things he'd done to her . . . He ran a shaking hand over his face.

And made her do to him.

How could he have been so wrong about her? *Because I'd been burning for more than a century. And she's paid for it.* "I told you before—she's *mine*."

She shrieked in fury. "Let—her—go!"

"*Never*," he bellowed back.

"You may not want a war, but you've got one." Calmer, she said, "I believe my sisters and I will go hunting for Celts' pelts."

The line went dead.

17

"Your brother's in Louisiana, my liege."

Lachlain's fingers paused on the last button of his shirt. *"Louisiana?"* After a quick shower to wash away evidence of the fight, Lachlain had called Harmann back to his room and asked where Garreth was. *Of all the places in the world.* "What in the hell is he doing there?"

"Louisiana is packed with the Lore, and many Lykae live there now. I'd say half your number reside in Canada and the United States. Most in Nova Scotia, but with a number farther south."

This news bitterly disappointed Lachlain. "Why did they leave their homes?" he asked, taking a seat near the balcony. A breeze blew in, smelling of the forest and of the sea that abutted his land miles and miles away. He was actually in the Highlands, looking out over the grounds of Kinevane. With his mate in their bed.

Harmann pulled up a chair as well, shifting into his normal shape, that of a behorned, large-eared Ostrander demon, so named for his extended Ostrander family. "When the clan thought the vampires had killed you, many refused to stay so close to their kingdom in Russia. Your brother assisted them with the journey, then stayed on in New Orleans to help them rebuild what they could."

"New Orleans?" This just got better and better. "Can you no' contact him? It so happens that I've got a coven of Valkyrie, in *New Orleans*, intent on peeling my family." And Garreth was the last member of his immediate family still living. Demestriu had seen to that—Lachlain's father dead in the last Accession, his mother dying of grief, and his youngest brother, Heath, setting out to avenge them all. . . .

"Valkyrie?" Harmann frowned. "Dare I ask?" When Lachlain shook his head, Harmann said, "Garreth made me vow to contact him the minute I learned anything of you. He was . . . well, he didn't take the news of your presumed death as we'd hoped, especially after losing so many of his . . . of your . . ." He trailed off, then said, "So, of course, I tried to reach him as soon as I closed the gate behind you. But I was told he's gone off by himself for a few days."

Lachlain had a flash of worry for Garreth, being alone and unwarned. *Hunting for Celts' pelts.* No. No way could they catch him. Garreth was as wily as he was fierce.

"It's imperative that I find him. Keep trying." His brother was the only one he would trust to protect Emma while Lachlain went to mete out his revenge. "I want all the information you've accumulated on the Horde since I've been gone, and anything we might have on the Valkyrie. I want any media that will help me acclimate to this time. And keep my return secret from the elders for now. Only my brother knows."

"Aye, of course, but may I ask what you mean by acclimating to this time? Where have you been?"

Lachlain hesitated, then admitted, "In the fire." There was no need to describe the catacombs. He could never convey how horrific it was.

Harmann's ears flattened, and as often happened when he was distressed, the last shape he'd shifted into wavered over him. For a moment he looked like the young human male he'd presented to Emma before he returned to his wiry, demon frame. "B-but that's just a rumor they spread."

"It's true, and I'll tell you of it another time. Right now, I canna think of it. I've got only four days, four *nights*, to convince Emma to stay with me."

"She doesn't want to stay?"

"No, no' at all." A vague memory of her trembling in the shower, eyes squeezed shut to what he was doing to her, flashed into his mind. His claws sank into his palms. "I have no' been . . . good to her."

"Does she know how long you've waited?"

"She does no' even know she's my mate."

Time was dwindling. Lachlain would need her so badly with the coming full moon. He knew about the effect it had on any Lykae who'd found his mate. Lachlain figured if he hadn't scared her away by then, he certainly would on that night, unless she was more used to him.

And no longer virgin. He would never have thought he would be so dismayed to find out his mate was untouched. Emma was so soft and gentle, and the thought of spilling her virgin's blood when she was still healing and he was in the grip of the moon horrified him.

Soon the elders would descend upon Kinevane with their hatred toward her undisguised. He and Emma had to be joined by then. She had to be marked by him so they knew they couldn't harm her.

Yet how could he expect her to face these things with him when he hadn't begun to make up for all that he'd done to her? "I want you to find everything a twenty-four-year-old female would desire in her home—anything that would appeal to her."

If she was truly part Valkyrie, and the rumors of their acquisitiveness were true, then perhaps she could be softened with gifts. Hadn't she been intent on getting to her jewelry? He could give her a new piece every day for decades.

When Harmann picked up the clipboard and pen he always carried, Lachlain said, "Study her clothing and buy her more in similar sizes and styles. Replace anything that has been damaged." He ran his hand over the back of his neck, thinking of all he had to do. "She must be protected from the sun."

"Aye, I thought of that. The drapes in your rooms are thick and will suffice for now, but perhaps shutters? That automatically open at sunset and close at sunrise."

"Get them installed—" Lachlain broke off and did a double take. "Automatic?" At Harmann's nod, Lachlain said, "Aye, then, as soon as possible. I want every window in Kinevane protected, and have porticos built over all exposed doorways."

"We'll begin work on it in the morn."

"And her music player, her . . . *iPod*? The vampires destroyed it. She needs a new one—truly needs it. In fact, she seems to like all the things of this time, gadgets, electronic objects. I saw you'd modernized my rooms. The rest of the castle—"

"Is completely modernized. I've retained the full staff here, from cook to maid to guard, and we've kept Kinevane ready in case of your or your brother's return."

"Keep only the most trusted servants on, and tell them who and what she is. Also inform them of what I will do if she is harmed in any way."

Lachlain must have begun to turn at the idea of her being hurt, because Harmann stared, then coughed into his hand. "O-of course."

After an inward shake, Lachlain said, "Are there any vulnerabilities I should know about? Anything concerning finances or encroachment?"

"You're richer than you were before. Exponentially. This land is still protected and hidden."

He exhaled with relief. Lachlain couldn't have found better than Harmann. He was honest and clever, especially with humans, using his shape-shifting abilities to appear to grow old around them. "I appreciate all you've done," Lachlain said—an understatement, for his home and his wealth had all been protected by this being. As always, Lachlain found it ridiculous that shifters were plagued with a reputation for dishonesty, called "two-faced" as an insult for so long that the term had finally migrated to the humans. "I owe you much."

"You've given me generous cost-of-living-index raises," Harmann said with a grin, then tilted his head at Emma. "The little one—she's truly a *vampire*?"

Lachlain crossed to her and tucked a blond curl behind her ear. "Half-Valkyrie."

Harmann raised his eyebrows at her pointed ear. "You never did like to do things the easy way."

Car alarms still resounded from miles away.

Though Annika had finally been calmed and the lightning that threatened to rupture the manor had quieted, that *thing* still had her Emma.

She tried to shake the rage free—vomiting energy as she had was only harming the entire collective of Valkyrie who shared power, a dozen of whom sat together right now in this great room. They looked to her for answers she would have to give. Answers Furie should be here to supply.

Regin was back on the computer, accessing the coven's database once more, this time researching this Lachlain.

Impatiently pacing, Annika let her mind wander to the day that Emma had first arrived. The snow outside had been packed so high it covered half the window. Not surprising, in the old country. By the fire, Annika had cradled the baby, falling each second for the golden-haired girl with her tiny pointed ears.

"How are we to care for her, Annika?" *Lucia had murmured.*

Regin had sprung from her seat on the mantel to snap, "How can you bring one of those among us when they slaughtered my people?"

Daniela had knelt beside Annika, peering up at her, giving her a rare touch—and the stinging of ice from her pale hand. "She needs to be with her own kind. I know this well."

Annika had shaken her head determinedly. "Her ears. Her eyes. She's fey. She's Valkyrie."

"She'll grow to be evil!" Regin had insisted. "Damn if she hasn't snapped at me with her baby fangs. By Freya, she already drinks blood!"

"Trifling," Myst had interjected in a casual tone. "We eat electricity."

The baby had clutched Annika's long braid, as if saying she wanted to stay. "She was Helen's, whom I loved dearly. And her letter begged me to keep Emmaline from the vampires. So I am raising her and will leave the coven if that is your collective wish, but understand—she is as my daughter from now on." She re-membered how sad her next words had sounded. "I will guide her to be all that was good and honorable about the Valkyrie before time eroded us. She will never see the horrors we have. She will be protected." They'd all quieted, reflecting. "Emmaline of Troy." She'd rubbed noses with Emma and asked the baby, "Now, where's the best place to hide the most beautiful little vam-pire in the world?"

Nïx had laughed delightedly. "Laissez les bon temps roulez. . . ."

"Okay, here it is!" Regin said. "Lachlain, king of the Lykae, disappeared for two centuries or so. I'm just going to update the database and say that apparently he's back at the desk." She scrolled down. "Brave and vicious on the battlefield, and he appears to be in *every* battle the Lykae ever engaged. What was he doing? Trying to earn merit badges? And, uh-oh, careful, ladies, this big boy fights dirty. He'd just as soon end a sword fight with his fists and claws, and hand-to-hand with his fangs."

"What about his family?" Annika asked. "What does he care for that we can use?"

"He doesn't have much of a family left. Damn. Demestriu killed them all."

When she paused, continuing to read, Annika waved her on, until Regin exclaimed, "Ooh, the chicks in the New Zealand coven are *evil*. They've noted here that though they haven't engaged him, they've seen him fight vampires, and barbs about his family will make him go mindless with rage, making him easier prey for a skilled killer."

Kaderin laid one of her swords flat in her lap, her diamond hone file finally at rest. "He's hurt her, then. If he thought she was one of the Horde."

Regin said, "He'd had no idea she was a Valkyrie. She must be trying to protect us. Boneheaded little leech."

Lucia murmured, "Can you imagine how utterly terrified she must be?"

Nïx sighed. "The Saints aren't going to make it to the playoffs."

Gentle, fearful Emma, in the hands of an animal . . . Annika clenched her fists and two of the lamps closest to her—

just fixed along with the chimney by a Lore contractor today—burst, shattering glass twelve feet into the air. Valkyrie in the way casually sidestepped or lowered their faces, then shook out their hair and resumed whatever they'd been doing.

Not looking up from the screen, Regin said, "It's the Accession putting all these pieces into play. It's got to be."

Annika knew it was so. A protracted imprisonment had just ended for the Lykae king. Kristoff, the rebel vampire leader, had taken a Horde stronghold just five years ago and was dispatching soldiers to America. And the ghouls, led by a fierce and occasionally lucid leader, had begun making a power play by infecting as many people as possible to build their army.

Annika crossed to the window and looked out into the night. "You said Lachlain didn't have much of a family. Then who?"

Regin put a pencil behind her ear. "He's got one younger brother left. Garreth."

"How do we find this Garreth?"

Nïx clapped her hands. "I know this one! I know this one! Ask . . . *Lucia!*"

Lucia looked up sharply and hissed at Nïx, but there was no true venom behind it. She answered in a monotone, "He's the Lykae who saved our lives two nights ago."

Annika turned from the window. "Then I'm sorry that we have to do what we're about to do."

Lucia turned questioning eyes to Annika.

"We're going to trap him."

"How? He's strong, and from what I can tell, he's clever."

"Lucia, I need you to miss again."

18

Throughout the day, Lachlain stayed by Emma's side, sunproofing any hint of a crack in the thick curtains and checking her wounds to make sure they were healing.

He took no chances, though, even lying beside her, cutting the side of his neck and coaxing her to drink from him.

The wee vampire had softly lapped at him, sighing in sleep. She must have bewitched him, because it had felt like the most natural thing in the world.

By afternoon, when he removed the bandages, he found the wounds still tender and raised, but fully closed.

The worst of his worry abated, he mused on what he'd learned.

Now that he knew the truth about everything, he looked at Emma differently, though he had to admit he didn't feel any differently. He'd already accepted her as his mate even when he'd thought she was part of the Horde. Now he knew that not only was she not part of the Horde, she wasn't even exactly a vampire.

Over the long years alone, he'd envisioned his mate in a thousand different lights. He'd prayed she would be intelligent and attractive, prayed that she would be caring. And now Emma, a half-vampire, half-Valkyrie, was shaming even his wildest fantasies.

But her family . . . He exhaled wearily. Lachlain had never fought against them, thinking them beneath him, and had only seen them from a distance. But he knew the Valkyrie were weird, fey little creatures, swift and strong with lightning firing all around them—firing somehow *through* them. Rumor had it that they derived nourishment from *electricity*. As he'd discovered in Emma, they were known to be extremely intelligent. Unlike Emma, they were almost as violent and warmongering as the vampires.

Though the Valkyrie had few known weaknesses, it was said they could be mesmerized by glittering objects—and that they were the only species in the Lore that could die of sorrow.

In a quick perusal of what the clan had compiled on them, he was able to find a tale of their origin. The Lore said that millennia ago, Wóden and Freya were awakened from a decade of sleep by a maiden warrior's scream as she died in battle. Freya had marveled at the maiden's courage and wanted to preserve it, so she and Wóden struck the human with their lightning. The maiden woke in their great hall, healed but untouched—still mortal—and pregnant with an immortal Valkyrie daughter.

In the years that came, their lightning would strike dying women warriors from all species of the Lore—Valkyrie like Furie were truly part Fury. Freya and Wóden gave the daughters Freya's fey beauty and his cunning. They combined these traits with the mother's valor and individual ancestry. This made the daughters all unique, but according to the Lore, one could recognize a Valkyrie if her eyes fired silver with strong emotion.

Emma's had turned when she'd drunk from him.

If this legend was true—and Lachlain believed it was—

then that would mean Emma was the granddaughter of . . .
gods.

And he'd thought her beneath him. A strong Lykae king
saddled with a lacking mate.

He pinched his forehead, struggling with regret, but
forced himself to read on. He found brief descriptions of the
Valkyrie he knew were directly connected to her. Nïx was
the oldest, and some said a soothsayer. Levelheaded Lucia
was an expert archer, rumored to be cursed to feel indescribable pain whenever she missed a target.

Furie had been their queen, living under the same roof as
gentle Emma when she'd been a child. Now, the Valkyrie
suspected that Demestriu had trapped Furie at the bottom
of the ocean for an eternity of torture. Based on Lachlain's
experience, he could say without a doubt that she was
choking saltwater into her lungs somewhere in the freezing
dark right now.

But the entries on Regin and Annika troubled him the
most. Regin's mother's entire race had been exterminated by
the Horde. Annika, who was known as a brilliant strategist
and a fearless fighter, had devoted her life to destroying vampires.

When Emma's family voiced their hatred of vampires,
when they celebrated each kill, how could Emma not feel
like an outsider? How could she not inwardly flinch? The
Valkyrie were all centuries old to her mere decades, and
she was what the Lore called "other"—or outside one's
species. Emma was *other* from everything on the entire
earth.

Was this the root of the pain he'd discovered within her?
Did her family differentiate between what the Horde was
and what Emma was? He would have to be careful with that

himself. He could curse vampires to hell and not be thinking of Emma whatsoever.

The only positive thing he could find about the Valkyrie was that they'd always maintained an uneasy truce with the Lykae, reasoning that "the enemy of my enemy is my friend."

Until the Accession. When all immortals were forced to fight for survival in the Lore.

This news was a thousand times better than if her family was of the Horde. But it still had its share of problems.

Almost all creatures of the Lore had a mate for life in some fashion. Vampires had Brides, demons had Lovers, phantoms had Kindred, and Lykae had their mates. Even a ghoul never left the troop that had first infected it.

Valkyrie formed no such bonds.

They drew strength from their coven but were completely independent when away from it. It was said that the thing they wanted above all else was freedom. *You can never keep a Valkyrie when she wants to be free*, his own father had told him. And Lachlain was going to try to do just that.

He would try to keep her though she "must be terrified" of him. And her family didn't even know he'd attacked her. They only suspected he'd touched her as she'd never been touched.

Yet he had. And he would do it again under the influence of the moon. Like all mated Lykae, his need would be so strong then, his control weak. Since earliest memory, when a king was in residence with his queen at Kinevane, all others left the castle on the night of the full moon and the ones preceding and following, so the pair could give themselves up to its pull and surrender to it with abandon.

If only she could feel the same need and aggression, he

wouldn't frighten her so badly. He vowed he would lock her away, even as he knew nothing could stop him from getting to her. . . .

It would've been so much easier if his mate had been of the clan.

But then he wouldn't have *Emma*. . . .

Near sunset, two maids knocked to unpack and arrange her clothing. "Take care with her things," he told them as he rose from her bedside. "And doona touch her." Leaving them wide-eyed, he shrugged through the closed curtains to get to the balcony. He stared out at the setting sun, gazing at their home, the land and hills, the forest that he hoped she would grow to love.

When the sun set, he returned and frowned to find the maids a few feet from the bed, peering at Emma, whispering. But he knew they wouldn't dare touch her, and they were young Lykae who had probably never seen a vampire.

He was just about to tell them to leave when Emma opened her eyes in a flash and rose in that floating way. The maids screamed in terror; Emma hissed and scrambled to the headboard as the two fled.

Lachlain had known this wouldn't be smooth.

"Easy, Emma," he said, striding to her side. "You startled each other."

Emma watched the door for long moments, and then her gaze flickered over his face. Her skin paled and she turned away.

"Your wounds are mending well."

She said nothing, just brushed her fingertips over her chest.

"When you drink again, they should heal completely." He sat beside her, rolling up his sleeve, but she recoiled from him.

"Where am I?" Her gaze darted all around, finally resting on the foot of the mahogany bed. She focused on the intricately wrought carvings, then twisted around to view the headboard, scrutinizing the inlaid symbols there. The room was deepening into darkness, with only the fire lighting it, and the symbols seemed to move with shadow.

Craftsmen had begun constructing this bed on the day of Lachlain's birth, not only for him, but for *her*. He'd often lain just where she was, staring at the carvings with fascination, imagining what his mate would be like.

"You're at Kinevane. You're safe. Nothing can harm you here."

"Did you kill all of them?"

"Aye."

She nodded, clearly satisfied.

"Do you know why they would attack like that?"

"You're asking me?" She tried to rise.

"What do you think you're doing?" he demanded, pressing her back down.

"I need to call home."

"I called your home last night."

Her eyes went wide with apparent relief. "You swear? When are they coming to get me?"

He was disappointed by how happy the thought of leaving him made her—but he couldn't blame her. "I spoke to Annika, and now I know what they are. What you are."

Her face fell. "Did you tell her what *you* are?"

When he nodded, she turned away, flushing, he realized, with shame.

He tried to tamp down his anger. "It shames you for them to know you're with me?"

"Of course it does."

He grated, "Because you see me as an animal."

"Because you're the enemy."

"I've no quarrel with your family."

She raised her eyebrows. "The Lykae haven't fought against my aunts?"

"Only at the last Accession." Just five hundred years ago.

"Did you kill any of them then?"

"I've never killed a Valkyrie," he answered honestly. But he admitted to himself that this was probably because he'd never faced one.

She raised her chin. "And what about that *thing* inside you? What's it been up to?"

19

~

Emma still got chills thinking about what she'd seen in the midst of the vampire attack.

Unfortunately for her, she now knew exactly what Lachlain looked like when he changed. It had been like a shaky projector image, flickering over him, illuminating something feral and brutal that had peered at her with *absolute possession*.

And now she was in its bed.

"Emma, what you saw last night—that's no' what I am." The firelight cast shadows across his face, reminding her. "That's only a small part of me, and I can control it."

"Control?" She nodded slowly. "So you made a decision to attack me in the field and in the hotel room in Paris? You *meant* to strangle me?"

She thought he stifled a wince. "I need to explain something to you. You know I was imprisoned by the Horde, but you doona know that I'd been . . . tortured. It affected my behavior, my thinking."

She had known he'd been tortured, just not how. "What did they do to you?"

His expression grew guarded. "I will never burden you with those details. Why did you no' tell me you were part Valkyrie?"

"What difference would it have made? I'm still a vampire, and my aunts are still your enemies."

"No, they're no'," he insisted. "I doona count among my enemies wee fey women who live on another continent."

His dismissive tone rankled almost as much as if he'd admitted to being their enemy. "When is Annika coming for me?"

His eyes narrowed. "You made a promise to me to stay until the full moon."

Emma gasped. "You didn't . . . she isn't coming for me?"

"No' at this time."

Her lips parted as disbelief hammered through her. "Incredible! Because you're from the past, I'll hip you to some rules. One rule is that when Emma is nearly killed by vampires, she gets a get-out-of-jail-free card from the Lykae's little playdate." She held up two fingers. "Another rule? Now that my aunts know what you are, they will kill you if you don't send me to the coven immediately. Your best bet is to let me go as soon as possible."

"If they can find this place, they deserve to try."

Realizing how resolute he was about this, she felt her bottom lip trembling. "You would keep me from my family when I need them the most?" A hot tear tracked down her cheek. Before, he'd appeared revolted by her tears. Now he looked . . . tormented, quickly reaching forward to brush it away.

"You want to go home and you will, but no' for just a few days more."

Not bothering to hide her frustration, she asked, "What difference will a few days make?"

"I ask you the same."

She gritted her teeth, fighting aggravation, fighting her useless tears.

He cupped her face, stroking her cheek with his thumb. His voice sounding rough, he said, "Lass, if I have you here for such a short time, I doona want to quarrel with you. For now, let me show you Kinevane." He rose to cross to the thick curtains, opening them wide, then returned for her. Though she stiffened and leaned away, he lifted her into his arms, carrying her across the spacious room to the balcony. "You'll be surprised to know that it's still mine. No *Wal-Mart*."

Outside she saw the moon rising over a stately castle, lighting its ancient bricks and magnificent lawns. A fog was rolling in and carried a hint of brine.

He pointed off into the distance. "You canna see the walls surrounding the property, but know that whenever you are within them, you are protected."

When he sat her on the railing, her legs immediately threaded through its marble balusters even though he held her hips.

She saw he noted this with a frown but didn't comment on it. Instead, he asked, "What do you think?"

He appeared proud, as he should with a place like this. Amidst the stone frontage of the castle were stunning her-ringbone formations of brick that framed the windows and matched the walks and even the back of the huge fireplace in this bedroom. The gardens were immaculate, and if the rest of the castle was decorated as sumptuously as his bed-room, then this Kinevane was a testament to luxury. Her Valkyrie sensibilities couldn't help but appreciate it.

"Well?" He looked expectant. He wanted her to like it.

She turned, lifting her gaze above the tree line to regard

the moon. "I think I only have a few days left until the moon is full."

When she turned back, she found his jaw was clenched.

She pushed her knotted hair back and it felt gritty. "I want a shower," she said, ducking to glance around his torso, spying out a bathroom.

She squirmed, wriggling her hips from his hands, until he finally let her down.

"I'll help you. You're still weak—"

"A shower. Alone!" she snapped as she strode into the opulent—and modern—bathroom. She rushed to lock the heavy door behind her, having discovered to her horror that her nails were dirty.

She removed the shirt he'd dressed her in—his, she noticed—and stared at the ugly, raised marks winding down her chest. An involuntary moan escaped her as she swayed. For the rest of her life, she would never forget the look in that vampire's eyes just before he'd clawed her. She recalled she'd regretted head-butting him. *Now I'm going to get it,* she'd thought as his hand swung up above her. Why had she provoked him?

She turned on the shower, waiting until it steamed, then stepped under the water. A red stream ran as dried blood rinsed clean from her hair, and she focused on it, shivering. *Three vampires.* The red swirled round and round into the drain. *Why did I provoke him?*

But who was alive now?

She should be dead right now. But she wasn't. She'd survived them.

She frowned. She'd survived vampires. And the sun. *And a Lykae attack*—all this week. Her worst fears for dozens of years were becoming—she bit her lip—old hat?

"Emma, let me help you."

Her head whipped up. "You should buy stock in a lock company! I said alone!"

He nodded in agreement. "Aye, you usually say that, and I still stay. It's our way." His voice was calm, and though the idea was crazy, *he* sounded reasonable.

Privacy? You have none. . . . Her hand shot out to a shampoo bottle, *her* shampoo bottle that had already been *unpacked for her stay.* She hurled it at him, hard like a dagger throw, end over end. He ducked, just dodging it, and it flew into the next room. The sound of shattering felt like an accomplishment. Why was she provoking him?

Because it feels good.

He raised his eyebrows. "You'll reinjure yourself."

She reached blindly for the conditioner. "Not before you."

When she swooped up another bottle, Lachlain gave a quick, tight nod. "Verra well."

As he closed the door behind him, he thought that not doing exactly as he pleased in his own home was going to take some getting used to.

When he spotted the priceless mirror she'd broken, he remembered it had been at Kinevane for centuries and could've been the oldest one extant anywhere. He shrugged. At least she was getting her strength back.

For fifteen minutes, he prowled the hallway. As he listened in the unlikely case that she called for him, he wondered how to coax her to drink again. If his blood made her stronger, then she needed a surfeit of it. He'd see that she had it.

She was angry, wanting to return to her family, and he

understood her need. But there was no way he could send her home. And going with her? When he could never hurt any of them, even to defend himself?

He regretted having to be so hard with her, knowing how much she'd been through, but there wasn't any *time* for this.

When he returned to their room, she was showered—and dressed as though to go outside. "What do you think you're doing?" he snapped. "You need to be in bed."

"Going out. You told me it was safe."

"Of course it is, and I'll take you out—"

"The whole point is to get away from you. You might be able to keep me here for four more nights, but it doesn't mean I have to spend them with you."

He took her elbow. "Then you'll drink first."

She gave his hand a withering glare. "Let go of me."

"You're going to drink, Emma!" he bellowed.

"*Get bent, Lachlain!*" she screamed back at him, wrenching her arm away. When he caught her once more, she struck out so fast it was a blur. He barely caught her palm before it cracked across his face.

With a low, menacing growl, he put his hand behind her head and pressed her against the wall. "I've told you no' to strike me. Know that the next time you try, I *will* retaliate."

She kept her chin in the air, though she prayed his eyes wouldn't flicker. "One hit from you could kill me."

His voice grew rough. "*Never hit you.*" He leaned in and brushed her lips with his own. "Each time, I'll take a kiss as my due."

She felt her nipples harden and grew angered at her lack of control over her body—he seemed to have more control over it than she did. Even with all the confusion and panic of the last few nights, another slow brush of his lips across hers had her wanting him still. Even when she was terrified by what was inside him. What if he turned when they had sex? That thought made her break away.

"I know you want more than a kiss. Isn't that why you're forcing me to stay until the full moon? So you can sleep with me?" Like he'd warned her he would.

"I will no' deny that I want you."

"What if I said we should just get it over with? Tonight? So I could leave tomorrow."

She could sense him weighing his answer. "You'd sleep with me to leave me a few days early?" He sounded almost hurt by this. "Your body for your freedom?"

"Why not?" she asked, lowering her voice to nearly a hiss. "Just think of all the things I did in a shower in Paris for only a phone call."

She thought he flinched before he turned away. He limped to the fireplace, then lowered his head, staring at the fire. She'd never seen anyone gaze at one the way he did. Watchfully. While most seemed to lose themselves in the lulling flames, Lachlain did not. His wary eyes darted and flickered as though a play were being presented inside. "Know that I regret the way I've been with you, but I will no' let you go. For now, you're free to walk the grounds, and you'll be guarded."

Free to walk the grounds. The ones that were dark and should unnerve her; yet she'd been itching to explore them since first perceiving that scent of brine. And didn't she belong out there anyway? Without a look back, she crossed to the balcony, strode up the railing, then dropped off into the night.

The last thing she heard was him rasping, "And I know you'll come back to me before dawn."

20

Emma immediately sensed things following her as she moved into the mist.

So he'd really sicced guards on her? Considering his intrusive nature, they were probably more like spies. She figured a proud, independent woman would resent the intrusion. Emma? She reasoned that if this place wasn't as safe as he'd told her and vampires did attack again, Emma wouldn't have to outrun them—she would merely have to outrun the spies hiding in the bushes.

Unable to muster the desired outrage at being spied on, she explored for a while before stumbling upon a folly. Clustered all around it were wildflowers, which had bloomed during the day and now looked wilted and dismal. *Just missed 'em. Story of my life.*

Still, it was nice here, she supposed, with the fog-covered lake in view—or loch—or *whatever*. It kind of reminded her of home.

She closed her eyes at the thought of the manor. What she wouldn't give to be back there. She'd missed Xbox night last night. Tonight she was supposed to be riding horses through the bayou.

She hopped atop the folly's railing, following it, pacing round and round as she thought of everything that had happened to her. Before her trip, she'd yearned for something more. Now, being forced away, she realized how good she had it. Yes, she'd been lonely, feeling the lack of a partner in her life. Yet now that she had to deal with a stubborn, over-bearing male every day, was being held captive by one, she thought partners were spectacularly overrated.

And, yes, sometimes she felt like an outsider—like not knowing where to look or how to act when her aunts shrieked about vampires—but often she didn't. Sure, they taunted her unmercifully, but looking back, she realized they taunted *everyone*. Like her aunt Myst. Years ago, after the in-cident with the vampire general, the coven had dubbed her Mysty the Vampire Layer. *How do you separate Myst from a vampire? With a crowbar.*

Emma's lips parted in surprise. They might treat her dif-ferently, but they did *not* treat her like an outsider. Had her own insecurities colored how she saw them? She recalled her memory of the day her hand had been burned, and now she saw even that differently. At first the memory had hurt her and shocked her anew. Now she remembered two dis-tinct things: Regin had dived for her and shuddered at the close call. And Furie had announced to them all that *Emma was just like them*.

Emma felt her lips curling. Furie had said that. Their queen.

Excitement began to build in her, and she grew impatient to return home to see it with new eyes. Now she ached to appreciate all the things she'd taken for granted—or had been blind to. She wanted to fall asleep awash in the com-forting sounds of bayou insects and her family's shrieks. She wanted to lie in her own blankets piled under the princess bed in her room—not in Lachlain's massive bed. She'd gotten the feeling that those carved symbols told an ancient story and, Freya help her, she sensed that as long as she was in that bed, she was a part of it. . . .

When she skimmed around a column, her palm caught a large splinter. In the past, she would've howled from the pain. Now she sighed. *Everything's relative.* Compared to having her chest ploughed like a vegetable patch, this was a mere annoyance.

She tilted her head and stared at the sliver, frowning as a memory flooded her. She must have dreamed of him again. Today.

When she'd slept, she'd seen their last . . . sexual encounter, from *his point of view.*

As she stared at the small trickle of blood around the white wood, she went awash in the dream, feeling splinters from the *headboard* digging into *his* palms as he crumbled it. But he didn't care about the pain. He *had* to keep his hands there. Had to.

His need to touch her warred with his desire to earn her trust. Emma *felt* how strongly he'd wanted to put his hands on her—felt the lust welling up in him, the urge to thrust against her—and admitted to herself that if the situation had been reversed, she'd have said, "Screw it," and pawed him.

Now she grew dizzy, overwhelmed by the sheer hunger he'd felt, confused that *she* saw the hotel's patterned ceiling as he threw his head back, struggling not to come.

But her hair brushed over him, and her hips bucked relentlessly against him, and her breasts pressed into his chest. He felt her sucking him greedily and knew it was over. . . .

She swayed as she suddenly left the memory, then blinked.

He'd acted honorably. He'd kept his word even under that onslaught of need. Now she wanted to go back to that night and give him what he'd desperately needed. But she couldn't, because it was just a dream. *Or a memory.* She fell from the rail. Instinct landed her on her haunches, yet she sank to the ground just after.

Just like the dream of the necklace.

She was going mad. Like Nïx, who saw things that she *shouldn't.*

Lachlain, what have you done to me?

There she sat in the wet grass in a strange country with the stars above off-kilter as though the world had dropped a notch. With no one to confide her suspicion to.

Emma didn't return at dawn.

The guards had watched her return to the house and protected the entrances afterward, but it had taken a frantic hour before Lachlain found her curled up, asleep under the stairs in a broom closet. Had she known that the ammonia and polishes stored there would cloak her scent from him?

Now he gnashed his teeth to find her shivering in the dust, his worry turning to ire in an instant. "Goddamn it, Emma," he snapped, scooping her up. What in the hell had she been *thinking*? He would lay down the rules, and, by God, she would—

Sun flooded the hallway, and he shoved them into a corner, covering her with his body. *"Shut the fucking door!"*

"My apologies," a familiar voice drawled from behind him as the door closed. "Dinna know there were going to be vampires about. You should have a sign."

Back in the low light, Lachlain turned to find Bowen, his oldest friend. His pleasure at seeing him dimmed when he noticed how much more weight Bowe had lost. Once Lachlain's size, he was now rangy and gaunt.

"And here I was surprised to see you alive, but looks like you've another surprise there." Bowe approached, rudely inspecting Emma as she lay in Lachlain's arms, picking up her hair and chucking her chin. "Wee beauty. Bit dirty."

"From sleeping under the stairs this morning." Lachlain shook his head, incapable of understanding her. "Meet Emmaline Troy. Your queen."

Bowe raised his eyebrows, demonstrating the most emotion Lachlain had seen from him since his mate had left him. "A *vampire* queen? Fate must hate you." More examination while Lachlain scowled. "Her ears are pointed?"

"She's half-Valkyrie," Lachlain explained. "Raised in a coven of them and kept from the Horde."

"Then things around here just got interesting," Bowe said, but he displayed little interest.

Emmaline shivered and buried her face in Lachlain's chest.

Bowe studied him. "Doona think I've ever seen you look so exhausted. Go bathe your freezing, wee . . . *valkire* and get some sleep." Though it was not yet eight in the morning, he added, "I'll help myself to whiskey."

Lachlain was out of his bloody mind, Bowe concluded by late that afternoon.

As he poured another scotch, thinking and drinking, Bowe admitted to himself that he should be the last one to doubt a mate being *other*, but this was too far-fetched. No two species were greater foes than the vampires and the Lykae, yet Lachlain thought to take one, or a halfling born of one, as his queen?

Wherever he'd been for the last one hundred and fifty years had clearly warped his brain. . . .

Bowe raised his face, briefly distracted by the scents wafting from the busy kitchens. All who worked here were preparing for the rising of the full moon, cleaning, cooking in abundance, readying to vacate the castle. The smells from the ovens were just as he remembered from growing up here. In fact, the kitchens had been his favorite place. Now he frowned, trying to recall the last time he'd eaten. Perhaps he should commandeer the vampire's share of the food. She wouldn't miss it—

Lachlain greeted him with a censorious expression as he finally returned to the study. "Christ, man, you've been at it since morn?"

"Can I help it? Kinevane always kept the best liquor. Nothing's changed." Bowe poured a glass to the rim for Lachlain.

Lachlain accepted it, then sank down behind his desk, somehow appearing more exhausted than before, though his clothes were rumpled as if he'd just woken. And he had a nick on his neck. *No. No way he'd allow that depravity. What the hell has gotten into him?* Giving it a second thought, Bowe slid the decanter over the desktop to him as well.

When Lachlain raised his eyebrows, Bowe said, "Have a feeling you'll need it when you tell me where the bloody hell you've been that we could no' find you for decades." Bowe noticed he sounded angry. As if he blamed Lachlain for his disappearance.

"You never would have found me. No more than I was able to find Heath," Lachlain said, his voice deadened as usual when he spoke of his youngest brother.

Bowe shook his head, remembering Heath. Hot-tempered

to a fault, he'd set off to avenge his father's death, not comprehending that those who set out to kill Demestriu didn't return. Lachlain had refused to believe he was dead. "You were in Helvita?"

"For a while."

"He was no' there?"

Lachlain's expression was bare—pure pain. "The Horde . . . dinna take him alive."

"I'm sorry, Lachlain." After a long moment, Bowe frowned and broke the silence. "You said, 'for a while.' "

"Then Demestriu decided on the catacombs."

"Catacombs?" There were rumors among the Lore that the Horde had an everlasting fire deep beneath Paris, kept solely for the purpose of torturing the immortals who could never quite die from it. Bowe's gut began to churn, the liquor roiling on his empty stomach.

When Lachlain said nothing, only drank, Bowe's face tightened. "The fire is real? How long?"

"The dungeon for a decade. The fire for the rest."

At that, Bowe had to drain his glass and snatched back the decanter. "How the fuck have you stayed sane?"

"You never did mince words." Lachlain leaned forward, brows drawn as if he was struggling to voice his thoughts. "I was no' when I escaped. I went from one rage to the next, destroying anything unfamiliar, experiencing few lucid thoughts. I still was battling these rages when I found Emma," he admitted.

"How did you get free?"

Lachlain hesitated, then hiked up his pants leg.

Bowe leaned forward to see, then whistled out a breath. "You lost it?"

Lachlain brushed the fabric down. "There was no time.

The fires had abated and I scented her on the surface." He swooped up his glass and drew deeply. "I feared losing her after so long."

"You . . . took your leg?"

"Aye."

Seeing Lachlain about to crush his glass, Bowe changed the subject. "How are you with her?" *After what they did to you*.

"At first I terrified her. Lost control again and again. But I believe it would have been even worse if she had no' been there. I think I would no' have recovered at all. She calms me, and my thoughts are so focused on her, I've little time to think of the past."

The beauty calms the beast? "And where did you find your Emmaline Troy that you had no' been able to for so long? Where was your wee queen hiding?"

"She was no' born before seventy years ago."

He raised his eyebrows. "So young? Is she everything you'd hoped?"

"Much more than I'd hoped." Lachlain ran his fingers through his hair. "I could never even conceive of a mate like her. Emma's clever, with a mind so tricky and complicated, I know I'll never figure her out. And she's far too beautiful and frustratingly secretive and no' like any other woman I've ever met." He took a swig from his glass, this time savoring it. "The more I understand her phrasings, the more I realize my mate is a witty, droll lass." His lips curled absently, no doubt as he remembered some amusement. When he finally faced Bowe again, he said, "I had no' expected her humor, but welcome it gladly."

Bowe knew something extraordinary was at work for Lachlain even to approach a smile so soon after his torture. If Bowe had been convinced that Lachlain was confused and mistaken about his mate, he was no longer. Lachlain was lost for this Emmaline. Obviously, she was *his*. "So how do you plan to keep her? Seems her care and feeding would be verra involved."

"She drinks from me. Has never taken from another living being."

Though he'd seen the nick, Bowe was still surprised. "So she does no' kill?"

"Never," Lachlain said in a proud tone. "I'd wondered about that as well, but she's gentle—would never hurt a fly. I had to force her to take from me."

"That's why your leg is no' healing as it should," Bowe observed.

"A verra small price to pay."

"And what's that like, when she drinks?" As Lachlain formulated an answer, Bowe said, "The expression you're trying to hide says much." Christ, Lachlain *liked* it.

He ran his hand over his mouth. "The act is intensely . . . pleasurable. But besides that, I believe it bonds us. Connects us. As least, it has me." In a lower voice, he admitted, "I've come to crave it more than she does, I believe."

Lost for her. Vampire or not, Bowe envied him the feeling. "And how is such a young immortal handling the epic destiny of being your queen?"

"She does no' know it."

At Bowe's look, he said, "She would no' be pleased. As I said, I was . . . I have no' treated her as I should. I have no' shown her respect and dinna bother hiding my feelings about a vampire's nature. She only wants to return to her home, and I doona blame her."

"I'd wondered why you had no' marked her. This is a vulnerable time."

"I ken that. Believe me. I've spent centuries imagining how I would spoil and protect my mate, and yet I've made Emma's life into a living hell."

"Then why were you angry with her this morning, Lachlain?" He narrowed his eyes. "I canna tell you how ill-advised that is."

"I was worried and became angry. I'm no' now."

"You've no' claimed her—you could lose her."

"Is that what happened to Mariah?"

Lachlain knew better than to speak of her around Bowe. Mariah had been Bowe's fey mate who'd died *fleeing* him.

When Bowe cast him a savage look, Lachlain said, "I ken you never talk about it, but in this case, do I need to know something?"

"Aye. Your Emma's *other* and will always be so. Doona be stubborn and stupid. And doona try to force her to our ways." Bowe added in a low voice, "Else end up a cautionary tale like me."

Lachlain began to say something, then hesitated.

"What? Ask me what you will."

"How do you do it? Continuing on for so long? Now that I fully understand what you have lost, I doona know that I could."

Bowe arched an eyebrow. "And I doona think I could have my flesh burned from me every day for decades and stay sane." He shrugged. "We all have our petty torments." But the two were not equal and they both knew it. Bowe would gladly go to hell to get Mariah back.

"Do you believe Mariah might . . . ?" Lachlain trailed off, brows drawing together. "You saw her die, did you no'?"

Bowe turned away, but not before he felt his face leached of color. In a voice barely discernible, he said, "I . . . buried her." He had, and he knew she was gone. But he also knew the Lore couldn't be predicted and the rules were often fluid. He now spent his life looking for the key to bring her back.

What else did he have?

Analytical Lachlain was putting him under scrutiny. "You canna get her back."

Bowe faced him again. "No one escapes the vampires. Lykae canna have a mate who's part vampire. There's no such thing as a vampire/Valkyrie creature. Who are you to tell me what's possible?"

Lachlain said nothing, no doubt viewing this as a delusion, a weakness. Bowe wondered if Lachlain would just let him have it.

"You're right," he finally agreed, surprising Bowe. "Things happen that we doona understand. If you had told me two weeks ago that my mate was a vampire, I would have called you sick."

"Aye, so doona concern yourself with me. You've enough on your plate. Harmann told me you were ambushed by three vampires the night before last."

He nodded. "Recently the vampires have stalked Valkyrie all over the world. But they might have been after Emma."

"Could be. She's the first vampire female I've heard of in centuries."

"Then I have even more incentive to destroy the Horde. I will no' let her be taken by them."

"What do you plan to do?"

"I can find the catacombs once more, and we will wait until the guards return. Force them to tell us where Helvita is."

"We've tortured vampires before and were never able to extract that information from them."

A deadly expression hardened Lachlain's face and his eyes turned sharply. "They've taught me much about torture."

Lachlain might be healing on the outside, but inside he was still being tormented. He was right—if he hadn't found his mate when he did . . . So what would happen to Lachlain if he *left* her to seek this revenge?

"Are you up for a war?"

Bowe gave him a bored expression. "When have I no' been? Curious, though, what the hurry is. Are you so anxious to leave your new mate just now?"

"I've told you I've little time to think of the past, but after I claim her and convince her to stay with me, then I will have to seek out this revenge."

"I understand."

"I doona know that you do. I canna ignore the vows for revenge that I made to myself every day in hell." The glass of scotch shattered. Lachlain stared down at the glinting shards and rasped, "That was all I had."

"Lachlain, you ken I'll fight by your side. Garreth and others will gladly. But I doona believe we can win. As long as they can trace, it does no' matter if we are stronger or have more numbers. We will always lose."

"Do we have more numbers?"

"Oh, aye. Hundreds of thousands now."

At Lachlain's disbelieving expression, Bowe said, "A continent away from the vampires is very comfortable for the clan. They've gone back to the old ways, having seven, eight, even ten bairns in a family. The only problem with America is that that's where two Valkyrie covens reside." He smirked. "You know how territorial your in-laws can be."

Lachlain scowled. "Doona remind me."

"By the way, if I, with my limited social engagements, heard rumors of activity up at the castle, I'm sure others did as well. You doona have a lot of time. Can you no' charm her?"

His expression stark, he admitted, "Just two nights ago, I . . . I almost strangled her to death while I slept."

Bowe winced, as much from the deed as from Lachlain's palpable shame.

"The same night she saw me turn against the vampires."

"Christ, Lachlain. And how'd she react to the change?"

"Found it terrifying, of course. She's even more wary of me now." He ran a hand over the back of his neck.

"Why do you no' tell her what happened to you—"

"Never. I have to believe she'll come to care for me. And if she does, that knowledge would pain her. I feel she'll come around, but I need more time. If I could just speed up the process."

Bowe drained his glass, then contemplated the bottom of it. "Get her drunk. Human males do it all the time. One night of lowering her inhibitions . . ."

Lachlain almost grinned, then saw Bowe was serious. "You think if I was, then she would become so?"

"Why no'?"

Lachlain shook his head. "No. No' while I've still got a chance."

When Bowe saw Lachlain repeatedly glance to the window, no doubt noting that sunset neared, he said, "Go. Be there when she wakes."

Lachlain nodded and rose. "I actually want to be there before she rises. My lass prefers to bed on the floor, but I've fought her on it. I will no longer—"

"*You bloody bitch!*" a woman screamed from the gallery downstairs.

21

Lachlain sprinted for the railing to spy out the gallery below.

"Cassandra's arrived," Bowe murmured from behind him, stating the obvious, because Cassandra now had Emma pinned under her trying to *strangle* her. Lachlain shoved his hand to the railing to jump, but Bowe hauled him back.

"Doona fucking do this, Bowe. Cass hurts her and I'll have to kill her."

When he didn't let go, Lachlain swung a fist at Bowe—out of habit, his weaker left fist. Expecting it, Bowe caught it and wrenched his arm back. "*Still* feel guilty for that one punch when we were boys? Again—I eventually woke. Now, look and give your mate more credit."

Lachlain did, but at the same time he raised his other elbow to jab it back in Bowe's face.

Emma slammed her forehead against Cass's nose. Lachlain hesitated.

"Your Emmaline is no' even the least bit out of breath. And if she does no' do this now, she'll be constantly challenged. You forget, *we're a vicious breed that worships strength*," Bowe added the last in a sneer as if he was quoting someone.

"Damn it, it does no' matter, she's small. She's coming off injuries—"

"She's wily and someone's trained her," Bowe observed coolly, releasing Lachlain when Emma gained room beneath Cass, then kicked out with both feet so fast it was a blur. She connected solidly with Cass's chest, sending her across the room. Lachlain shook his head, disbelieving his eyes.

Bowe in the meantime had gotten a scotch and pulled up chairs.

Cass threw her hair out of her face. "You'll pay for that one, leech."

Emma gave her a bored look as she gracefully stood, but her eyes had fired silver. "Bring it on."

Bowe was right—she wasn't out of breath whatsoever.

Cass rose to the challenge. She leapt at Emma, tackling her with her larger size, then gave a sharp jab at Emma's mouth.

Lachlain roared with fury, vaulting over the rail. Before he could reach them, Emma slashed out her claws at Cass, wriggled out from under her, then leapt to her feet to fully swing the back of her hand.

Lachlain knew that hit.

Cass landed against the opposite wall, a tapestry collapsing over her. She didn't get up.

Bowen dropped down behind him, exhaled, and added, "The only thing that could've made that wrestling any better was Jell-O."

When Lachlain reached Emma, he took her by the shoulders, but she jerked in reaction and punched out at him, connecting with his right eye. He clenched his jaw, shook it off, and ran his gaze over her, examining her for injuries. He winced to see the cut marring her bottom lip and yanked out his shirttail to brush against it, but she hissed in a breath.

"*That* hurts you?"

Bowe helped Cass up and dragged her over.

"What the fuck is going on here?" Lachlain bellowed at Cass, then immediately turned to Emma and said, "I apologize."

She frowned at him. "So put a quarter in the cuss jar. Whatever." She pressed the back of her hand against her still bleeding lip.

"Lachlain, you're alive!" Cass cried, running for him. The look he gave her made her slow, expression confused, then stop completely.

"What happened to you?" she asked. "And who is this vampire that has free run of Kinevane?"

Emma looked from Cass up to Lachlain as if she couldn't wait to hear this one.

"She's to be treated as an honored guest."

While Cass gaped, Bowe turned to Emma and said, "I am Bowen, an old friend of Lachlain's. I've spent the afternoon hearing all about you. Pleased to meet you."

While Emma tilted her head at him, wary, Cassandra finally managed, "And when did leeches become guests?"

Lachlain grabbed her elbow. "*Doona ever call her that again.*"

At the insult, Emma's eyes turned silver once more. As she turned on her heel for the door, Lachlain heard her mumble in an odd voice, "Screw you guys . . . I'm going home."

With a last glare at Cass, he followed, in time to see Emma catch her own reflection in a mirror.

She jumped back, startled.

Her hair was wild and the silver in her eyes glittered and moved like mercury. Blood streamed down her chin, and her fangs, though small, looked wickedly sharp. One tear drop had streaked down her temple, leaving a line behind. He saw her pat her face as if she couldn't believe her reflection. Then she gave a short, bitter laugh. Their eyes met.

He knew what she was thinking. And it saddened him, even as he knew it helped his cause.

She was thinking she was just as much a monster as he was.

"This is no' finished, vampire," Cass said.

Emma shot around with an expression so menacing it gave him chills. *"Not in any way,"* she hissed, and stalked off.

It took Lachlain a moment to form words. "Bowe, take care of this," he said without taking his eyes from Emma.

"Aye, but you need to tell her," he called after. "Now."

Emma looked creepy.

As she stared into the mirror in her bathroom, washing her hands and face, she noted that though her fangs had receded, her eyes wouldn't return to their usual color and her lips were redder than usual.

Creepy. Just like the thing that had faced her in the mirror downstairs, the thing that was straight from a creature feature. When she'd patted her face, she'd found blood on her nails from where she'd swiped the Lykae across the belly.

Red of tooth and claw? *I'm your girl. . . .*

She recalled Lachlain in his changed form, and didn't shudder at the image as she usually did. Because wasn't it all relative?

A knock on the door. She'd known he would come after her, but she'd hoped he would at least take time to explain things to the other two. Apparently, he'd dissed them to come right after her.

Still . . . "Go away!"

"I ken you want your privacy, but—"

"Go—away! I don't want you to see me like this—"

And just like that, the door burst open.

She quickly closed her eyes. "What did I *just* say?"

"Wanting your privacy is one thing, but hiding your face from me will no' do, Emma." He turned her to him.

She was mortified even more because he knew she was. Her aunts' eyes turned this way, but it looked so normal in them, expected even with sharp emotion.

"Open your eyes."

When she wouldn't, he said, "This is no' the first time I've seen them like this."

That got her to open them. Wide. "What do you mean?" She could tell by the way he stared that they were *still* that freaky color. "Look at you staring! This is what I wanted to avoid. When have you ever seen them like this?"

"They turn when you drink from me. I'm staring now because if your eyes even flicker silver, I want you."

"I don't believe—"

He placed her hand on his rigid erection.

The memory from the night in the hotel bloomed in her mind, and her fingers curled around it, about to stroke. . . . The memory—the confusing memory from *his* point of view. She wrested her hand away.

"But my eyes are weird," she insisted, unable to face him. "And I can't control it."

"I find them beautiful."

Damn it! Why did he have to be so damn accepting? "Well, I didn't find *your* change as appealing then."

"I know. I can live with that if you can."

"Great. Not only do you seem to have gotten past your

prejudice with me, now you're accepting that I don't accept you. Are you trying to make me feel like an ass?"

"Never. I just want you to know that I am sorry for what happened."

"I am, too." Yes, she might have just spanked that Lykae, but it didn't mean she *liked* that she had to. And she didn't necessarily blame Cassandra for attacking. If Emma had seen a vampire strolling about the manor, admiring paintings, she'd have attacked, too. That did *not* negate the fact that this Cassandra was still a bitch.

Emma was shaken by the incident. All the training her aunts had forced on her seemed to have rushed to the forefront, finally clicking into place, and she'd felt like a different person. She'd actually *won*! Against a freaking Lykae!

Yet even as she felt like Frau Badass, she didn't forget the first staggering thought that had entered her mind when she'd suddenly hit the stone floor and found the Lykae standing over her.

Emma had wanted Lachlain.

And knew he would always come to her rescue.

He tucked a curl behind her ear. "Ach, you've cut your wee ear." He leaned down and kissed it, making her shiver. "And your lip." He kissed that as well, then stroked her cheekbone, and she couldn't quite feel the urgency she'd had that he shouldn't be touching her. "I canna forgive her for marking you."

"Fine by me," she said in a surly tone.

"You had no fear down there," he said, sounding impressed, and Emma had to admit that the next best thing to having Lachlain nuzzle her and kiss her wounds was him acting as if she'd just fought off Armageddon.

"What has changed you? Is it my blood?"

Record-needle scratch back to reality. The nerve! "Don't flatter yourself! I've just realized a lot about myself. You know, having survived continuous *Lykae attacks*"—he flinched at that—"a sunbath, and a dissection via vampire, I've had to ask, 'Is that it? Really. Is that all life has to throw at me?' Because if that's the worst and I keep bouncing back. . . ."

"Aye, I see. Your trials are making you stronger."

They were. Damn it, why did he have to look so *proud* of that fact? When had he begun acting so differently toward her? She knew why she'd changed, but why had he? If he kept looking at her like this, she'd start wondering if she was strong enough to handle *him*.

"You woke well before sunset? I was just coming for you when we heard Cass."

Emma had been up with plenty of time to shower—and to rant about the weird pang she'd felt to find that, for the first time, Lachlain wasn't there when she woke. "I don't sleep well—*in that bed.*"

"Is that why I found you in the stairwell?"

Emma blushed. Dark and cloistered and cavelike, the stairwell had seemed like a good idea at the time. Since she'd been *insane*. "Who's the woman?" she asked to change the subject, though she knew, had known at first sight.

"Cassandra. She's a friend from the clan."

"Only a *friend?*"

"O' course. And that is tenuous, after she hurt you."

"You'd take my side over hers? When you've known me for so short a time?"

He caught her gaze. "I will always take your side. Over anyone's."

"Why?"

"Because I know you will be in the right."

"And the bleak one? Bowen? What's his damage?" At Lachlain's frown, she added, "Why does he look so bad?" With his jet-black hair and intense golden eyes, the guy would be a hottie—if he weren't heroin-addict gaunt and evil-looking.

"He lost someone verra close to him."

"I'm sorry," she said softly. "When did it happen?"

"Early eighteen hundreds."

"And he *still* hasn't recovered?"

"He's gotten worse." Lachlain rested his forehead against hers. "It's our nature, Emma." She knew he was waiting for something from her. Something more.

He'd seen her in her worst state, and he still wanted her. Seeing her like that hadn't stopped him from following her directly to kiss her ear and commiserate. This gorgeous, walking fantasy of a male wanted something more. From *her.* Was she ready to give it? She felt bold and high from her first victory, but was she ready to brave taking Lachlain into her body and to risk seeing the beast rise inside him again?

Right at this moment, she thought she might be.

"Lachlain, if someone like you were to . . . to make love to someone like me, could he be easy with her? Take things slowly?"

His body shot tight with tension. "Aye, he could vow it."

"He wouldn't . . . he wouldn't turn?"

"No, Emma. No' tonight," he said, his voice so low and rumbling it made her shiver, made her nipples go tight. She needed him—desired him—knowing fully what he was.

When she raised her fingers and gently brushed the backs over his face, he gave her a disbelieving look before his lids closed briefly with pleasure. "Lachlain," she murmured, "I struck you."

His expression was unreadable. "So you did."

"Aren't you going to . . . retaliate?"

He groaned, and as he took her mouth, he lifted her onto the counter and pressed himself between her legs. His hands palmed her backside and yanked her against his unyielding hardness.

When she gasped, he touched his tongue to hers and she met him, wanting him to take her mouth deeply, to kiss her as he had that first night in the hotel. But it was better than even that. He was aggressive but masterful. He made her melt for him, undulating her hips up to his erection, seeking more.

He growled low, then rasped against her lips, "I canna stand to see you hurt. I will no' let you be hurt again."

She leaned forward, now kissing him, twining her hands in his thick hair. Her legs had wrapped themselves around him as he squeezed her backside, grinding her against him.

She attempted his buttons with tremulous fingers and made a sound of frustration. Instantly, he ripped off the shirt, and she wanted to thank him for displaying the muscles flexing and tensing beneath her palms. Aroused even more, shameless with it, she glided her hand down past the waist of his pants to grasp him.

He put his head back and yelled out, then snatched her sweater and bra up just above her breasts. He nuzzled her nipples, his breath hot against them, then suckled them until she thought she'd die with pleasure.

Screw the future and commitments and fears and whatever else. "I want you," she said on a breath, thumbing the moist head of his penis. When he took her nipple between his teeth and growled against it, she cried in response, "*All of you.*"

He groaned against her damp breast, then rose up to face her with an incredulous expression. "You canna know how much hearing that pleases me."

With her free hand, she unzipped her pants. He reached down to pluck off her boots, then snagged the ends of her jeans and tore them from her with one movement.

Then he went back to kissing her as if he knew she would lose her nerve, making her arch her back to him as she ran her hand along his impossibly large shaft. Shuddering, he lifted her legs to place her feet flat on the counter. Spreading her knees wide, he pulled aside her panties, groaning at the sight of her bared flesh.

For some reason she wasn't embarrassed as he stared, his eyes dark and hungry. In fact, his gaze made her tremble, made her wetter.

"How long I've waited." His voice was husky. "Canna believe it," he said, before taking her mouth so thoroughly, she was left panting and stunned.

He sucked one nipple, then the other between his lips to tongue them. Her hand squeezed his shaft, and her shaking intensified as her body throbbed for release. Why wasn't he touching her? Thrusting inside her? Why had she ever said to take this slow?

She was close, she felt it, on the verge of finally knowing the pleasure she'd never experienced, had only imagined.

Did he want her to ask as he had in the shower? She was no longer above it. . . . "*Please touch me here,*" she begged as her knees fell open in surrender. "Touch me. Kiss me. Whatever you want to do. . . ."

He groaned. "I'm going tae do it all," he bit out. "I'll make this good for you. . . ."

She gave a sharp cry when his fingers gently caressed her sex.

"So wet," he rasped. "You feel like silk." Fingers up and down slowly, leaving her flesh trembling in their wake, coaxing her even wetter. Then one dipped fully inside her, giving her no quarter as he had before, forcing her body to accept it, pressing her back into the mirror. Nothing could feel that good. She moaned in bliss, running her fist up and down his rigid erection.

"Why did you never make love before?" he rumbled in her ear, then hissed in a breath when she cupped his heavy sack.

He knew? Could he feel? "There's no one . . . For what I am, there was no one who . . ." She struggled for a word that meant *no one my family wouldn't kill*. "No one—"

"Who was no' disqualified from the competition." His lips curled. Wicked grin. Wicked Lykae. With his slow, hot touch.

"Uh-huh."

"Then it's good we found each other." He grasped her neck, holding her to face him. With his other hand, he thrust his finger and stroked his thumb over her clitoris. She was glad he held the back of her neck or her head would've lolled. "Look at me."

Her eyes fluttered open.

"You're mine, Emma," he grated between ragged breaths. "Do you understand what I'm telling you?"

Another thrust. Her hips lifted to meet it this time, and she ground into his hand, needing release, needing him deeper.

"Do you understand me? Always."

Her brows drew together. "You have someone else—"

"It's you, Emma. It's always been you."

His words were like a promise, like a . . . vow. She whispered inanely, "Not Australian for buddy?"

He shook his head slowly, his thumb stroking her, making it difficult to comprehend what he was telling her.

"B-but you said . . ." Why'd he have to tell her this now, while he made unhurried, perfect circles with his thumb? She vaguely understood what he was saying, and still she wanted his fingers playing, wanted him full and thick inside her. "You . . . you lied to me?"

He hesitated, then said, "Aye, I lied to you."

She groaned with frustration. Damn it, so close! "Why are you telling me this now?"

"Because we begin this tonight. With the truth between us."

"Begin this?" she asked in a bewildered tone. "What do you mean? Like our lives together or something?"

When he didn't disagree, she tensed. *Lives together.* For a Lykae, that meant *forever*, and forever for an immortal was literal. She scrambled away from him, pulling her panties back, and curled her legs under her. "You never intended to let me go." She worked her shirt and bra down, shivering when the material covered her nipples.

"No, I dinna. I had to keep you with me. And I'd planned to entice you to stay by then."

She repeated dumbly, "*Had* to keep me with you?" Her unfulfilled desire was making her body feel *wrong*, burning out of her control.

"In all the years that have passed, I have waited for the one woman who was meant to be mine alone. You are that woman."

"Are you still crazy?" she snapped, angered that her body felt bereft of him. "I'm not that woman. I'm just *not.*"

"You will realize soon enough that you were given to me above all others. You'll understand that I've searched relentlessly for you in every age that I have lived." His voice went low and gravelly. "And, Emma, I've lived and I have searched a verra long time."

"I'm a vam"—she patted her chest—"pire. Vampire. You've forgotten that."

"It stunned me as well. I dinna accept it at first."

"No kidding? I never would have known! What if you were correct then? You could be wrong now," she said desperately. "How can you be sure?"

He leaned over her. "I scented you from . . . afar, and it was beautiful and eased my mind. I saw your eyes for the first time, and I recognized you. I tasted your flesh, and"—he shuddered violently above her and his voice went guttural—"there is no way to describe it. But I can show you if you let me."

"I can't do this," she said, trying to dislodge herself from her pinned position, disgusted that when he'd shuddered, she'd gone soft for him once more.

Dawning horror. Her suspicion that she'd harbored and resisted was true. How could she have been so stupid— She stopped herself. No, the idea had been easy to discount because how could she, a half-creature who was part *vampire*, be a Lykae's mate? A vampire and a Lykae bound together?

And then there had been his convincing, ego-crushing lie. . . .

"So what had you planned to do with me?" She feinted right, then ducked left out from under his arms, snaring her jeans. She knew he'd *allowed* her to get away and faced him, shaking with anger. "*Really* planned? Am I to, say, live with your pack? The one you were quick to point out will rip me to bits?"

"*No one* will ever hurt you again, from my clan or outside of it. But you will no' live among them, because I am their king, and our home is here at Kinevane."

"Wow, I landed European royalty! Somebody call *People!*" She stormed from the bathroom, then wriggled into her pants.

What she wouldn't give to be able to trace, to disappear her ass out of this castle. She hated being lied to. Since she could never lie back.

Mimicking his accent, she said, " 'Ye're no' my mate, Emmaline. Nothing so serious as *my one mate*, but I would no' mind keepin' ye for my mistress. I want ye, but no' for *that*.' How condescending you were!"

He followed, gripping her arm and forcing her to face him. "I regretted having to lie, but what's done is done. I want you to at least listen to what I have to say."

"And I want to go home and see my family." And get her mind straight and ask them, *Why do I dream his memories? Why am I always overwhelmed and confused, like someone put a chaos spell on my life?*

"Will you no' even consider that this could be true? You would leave me, even knowing what we could have?"

She frowned as a sudden thought occurred. "You said 'every age that I have lived.' So how old are you? Six hundred? Seven hundred years?"

"Does that matter?"

She shook his hand free. "How—old?"

"Roughly twelve hundred years."

She gasped. "Do you know what 'robbing the cradle'

means? I am almost *seventy-one*. This skeeves me out!"

"I knew it would be difficult to accept, but you'll come to see it in time."

"Come to see what? That I want to live in a foreign country away from my family and friends in order to stay with the dishonest, unbalanced Lykae who keeps lying to me?"

"I will never lie to you again, but your place is with me. Here."

"Here. In northern Scotland. And we're coming up on summer. Gee, Lach, how long are the days in the summer way up here?"

"I've thought about that. We'll go to wherever you can be comfortable in the summer. And the nights are longer in the winter. Do you think I would no' take you where I could have more hours with you?"

"You've got it all figured out. You're going to make me say 'I do' whether I do or don't."

"I do?" He frowned. "As in marriage? This is much more serious than marriage."

"That's about as serious—"

"Marriages can end."

Her lips parted. "Well, that certainly puts it into perspective. No way out for eternity. Did it ever occur to you that I might like to take one day at a time? I'm young, and this is *everything*. You're asking me for—no, you're demanding—*everything*, and I've only known you a week. You may have this cosmic certainty about me, but I don't have the same about you."

"If I asked you, would that make a difference? Will you stay with me?"

"No, I won't. But I'm not saying we would never see each

other again. I'll go home and we'll take things slowly, get to know one another."

He closed his eyes. When he opened them, they were full of pain. Then his face hardened. "I canna allow that. You'll remain here until you can answer that question differently."

"You would separate me from my family?"

He seized her arm, hard. "You have no idea how ruthless I will be to keep you, Emma. I'd do that and more. I will do whatever it takes."

"You'll never hold me prisoner here."

For some reason, that clearly angered him more than the rest. His body tensed and his eyes flickered blue. "No, I canna. You're free to go. But you doona get a car. You doona get to direct someone here to pick you up. We're a hundred miles from the nearest town, which is inhabited almost solely by the clan, so walking out of here is no' recommended."

At the door, he turned back. "I canna keep you a prisoner here. But the sun can."

22

"Nïx!" Emma cried into the receiver when her aunt picked up the phone.

"Why, Emma, how are you? Enjoying Scotland?" she asked in a distracted voice.

"Just let me talk to Annika."

"She's indisposed."

Emma inhaled a deep breath, drumming her nails on the desk in the small office she'd found. "Nïx, this isn't a game. I don't know when I'll be able to make another call, and it's imperative that I speak with her."

"Indisposed."

"What do you mean?" Emma demanded. "She's either there or she's not."

"She's negotiating with the wraiths right now."

Stunned, Emma sank into a cool, leather chair. "Why would we need them?" The wraiths were a final measure when a coven was in grave danger. Their price to circle the manor, protecting it from outsiders with their ghostly power, was steep.

"We were attacked!" Nïx said delightedly. "Ivo the Cruel's vampires ambushed the manor and attacked us—not me, actually, because no one woke me for this, understand, and I'm quite put out. And they weren't all vampires exactly. One was a demon vampire. I want to call it a dempire from now on, but just to be contrary, Regin insists on naming it a vemon. Oh, and then Lucia's arrow missed the dempire and I heard she dropped like a rock, screaming, which burst every light in the house. But in the dark this Lykae came to the rescue, prowling inside. Lucia's screams seemed to really put *him* out. Hmmm. . . . So he stalked in and he and Regin united and fought side by side to slay the vampires. Except Ivo and his dempire escaped. Anyhoo. Vampires, Valkyrie, and Lykae, oh my. Or as Regin calls it—the 'fucking monster mash.' Hilarity ensued."

Nïx had finally lost it. Dempires? Lucia missing her target? Regin fighting side by side with a "dog"? Emma gritted her teeth. "Tell Annika I'm on the phone."

"Hold on, let me just finish up here."

Emma heard typing sounds and asked slowly, "Why are you on the computer?"

"I'm blocking all e-mails from your accounts and any that have the extension 'uk,' like from Scotland. Because I'm clever like that."

"Nïx, why are you doing this to me?" she cried. "Why are you stranding me here?"

"You can't possibly want Annika to come get you now."

"Yes! Yes, I can."

"So, the leader of our coven is to come after you, when we're under siege, Myst and Daniela are missing, and Lucia is in pain and alarmed by her when-animals-attack admirer? If you can tell me you fear for your life, then maybe, but otherwise you'll just have to take a number."

"You need me there! Nïx, you won't believe this, but I've got madskills going on. I can fight. I beat up a Lykae female!"

"That's wonderful, sweetling, but I can't talk much longer

or this GPS thingy Annika has attached to the phone might actually track your call."

"Nïx, she needs to know where—"

"You are? Emma, I've known precisely where you are. I'm not insane for nothing."

"Wait!" She gripped the phone with both hands. "Do you . . . do you ever dream others' memories?"

"What do you mean?"

"Have you ever dreamed things that have happened to someone else in the past—events that you couldn't have any knowledge of?"

"From the *past*? Of course not, sweetling. Now, that's just crazy."

Lachlain returned to his study, pinching his forehead and favoring his good leg. His injury was killing him, and after the buildup with Emma and its bitterly disappointing ending, weariness washed over him.

Bowe had already returned to the scotch. "And how'd that go?"

"Poorly. Now she believes I'm a liar. Probably because I lied to her." He sank into his chair, massaging his leg. "I should have told her the news *after*."

When Bowe raised his eyebrows, he explained, "I had to convince her earlier that she was no' my mate. Scoffed at the idea to convince her. She was sure to mimic that."

"You look like hell."

"I feel it." Explaining the fire to Bowe earlier had been excruciating. Though Lachlain had said little, merely having to revisit the memories pained him. And that had been before he'd seen his mate get struck in the face and strangled by a fellow Lykae.

"Do you want to hear more bad news?"

"Why the hell no'?"

"My discussion with Cass went poorly as well. She dinna take the news as well as we might have hoped. The idea of no' having you is bad enough, but to be beaten out by a vampire appears to be intolerable for her."

"I could care less about that—"

"She brings up issues that the elders will. She pointed out that vampire females are usually infertile. . . ."

"We canna have bairns. And I for one am glad of it. Anything else?" He *was* glad she couldn't have children. Shocking for a man who'd craved a family almost as much as his mate, but there it was.

After twelve hundred years of searching for her, he wasn't about to share her.

Bowe raised his eyebrows. "Aye. Do you see that red button on the phone there? Means someone's on the line. I just passed Harmann, and Cass would have a cell phone. Looks like your queen's phoning home."

Lachlain shrugged. "She canna give them directions to this place. She was unconscious until we got to the gate."

"They keep her on the phone long enough and she will no' have to. Lachlain, they can track where this phone call is coming from. Satellites above us and such."

Lachlain exhaled and mentally added "satellite" to his list of things he didn't bloody understand and would look up later. He'd thought satellites were for tele*vision*, not for tele*phones*.

Bowe continued, "Depends on how high-tech they are, but they might need as little as three minutes—" The light went off. "Good, then, she hung up—" The light resumed. "She's calling again. You truly might want to stop her." The light went on once more, then off, repeating several more times while Lachlain and Bowe watched in silence.

"Does no' matter," Lachlain finally said. "I will no' forbid her to speak with her family."

"They'll descend on this castle like the plague."

"If they can find it, and get past our protections, then I'll think of something to pacify them. Are they no' obsessed with shiny things? A bauble or two should suffice."

Bowe raised his eyebrows. "Let me know how that works out for you."

Lachlain scowled, then limped to the window, gazing out. He saw her a moment later, gliding out across the greens.

"Ah, I see you've spotted her."

"How do you know?" he asked without turning.

"You tensed and leaned forward. Doona worry. Soon you will be out there with her on nights like these."

As if she felt his gaze, she turned to the window. She was eerily beautiful with the fog swirling about her, her face as pale and captivating as the moon above her. But her normally expressive eyes now revealed nothing to him.

He wanted her so badly, but knew the harder he tightened his grasp, the more she would slip from it like quicksilver. The only thing about her that responded to him was her body—tonight her need had been strong—and he could use that.

She turned from him and stole into the night. She was born to haunt this place. To haunt him. He continued to stare long after she disappeared.

"Maybe you should just tell her why there's an element of time," Bowe offered.

He exhaled. "She's no' been with a man." Lachlain had debated telling her the truth again and again, but the truth involved admitting he was desperate to have her so he wouldn't *hurt* her. "So should I say, 'If you cooperate, then I will no' hurt you as badly'?"

"Christ, I dinna know she was innocent. No' many of those left in the Lore. Of course you canna tell her, else you'll terrify her and make her dread the night—"

"Bloody hell," Lachlain bit out when Cassandra followed in Emma's direction.

Bowe moved to another window facing out. "I've got this one. Why do you no' relax for a while."

"No, I'll go." He lurched for the door.

Bowe put his hand on Lachlain's shoulder. "Cass would no' dare hurt her after you made your wishes clear. I'll get rid of Cass and then talk to Emma. It canna hurt."

"No, Bowe, you might . . . frighten her."

"Oh, aye." Bowe raised his eyebrows, mocking expression in place. "After tonight, I see you've a verra delicate sparrow on your hands. I'll be sure to loosen up my jaw for her in case she wants to backhand me."

Emma leapt up to the roof of the folly to pace along the edges. She wanted her iPod so badly she would almost sleep with the liar for it.

She supposed it didn't matter that it had been trashed by the vampires, since even her "Angry Female Rock" tracks would sound insipid compared to her own ranting.

How dare he do this to her? She'd just gotten past the vampire attack, and then his change, and *then* the Cass attack, and now he had to go and throw this . . . this lie at her.

Every time she settled in with him, became even somewhat comfortable, he threw her a new curveball. The changes around her—for someone who rarely left home and didn't consider herself an adapter—and the changes *within* her frightened her. If she could just find one constant in this bombardment of variables. Just one thing to trust—

"I can get you away."

With a hiss, Emma leapt backward, clearing the weather vane to land perched on a gable top. Seeing Cassandra on the roof of the folly, she hunched down, ready to spring for her. Whenever she thought about this gorgeous, brick-house-built Lykae being in love with Lachlain for centuries, Emma wanted to scratch her eyes out.

"I can get you a car," Cassandra continued. A small breeze blew, just enough to stir the fog and brush her pretty sun-streaked hair back from her normal ear.

She had the lightest freckles on her nose, and Emma be-grudged her every one. "And why would you do that?" Emma asked, though she knew why. *The skank wants Lach-lain.*

"He seeks to keep you a prisoner. Bowe told me you are part Valkyrie, and I know your Valkyrie blood boils at the thought of being held here."

Emma felt a surge of embarrassment. *That is correct, sage foe, for my Valkyrie blood demands my absolute freedom,* had not been on the tip of her tongue. That hadn't even been her main concern. She was just ticked that Lachlain had lied. And ticked that Nïx had thrown her under the bus, hanging up on her *ten times.* "What's in it for you?" she asked.

"I want to save Lachlain from making a huge mistake, from alienating a clan that will *never* accept you. If he was no' coming off nearly two hundred years of torture, he would be able to see that you are no' his mate."

Emma assumed a thoughtful expression and tapped her

finger against her chin. "He wasn't just coming off torture"—wait for it—"when he saw that *you* are not his mate."

Cassandra almost stifled her wince.

Emma sighed at her own behavior. This wasn't her. She
wasn't usually so bitchy. She got along with all the Lore
creatures that were constantly tromping or floating in and
out of the manor. The witches, the demons, the fey—all of
them. She chalked this up as yet another example of
changes within her that she didn't understand.

What was it about this female that grated so much? Why
did she have a nearly undeniable urge to fight her? Like she
should be on *Jerry Springer,* screaming, "That's *my* man!"

Was she jealous of the time Cassandra had spent with
him?

"Look, Cassandra, I don't want to fight with you. And,
yes, I do want to leave, but it would take a life-or-death situation for me to trust you with my escape."

"I would vow no' to double-cross you." She glanced
down, then back. They both heard someone approaching.
"You canna win here, vampire. You'll never be queen of our
clan."

"Apparently I already am."

"A true queen would be able to walk in the sun with her
king." Cassandra's smile was too pleasant. "And give him
heirs."

Emma didn't come close to stifling a wince.

23

Cassandra passing time with the vampire boded ill.

Bowe vaulted to the roof to move between them, staring Cassandra down with a menacing expression. "What are you speaking about?"

Cassandra said airily, "Girl stuff."

That made Emmaline's face pale.

"I've discussed this with you once already. You must accept what's happened." Bowe wasn't known among the clan for his subtlety, and certainly not for taking the time to explain things twice. If Cassandra had hurt the situation between Lachlain and Emma, Bowe would do his best to rectify it. He crossed to just inches in front of her. "Go away, Cass. I'll speak to her alone."

She put her shoulders back. "No, I doona—"

He made his eyes turn as he growled low. He would do whatever was in his power to prevent his oldest friend from becoming like him, including hurling Cass from the roof. "Leave us."

"I was through here anyway," she said evenly, though she was backing swiftly away. "I'll just go visit with Lachlain while you two chat."

Bowe was relieved to see that the vampire didn't like that idea at all, her brows drawn together, her eyes flickering. He thought he'd never been so gladdened to see a woman's distress. Though he willed her to protest, Emmaline said nothing.

Before she dropped down, Cassandra called over her shoulder, "Remember my offer, vampire."

When they were alone, Bowe asked, "And what did she offer?"

"It doesn't concern you."

He gave her a threatening look as well.

But she just shrugged. "That has no effect on me. I know you can't hurt me or Lachlain would kick your ass six ways to Sunday. 'Kay?"

"You speak strangely."

"If I had a dollar . . ." she said with a sigh.

Why had Lachlain made this creature sound *retiring* when he'd described her? "So if you will no' tell me whatever malicious seed Cassandra has planted, then do me the courtesy of walking with me awhile."

"No, thanks. I'm busy."

"Busy pacing a folly roof on a foggy night, ranting to yourself?"

"You've a keen gift for observation," she said, turning from him.

"Speaking of gifts—one arrived for you during the day."

She froze, turned slowly, and tilted her head at him. "A present?"

He barely concealed his surprise. Damn if the Valkyrie weren't as acquisitive as the Lore said.

"If you take a turn with me and listen, I'll show it to you."

She nibbled her red bottom lip, fang showing, reminding him that she was still a vampire. The only other times he'd spoken with a vampire had been when he was torturing one.

"Okay. Five minutes. But only so I can see the gift."

He reached out to help her down, but in one of the strangest movements he'd ever seen, she stepped from the roof, her next footfall as regular as if her last hadn't been fifteen feet above, but fifteen inches.

He stared, shook himself, then followed. As he started toward the stables, he began, "I ken you're angry with Lachlain. Is it more for lying to you, or because you found out what you are?"

"Not what I *am*, but what you people seem to *think* I am. As for my anger, split it down the middle—call it a day."

"He lied for a reason. He is no' a dishonest man, in fact is known as the opposite, but he'll go to new lengths to keep you with him. And you *are* his mate."

"Mate, schmate. I'm tired of hearing that!"

"I've warned Lachlain no' to be stubborn or stupid, and it sounds like I'll have to warn you as well."

Her eyes fired silver with anger. Undaunted, he took her elbow and steered her into the stables. "Let's cut through the details and get to the meat. He's no' letting you go. Your family is going to want you back. There will be conflict. Unless you can convince them no' to fight."

"You don't get it!" she snapped. "I won't have this problem because I don't want him!" She flung herself free. "And the next Lykae that grabs my elbow to steer loses a paw."

She strode ahead of him down the lengthy run of stalls. Without any indication from him, she stopped and did a double take at the mare that had arrived this morning, then crossed over to gently run her hands down her muzzle. Strange that Emmaline would gravitate to the one that was hers alone. Damn grasping Valkyrie.

Her gaze flickered over the horse and she murmured,

"Hey, gorgeous," and "Aren't you a sweetie?" She looked as if she was in love.

Irrationally feeling as though he was interrupting, Bowe continued, "I thought vampires had an innate ability to cut through bullshite. He's no' letting you go. He's a wealthy, attractive male, a *king*, who would spoil and protect you for the rest of your life. All you have to do is accept it."

"Look, Bowen, I'm in no way a realist." She'd leaned back against the stall gate with a knee drawn up, as if she'd been here a thousand times. Her arm curled under the mare's neck to pet the side of her face. "I can pretend with the best of them. I can pretend Lachlain's dishonesty didn't hurt. I can pretend I like it better here than I do in my own home and my own country, and I can even ignore the fact that his age is a *multiple* of mine. But I can't pretend that his entire clan won't hate me or that Lykae won't keep attacking me. And I can't pretend that my family will accept him, because they never will, and I would be forced to choose anyway."

As she'd spoken, her expression had slowly ebbed from furious to stark. She wasn't telling him half of it. Her eyes were haunted. Lachlain's mate was spooked. Badly.

Just as Mariah had looked.

"What else is happening? Something else is upsetting you."

"It's just . . . everything's . . . *overwhelming.*" She whispered the last.

"What is?"

She shook her head and her face turned hard. "I'm a private person and I don't even know you. Not to mention that you're Lachlain's best friend. I'm not telling you anything."

"You can trust me. I will no' tell him anything you doona want me to."

"I'm sorry, but right now Lykae are not exactly in my to-be-trusted column. What with all the lies and those pesky stranglings."

He knew she was referring to Lachlain's actions as well, but said, "You held your own against Cassandra."

"I don't want to live in a place where I have to *hold my own*. I don't want to live in a place where I'm attacked *or* bullied."

Bowe sank down onto a bale of hay. "Lachlain canna find his brother. Cassandra is proving to be like a gnat in his ear. His leg ails him, and he can scarcely keep up with this new time he's been thrown into. Worse for him is that he canna make you happy." He snared a piece of straw out and chewed the end, offering her another.

She glared. "I don't masticate, thank you."

He shrugged. "I can take care of Cass. His leg will heal, he'll acclimate, and eventually Garreth will turn up. But none of this will matter if he canna make you content here."

She turned to touch her forehead to the mare's and said in a soft voice, "I don't like that he hurts or is worried, but I can't simply tell myself to be happy here. It's just got to come."

"It will if you give it time. Once he can shake off more of his past . . . troubles, you will find he's a good man."

"I don't seem to have a choice in the matter, do I?"

"No' at all. So in the meantime, do you want me to tell you how to manage him better?"

"*Manage* him?" she asked, facing him.

"Aye."

She blinked at him. "I might have to hear this."

"Understand that anything he does, he does with the ultimate goal of your happiness." She parted her lips to disagree, but he spoke over her: "So if you are displeased with any measure he takes toward that end, you need only to voice that it's made you *un*happy."

When she frowned, he asked, "How'd his lie make you feel?"

She looked down at the toe of her boot drawing circles in the packed dirt, and finally mumbled, "Betrayed. Hurt."

"Think about this for a moment. How do you think he'd react if you simply told him that he'd hurt you?"

She lifted her head, staring at him for many moments.

He rose, dusted off his pants, then turned for the door, only pausing to say over his shoulder, "By the way, that's your horse."

Before he faced forward, he saw the mare nose her hair and nearly knock her down.

"You will no' embrace an old friend?" Cassandra asked with a pout.

"If she were content to remain as such," Lachlain answered impatiently. How long was Bowe going to be? He trusted Bowe with his life, and if pressed, he'd say even with something so important as his mate, but he was still restless waiting here.

Her arms were still opened. "It's been centuries, Lachlain."

"If Emma walked in and saw us 'embracing,' how do you think that would make her feel?"

Her arms dropped and she sank into a chair across from the desk. "No' like you think. Because *she* feels nothing for you. While I mourned your death as a widow would."

"A waste of time on your part. Even if I'd died."

"Bowe explained where you've been and what she is. She has no place here. You've been unwell and canna see how wrong this is."

He couldn't even bring himself to anger, because he'd never been surer of anything than he was of Emma. He realized now that the reasons he'd continued to befriend Cassandra over the years no longer applied.

In the past, he'd felt sorry for her. Like him, she'd gone centuries without finding her mate, and he'd thought that, like him, she reacted to the lack in an unhealthy way. But whereas he'd sought out enemies, eagerly taking the forefront of every war and volunteering for any dangerous task abroad where he might stumble upon his mate, Cassandra had seized on him.

"Who was there for you when your da died? Your mother? Who helped you search for Heath?"

He exhaled wearily. "The entire clan."

Her lips thinned, then she seemed to rally. "We have a history together. We are of the same *species*. Lachlain, what would your parents have thought about you taking a vampire as mate? And Garreth? Think of the shame this will bring him."

Truthfully, Lachlain didn't know how his parents would have reacted. Before they'd died, they'd regretted that their sons had been unable to find their mates for so long, and had understood Lachlain's, the oldest son's, more obvious pain. But they'd also abhorred vampires—thought them malicious parasites and a blight on the earth. He couldn't say for Garreth, either. So instead, he answered, "I look forward to the day when you find your mate and you can think back on this and truly comprehend how ridiculous I find your words."

Bowe ambled through the doorway then. At Lachlain's raised eyebrows, Bowe shrugged, as though the conversation with Emma hadn't been overly encouraging.

Harmann bustled in just after, perspiring, hectic, the complete opposite of cool, uncaring Bowe. "The staff is departing. I just wanted to check to see if you need anything else before I leave."

"We'll be fine."

"If you need anything, my number is programmed into the phone."

"As if that helps me," Lachlain muttered. He thought he'd been doing so well with learning the tools of this time, but the sheer amount of technology was daunting.

"Oh, and the packages that arrived today for your queen have been unpacked."

"Harmann, go," he ordered. Harmann looked as if he was ready to pass out.

He cast Lachlain a grateful expression and strode out the door.

"Gifts will no' sway her," Cassandra pointed out in a churlish tone.

"I disagree," Bowe answered, pulling a red apple from his jacket pocket and shining it on his shirt. "I've learned the *queen* does so like her gifts."

When Lachlain raised his eyebrows, Bowe said, "Showed her the horse. Regret stealing your thunder." He displayed no sign of regret.

Lachlain shrugged as if unconcerned, though he had wanted to see her reaction and capitalize on any gratitude she might have demonstrated.

"The good news is that she dinna like the idea of Cass up here talking to you. Distressed the wee creature."

Could Emma have been *jealous*? Lachlain knew she could never feel the soul-deep possession he felt for her, but he'd take anything. He frowned. He didn't want her distressed. "Cassandra, you will leave here. No' to return until invited by Emmaline herself. I will no' be moved from this."

She gasped, truly shocked, but how could she be?

She shot to her feet, shaking, her voice sharp. "It may never be me, but when you are well, you'll see it never could be that *vampire* either." She flew to the door.

"I'll make sure she leaves," Bowe offered. "Just after a quick detour to the kitchen. They cooked for an army." He hesitated, then said, "Good luck."

Lachlain nodded, lost in thought, hearing cars departing down the long drive.

A king was in residence with his queen, a Lykae had his mate after a millennium, and the moon was waxing. Everyone here knew what that meant. Everyone except Emma.

He'd run out of time. He'd run out of options. His gaze fell to the sideboard, to the crystal glinting in the light.

24

When Emma woke, she was in Lachlain's arms, with her face tucked against his chest and his fingers gently sifting through her hair. Just before she went irate at the thought of him moving her to the bed again, she realized he was in her blankets on the floor.

Then the dream came back to her in a rush.

She'd seen Lachlain in some kind of war long ago, passing the time between charges. Garreth and Heath—his brothers?—and some other Lykae males talked about finding their mates, musing on what they would look like. They spoke in Gaelic. She understood the words.

"I'm just saying it would be nice if she's fair of form," one called Uilleam said. *He indicated what he meant by cupping his hands in front of his chest.*

Another said, "Just give mine a sweet arse to hold on to in the night—"

They quieted when Lachlain walked by, not wanting to talk of such things in front of him.

Lachlain was the oldest, and had waited the longest. Nine hundred years he'd waited.

He continued to a stream by their camp, bounding easily over boulders even under the weight of chain mail. He knelt on the shore by a becalmed pool and leaned down to cup water to his face.

His reflection wavered for the briefest second. He hadn't shaved for days and he had a long, winding cut down his face. His hair was long.

He was absolutely stunning to Emma, and she reacted viscerally to this remembered image from the dream.

When he'd sat back on his haunches and gazed up at the blue sky, Emma had felt the startling warmth of the sun as though she'd been there. Then a wave of emptiness had hit him. *Why can I no' find her . . . ?*

Emma blinked open her eyes. She was *her*. The one he'd longed for. . . .

She'd seen him with rage in his eyes, with confusion, with hatred, but she'd never seen hopelessness as she had in his reflection.

"Sleep well?" he said, rumbling his words.

"Did you sleep with me? Here?"

"Aye."

"Why?"

"Because you prefer sleeping here. And I prefer sleeping with you."

"And I have no say in the matter."

Ignoring her comment, he said, "I want to give you something," then reached behind him, drawing out . . . the gold necklace from her dream. Her eyes locked on it, mesmerized. It was more beautiful in reality.

"Do you like it? I never knew what you would prefer and guessed again and again."

Her gaze followed it as it swung like a pendulum. This was proof that she was going loopy, and yet she still had an inward evil grin. "I'll be sure to wear it in front of Cassandra," she murmured absently.

He caught it in his palm, breaking her stare. "Why would you say that?"

As she often did when she wanted to lie and couldn't, she asked a question. "Wouldn't she be jealous to see you'd bought me jewelry?"

He was still frowning at her.

"It's clear she wants you for herself."

"Aye. That's true," he said, surprising her with his honesty. "But she's gone. I've sent her away, no' to return until it pleases you, or never. I will no' have you uncomfortable in your own home."

Through gritted teeth, she said, "It's not my home." She pushed away, but he held her by her shoulder.

"Emma, it's your home whether you accept me or no'. It has always been and always will be."

She jerked from his hand. "I don't want your home and I don't want you," she cried. "Not when you've hurt me like this."

His body went tense and his expression turned bleak. As though he'd *failed*. "Tell me how."

"When you lied, it . . . it hurt."

"I dinna want to lie to you." He brushed her hair from her face. "But I dinna think you were ready to hear everything, and I already sensed a threat from the vampires and feared you would run away."

"But now keeping me from my family pains me even more."

"I will take you to them," he said quickly. "I have to meet with some of the clan and then I must go away for a short while. After that, I will take you there myself. But you canna go alone."

"Why?"

"I am uneasy. Emma, I need you to cleave to me. I know you doona and I fear losing you. They will talk you from any headway I may have made with you."

Annika would, in fact, remind Emma that she'd gone insane.

"I know the minute you enter that coven alone, I will have hell to get you back."

"And you *have* to get me back."

"O' course I do. I will no' lose you just when I've finally found you."

She rubbed her forehead. "Why are you so certain about this? For someone who's not a Lykae, this all seems really extreme. I mean, you've only known me for a *week*."

"While I've waited my entire lifetime."

"That doesn't mean you were right to have. It doesn't mean you should have."

His voice went low. "No, but it means having you here now feels verra, verra satisfying."

She ignored the warmth his words conjured, ignored her dream of him.

"Emma, will you drink from me?"

She scrunched her nose. "You smell like alcohol."

"I had a dram or two."

"Then I'll pass."

He was silent for a moment, then held up the necklace again. "I want you to wear this." He leaned forward to reach around and fasten it. Which placed his neck directly before her lips.

She spied a nick just inches from her mouth. "You've cut yourself," she murmured in a daze.

"Did I, then?"

She licked her lips, trying not to succumb to the temptation. "You're, oh, God, *move your neck,*" she whispered, panting.

The next thing she felt was his palm on the back of her head, pulling her to him, forcing her mouth against his skin.

She pounded her fists against his chest, but he was too strong. She finally surrendered, unable to stop herself from darting her tongue out. She licked him slowly, savoring his taste and the way his body tensed, she knew, with pleasure.

Moaning, shuddering, she sank her fangs in and drew.

25

As she drank, Lachlain squeezed her in his arms and rose to sit on the edge of the bed. He lifted her onto his lap, making her straddle him.

He knew she was lost, clinging so sweetly to him, her elbows on his shoulders, her forearms crossed behind his head. The necklace was cold against his chest as he pulled her closer.

She drew in deep.

"Drink . . . slowly, Emma."

When she didn't, he did something he wouldn't have thought he was capable of. *He* broke away from her.

She swayed immediately. "What's happening to me?" she asked in a slurred tone.

You're drunk so I can take advantage of you. . . .

"I feel so . . . strange."

When he rolled up her nightgown, she didn't stop him, even when he palmed her between her legs. He groaned anew to find her so wet. His erection was about to rip through his pants.

She was breathing hot and fast against his skin where her lips and teeth had been. She licked him there when he thrust his finger inside her tight sex, then ran her face against his, moaning softly.

"Everything's spinning," she whispered.

He felt guilt, but he knew what they needed and would take them headlong to it, damn the consequences. "Spread your knees more. Rest on my hand."

She did. "I ache, Lachlain." Her voice was throaty, sexy as hell.

She whimpered when he leaned down to drag his tongue over her nipple. "I can ease it," he bit out as he unfastened his pants with his free hand and his cock sprang forth just beneath her. "Emma, I need . . . tae be inside you. I'm going tae press you down on me."

He forced her hips lower and lower. *Gentle. First time. So small.*

"And then I'm going to take you until neither of us aches like this," he said against her nipple. Just when he was about to touch her wetness, when he could perceive her heat, she flung away from him, scrambling to the headboard.

He growled with frustration, yanking her right back, until she pummelled his shoulder.

"No! Something's not right." Her hand flew to her forehead. "Feel so dizzy."

Put the beast back in its cage. He'd made a vow to her, never to touch her when she didn't want him to. But her gown was barely covering her, red silk teasing against her white thighs, her nipples hard. He couldn't catch his breath . . . needed her so badly. . . .

With another growl, he reached over and tossed her to her front. As she struggled, he held her down to bare her generous, perfect arse.

Groaning, he brought his hand down on her curves, not a slap, more a pawing that landed hard. Since he'd met her, he'd brought himself to spend each day in the shower. With her scent fresh in his mind and his hands still warmed from her skin, it was always violently powerful.

She gasped when he kneaded her curves. It would have to be enough.

Time to shower.

Emma still felt his hand against her. It hadn't been a hit or a slap, but—Freya help her—an exquisitely delivered message.

What was wrong with her? Why was she thinking this way? She shivered and moaned. The beast in the cage?—that's what he'd told her. Well, the beast had just swiped a hand out of the cage and delivered a good smack on her backside. It was a masterful, masculine touch that made her want to dissolve, and left her rolling her hips against the bed.

The urge to touch her sex was overwhelming. She wanted to *beg* to ride him. Her body twitched as she fought it.

The necklace he'd fastened around her was actually a choker that had gold strands and jewels cascading down over her breasts. It was heavy on her and felt sexy and forbidden. When she moved, it swayed and tickled her nipples.

Something about this necklace and the way he'd pressed it upon her signaled . . . possession.

He'd done something to her tonight. The bed spun, and she felt like . . . giggling. She also couldn't seem to stop running her hands up and down her body. When her thoughts came, they were clear, but soft and slow. . . .

She didn't know how much longer she could take him touching her without begging for him. Right now on the tip of her tongue, "*Please.*"

No! She was already different from others in her coven—part hated foe, weak compared to her aunts.

If the timid vampire Valkyrie returned home aching for her *Lykae*?

The disgust and disappointment they would feel. The hurt in their eyes. Besides, she believed if she gave this up, she'd have no power between her and Lachlain—surrendered with a whispered, "Please." If she succumbed, she wouldn't be going home. Ever. She feared he had the power to make her forget why she'd ever wanted to.

The bed spun more wildly. She frowned as realization hit her.

He'd gotten her drunk.

The bastard had gotten himself . . . so that she would . . . when she drank . . . Oh, that son of a bitch! She hadn't even known this was possible!

She'd get him back for this. Uncalled for, tricking her like this. She couldn't trust him. He'd said he wouldn't lie, but she found this just as dishonest.

In the past, she would've just accepted this, taken it meekly as yet another time her wishes and feelings were ignored, but now *she refused*. Lachlain needed to learn a lesson. He needed to learn that sometime in the last seven days, she'd become a creature with which one did not fuck.

When she licked her lips for the thirtieth time since he'd gone, a nebulous idea formed.

A wicked, evil idea. She glanced around, embarrassed, as if someone could hear her thoughts. If he wanted to play dirty, if he wanted to throw down that gauntlet, she'd swoop the thing up. . . .

She could do it. Damn it, she could be evil, she *could*.

A hazy memory arose of when she was younger, asking

her aunt Myst why the vampires were so evil. She'd answered, "It's their nature." Now Emma grinned drunkenly.

Time to get back to nature.

Emma woke to the sound of the phone ringing. No phone in the history of telephonics had ever sounded so annoying. She yearned to crush it with a ball-peen hammer.

She blearily opened her eyes, turning in her blankets to see Lachlain leave the bed and limp over to answer it.

She reached a hand up and ran it over the warmed bedcover. He'd been lying there, stretched out on top of it. Had he been watching her sleep?

Lachlain picked up, then said, "He's still no' returned? Canvass farther out then. . . . I doona care. Call me the minute you find him." He hung up the phone and ran a hand through his hair. She couldn't remember the last time she'd seen anyone look so exhausted as Lachlain. She heard him exhale wearily and noticed his shoulders were tense. She knew he was searching for his brother and was sorry that he didn't know where he was. After all these years, Lachlain still wasn't able to tell his brother he was alive. She felt sympathy for him.

Until she rose.

Her head began pounding in a rush, and as she stumbled to the bathroom, she realized her mouth was bone dry. Brushing her teeth and showering helped her head and mouth, but had minimal effect on her dizziness.

He'd given her the mother of all hangovers—a run-in with the wrath of grapes. Her very first. If he'd truly had "a dram or two," surely she wouldn't have been *that* tanked and wouldn't be this hungover now. Last night, as she'd dressed and set out to explore once more, she'd been buzzed all the way up until she collapsed in her blankets at dawn. And the floor of the massive castle had spun. She was sure of it.

He must have drunk like a frat pledge before coming to her.

Bastard.

When she exited the bathroom in her towel to go to her closet to dress, he followed, leaning against the doorframe as she picked out clothes. There were new pieces everywhere. Purses and shoes as well.

She padded along, checking out the offerings, analyzing them with a discerning eye. She was picky about her clothes and had always eschewed anything that didn't conform to her hipster/contrarian fashion style. She'd found that any garment not vintage or D.W.O.T.B—*damn well off the boat*—didn't conform. . . .

"Do you like everything?" he asked.

She tilted her head, a flare of anger bubbling up when she saw that her own luggage was conspicuously absent. "Oh, I'll be sending for everything when I go home," she answered with absolute honesty.

With her forefinger pointed down, she made a spinning gesture indicating he should turn around. When he complied, she hastily donned underwear, a bra and jeans for running, and a loose sweater.

She ambled past him and sat on the bed, only now noticing that every window was covered in shutters. Of course, he'd had this done. After all, he didn't believe she was going anywhere—because he didn't think she could escape him. "When did these come?"

"Installed today. They will open automatically at sunset and close at dawn."

"They're closed."

He eyed her. "Sun's no' fully set yet."

She shrugged, though she did wonder why she'd been rising so early. "You haven't asked me to drink."

He raised his eyebrows. "Will you?"

"Right after a Breathalyzer test." When he frowned, she said, "Measures how drunk you are."

He did not even look guilty. "I've had no liquor tonight and only want you to take." He sat down, too close beside her.

"Why did you rush to the shower last night? Do you find the act so unclean?"

A short laugh. "Emma, it's the most erotic thing I've ever experienced. In the shower, I took release so I doona break my vow to you."

She frowned. "You mean you—?"

"Oh, aye." His lips curled as he looked down into her eyes. "Every night you've got me like a randy lad."

He was completely unembarrassed to admit he'd stroked himself to orgasm mere feet away from her. At that exact time she'd been rolling in his bed, struggling not to touch her own body. How . . . titillating. She blushed as much from his admission as from her own thoughts. *I wish I'd seen him doing that.*

No, no, no. If she kept staring at his sexy smirk, she'd forget her plan, forget the hurt she'd felt upon realizing he'd nicked himself and tricked her and *held her in place* against him until she drank.

Consequences. Messing with vampire Emmaline Troy now brought consequences.

When the shutters opened with a smooth hum, revealing the night, she said, "Lachlain, I have an idea." Did she truly have the mettle to retaliate? Consequences. Paying in kind. Surprising herself, she found the answer was yes. "I think there's a way we could both 'take release' while I drink."

"I'm listening," he said quickly.

"I mean from the act itself." Her voice was a purr as she glided to the floor to kneel before him. With delicate, pale hands, she tentatively eased open his knees.

His jaw slackened as realization hit him. "You doona mean—?" He should be recoiling. His cock stood stiff as a pole.

"I want all of you, Lachlain." Purring words. Lovely Emmaline with her plump lips gazing up at him with beseeching blue eyes. "All that you have to give."

He wanted to give her anything she desired. Anything. With a shaking hand, she unfastened the top button of his jeans.

He swallowed hard.

Shouldn't he at least be *hesitant* about this? Lord help him, he was fighting to keep his hands off the back of her head to rush her. He sensed she could easily lose her nerve, knew she had never before given a man this pleasure. To begin the night of the full moon with this . . . ? He was dreaming.

She slowly unzipped his jeans, gasping when he sprang forth, then gave him a shy but seductive smile, seeming pleased by his erection. She held it with two hands as if she'd never let him go.

"Emma." His voice was broken.

"Hold out for as long as you can," she said, stroking his length once. His eyes closed with pleasure.

He felt her breath first, making him shudder. Then her

slick lips, then her tongue darting and flicking over his flesh. Ah, she had a wicked little tongue—

Sweet God, her *bite*.

He gave an anguished groan, falling back on the bed, only to immediately raise his hand to cup her face and his head to watch her mouth on his cock. He was a twisted man. . . . "I had . . . no idea. *Always like this*," he growled. "*Always*."

He didn't know if he was going to come at once or pass out. Her hands were everywhere, cupping, teasing, driving him wild. She moaned against him, and her sucking grew greedy. She'd never taken this much, but if she needed, he would give. He was weakening, yet he never wanted it to end. "Emma, I'm going to—" His eyes rolled back in his head and everything turned black.

26

*D*on't look back, put on my shoes in the car. Run like hell.

She did. Straight to the extensive garage, scanning for keys to the many cars, finding nothing. Frustration welled up. But then words were whispered in her head, like silk fluttering down.

Run.

She was trying to! No keys. She sprinted back and scanned around the castle for a work truck, a freaking tractor at this point.

She stilled and frowned, feeling warmth from just above the horizon. As if in a trance, she lifted her face to it. The full moon. Rising tonight.

She *felt* the light. Like she'd always imagined people did with the sun.

Her hearing was sensitive; things called to her from the forest beyond. She'd avoided that dark place in all her exploring. The sight of it had defeated even her newfound sense of courage.

Run there.

She had to fight the urge to sprint headlong into the abysmal-looking forest. Lachlain would catch her there—he was a hunter, a tracker. That's what he did. She had no chance of escaping.

Still her body twitched from the battle, as if she missed running within the forest, though she'd never been. Was she going mad even to think of this?

Run!

With a cry, she dropped her shoes and obeyed, fleeing the manor and a soon-to-wake, irate Lykae. She plunged into the woods and realized she could see. Her already strong night vision was perfected.

But why was *she* seeing? Did his blood affect her so much? She'd taken a lot. Now she knew Lykae could see as well at night as by day.

She smelled the forest floor, the moist earth, the moss. She even smelled rocks wet with dew. Dizzying. She might have swayed, but her feet fell perfectly placed to the ground as if she'd run this way a thousand times.

The scents, the sound of her breaths and her heart beating, the air rushing over her . . . heaven. This was like heaven.

Then she became aware of something new. The running was an aphrodisiac, with every footfall vibrating up her body like a long stroke. She heard his bellow of rage echoing from miles away at the manor, seeming to shake the whole black world around her. As she heard him crashing after her, she felt the need for release. Not fear of what he would do to her when he caught her, but anticipation. She could hear *his* heart pounding furiously as he neared. Even when weakened, he ran headlong for her.

He would chase her forever.

She knew this as if he'd spoken it in her mind. He would claim her and never let her go. That was what his kind did.

You're his kind now, her mind whispered. No! She wouldn't give in.

A Lykae mate would've let herself be caught. Would be waiting for him, naked and spread in the grass or leaning back against a tree, hips offered up and arms overhead, reveling in the fact that he was chasing her, anticipating his ferocity.

Emma was going insane! How could she know these things? She would never welcome ferocity. *Give a cry early, at the first sign of pain.* That was her rule.

She'd just reached a clearing when she heard him lunge for her. She tensed for the impact with the ground, but he turned and took it on his back, then moved her bodily to lie in the grass. When she opened her eyes, he was above her, on all fours.

He was larger. His eyes weren't their golden color. That eerie blue flickered across them. His exhaled breaths were low rumbling growls. She knew his body was weakened, *she* had felt how much so when he ran, but his obvious intent made him strong.

"Turn . . . over," he bit out. His voice was distorted, grating.

Lightning streaked the sky above him. He didn't seem to notice it, but she stared at it like one might a comet. Could she be more Valkyrie than she knew?

Sane Emma said, "No."

The lightning also illuminated in flashes what he was inside. Fangs of his own, the ice-blue eyes, his already incredibly powerful body rippling with more muscle. He yanked her bag and jacket from her, sliced open her clothes to strip her, snarling and growling while she beheld the lights above in a daze.

"Arms . . . over . . . your head," he grated, while tearing his jeans from himself.

She did this. He was still positioning himself over her, bending down to kiss or lick, moving a hand or a knee. Something was happening that she didn't understand. This wasn't just random movement, this was . . .

Ritual.

As he moved above her, the urge to go to her hands and knees grew overwhelming. To brush her hair aside and present her neck. He dragged a tongue across her nipple and her back arched.

"Turn . . . over."

As if someone else were in her body, someone carnal and aggressive, she did as he commanded. Movements behind her that she couldn't see. She could feel his huge erection slide against her backside, then prod against her thigh.

Smell the night, feel the growing moon bathe your skin. She was going insane . . . knew it when she pressed her chest down into the grass, arms in front of her, and raised her ass up. He growled as if pleased, then immediately kicked her knees open with his own. She could feel herself getting wetter though he wasn't touching her.

She ached. She felt empty. She knew she could *feel* the scents of the earth if he would just enter her. She rocked back as if to attract him.

"*Doona do that,*" he hissed. His hand landed on her backside, then clutched, holding her in place.

She moaned, her eyes rolling back in her head.

"With the moon . . . I canna . . . be as I should. If you knew what I was thinking right now—"

She spread her knees wider, though a beast was at her back about to go mad from the moon, with a shaft that could rend her in two. She should be curled in a ball with her hands over her head. Not rocking front and back trying to attract him.

"Ye've no need for that. Ever. Can barely . . . keep from . . ."

She perceived him moving, then . . . felt his mouth on her sex. She cried out with shock and pleasure. He was lying on his back beneath her, her knees spread over his face, his arms wrapped over her back, hugging her down. She couldn't move if she tried.

He groaned against her, arms tightening if possible. "Dreamed of tasting you again," he growled. "Almost as much as fucking."

Her claws dug into the grass and the cut blades erupted in scent. He suckled her and she screamed. Lightning split the sky like a whip. She couldn't move, she couldn't rock her hips into him like she needed to. She didn't feel the ground abrading her knees as she knew it must be. Going insane.

"Oh, God, yes! Lachlain, *please.*"

He drew his tongue from her, entering his finger. "Please what?"

She was panting, near mindless. "Please make me for once . . . please let me have—"

"Come," he commanded, with a palm coming down on her ass and a thrust of his finger as he resumed sucking and licking. She screamed and her body clenched instantly, shuddering her through her first orgasm, making her accept the explosion of pleasure. His hands were on her, roughly palming her cheeks, shoving her against his mouth, licking relentlessly.

And all the while she watched the sky as she moved the only way she could, by arching her back, until she could take no more.

When she was spent and fell limp with a whimper, stunned by the pleasure she'd never known, he eased her to the ground and stood. Trembling, she gazed up at him, silhouetted against the lightning still firing though not as furiously. He was like a god. He awaited something.

Ritual. She was on her knees before him. Gazing up at him, she drew him into her mouth as best as she was able, adoring his flesh with her tongue as she should've done before. He cupped her face with shaking hands, groaning. His expression was one of ecstasy mingled with disbelief as he watched her. She reached up to scratch down his torso, nails digging into his flesh, and he shuddered. She could taste him already salty and slick at the tip.

"Canna do this . . . need to claim you. Here. It will be here. . . ."

She resisted him taking his shaft from her mouth, licking her lips for it even as he moved behind her, kneeling between her legs. He bent down, tonguing her again while trying to fit two fingers inside her. When he was able, he released her, then his whole hand was on her head guiding her down onto her hands. She looked back, saw him holding his erection about to put it inside her. She began shaking in earnest, yearning.

Need. Attract. She pressed back, but he held her still, spreading her flesh and placing the tip against her. A hand roughly ran down her back, making her arch down with pleasure.

"No' a dream," he murmured in a stunned tone. "Emmaline . . ."

She was panting, repeating "please" again and again.

He put one arm solidly around her waist. *"Waited so long to be inside you."* He ran his other arm under her, over her breast, and clenched her shoulder from underneath, holding her immobile. "*I claim you for my own.*" He plunged into her.

She screamed again, this time in pain.

"*Ah, God,*" he groaned. "So tight," he bit out with another buck of his hips. She was so clenched around him he could scarcely move.

She gasped, her eyes watering from the searing pain. She'd known they wouldn't fit.

To her relief, he stopped thrusting, though she wondered how he had when she could feel his body shaking all around her, his shaft so huge and throbbing within her.

He drew her up as he went to his knees, putting her back against his chest and taking her arms to guide them up around his neck, locking them there. "Hold on tae me."

When she nodded, he skimmed his fingers from her shoulders over her breasts and down, then dipped both of his hands to cup and stroke her between her legs. When her wetness returned in a rush, he still refrained from thrusting. Instead he thumbed her nipples and palmed her breasts for long, long moments until she was panting again, feeling a desperate lust like she had when he'd teased her that night in the bathroom. No, worse than that, because now she knew exactly what she was missing.

Remembering her frustration that night and fearing he'd subject her to that again, she wriggled her hips against him.

He growled low at her ear, "Do you want more?"

"Y-yes."

"Go tae your hands again . . . let me give it tae you."

As soon as she did, he clutched her hips, slowly withdrew, then eased deeper within her. She cried out, this time in pleasure. When she arched her back and worked her knees wide again, he groaned her name in answer, but his voice had changed. Still as deep but guttural, grating. Almost . . . snarling.

Another thrust inside her, this time more forceful. Groans, growling. Hers as well?

Thoughts were growing dim as the pleasure increased. Each measured withdrawal made her whimper, each time his skin slapped against hers as he bucked into her made her cry out for more. Her lips curled when the air charged with electricity, and she gloried in the sky, in the scents, in Lachlain wedged deep inside her. He stretched down over her back, and she felt his mouth on her neck. Felt his *bite*, but not like hers, not piercing the skin, but she reveled in it as if she'd accomplished it.

"Going tae come so hard," he snarled against her skin, "you'll feel it like a thrust of my cock."

She climaxed once more, screaming in ecstasy to the sky, throwing her head back to his shoulder, wanting his mouth at her neck.

"Ah, God, yes," he yelled, then returned to his bite. . . . She did feel him ejaculate, forcefully, pumping his seed so hotly inside her.

Yet when he was finished, he didn't stop thrusting.

He'd come harder than he ever had, but felt no relief. If anything, the need intensified. *"I canna stop."*

He tossed her to her back, pinning her hands above her, still driving into her. Her hair fanned out, haloing her head, and the scent of it exploded within him. He swayed from the power of it. He was claiming her. At last. He was inside his mate. *Emmaline.* He gazed down at her face. Her eyelids were shuttered, her lips glistening. So beautiful it pained him.

The moon, completely risen now, fired light, casting silver over her body as she writhed beneath him.

Any control he'd had was disappearing, an animal feeling of possession taking its place.

Possession. Claim.

He could feel the moon on his skin as he never had before and his thoughts came frenzied, ungovernable.

But she'd run from him. She'd thought to leave him. Never.

Control slipping . . . Christ, no, he was . . . *turning,* fangs sharpening. To mark her flesh. *Claws to seize her hips when he spent into her body over and over.*

Possess her completely.

She was his. He'd found her. He *deserved* her. Deserved to have everything he was about to take from her.

Plunging into her soft, giving body with the moon at his back. Pleasure as he'd never known.

Make her surrender everything.

Licking, biting, suckling her, slaking his lust on his mate. Unable to tamp down yells, growls, his need to taste her wet flesh. Too rough with her. Needed to fuck her harder. Couldn't stop driving into her.

With the last of his will, he shoved himself away from her.

Her claws rent the ground in frustration, her hips undulating for him. "Why?" she cried.

"Canna hurt you." His voice was not his own.

"Please . . . come back inside me."

"You want this? Like I am?"

"Yes . . . need you . . . exactly as you are. *Please, Lachlain! I feel it too.*"

The moon had claimed her too? At her words, he gave himself over to it.

His vision went hazy, seeing only the silver of her eyes as they stared up into his and the attracting deep pink of her plump lips and nipples. He stalked over her, caging her in with his body, compelled to lean his head down to tongue and suck her nipples, then take her mouth. He clutched her from beneath, holding her in place as he rose up on his knees. "Mine," he growled with a brutal thrust.

As though out of his body, he heard the low, guttural sounds erupting from his chest, the snarls that accompanied each frenzied thrust. Her breasts bounced, and his eyes were riveted by the tight, hard points, wet from his furious suckling. He felt her claws dig into his skin as the pressure in his cock built and built. Her head thrashed.

"Mine. . . ." *She thought to leave him?* He fucked her with all his strength.

She accepted it, trying to meet him.

He cupped the back of her neck, yanking her up to him. *"Surrender to me."*

Her eyes flashed open when she came again. Dazed. Mirrors. He could feel her squeezing around his cock, milking him.

When he followed, yelling out, his seed shot from him, pumping into her . . . hot . . . relentless. All he comprehended was that she arched her back and spread her legs wider for him as though she loved the feeling of it.

At moonset, when she could come no more, she fell limp. With a last shuddering groan he fell on top of her, but it wasn't uncomfortable.

Finally he planted a knee and raised up, turning her to face him. He lay on his side and brushed her hair from her lip. Now that the night's frenzy had passed, she felt an overwhelming joy that he'd claimed her, as if she'd waited as long as he had.

She turned to her back and stretched, gazing up at the sky, then to the trees just beyond them. The grass was cool beneath her and the air was as well, but she felt burning hot. As if her eyes couldn't stray for long, she turned back to stare up at his face once more. She felt *connected* to everything, as though she belonged, a feeling that had always eluded her.

Contentment surged through her, and she wanted to weep with relief that he'd caught her and still wanted her. She found she couldn't stop touching him, as if she feared he would disappear, and wondered how she could possibly have acted cruelly toward him.

She recalled that she'd been angry with him and had run, but couldn't quite recall why. She could never stay angry with a man who was looking at her like he was.

He stared at her as though awed.

"I dinna want to hurt you. I tried no' to."

"It was fleeting. I tried not to hurt you, either."

He grinned, then asked, "Did you hear something inside you? You knew things. . . ."

She nodded. "It was like . . . instinct, but instinct I was clearly aware of. It scared me at first."

"And then?"

"And then I came to understand it was, I don't know how to put it, but it was guiding me . . . rightly."

"How did the moon feel on your skin?"

"Almost as good as it felt to run. It was like . . . heaven. Lachlain, I *felt* scents."

His body was shaking and he sank back, pulling her over him to lie on his chest, straddling his hips. "Sleep." His lids were heavy, but he kissed her. "Tired from sating my young mate. And from your trick."

Now she remembered the night before, and stiffened. "I only retaliated against yours." If he took her to task about her actions—

"Aye. I like that you give as you get." His voice was drowsy as he said against her hair, "You are teaching me, Emmaline."

At that, the outrage she'd wanted to feel at his actions—or felt she *should* feel like other, stronger women would—deflated to nonexistence. She was a spineless wuss, she knew it. Because after one mere cataclysmic night in the grass, her first through fifteenth orgasms, and a couple of awed looks, she was tempted to latch on to this strong, bighearted Lykae with two hands and fangs and never let go.

As if reading her mind, he murmured, "Need to sleep. But when I get my strength back, I'll be able to give you this"—he thrust into her, still semihard—"and all the blood you can drink."

Her flesh spasmed around him at the thought.

He grinned. "Every night. I promise you." He kissed her forehead. "Rest for a while."

"But the sun will be up soon."

"I'll have you in our bed well before then."

Her body was warm and relaxed under his hands, but her mind was in a panic. Yes, she wanted to rest in an open field on top of him near the earth they'd torn apart during hours of sex. But an open field—like a parking lot or a football field or, God forbid, a plain—was a death trap. Sleeping under the stars? Avoid at all costs. She craved cover, thick canopy, a cave or some way to get lower in the earth, farther from the sun.

And still the pull to remain here was strong, conflicting with her need for self-preservation. The Lykae Instinct he'd given her was beautiful, compelling, but there was one problem.

She was a vampire.

He rolled over in sleep, tucking her into his side. He put his knee over her to pull her close and then crooked his arm around her head. Protectively. All around her. Better. Maybe just surrender.

"Mine," he growled softly. "Missed you."

Yes. Apparently she'd missed him, too.

Surrender. Trust him. Her eyelids drifted closed. Her last thought was, *Never knew day. Or night.* . . .

27

In their bed, Lachlain lay on his side, stroking the backs of his fingers from her navel up between her soft breasts and down again. He felt electricity charging the air and after last night, he now knew it was for her.

He didn't understand how she could still desire him or why she seemed so pleased with him. He'd woken with a heavy regret for his actions. She had been more than he'd ever dreamed, so beautiful, so passionate, and he'd finally claimed her. Again and again. Beneath the full moon, she'd given him unimaginable, mind-boggling pleasure—and a soul-deep feeling of connection with her.

She'd given these things, but he'd taken her virginity on the ground in the woods like the beast she thought him, shoving into her delicate flesh. He thought . . . he thought he'd made her *scream with pain*.

Then he'd marked her neck savagely. She could never see his mark—no one but a Lykae could—or feel it, but she would carry this frenzied brand forever. The Lykae would forever know upon seeing it that he had been out of his mind with lust for her. Or they would reason he'd done it to such a degree as an overtly hostile threat to other males. Both would be true.

Yet in spite of all this, the lass seemed pleased with him,

chattering happily, reaching up with a dreamy expression to caress the side of his face.

"You have no' drunk today. Are you thirsty?"

"No. For some reason, no." Then she smiled brightly. "Probably because I stole so much yesterday."

"Saucy lass." He leaned down and nuzzled her breast, making her jump. "And you know it's freely given." He grasped her chin and met her eyes. "You do know that, do you no'? Anytime you need to drink, even if I'm asleep, I want you to take."

"You really like it?"

"Like is no' the word I'd use."

"You'd heal faster if I didn't."

"Maybe, but my recovery would no' be so sweet."

Still she was insistent. "Lachlain, sometimes I feel like a ball and chain around your ankle." Before he could protest, she said, "You asked me the first time I drank if I thought you would turn me to a Lykae. Could you?"

He tensed when he saw she was serious. "Emma, you know no living being can change without dying first." The catalyst for the transformation among the vampires, the ghouls, the wraiths, among all of them, was death. "I would have to turn fully, give myself up to it, and then *kill* you, hoping that you got infected so you could be reborn." Praying that she accepted a piece of the beast into her body and that it would roar to life within her—but not too strongly. "And if you survived, you'd be locked away for years until you could control the . . . possession." Most took a decade. Some never gained control.

With her shoulders curving in protectively, miserably, she muttered, "And still it almost sounds worth it to me. I hate being a vampire. I hate being hated."

"Becoming a Lykae would no' alter that—just would alter you to a new set of enemies. We're no' exactly universally loved in the Lore. Besides, even were it done with the snap of my fingers, I would no' do it."

"You wouldn't change that I'm a vampire?" she asked, her tone disbelieving. "It would be so much simpler!"

"Bugger simple. It's made you what you are, and I would no' change a single thing about you. And besides, you're no' even wholly a vampire." Going to his knees, he scooped her up against his chest. He ran the tip of his finger over the small sharp point of her ear, then nipped it with his teeth, making her shiver. "Think you I dinna see the sky you gave me last night?"

She blushed, a shy smile coaxed forth, then buried her face in his shoulder.

If he hadn't seen it, he'd never have believed it. Crystal clear sky, moon heavy, yet lightning streaked wildly over it like a net, the light fading so slowly from each bolt. It had taken him a long moment to realize they mirrored her cries. "That's always been rumored to be a Valkyrie trait, but none of us knew for certain."

"The men who see it don't usually, well, *live*, if they're the type to tell about it."

He briefly raised his eyebrows at that, then said, "You are no vampire. You have your lightning and your eyes grow silver. You're unique to all the world."

She grimaced. "In other words—a freak."

"No, doona say that. You're just your own entity, I believe." He eased her back in his arms and the corners of his lips quirked up. "You're my wee halfling."

She punched his shoulder.

"And I like the lightning. I'll know you're never feigning it." He kissed her, but he was grinning and she punched him again. He seemed to think this was hilarious.

"Oooh! I wish you'd never seen it!"

He gave her a lewd smirk. "And if I'm outside and feel a charge in the air, I'll know to come running to you. You'll have me trained in a day." He was clearly thinking of all the scenarios. "I'm glad we live so far from towns."

We live.

He frowned. "But you were in a coven. Everyone would know if late one night you brought yourself to come. No' a lot of privacy."

He spoke so bluntly—he was so aggravating! Face back against his chest, she snapped, "I didn't have to worry about that!"

"What do you mean? You never saw even when you touched yourself?"

She gasped, glad he couldn't see her face. But of course, he leaned her back, not letting her look away. "No, Emma. I want to know. I need to understand everything about you."

She was secretive, shy. Those damn voices were insisting she *share*.

"Lightning is constant over the manor—any marked emotion triggers it, and so many live there. And anyway, before last night, I've never, um, well"—she struggled with the word—"come."

His eyes widened, and she could tell he was . . . delighted.

"It was very distressing for me."

"I doona understand."

"I've heard that the most twisted vampires have subjugated that need. Blood is all they desire, and those are the ones that decimate villages and drink to kill with such greed. . . ." She stared past him. "To not be able to was terrifying for me. Every day I feared I would be like them."

"No' able to." He brushed her hair back from her forehead. "I dinna know. I thought you had some kind of Valkyrie control over yourself . . . I dinna know it was involuntary."

She must be using a gallon of blood blushing tonight.

"It's no' surprising you could no'."

She looked at him with hurt.

"No, no, if you were young and dinna know how and then it dinna happen . . . you would start to feel pressure each time."

She nodded, stunned he saw so much. That was exactly what had happened.

"You will never be like those vampires. Emma, you are nothing like them."

"How can you be so certain?"

"You are kind and gentle. You feel compassion. I would no' want you so strongly if I dinna know you are these things."

"But the Instinct *forces* you to want me. You said before that you *had* to keep me with you."

"Is that what you think?" He cupped her face. "The Instinct *guides* me to what I want and need. It directed me to the one woman I could make a life with. No matter what, it would always be you for me, but without the Instinct, I would never have recognized you as my mate because you are other. I would no' have given us a chance—and never forced you to."

"You say all of this like my mind's made up."

His expression grew grave, his eyes bleak. "Is it no'?"

"Well, what if it wasn't?"

He palmed the back of her neck, his eyes flickering blue. "You canna speak lightly of this."

"Has it never happened?" she whispered.

"Aye. Bowen."

She wriggled from his grasp, curling up against the headboard. "I thought you said his mate died."

"She did. As she ran from him."

"Oh, my God. What did he do?"

"He became void of feeling, more a walking corpse than Demestriu even. You would doom me to that."

"But if you want to build a life with me, mine involves my family. You said you'd take me there. Why not now? Just get it over with."

"I have to do something first."

"You're going to get revenge, aren't you?"

"Aye."

"It's that important to you?"

"I canna be right without it."

"What Demestriu did to you must've been awful."

A muscle ticked in his cheek. "I will no' tell you, so doona play to find out."

"You always want me to tell you my secrets, but you won't share one that affects both of us."

"I will never share this."

Giving him her side, she hugged her legs tighter to her chest. "You want your revenge more than you want me."

"I will no' be what you need until I set this right."

"People who go after Demestriu don't come back."

"I did," he said smugly, with all his considerable arrogance.

Could he be lucky twice? He couldn't *not* come back. "So, do you plan to leave me here when you go mete out your retribution?"

"Aye, I would trust your safety only to my brother Garreth."

"Leaving the little lady back at the keep?" She laughed, but it was a bitter sound. "Sometimes I'm stunned by what a time capsule you are." He frowned, obviously not understanding her. "Even if I could be convinced to kick my heels up here, this plan has a flaw. The coven is busy with their own difficulties, but there's only so much time before they will come for me. Or worse."

"What do you mean, or worse?"

"They'll find a way to hurt you. Find a weakness and exploit it *like a scourge*. They just won't stop. Isn't there a group of Lykae living in the next parish over? My aunt, the one I love best in the world, could attack them with a viciousness that would stagger you."

He ground his teeth. "You know what bothers me most about what you said? I should be the one you love best in the world. *Me.*"

She gasped at the words and the surprise feeling that flashed through her all the way to her toes.

"And of the other, if anyone in my clan is weak enough to be captured or killed by wee fey . . . women, then they needed to be culled from the pack anyway."

That statement brought her crash-landing back into the conversation. "They are small and fey *looking*. They also kill vampires regularly. My aunt Kaderin has destroyed more than four hundred of them."

His lips curled. "An auntie tells you tales."

"There's proof."

"Did they sign a paper right before she worked their heads off?"

She sighed, and when she didn't answer, he leaned forward and squeezed her foot. "When Kaderin kills, she snaps out a fang—to be strung with the others. The line runs the length of her room."

"All you're doing is endearing her to me. Remember, I'll see every one of them dead."

"How can you say that when I am one? Or part of one. Whatever you want to call it! One of them is my father." He opened his mouth to speak, but she said, "You can't spare him only. Because I don't know who he was . . . or is. That's why I was in Paris searching for information."

"What of your mother?"

"I know more about what she was doing a thousand years ago than I do about when she was pregnant with me. We do know that she lived in Paris for some time with my father. Just the fact that I insisted on traveling alone should tell you how important it was to me."

"Then I will help you. When I return and after you see your family, we will solve this."

He was so assured it would be done. *So says the king.*

"What was your mother's name? I know the names of about twenty or so Valkyrie. Even know some legends told around a fire. Was she another bloodthirsty witch like Furie? Does she have a trailing name like Myst the Coveted or Daniela the Ice Maiden? The beheader, perhaps? The castrator?"

She sighed, weary of this. "Her name was Helen. Just Helen."

"I never heard of her." He grew quiet, then said, "And your last name? Troy? At least your aunts have a sense of humor."

Her gaze flickered over his face.

"Oh, no. No' going to believe that one. Helen of Troy was

human at best. Most likely a myth or a character in a play."

She shook her head. "Nope. She was Helen of Troy by way of the country of Lydia. She's no more a myth than my aunt Atalanta in New Zealand or my aunt Mina, of Dracula legend, in Seattle. They came first. The warped stories come after."

"But . . . Helen? At least that explains your looks," he muttered, clearly shocked, then frowned. "Why in the hell would she stoop to a vampire?"

She flinched. "Listen to your disgust. Stoop to *my father*, you mean." She grasped her forehead with her fingers. "What if he is Demestriu? Have you ever thought about that?"

"Demestriu? I know that is no' the case. I will help you find your father—you will have your questions answered. I vow it. But you are no' his."

"How can you be so sure?"

"You're gentle and beautiful and *sane*. His issue would be like him." His eyes grew blue. "Malevolent, filthy parasites that belong in hell."

A chill crept up her spine. To hate so *deeply* . . . it would have to spill over to *any* vampire. "We're kidding ourselves, Lachlain. This will never work between us," she said, in a tone that even she recognized was utterly defeated.

His brows drew together at her words as if astounded she felt that way. But how could he be?

"Yes, it will. We've trials to overcome, but *they will be overcome*."

When he said it like that, when she couldn't sense even the minutest hint of doubt, she almost felt herself believing disparate beings like themselves could make this a go. Almost. She ventured a reassuring expression for him, but didn't think she pulled it off.

He suddenly rasped, "Christ, lass, I will no' argue with you when I've been too long to find you." He reached forward to cup her face with both hands. "Let's speak of this no more. I have something I want to show you."

He lifted her from the bed, setting her on her feet, then began leading her to the bedroom door though she was naked.

"I need to put on a nightgown!"

"No one's here."

"Lachlain! I'm not walking around willy-nilly naked. Okay?"

His lips curled as if he found her modesty endearing. "Then go put on the silk I'll soon be ripping from you. You've no respect for your clothing."

She glowered, crossed to her dresser, and chose a gown. When she turned back, she found he'd slung on a pair of jeans. She'd realized that about him—he'd begun trying to make her feel more comfortable. Of course, he still often insisted that she "stretch herself."

He led her downstairs, then past the gallery, until they approached what had to be the end of the castle. There he covered her eyes with his hands, leading her into a room that felt moist and smelled decadent and lush. When he removed his hands, she gasped. He'd taken her to an ancient solarium, but now the light it captured was the moon's, illuminating all that grew within.

"Flowers. *Blooming* flowers," she breathed, staring in disbelief. "A night garden."

Emma turned to him, bottom lip trembling. "For me?"

Always for you. All things for you. He coughed into his fist. "All your own."

"How did you know?" She ran to him, leaping up into his

arms. As she hugged him tightly—she really was getting to be a strong wee lass—she whispered her thanks in his ear, with little teasing kisses, easing the empty, feral desperation still clinging to him. He'd been stunned to realize how convinced she was that they would end.

After last night and today, he'd hoped their bond had been cemented. For his part, he was lost for her. Yet she dared envision a future without him? When she scrambled down, he reluctantly released her.

He simply had to use every means at his disposal to convince her. As she flitted back and forth among the plants, gently skimming her fingertips down the slick leaves, he wanted to convince her right then and there. When she brought one bloom to her lips and brushed it over them, closing her eyes in bliss, his gut tightened with want. He forced himself to lie back on a long chair, but felt like a voyeur as he watched her.

She crossed to a marble counter lining one of the glass walls and stood on tiptoe against it to reach the hanging plants strung above. Her short shift rose with each of her reaches, flashing him glimpses of her white thighs until he could take it no longer.

He stalked up behind her to clench her hips, and she stilled.

In a breathy voice, she asked, "You're going to make love to me again, aren't you?"

In answer, he lifted her onto the counter, tore off her shift, then pressed her naked body back into the blooms.

28

"So I'm, uh, like a queen now."

"All hail Queen Emma!" Nïx cheered. "Is your coronation the reason you couldn't call for five days?"

"Or perhaps it was being hung up on repeatedly the last time I tried?" Emma didn't mention that two days ago she had called and found Nïx wasn't lucid. "Besides, I'm serious," Emma said, shaking her nail polish bottle. The color was *I'm Not Really a Waitress* red.

"So am I. And who are your people? Hopefully not all the other vampire Valkyries, or you'll have no one to tax. Or are they the Lykae?"

"Yep, I'm like queen of the Lykae." She hopped onto the bed, then stuffed cotton between her toes. "Aren't you going to congratulate me for fulfilling my destiny?"

"Hmmm. How do you feel about it?"

At the surprise fluttering of disappointment, Emma accidentally painted a stripe on her toe. She frowned, feeling as if she should have *done* something. As it was, her fate was no more than a quirk of the same. A quirk that had made her the queen of someone great. "I went from co-ed to queen. I'd have to be happy, right?"

"Uh-huh," Nïx said in a noncommittal tone.

"So is Annika there?"

"Nope. Out working on, er, a *pet project.*"

"How's she taking this?"

"Luckily, she's up to her ears with work. Otherwise she'd be more of a wreck since 'a dog has her Emma.'"

Emma winced. "Will you not tell her that I'm here voluntarily?"

"Right. She'll believe that over the other options. A. You're delusional. B. He's terrified you into submission."

Emma exhaled, then said, "What's going on around the coven?" She hoped Nïx could talk for a while.

Since Lachlain had king stuff to do—land disputes, punishments for bad behavior, overarching improvements for the region—Emma had time, even *day* time. They'd discovered that, like Lachlain, she now needed only four or five hours of sleep in a twenty-four-hour span.

Though the nights were for them alone—each sunset they sent everyone away so they could have the run of Kinevane, literally—the days could get boring. He'd been concerned about that and had asked her if she could content herself by "buying goods via the computer." She'd batted her eyelashes up at him and answered, "I'll endeavor for you."

"You're far too far behind, Em," Nïx said. "You'll never catch up with this soap."

"Come on, gimme dish."

Nïx sighed and Emma heard her shaking her own polish. The Valkyrie loved painting their nails, since it was the only way they could semipermanently change their appearance.

Polish shaking meant Nïx was settling down for a long talk. This afternoon Lachlain was taking a break from meeting with Lykae and the Lore creatures that seemed to surround Kinevane and the village in droves, but only to read numerous abstracts on the computer. He abhorred the computer, and his big hands, which were so skilled with her, were clumsy on the keyboard. He was on his third one.

"Very well. Dish as follows. . . ." Nïx said as though put out, but Emma knew she loved to gossip. "Myst and Daniela never returned from their vampire hunt. Myst could be out tomcatting, for all we know. Now, Daniela is more of a mystery. For her to go walkabout for a while? Odd. . . . Oh! Speaking of walkabout—Kaderin's gearing up for the Talisman's Hie."

The Talisman's Hie was the equivalent of an immortal Amazing Race, with the winner garnering power for their faction in the Lore. Kaderin the Coldhearted *always* won. "I guess it's silly to ask if she's excited," Emma said. Centuries ago, Kaderin had spared a young vampire's life and lost her two sisters because of it. She'd wished to be unfeeling, to never let emotion sway her judgment, and some power had unexpectedly granted her wish, thereby blessing—or cursing—her forever.

"No symptoms of excitement. But I did find her at the window, forehead and palm pressed against it, staring out into the night. As though she had feelings. As though she *longed.*"

"I used to do that," Emma murmured. She'd yearned for more, ached for something unknown. Had it always been for Lachlain?

"But no longer. I suppose things are going well with your Lykae?"

"Nïx, I think I . . . like him." When he wasn't doing king stuff, they watched TV with him propped up at the headboard, her lying between his legs, her back to his chest. They watched soccer, which he loved. She watched the ball, everyone did, but he really, *really* watched the ball—much like he watched her legs whenever she crossed them.

He enjoyed adventure films, but he especially liked science fiction, because, as he said, "Everything in those movies gets explained as if everyone else knows as little as I do."

So she'd made him watch every *Alien* movie. Most of the goriest scenes were accompanied by his dialogue: "Ach, that's no'—that's just no' right. . . . Bloody hell, this canna be right."

"He's a bit stubborn and aggressive, but I can wiggle around that. Though I'm not planning on bringing him home for dinner anytime soon."

"Smart. There'd be all those attempts on his life. Plus, we don't eat."

Emma edged off the bed to hobble on her heels over to her polish remover. "Why hasn't Annika sent a retrieval party?"

"Now, don't feel slighted—I'm sure she will soon—but right now she's focused on finding Myst. She figures if Ivo is looking for a Valkyrie, it'd have to be Myst. Remember, she was in his dungeon only five years ago? And had that *incident* with the rebel general?"

Like Emma would ever forget. Myst herself had confided to Emma that she might as well have been caught freebasing with the ghost of Bundy.

"See," Nïx said, "other Valkyrie like the forbidden fruit as much as you do."

"Yes, but Myst stopped herself," Emma said. *Unlike my own mother.* "She got past it."

Nïx chuckled. "Just because you *slept* with the Lykae doesn't mean you can never leave him."

Emma blushed and tried to say lightly, "Yeah, yeah, I gave it up."

"So. Do you *wuv* him?"

"Shut it."

"Would you run into his arms?" Nïx asked. Her aunts believed that a Valkyrie would always know her true love when he opened his arms to her and she realized she would forever run to get within them. Emma had thought it a quaint legend, but her aunts swore by it.

"We've only been together for two weeks." The only thing she knew for certain was that he made her happy. Because of Lachlain, she could now determine that she enjoyed—in addition to getting gifts from vending machines and popping bubble wrap—showers big enough for two, stripping to his riveted gaze, drinking straight from the tap, and night-blooming flowers. Oh, and daily gifts of priceless jewels.

"Do you enjoy it there?"

"It's a sweet setup, I'll admit. For all that the maids *still* show up each day with jumbo crucifixes, jumpy movements, and eyes red from crying over the short straw that drew them vampire duty." Yesterday, she'd just stopped herself from raising her clenched hands above her head and chasing one of them around the room groaning, "I vant to suck your blood."

"If that's your only complaint. . . . Or are your memory dreams a problem? I'm assuming the ones you spoke of were Lachlain's memories."

"Yeah, I can see things from his eyes, smell scents he smelled." Just the thought of those memories made her mood turn serious. "In one dream, he was buying this gorgeous gold necklace, and when he picked it up, I felt the metal warming in my hands. I know, I know, it's crazy."

"Are they all old memories? Or do you experience what he remembers about you?"

"They all seem connected to me somehow, and yes, I've heard him thinking to himself about me."

"Nice things, I hope?"

"Very nice things. He . . . he thinks I'm *beautiful*." In her dream just today came the memory of him watching her pad into the shower one night, his eyes glued to the ribbon swaying down from the string waist of her Strumpet & Pink thong. Back and forth.

She now knew he liked her elaborate lingerie, liked that *he alone knew what was beneath her clothing*. Back and forth went the ribbon. He growled so low she didn't hear him.

She has an arse men should write sonnets to. . . .

Her toes still curled to think of that one.

"How welcome that must be for someone so irrationally insecure as you."

It was. "There's only one drawback—"

"Seeing him in the past with another woman?"

"Bingo. I think if I saw that, I'd lose it. I fear that I will see that." To know his thoughts and his pleasure as he touched another?

"You know, I never see what I truly don't want to see."

"Like the death of a Valkyrie." Nïx had never been able to. She could predict much about their charges, could often see the Valkyrie's upcoming injuries, but never to the point of death. To Cara's great despair, Nïx couldn't see Furie's fate.

"Yes. It's likely that you will never see these things because your mind knows you might not recover from it."

"I hope. Why do you think this is happening?"

"Why do you?"

"I, uh, well, the thing is that . . . I drank directly from him," she finally confessed. "I fear it's related to that."

"Emma, I've heard that all vampires can take memories from the blood, but only some can interpret them and *see* them. Looks like you just found a new talent."

"Great. Why couldn't I be good at underwater origami or something?"

"Have you told Lachlain?"

"Not just yet. But I will," Emma added in a rush. "It's not like I could *not* tell him, right?"

"Right. Now, on to a much, much more important subject. . . . Did you get the gold necklace you saw him buy?"

29

"I think your queen misses her coven," Harmann re-marked when Emma had been at Kinevane for her second week.

"Aye, I gathered as much," Lachlain said, glancing up from papers strewn all about his desk. Missing her family was a blight on her happiness, but one soon rectified. As would be her marked dread of meeting other Lykae. She'd told him she was "shooting one in three with Lykae" and "wouldn't take that to the track." They were arriving in just three days. "But what makes you say that?"

"She dragged a maid into her drawing room to play video games. Then they painted each other's toenails. Blue."

He leaned back. "How'd the girl react?"

"Scared at first, but growing more comfortable. They all are. She could actually win them over." With a proud smile, he confided, "She calls me Manny."

Lachlain grinned.

"She didn't even ask me to do impressions." Harmann frowned to himself, and muttered, "They *always* ask me to do impressions."

"Does she have everything she needs?" he asked, though he knew she was growing content. When happy, she'd sing softly, absently. Oftentimes, he heard her voice lilting up from the "lunarium," as she called it, while she tended her garden. He could almost wager she liked the jasmine better than the jewels.

"Oh, yes. She's, uh, quite the talented, efficient, and, dare I say, *aggressive* shopper."

Lachlain had noticed her purchases himself and suspected he stood a little taller now that she was filling their home with things she liked or needed, making it her own. He found it deeply satisfying to see it taking shape. Did he even pretend to know why she needed hundreds of bottles of nail polish? No, but he liked that when he kissed her wee toes, he never knew what color they'd be.

For his part, Lachlain was healing, feeling stronger every day. His leg was nearly back to normal and his power was returning. His own sense of contentment—even in light of everything that had happened—was shockingly strong. And it was all because of her.

The only blight on *his* happiness was the fact that he would soon leave her, which was unbearable in itself, but now she'd begun insisting on going with him. She'd told him that she would go and fight by his side and "not let all this considerable badassness go to waste," or she would return to her coven.

She refused to remain behind at Kinevane. He knew he could talk her from her ultimatum. Surely, she could be brought to see things logically. Yet every day as she got stronger, he was a bit less confident. If she remained resolved in this, his choices would be to give up his revenge or possibly lose her to her coven. Both were untenable, in his mind.

He and Harmann finished speaking of some other business details, and shortly after Harmann scuttled off again, Bowe rapped on the door.

"You know where the scotch is," Lachlain said.

Bowe had apparently just come from the kitchen and was licking his thumb of something sweet-smelling on his way to the bar. When he poured one for his host, Lachlain emphatically shook his head.

Bowe shrugged and lifted his own. "To creatures that are *other*."

"They do make life interesting." Lachlain realized Bowe was almost not in evident pain. "Are you relieved?"

"Aye. Spotted her tending her plants downstairs, and when I saw you'd claimed her, I was glad for you." After a swig, Bowe observed, "You marked her a bit . . . hard, did you no'?"

Lachlain scowled.

"By the way, do you know what 'heroin chic' is? She said I should be aware that it's *so* last year." When Lachlain shrugged, baffled, Bowe turned serious. "The elders want to know what happened to you. Have been pestering me."

"Aye, I understand. When they come here, I'll tell them everything. I need to anyway so we can begin this."

"You think it wise to leave her so soon?"

"No' you, too," he snapped.

"Just want it noted that leaving her behind is a risk I myself would no' take. And they've no' found Garreth anyway."

Lachlain ran a hand over his face. "I want you to go to New Orleans. Find out what the hell is going on."

"Have to check my schedule." At Lachlain's look, he said, "All right. Leaving in the morning. Now, would you like to view the latest in vampire intelligence?" He tossed a file on the desk. "Courtesy of Uilleam and Munro, who look forward to seeing you soon."

Uilleam and Munro were brothers and two of Lachlain's

oldest friends. He'd been pleased to hear they were doing well, though both still had not found their mates. Probably a good thing for Munro, since ages ago a clan seer had once predicted he would have a harridan for himself.

Lachlain scanned the file, astonished by the developments within the Horde in the last one hundred and fifty years.

Kristoff, a rebel vampire leader, had taken Mount Oblak castle, one of the five Horde strongholds. Lachlain had heard rumors of Kristoff, had heard he was Demestriu's nephew, and now members of the clan had uncovered the entire story.

Kristoff was the *rightful king* of the Horde. Just days after he'd been born, Demestriu had attempted to have him killed. Kristoff had been smuggled out of Helvita, then raised by human guardians. He'd lived among them for hundreds of years before he learned who he truly was. His first rebellion had been seventy years ago and had ended in failure.

"So the legend of the Forbearers is true?" Lachlain asked. They were not merely abstainers. The Forbearers were Kristoff's army, an army he'd been secretly *making* since antiquity.

"Aye, he's created them from humans, stalking battlefields for the bravest warriors who'd fallen, sometimes turning entire families of worthy brothers. Think of it, you're a human lying in the dark nearly slain—I'd consider that a bad day—and then a *vampire* appears, promising immortality. How many do you think really listen to the conditions of his dark offer—eternal life for eternal *fealty*?"

"What's his agenda?"

"No one in the Lore knows."

"So we canna predict if Kristoff will be worse than even Demestriu."

"Is it possible to be worse than Demestriu?"

Lachlain leaned back, mulling the possibilities. If this Kristoff had taken Oblak, then he'd want the royal seat of Helvita as well. It was possible that Kristoff could kill Demestriu for them.

Yet there was another twist. Oblak had been the hold of Ivo the Cruel, the second in command of the Horde. For centuries, he'd had his sights on Helvita and the crown, and he'd apparently survived the taking of his castle. He'd been eyeing Helvita when he had his own holding; now robbed of it, he must be aching for Helvita. Would he make a play for it, even knowing the Horde had never recognized a leader without royal blood?

Three unpredictable powers, three possibilities. Lachlain knew Ivo's vampires were stalking Valkyrie all over the world, obviously searching for one among them, but was Ivo doing Demestriu's bidding or acting alone? Would Kristoff take the offensive and seek out the target who was clearly so important to the Horde?

Though there was speculation, no one could say with certainty who this person was.

Lachlain feared he could. One or even more of these factions were searching for the last female vampire.

That night Emma lay under his arm as he slept. He held her like a vise, as if he dreamed she was leaving him. When, in fact, he was going to leave her. Uneasy, she ran one fang along his chest and lapped for comfort. He groaned softly.

After kissing the mark she'd just drawn from, she drifted into a fitful sleep full of dreams.

In one, she saw Lachlain's office from his eyes. Harmann stood at the door with a pensive expression, clipboard in hand.

Lachlain's voice rang in her head as though she were there. "There's no chance of it, Harmann. We will no' have bairns," he said.

Expeditious Harmann had wanted to make preparations for the arrival of children, because as he'd said, "If you have vampire little ones, they will need special amenities. We can't begin preparing soon enough." He appeared anxious, as though he was already behind.

Lachlain believed he and Emma would have had incredible children—*brilliant lasses with her beauty, and braw, wily lads with his temper.* He might have felt a whisper of regret, but then he pictured her upstairs sleeping in his bed. How she would sigh in contentment when he joined her, and how he could coax her to take blood from his neck in her sleep.

She'd never known this—why was he doing it?

She heard his thoughts: *Must make her stronger.*

When he watched her sleeping, he often thought, *My heart lies vulnerable outside my chest.*

Emma flinched with shame. Her weakness made him worry about her constantly, worry so much that it even made him ill sometimes. He was so strong, and she was a liability.

He hadn't told her he loved her, but his heart hurt—she felt it—with love for her, for *his Emmaline.*

Children? He would give up *anything* for her.

Could he give up his revenge? If he did, he would become a shell of himself. . . .

The dream changed. Lachlain was in a dark, foul place

that smelled of smoke and sulfur; his body was a knot of agony that she felt. He tried to stare down the two vampires, with their red, glowing eyes before him, but he could scarcely see from his own battered eyes. The vampire with the shaved head was Ivo the Cruel. The blond, tall one she knew through Lachlain's hatred was . . . *Demestriu*.

Emma's body tensed at the sight of him. Why did he seem familiar to her? Why did he stare into Lachlain's eyes as though he were seeing . . . *her?*

Then came the fire.

30

Emma raised her face to the warmth of the rising moon as it filtered through the trees. She and Lachlain sat on opposite sides of a small fire he'd built to warm her further. The breeze that wisped through the great forest of Kinevane was chilly.

She knew others would enjoy such a romantic situation—two people alone, a fire crackling in the Highlands—but she was on edge and Lachlain clearly was as well. His gaze was locked on her every movement, no doubt scrutinizing her for a hint about what she'd dreamed.

She would love a hint, too.

Near sunset, she'd shot up in bed with hot tears streaming down her face and the entire castle *quaking* under an onslaught of lightning. Face drawn with panic, Lachlain had clasped her arms, shaking her and yelling her name.

Yet she didn't remember the dream. Nïx had told her that people couldn't remember what they couldn't handle. So what had been so bad that Emma had almost toppled a castle with lightning, then wiped it from her memory? All night, she hadn't been able to shake an underlying feeling of dread. Just how heavy was this other shoe she sensed was about to fall?

"What do you think of that makes your expression so serious?" he asked.

"The future."

"Why no' relax and enjoy the present?"

"As soon as you let go of the past," she countered.

He exhaled wearily and leaned back against a tree. "You ken I canna do that. Can we no' speak of something else?"

"I know you won't speak of the . . . torture. But how did Demestriu come to capture you in the first place?"

"Demestriu faced my father in the last Accession and slew him. My younger brother Heath could no' handle the rage he carried. He obsessed on the fact that Demestriu took our father's life—and then stooped to steal his ring, which had been passed down since metal was first forged. Heath told us he'd rather die than feel that way. He set out for Demestriu's head and that damned ring, uncaring if we followed or aided him."

"He wasn't scared? To face him alone?"

"Emma, I believe in times of adversity there's a line that is sometimes drawn, a line that separates your old life from your new. You cross the line, you'll never be the same. Heath's hatred made him cross the line, and he could never go back. He'd sealed his fate to one of two outcomes: Kill Demestriu, or die trying."

His voice went low. "I searched everywhere for him, but Helvita is hidden mystically, like Kinevane is. I used everything I'd ever learned about tracking, and I believe I got close. That's when they ambushed me." His eyes were faraway. "Like a nest of vipers they rose up, attacking, then tracing, so I could no' retaliate. There were too many." He ran a hand over his face. "I later learned that they had no' taken Heath alive."

"Oh, Lachlain, I'm so sorry." She sidled over to kneel beside his outstretched legs.

"It's the way of war, I'm afraid," he said, tucking her hair behind her ear. "I'd lost two brothers before Heath."

How much pain he'd endured, most of it at the hands of Demestriu. "I've never lost anyone I've known. Except Furie. But I can't believe she's dead."

He stared past her to peer into the fire.

"What, Lachlain?"

"She might wish it so," he finally said, but before she could speak, he asked, "Is Furie the one who burned your hand?"

She gasped, staring down at it when he cradled it in his own. "How did you know someone burned it?"

He ran his fingertips over the back. "It seemed to explain the pattern of scarring."

"When I was three, I almost ran into the sun." Emma supposed she hadn't learned her lesson as well as she'd thought. Every day here, she secretly returned to a hidden shaft of light and exposed her skin to it. Did she plan to book a cruise to St. Tropez anytime soon? No, but each time she could withstand it longer, and maybe in a hundred years she could walk in the twilight with him. "Furie ordered it done."

His face turned hard. "They could no' have found another means to teach you? The day a child is hurt so in this clan will be a day of reckoning."

Emma flushed, embarrassed. "Lachlain, the Valkyrie are . . . different. Violence doesn't affect them like others, and their beliefs are not like yours. Power and fighting are what they revere." She left out shopping, suspecting it might detract from the point she was trying to make.

"Then why are you so gentle, lass?"

She bit her lip, wondering why she kept letting him think she still was. No longer. Tonight she would tell him about the dreams, and of her new decision. . . .

"Lachlain, if you leave on your quest without me, then know that I'm going to resume mine."

He ran his hand over his face. "I thought you wanted to go to your coven."

"I've realized I don't have to think of my life in terms of either the Valkyrie or you. I began something and I want to see it done."

"Never, Emma." His eyes flashed blue. "There is no way in hell you'll return to Paris—to search out a *vampire*—when I am gone."

She raised her eyebrows. "Seems like you won't be here to have a say."

He grabbed her arm and pulled her to him. "No, I will no'. So I'll do what men did with their women in times past. Before I go, I will lock you away until I return for you."

Her lips parted. He was . . . *serious?* The time capsule was deadly serious. Two weeks ago, she would have made excuses for his behavior and placed herself in his shoes. She would have convinced herself that he'd been through so much and deserved some latitude.

Now, she cast him the look his words deserved, twisted from his arms to stand, then walked away.

Lachlain stared long after she'd gone, debating whether he should go to her. He sometimes felt like he crowded her, overwhelmed her even, and decided to let her be alone now.

That left him—and the fire. Though he was improving,

he was still uneasy every time he was near one. She could never know this. And so she could never understand why he couldn't allow Demestriu to live—

A loud groaning sounded. He leapt to his feet, every muscle tensed. The unfamiliar sound echoed again from miles away.

He stood, head cocked, trying to make it out. Then . . . realization.

Like a shot, he sprinted down the path, spying her just ahead.

"Lachlain!" she cried when he swooped her into his arms before racing for the castle. He was dragging her into their room minutes later.

"Stay in here!" He charged across the room, retrieving his sword. "Doona come out for any reason! Promise me."

Some being trespassed on the grounds of Kinevane—and in a fit of groaning metal and screams had somehow taken down the massive gate to do it.

If it got past him . . .

"But, Lachlain—"

"Goddamn it, Emma. Stay here." When she still protested, he snapped, "Did it ever occur to you that on occasion you'd be *right* to be afraid?"

He slammed the door on her shocked face, then tore off to the front entrance. There he stood tensed, waiting, clutching his sword—

The front door to Kinevane Castle was kicked down for the first time in history.

He looked at the kicker—a blond woman with glowing skin and pointed ears. He glanced at the fallen door, then back at her.

"Pilates," she explained with a shrug.

"Let me guess. Regin?"

When she smirked, another Valkyrie passed in front of her, marching up to him, raking her gaze over him. *"Hubba, hubba,"* she growled with a wink. "Emma caught herself a wolf." Her eyes zeroed in on his neck where Emma had drunk earlier, and she tilted her head. "Hmmm. You wear her bite like a badge you've earned."

"And you must be the soothsayer—"

"I prefer predeterminationally abled, thank you." Her hand shot out, ripping a button from his shirt, so fast it was a blur. She'd taken the one closest to his heart, and for a moment her face turned very cold. She'd made a point—she could have gone for his heart.

Then she opened her hand and gasped in surprise. "A button!" She smiled delightedly. "You can never have enough of these!"

"How did you find this place?" he demanded of Regin.

"A phone tap, satellite imaging, and a psychic," she said, then immediately frowned. "How do *you* find places?"

"And the barrier?"

"That was some serious Celtic cujo mojo." She jerked a thumb over her shoulder at their car. "But we also packed the most powerful witch we know, just in case." A nondescript woman waved brightly from the front seat.

"Enough of this." He stalked toward Regin. "You'll be leaving our home. Now." He raised his sword, but a blur swept past him. He twisted around and found another one perched on the grandfather clock, having landed so gracefully that the chains were undisturbed. She had a bow pulled taut, an arrow trained on him. Lucia.

Didn't matter. He wanted these creatures gone—they'd come here with one objective. He charged the door. An arrow tore through his sword arm like a bullet, exited with a rip, then buried itself a foot into the stone wall.

Severed tendons and muscles in his arm made his hand go limp. The sword clattered to the ground. Blood seeped down to his wrist. He wheeled around and found her with three arrows notched at once, bow horizontal, aiming for his neck. To take off his head.

Regin said, "You know why we're here. So don't make this get ugly."

Brows drawn, he followed her gaze down until he saw a razor-sharp sword inching up between his legs. Another Valkyrie that he'd never even seen enter wielded it from the shadows.

"Better hope Kaderin the Coldhearted doesn't sneeze with her sword like that," Nïx said with a chuckle. "Kitty-Kad, do you feel allergyish? I dunno, you look twitchy to me."

Lachlain swallowed, then chanced a glance over his shoulder. This Kaderin's eyes were blank, no feeling—only pure intent.

Lachlain had known they were vicious, but to see it, to feel it with an arrow through his arm and a sword tucked against him . . .

He would never let Emma near them again.

Just then, Cassandra crossed over the flattened door, warily eyeing the Valkyrie.

Lachlain snapped at her, "Why are you here now?"

"I heard talk of these . . . creatures cruising through the village, pumping bass and whistling at men on the street, before turning for the castle. Saw the gate *mangled* and thought you might need some help. . . ." She trailed off, eyes widening at the sword.

Regin said, "Where is she, Lachlain?"

Nïx added, "We're not leaving without her. So unless you want permanent houseguests of the destructive sort, just hand her over."

"Never. You're never to see her again."

"A lot of nerve saying that when you're about to bloody Kaderin's sword," Regin said with a smirk. Then her ears twitched and her voice suddenly turned saccharine. "But what do you mean, you don't ever want us to see her again?"

"Never. I doona know how she became what she is after growing up in your vicious coven, but you'll no' get a second chance to twist her."

Regin visibly relaxed at his words. Lucia dropped down and strode to the door, casually, as if she hadn't just *shot* him and as if she weren't mere feet from a Lykae itching for a kill and two seconds from turning.

"Lachlain?" Emma murmured from the stairs. He twisted his head around, saw her brows drawn. They'd wanted him to repeat his decree for her benefit. "Had you always planned to keep me from my family?"

"No, no' until I met them," Lachlain explained, as though that made it better.

She surveyed the room, then her aunts. Just what had they done since that door had been kicked down? She could only imagine—

And what the hell was Cass doing here?

Emma spotted Kaderin behind Lachlain, sword in place. "Kaderin," she murmured. "Annika sent you?" Kaderin was a deadly, skilled, and *unfeeling* assassin. A perfect killing machine, she didn't get dispatched on recovery missions. "Lower your sword, Kaderin."

Regin said, "Come down, Em, and nobody has to get hurt."

"Kad, lower it!"

Regin reluctantly nodded, and Kaderin retreated into the shadows. Lachlain immediately strode up the stairs, reaching for Emma, but she gave his hand a withering glare and shook him off. He appeared dumbfounded.

Regin cast Emma a guilty smile. "Annika just wants you away from him, Em."

Emma marched down the stairs to point a finger in Regin's face. "So, Lachlain plans to forbid me from seeing you, and Annika plans to kill the man I'm sleeping with without even asking me if this is a good idea?" These people were treating her like the old Emma, with everyone jockeying for the right to control her. And that simply did not apply any longer. "I wonder what *I* plan."

"Tell us!" Nïx cried breathlessly.

Emma glared at Nïx. *Rhetorical, here!* She had no idea what she planned—

"*He seeks you,*" a vampire intoned from the doorstep, his eyes on her.

Emma's lips parted. The Valkyrie did not believe in coincidence, only in fate. And sometimes fate didn't even bother being subtle.

Lachlain leapt for the vampire just as others appeared. Cass ran headlong into the fight beside him. Emma watched it all as though in slow motion, feeling the vampire's red eyes returning to her again and again.

Suddenly her back met the floor, her legs kicked out from under her.

Lachlain had tripped her? "*Get back, Emma!*" he roared, shoving her away, sending her flying far across the polished floor.

As she glanced up through the melee, she saw that the vampires kept their gazes trained on her.

Here for her. What if her father knew about her? Had sent them to find her?

But who . . . ?

Suddenly, dreams—nightmares—seeped into reality. Lachlain's memories.

An image of a golden-haired man flashed into her mind. Demestriu. Casually watching Lachlain suffer.

Everyone always says my features are my mother's, but Helen had black hair, black as sable, and dark eyes. The man in the dream is blond, with his sword sheath on his right, indicating he's left-handed.

Emma was a southpaw herself.

No. No way.

Lightning whipped outside. Fatalistic. That was it, she was simply being fatalistic, since this was the absolute worst scenario that could be. Her father couldn't have tortured Lachlain.

Like an acid bath, Lachlain's memory of the fire washed over her—torture that was now her own forever. His rage boiled within her, and she gave herself up to it—just as he had—to get through the pain. . . .

She shuddered, couldn't stifle a whimper. Her thoughts grew dim, distant. . . . She couldn't separate reality from nightmares. Like the way she somehow knew that, deep down in Lachlain's mind, utterly unacknowledged by him was a new suspicion that she was Demestriu's. . . .

She recognized the monster for what he was. Father. Shaking, still on the floor, she gaped at her aunts fighting so valiantly, so perfectly, with all their innate grace and ferocity. Demestriu had taken their queen from them.

Filthy parasite.

Lightning rained down again in a crowded volley.

Fighting all around, and she was frozen. Not with a fear of dying, but with grief and pain. Grief that what she'd wanted so badly—a life with Lachlain, and the love of her coven—was being threatened by the blood running, now itching like poison, in her veins.

Watching these heroic warriors fighting to protect her, when they had no idea what she really was, was killing her. She was unworthy of all of them.

A vampire slumped to the ground. Laughing in delight, Nïx flew on top of him, stabbing her knees into his back, and snatched his hair to lift his head, baring his throat. Poised for her deathblow. The vampire caught sight of Emma. He reached out.

She felt unclean; her veins burned. Unworthy.

But I could make it right. Or at least better.

Nïx caught her gaze across the floor. Winked at her.

Clarity.

"Will I die?" Emma whispered.

"Do you care?" Nïx countered, her words as clear in Emma's ears as if they were right next to each other.

"He seeks *you*," the thing gasped, reaching for her.

"I seek him, too." Emma wanted to take his hand, but he was so far away— Suddenly, she found herself mere feet from him.

Dizzy. . . . Had she traced? Like a vampire. For the first time . . . ?

Nïx slowly raised her blade, and Emma crawled forward.

She heard Lachlain inhale sharply, knew he'd spotted her. "Emma," he rasped, diving for her, then bellowed, *"Goddamn it, Emma, no!"*

Too late. A line had been drawn, just as with Heath. No, not drawn—it'd been seared into her mind. Lightning shot down to punctuate her decision. That which she had been born to do.

She stretched out her hand. Met eyes with the vampire. *You have no idea what you're dragging home.*

Lachlain roared with fury as that thing—the last one left alive—took Emma. He couldn't comprehend it. She had sought him out?

He clenched Nïx's shoulders. "Why did you hesitate? I saw you hesitate!" He shook her until her head lolled, while she grinned and said, "Wheeee!"

"Where the fuck have they taken her?" he thundered.

One of the Valkyrie punted his bad leg, buckling it, making him release Nïx.

Cass raised her sword again. "You let them in!" she snapped to Regin. "Left Kinevane unguarded."

Regin tilted her head in Lachlain's direction. "He stole a daughter from her foster mother and kept her from the protection of our family."

"Turnabout's a bitch," Kaderin added, dropping down to collect fangs from the severed heads as trophies.

"They fucking have her!" He punched the wall. *"How can you be so calm?"*

"I can't feel raw emotion, and they won't indulge in the luxury of feeling sorrow," Kaderin explained. "Sorrow weakens the entire collective. It will weaken Emma herself. And we won't borrow trouble."

Lachlain shook with rage, about to turn, about to kill them all—

Suddenly, some hideous noise erupted. Kaderin put her

bloody fangs away and dug in her pocket, pulling out a phone. "Crazy Frog," she hissed as she flipped it open. "Regin, you are a fiend."

Regin shrugged as Lachlain grappled with confusion. Nïx yawned loudly, muttering, "This is a rerun."

"No," Kaderin said into the phone. "She went voluntarily with the vampires." She related this information as if she were reciting a weather report, even over the growing shrieks Lachlain heard from the phone.

Lachlain's hand shot out, yanking the phone away from her. At least someone reacted as they should.

Annika. *"What's happened to her?"* she screamed in fury. "Dog, you will beg for death!"

"Why would she go with them?" he bellowed back. "Goddamn it, tell me how to get to her!"

As Annika screeched on the phone, Kaderin gave him a thumbs-up sign and mouthed, "Keep it." Then, as he and Cass gaped, the four Valkyrie turned for their car and strolled from the castle as if they'd come over to drop off a basket of scones. He loped after them.

The bow shot up once more.

"Shoot him if he follows," Nïx ordered.

"Shoot me full of them, then," he grated.

Nïx turned to him. "We don't know anything to help you, and I think you're about to need your strength, huh?" To the three others, she said, "I *told* you, we are *not* bringing her back on this trip."

And then they were gone.

"Where the fuck did that vampire take her?" he snapped into the phone.

"I—don't—know!"

"Your Valkyrie let them into our home—"

"That's not Emma's home. *This* is her home!"

"No, no longer. I vow to you, witch, that when I find her, I'll never let her near you again."

"You will find her, won't you? You're a hunter who'll be after your most prized possession. I could ask for no better." She sounded calm now, even serene. He could *hear* her sneering. "Yes, you go find her, and then I'll tell you what. When you bring her here safe and sound, I'll scratch my new pet behind his ears instead of peeling him."

"What are you speaking of, woman?"

Her voice was pure evil. "Your brother's neck is beneath my boot right now. Garreth for Emma."

The line went dead.

31

Emma felt like an offering on a dark altar.

The vampire had traced her into a dim corridor just outside a heavy wooden door. He unlocked the door and opened it, then shoved her into a room with such force that she tripped to the cold stone floor. Lightheaded from his tracing, she'd lain where she'd fallen—at the foot of a towering arched window reaching at least twenty feet high. Its glass was stained obsidian, with gold inlays gracefully twisted into symbols of the black arts.

The vampire had abandoned her with only the warning, "Do not try to escape. No one traces into or out of his rooms but him," then he locked the door once more.

She shivered, dragging her eyes from the window, and rose dizzily to her knees to examine the room. A study, a working one—with papers atop the desk—though it was dank and redolent of the scent of old blood.

Screams sounded from somewhere in the bowels of the castle, and she shot to her feet, turning in wary circles. What in the hell had she done?

Before regret could overwhelm her, memories of the fire returned. The scene was as clear as if she'd been there.

Lachlain's lungs had filled with fire, and he'd reacted more violently to that than even the skin burning from his legs as the fire grew. He'd never given them the pleasure of hearing him roar with pain. Not the first time he died, or the second, or any other time over the next fifteen decades when he'd burned and woken into a fresh hell. His hatred was the only thing that kept him remotely sane, and he'd clung to it.

He clung to it when the fires abated. He clung to it when he realized his leg alone kept him from her, and when he forced himself to snap the bone, and then when he . . . let the beast rise up so he could . . .

She hung her head and retched. He'd clung to it until he'd found her—the one he'd sensed on the surface, the one who was supposed to *save* him. . . .

Then he'd fought it for their sake.

She wondered how he hadn't killed her, how he hadn't given in to the confusion and hate that mixed with his need to claim her and find oblivion. How had he *not* taken her savagely when his skin still burned?

He hadn't wanted her to know about his torture, and she understood why. She'd known she would have to tell him about the dream memories, but what could she say about this? That she had an apocalyptic case of TMI? That she finally knew the nature of his torture, and she was certain it was the worst any being had ever been subjected to?

How to tell him that her father had done it to him?

Malevolent, filthy parasites that belong in hell.

She almost threw up, but choked it back. She didn't think Lachlain could hate her for this, but it would burn, seethe like a tiny drop of acid on the skin. Always wearing away. Her father had destroyed almost his entire family, a family that he'd clearly loved.

Now that she knew everything Lachlain had been through, knew his thoughts, his vows for retribution, hot shame suffused her for fighting him about his revenge.

Especially now that she was about to take it from him forever.

Her resolve was, well, resolved. As she lay on Kinevane's cool floor amid all that carnage, her mind had raced. Her bitter shame had been beaten down by the notorious Valkyrie pride and sense of honor that had *finally* roiled within her. *Unworthy. Frightened. Weak.* Emma the Meek. No longer.

Because—and here was the baffling thing—now that her emotions had stabilized and she could think more clearly, she *would still do the same thing.*

It frightened her how determined she was about this. Yes, the old Emma still lurked in the background of her mind, squeaking about how stupid this was: *Hey, how do you like my new meat pants? Now, where is that tiger cage?*

True, it was foolhardy.

But the new Emma knew she wasn't too stupid to live; she was too ashamed to care. She needed to do this to make things right with her coven and with Lachlain.

Lachlain. The bighearted king she had fallen helplessly for. And for him, she'd fight relentlessly.

Her father, her burden. She'd come to slay Demestriu.

For the hellish hour it took Harmann to drive him to the private airport, Lachlain fought to keep from turning, never quite able to pull back from the razor-thin boundary—or to reason as clearly as he needed to. Vampires had Emma, and the Valkyrie had Garreth.

The curse of the Lykae. The strength and ferocity that they carried into battle was a detriment in all other scenarios, and the more they cared for something, the more the beast wanted to rise up to protect it.

He was gambling that they'd taken Emma to Helvita, back to Demestriu, though it could have been to Ivo or even this Kristoff. He'd dispatched Cass to find Uilleam and Munro and as many Lykae as they could readily assemble to travel to Kristoff's castle. Lachlain knew she would do it. She'd taken one look at his eyes after Emma was gone and finally understood.

But what if Lachlain was wrong about where they'd taken her? What if he couldn't find Helvita this time either? He couldn't seem to think now that the full situation had hit him.

The full situation. Garreth had been taken, too. Somehow captured. Somehow? After palpable demonstrations of Lucia's skill, Regin's strength, Nïx's speed, and Kaderin's single-minded malice, Lachlain knew he'd underestimated an enemy.

"They have Garreth," he'd told Bowe, calling from the car as Harmann sped down foggy Scottish roads. "Get him back."

"Bloody hell. It isn't as easy as that, Lachlain."

It was that easy. Lachlain wanted Garreth free. Bowe was a powerful Lykae known for his ruthlessness. *"Free—him,"* he'd growled.

"We canna. I dinna want to tell you this, but they have goddamned *wraiths* guarding them."

Garreth, last of his blood family, behind the guard of an ancient scourge, in the hands of an insane, vicious being.

And . . . Emma had left him.

Purposely left him. Made the conscious effort to forsake him, and crawled to a vampire's fucking outstretched hand to do it.

Haze.

No, need to fight it. Again and again he struggled to examine everything he knew about her, looking for a clue as to why she would do this.

Seventy years old. College. She'd been hunted by the vampires. It was her they wanted all along. For what purpose? Which faction? Annika's her foster mother. Emma's blood mother was of Lydian descent, she said. Helen. That's where she got her looks from.

As they neared the airport, the sun rose. Lachlain roared with frustration, hating it, wanting never to see it rise again. She was out there without him to protect her, could be staked to a field at this moment. His palms were bloodied from his claws digging into them, his arm wound unchecked.

Think! Replay anything he'd learned about her. *Seventy years old. College. . . .*

He frowned. He'd met Lydian women before. They had pale skin like Emma's, but dark, dark hair and eyes. Emma was fair-haired, her eyes blue.

Then her father would be as well—

Lachlain froze. No.

Not possible.

"What if he's my father?" Emma had asked.

And Lachlain had answered . . . he'd answered that Demestriu's issue would be *malevolent, filthy parasites.*

No.

Even if his mind could assimilate that she was the daughter of Demestriu, Lachlain couldn't accept that she was in his power right now, could have been pushed there by his careless words.

Pushed to go to Helvita, to Demestriu, who would tear his own daughter limb from limb while she begged for death, and never blink his red eyes.

If Lachlain didn't reach her quickly . . . Now he had to not merely find Helvita, but find it fast. He'd hunted and tracked through that region of Russia with no success. He might have gotten close to it last time, just before he'd been discovered and beaten bloody by a dozen tracing vampires.

He would fly to Russia and get that close again—

The memory arose of her beneath him just yesterday when her head had thrashed on her pillow, sending him awash in the exquisite scent of her hair. He would never forget her scent, had taken it into him forever from the first night he recognized her. The memory came as a reminder for him to *use* it.

He could find her. He had before. Put him anywhere in her vicinity, and he could track her straight to Helvita.

She was meant to be found by him.

A deep voice in the shadows said, "So let's see what my general's been after."

Her eyes followed the direction of the sound. She knew she'd been alone as of a second ago, yet now she spied him sitting behind his large desk even before he lit a lamp. The light glinted off red eyes.

Tension seemed to radiate from him, and he stared at her as if seeing a ghost.

She'd been forced to wait alone here in this eerie castle, with the screams from below erupting every so often, until hours after sunup. In that time, she'd gone through a type of catharsis, her thoughts calming, her resolve sharpening till crystalline. She felt the way she imagined her aunts did before a great battle. Now she waited patiently to end this one way or another, and knew only one of them would leave this room alive.

Demestriu summoned a guard. "Do not let Ivo in when he returns," he commanded the vampire. "Not for any reason. Do not speak of finding her. If you do, I'll keep you years without viscera."

Well. She'd grown up hearing the threats so popular among the Lore—the ones that began with *if this action does or doesn't occur,* and ended with *then you'll suffer this consequence*—but this guy was good.

Demestriu traced to the door to bolt it behind the guard.

So . . . no one can trace in or out, and now no one can walk out either?

When Demestriu returned to his seat, any surprise he might have shown was gone. He studied her with dispassion. "Your face is exactly like your mother's."

"Thank you. My aunts have often said so."

"I knew Ivo was up to something. Knew he searched and that he'd lost dozens of our soldiers—three in Scotland alone. So I thought to take from him whatever he'd gotten close to. I didn't expect him to be after my daughter."

"What's this guy want with me?" she asked, though she had a pretty good idea—now that she'd realized her freaking *pedigree.*

"Ivo's spent centuries plotting, eyeing my crown. But he knows that the one thing the Horde holds sacred is its bloodlines. He knows he can't rule without a royal tie, and he just happened to find one. In my daughter."

"So he thought he would just kill you off and force me to marry him?"

"Precisely." A considering pause, then he asked, "Why have you never sought me out before this?"

"I just learned you were my father about eight hours ago."

Some emotion flickered in his eyes, but was so fleeting she thought she'd imagined it. "Your mother . . . didn't tell you?"

"I never knew her. She died right after I was born."

"So soon?" he asked in a low voice, as if to himself.

"I was searching for information about my father—you—in Paris," she said, irrationally trying to make him feel better.

"I lived there with your mother. Above the catacombs."

Any impulse to kindness vanished at the mention of the catacombs from which Lachlain had clawed his way free.

"Look at your eyes fire silver, just like hers." His red gaze flickered over her appraisingly for the first time.

Uncomfortable silence. She glanced around, struggling to remember the training Annika and Regin had forced on her. Beating up Cassandra was one thing, but this was a monster before her.

She frowned. *If he's a monster, then I'm a monster, too.*

Hey, I don't have to live. She'd known only one of them was leaving this room. Now she knew that was at the most.

Weapons on the walls. Crossed swords hanging upside down. The ones in the sheaths were actually more susceptible to rust. Rust meant weakness. *Gotta get the one without the sheath.*

"Sit." When she reluctantly did so, he held up a pitcher of blood. "Drink?"

She shook her head. "Trying to watch my points."

He gave her a disgusted look. "You speak like a human."

"If I had a dollar . . ." she sighed.

"Perhaps you just drank from the Lykae you'd been with?"

Even if she could, she saw no reason to deny it, and put her shoulders back. "I did."

He raised his eyebrows and regarded her with new interest. "Even I refused to take from an immortal like him."

"Why?" she asked, leaning forward, curiosity ruling her now. "That was the one instruction my mother gave my aunts when she sent me to them—that I never drink straight from a source."

He stared into his goblet of blood. "When you drink some-one to death, you take everything from them—down to the bottom of their soul. Do it enough, and soon the pit of a soul can be quite literal. You can taste it. Your heart turns black and your eyes redden with rage. It's a poison, and we crave it."

"But drinking from a source and killing are two different things. Why wouldn't I be warned instead not to kill?" This was so surreal. They were sharing a conversation, asking and answering questions even with the grueling tension between them, like Dr. Lecter and Clarice in that jail scene. *Courteous and responding to courtesy* . . . "And why do I get these memories?"

"*You* have that dark talent?" He gave a short laugh that had no humor. "I've suspected it's passed down through the bloodline. I think that's what made our line kings in the first chaos of the Lore. I have it. Kristoff has it. And has given it to every human he's turned," he added with a sneer. "But you inherited it from me?" He raised his eyebrows, as if still not quite believing her. "Your mother must have feared you would. Drinking beings to death makes you mad. Drinking and seizing their memories makes you mad—and powerful."

She shrugged, not feeling *mad*. Yes, she'd almost crumbled a castle in her sleep, but . . . "I don't feel that way. Will something more happen to me?"

He looked aghast. "*The memories aren't enough?*" he said, then composed himself. "To take their blood, their life, and all that they have experienced—that is what makes a true vampire. I used to seek out immortals for their knowledge and power, but I also suffered the shadows of their minds.

For you to drink one with so many memories . . . you play with fire."

"You have *no* idea how right you are about that."

He frowned, thought for a moment, then said, "Did I put the Lykae in the catacombs?"

"He escaped," she said smugly.

"Ah, but now you remember his torment?"

She nodded slowly. One of them was about to die. Was she prolonging the conversation to learn answers to questions that had plagued her? Or to live a little longer? Why was he complying?

"Imagine ten thousand memories like that clotting your mind. Imagine experiencing your victim's death. The moments leading up to it when *you* stalk him, when he explains away a sound, saying the breeze was stirring. When he calls himself a fool because the hair on the back of his neck stands up." He gazed past her. "Some fight against believing to the end. Others look on my face and *know* what has them."

She shivered. "You suffer from that?"

"I do." He drummed his fingers on the desk, and a ring caught her attention. The crest with two wolves.

"That's Lachlain's ring." Stolen from his dead father's hand. *My father killed his.*

He studied it, red eyes vacant. "I suppose it is."

He was insane. And she knew he would talk to her like this for as long as she wanted, because she sensed that he was . . . lonely. And because he believed these were the last hours of her life. "Given the history between the Valkyrie and the Horde, how did you and Helen get together?"

His gaunt face taking on a faraway expression, he began casually, "I had her neck in my hands, about to twist her head from her body."

"How . . . romantic." *One to tell the grandkids*.

He ignored her. "Yet something stayed me. I released her, but studied her in the following months trying to discover what had made me hesitate. In time, I realized that she was my Bride. When I seized her and took her from her home, she said she saw something good in me and agreed to stay. She was right for a while, but in the end she paid with her life."

"How? How did she die?"

"I'd heard from sorrow. Over me. That's why I was surprised she succumbed so quickly."

"I don't understand."

"Your mother tried to get me to stop drinking blood not just from a living source but altogether. She even convinced me to eat like a human, joining me to make it easier although she had no need for sustenance. And then came news of you, just as I was about to lose my crown from Kristoff's first rebellion. In the battle, I reverted to my old ways. I kept my crown, but lost everything I'd gained with her. I'd succumbed again. After taking one look at my eyes, Helen fled me."

"Did you ever wonder about me?" she asked, sounding too much like she cared.

"I heard tales that you were weak and unskilled, having received the worst traits of both species. I would never have returned for you even if I thought you would survive long enough to freeze into your immortality. No, this was solely Ivo."

She gave a theatrical wince. "Yeouch." But it did actually sting a bit, a sting that was escalating toward spectacularly pissed off. "Talk about a deadbeat dad—oh, now, that was just *awful*—" She fell silent as he rose, silhouetted by the stained glass, his hair as gold as the rich inlays. He awed her. Here was her father, and he was terrifying.

He sighed, looking her over, not as though seeing a ghost or a novelty, but like he leisurely mulled an easy kill. "Little Emmaline, coming here is the last mistake you will ever make. You should have known that vampires can always cut away anything that stands between them and their prize— anything else becomes secondary. My prize is keeping my crown. You are a weakness that Ivo, or any of the others, could exploit. So you just became *incidental.*"

Hit the girl where it hurts. "When a leech like you won't have me . . . I've really got nothing left to lose." She stood and brushed her hands on her jeans. "Works out for me, anyway. I've come here to kill you."

"Have you, now?" He shouldn't look *that* amused.

His chilling smile was the last thing she saw before he disappeared, tracing. She leapt for the unsheathed sword on the wall, hearing him behind her in an instant. She dropped down, snaring the sword, but he was tracing all around her.

She attempted it herself . . . unable . . . wasting precious seconds. Then turned to what she did best—fleeing—using her agility to dodge him.

"You certainly are spry," he said, appearing in front of her. Her sword shot out like a blur, but he easily dodged it. When she struck again, he plucked the raised sword from her, tossing it clattering to the ground.

Emma's gut clenched with the stark realization of what was happening.

He was *toying* with her.

32

Alone in a great Russian forest, Lachlain stood where it had all begun fifteen decades ago. He and Harmann had landed just hours before, then set out in a truck over the rough terrain to find the location of Lachlain's capture. When the roads became impassable, Lachlain had left Harmann behind. Both of them knew that once Lachlain scented Emma, Harmann could never keep up with him.

Even after so much time, Lachlain had been drawn to the spot unerringly. But now as he circled the clearing, desperate for a hint of her, he feared his judgment had been wrong. No one had ever located Helvita. And Lachlain had been unable to save his own brother in these very woods.

His decision to take this course could end her life—

Wait. . . . *She was here.*

The first night he found her, he'd gone to his knees to scent her again. Now he raced over miles of terrain, sword sheathed at his back, heart pounding. He rushed up a steep hill, then stared out from the height.

Helvita lay just beyond him. Desolate, sinister.

Under the watch of the sun, Lachlain took a direct path there. He swiftly scaled a sheer wall, then stalked along the broken-down battlements, moving freely along the empty walk. He entertained no feeling of accomplishment for having located it at last. This was merely a first step.

He froze when he heard her voice like a faint echo, but couldn't pinpoint the source inside, couldn't make out the words. The sheer immensity of the castle was staggering, and she was in the bowels of this foul place.

He couldn't understand what had made her come here, what would drive her to do something this mad.

Had she dreamed of Demestriu? Had she had a premonition in a dream that violent night? He fought to stay cold about this, but his mate was in this hell facing the most evil—and powerful—being ever to walk the earth. She was so gentle. Was she *afraid* . . . ?

No—he couldn't think like that. He'd found her, knew she was still alive. He could save her—if he was lucid, weighing, determining *possibilities*.

There was a reason the vampires always won. And Bowe had been wrong about it. It wasn't because they could trace. The vampires always won because the Lykae couldn't rein in their beasts . . . or because they so readily surrendered to them.

Emma shot backward over his desk, just missing his outstretched claws, staring in disbelief as he slashed the massive desk in two as if ripping a piece of paper.

The wood groaned as it parted, then thudded to the ground.

He appeared behind her before she'd even comprehended that he'd traced. She lunged away, but he clawed down her side, gaining a hold on her, piercing her skin. He propped her up in front of him as easily as if she were a rag doll. The torn skin of her leg and side funneled blood from her as he placed his forearms at her neck.

To take my head.

"Good-bye, Emmaline."

He's shielding me.

She drew in a breath and screamed. The thick black glass above shattered like an explosion. Sunlight fired in. He went motionless as if stunned that he was immersed in light. She hunched into him, using his body as cover. When he tried to escape, she fought to keep him there, but even as he began to burn he was too strong. He traced them into the shadows.

To where the sword was.

She dropped down, snatched the sword, and sprang up behind him. She plunged it into his torso, nearly gagging as she carved through bone, then forced herself to twist it inside him as she'd been taught.

He fell. She yanked the sword clear, leapt over him for another blow, and found him staring up at her with utter shock.

He struggled to one knee, which scared the hell out of her, so she rammed the sword back in, through his heart, as hard as she could. The force sent him reeling to his back and planted him on the stone floor.

Pinned through the heart, he lay writhing. He wouldn't die like this. She knew she had to take off his head as well. She limped to the other sword, shaking as she drew it down, still disbelieving what had just happened, what was *about* to happen. When she returned, her face scrunched up. Blackened blood pooled all around him. She'd have to *step* through it.

His face was changing, softening, becoming less macabre. The tight planes and shadows dissipated.

He opened his eyes . . . and they were blue as the sky.

"Release me."

"Yeah, right."

"No . . . mean for you . . . to kill me."

"Why?" she cried. "Why would you say that?"

"Hunger at bay. Memories at bay. No memories of their horror of . . . *me.*"

Pounding on the door.

He bellowed, "Leave us be." Then to her, he lowered his voice to say, "Sever head. Waist. Legs. Or I can still rise. . . . Furie's mistake."

Furie? "Did you kill her?" she shrieked.

"No, tortured. She wasn't supposed to endure this long. . . ."

"Where is she?"

"Never knew. Lothaire saw to it. Head, waist, legs."

"I can't think!" She paced. By Freya, Furie did live.

"Emmaline, do it!"

"Listen, I'm doing the best I can!" He wasn't supposed to go all Darth Vader, not supposed to *direct* her how to *really, really* kill him. The head was one thing, but the waist and the legs? Had he truly become that powerful? "And your impatience is not helping the situation!"

"Your mother died of sorrow . . . because we couldn't make it stop. You can end this."

With a deep breath, she stood over him, choking up on the handle. Yes, like baseball. *Never played baseball, freak. Oh, yeah. Kaderin always holds her swords loosely, wrists fluid. I am so not Kaderin. Think like the vampires. What is standing between you and the one you love and your family? Three clean chops. Just three swings.*

The more beseeching he appeared, the harder this became. His eyes were clear, his face rid of the twisting menace from before. He didn't look evil now. Just a creature in pain. She dropped to her knees beside him, heedless of the blood. "What about some kind of, like, rehabilitation—"

"Do it, daughter." He snapped his teeth at her, sending her scrambling back. More pounding on the door. "They can't trace into my lair, but they can break down that door . . . And when they do, they will catch you and hold you for food . . . until you die of sorrow. Or Ivo will make you kill and turn you."

Oh, hell, no.

"I will feed and . . . heal. Turn again and never stop until I've killed . . . the Lykae. Slaughtered his . . . clan."

That's my clan, too. The door was bowing now, wood splintering. The Instinct whispered, *Protect it.*

"I'm really sorry to have to do this."

A shadow of a smile, then he grimaced in pain. "Emma the Unlikely . . . the killer of kings."

She raised the sword and took aim, tears pouring from her as quickly as the blood from her leg wound.

"Wait! Emmaline, the head first . . . if you please."

"Oh, my duh." She gave him a sheepish, watery grin. "Good-bye . . . Father."

"Proud."

He shut his eyes and she swung. She got through enough to knock him out, but sadly, this sword blew—so dull she had to hack three more times at his neck to sever it. Then his waist took forever. She was streaked with blood before she even reached his legs.

The Mob was dead-on to call this stuff wet-works.

Just as she finished with the last of him, the door burst open. She hissed.

Ivo. She remembered him from Lachlain's memories. She lifted her sword again. Hey, as long as she was in the neighborhood . . .

Why was he looking at her that way, red eyes glued to her? As though he *adored* her for her kill. It was chilling. He asked in an unsteady tone, *"Are you truly Emmaline?"*

When more vampires crowded the door behind him, she realized one assassination might be enough for the day. She ripped Lachlain's ring from Demestriu's finger, then put her shoulders back. Myst always said, "It's not *if* you castrate an entire Roman legion, it's if they *believe* you did. Perception is everything."

In a voice ringing with strength she didn't have, she said, "I am Emma." *Own it, own it.* "The king killer."

"I knew you would be like this." He crossed toward her. "I knew it."

She raised her sword that totally sucked as if it were Excalibur. "No closer, Ivo."

"I've searched for you, Emmaline. Searched for years, ever since I heard rumors of your existence. I want you to be my queen."

"Yeah, I get that a lot," she said, wiping her face on her sleeve. There were two options. Into their hands, or out the window into the sun. "But I've already accepted a position elsewhere."

Maybe she could trace—hadn't been able to during the fight, but damn it, she'd done it once. She could disappear before she even hit the ground outside. In theory. But she was weak from Demestriu's attack. Couldn't go to Lachlain. Blood running freely. *You only went a few feet last time—not around the world. . . .*

One for two in terms of tracing. Didn't know if she could.

About to bet the farm. . . . But when they charged, she hissed weakly and jumped.

Flying! Tracing! No . . .

Landing on her ass in a bush. Spitting leaves in the sun. She leapt up, running for cover. She closed her eyes to the pain and thought of the bayou. . . . Still thinking. Bayou! Coolness. Wet.

Her skin caught fire.

One of his eardrums had ruptured from her scream even as he fought to follow the sound. Then, in a last echo through the castle, it was gone. His heart had seemed to stop with it, but he'd sprinted on in the same direction, following the winding stairs. Lachlain remembered that Demestriu's rooms were located high in the castle, and he charged ever upward.

Now he heard only his own ragged breaths. He tried to scent her, but the odor of copious amounts of blood drowned all other smells.

At the landing of the top floor, he slowed to stalk in the shadows. The kill was imminent. He was almost at the door. He would save her, take her from this place—

He scarcely comprehended the sight. Demestriu lay butchered.

He saw Ivo lunge, reaching into a shaft of *sunlight* as though he'd dropped a treasure from the window. "No!" Ivo bellowed. "Not into the sun!" He leapt back out of the light. "Traced away!" He visibly sagged with relief as he rubbed his skin, then his blinded eyes.

Ivo turned to his two henchmen. "She lives. Now, get the video! I want to find out everything about her."

Lachlain was stunned. She couldn't have jumped into the sun. . . .

He charged into the room, diving for the window, but saw only the empty field. She had truly disappeared. His mind was in turmoil. Had she killed Demestriu? Had she traced to safety? To Kinevane?

Behind him, Lachlain heard a sword being drawn.

"Back from the dead?" Ivo asked pleasantly.

Lachlain turned in time to see Ivo glance at the door to the adjoining room, through which the others had apparently exited. To get a *video?* Lachlain had learned there were surveillance cameras that were capable of secretly filming. "You spy on your king?"

"Of course. Why ignore the benefits of the modern age?"

"But now you're alone." Lachlain bared his fangs with pleasure. "You've got to fight me on your own. No' with the help of a dozen. Unless you want to trace from me?"

Lachlain burned to rush home, but Ivo, he realized, posed a considerable threat to Emma. She might not have needed Lachlain to kill Demestriu—*she* apparently had done that—and there was no need for rescue. But seeing the fanatical look in Ivo's eyes, Lachlain knew he would never stop sending out his minions to hunt her.

Ivo raked his gaze over Lachlain's injured arm, appraising his opponent. "No, I'll stay and fight for this one," he said. "I heard you think she's yours."

"There's no doubt of it."

"She assassinated my nemesis when no one else could, and is the key to my crown." Ivo's voice was low, thrumming as though in wonder. "That means she belongs to *me*. I will find her. I don't care what it takes, I will find her again—"

"No' while I live." He gripped his sword hilt in his left hand and charged, striking at Ivo's head. Ivo blocked and their swords crossed, ringing.

Several more charges, each parried. Lachlain was out of practice, especially with his left hand. He sensed the other two returning and growled in fury, blocking a stroke from the back and slashing out with his claws, dropping one of the henchmen.

The other two put Lachlain between them. Before he could even register what had happened, Ivo traced to mere inches from Lachlain, slashing out with his sword, then tracing away. The blow ripped across Lachlain's shoulder and chest, sending him spinning to the ground.

33

Damp ivy. Oak trees. Home. She'd somehow made it.
Or at least to the grounds of Val Hall. But her skin
still smoked, and she was weak as a babe from her injuries.
How much blood had she lost? Had she made it so far just to
die at dawn?

She tried to roll over in order to crawl, but failed. The
effort made her vision go blurry. When it finally cleared,
she spied a massive, black-haired man peering down at her.
Brows drawn, he scooped her up into his arms, then began
walking up the long drive to the manor. Emma thought
this was the drive. She could also be mistaken that it was a
man.

"Easy, girl. I know you are Emmaline. Your aunts have
been worried." Deep voice. Strange accent. European and
moneyed. "I am Nikolai Wroth."

Why did that name sound so familiar? She squinted up at
him. "You are a friend of my aunts?" she said, her voice
sounding faint.

"With *one*. And it seems only one." A short laugh with
no humor. "Myst is my wife."

"Myst married?" Was that where she'd been? No, no way.
"That's funny."

"The jest's on me, I'm afraid." As they reached the

manor, he bellowed, "Annika, call off the goddamn wraiths and let me in."

Emma stared up at the sky, seeing swirling red swaths of ragged cloth circling the house. Occasionally she spied a gaunt, skeletal face, but it would change to beauty if you met its eyes.

The price for their protection was hair from each of the Valkyrie within. The wraiths wove each lock into a massive braid, and when it grew long enough, they bent all living Valkyrie to their will for a time.

"Myst hasn't returned yet," someone called from the house. "But you know that, or else you'd both be naked and fornicating on the front lawn."

"The night's young. Give us time." To himself, he murmured, "And it was a *field* a mile away."

"Don't you have a tanning appointment to go to, vampire?"

Emma stiffened. Vampire? But his eyes weren't red. "Did you follow me?"

"No, I was awaiting Myst's return from shopping and sensed you trace into the woods."

A vampire waiting for Myst? He'd said she was his wife. She sucked in a breath. "You're the general, aren't you," she whispered. "The one Myst had to be pried from?"

She thought the corners of his lips quirked. "Is that what you heard?" At her solemn nod, he said, "It was mutual, I assure you." He glanced away down the drive, as if *willing* Myst to return, and said almost to himself, "How much lingerie can one female need . . . ?"

Suddenly Annika was shrieking, running for her, vowing to kill him ever so slowly.

Amazingly, his body was still relaxed. "If you do not cease

trying to take off my head, Annika, we will have words."

"What have you done to her?" she cried.

"Obviously, I clawed her, bloodied her, and burned her, and now, oddly, I offer her up to you."

"No, Annika," Emma said. "He found me. Don't kill him."

Through heavy-lidded eyes, Emma saw Myst returning then, dropping shopping bags full of lace—and leather—to run toward them in all her heart-stopping beauty. Gaze locked on Myst, the vampire finally tensed, and his heart sped up, beating loud like a drum.

Then Emma felt a very decisive yank as she went from his arms to Annika's.

"I was on fire," Emma told her. "I slew Demestriu."

"Of course, you did. Shhh, you are unwell."

When Myst reached them, she pressed a kiss on Emma's forehead.

"Myst, he found me," Emma said. "You shouldn't kill him."

"I'll try to refrain, my sweet," Myst answered in a wry tone. Curiously, no one raised a sword against this vampire.

The others gathered round until she was surrounded by her coven. When Annika stroked her face, Emma succumbed to the blackness.

Lachlain hauled himself to his feet, then sagged against the castle wall, still holding his sword out.

"Perhaps I shouldn't have pushed so hard to have you tortured," Ivo said. "But I can't tell you how many nights have been gladdened by the thought of your skin cooked from your bones."

He was baiting Lachlain, stirring up the beast to render him thoughtless.

"I can't let you leave here alive. A Lykae after his mate . . ." Ivo tsked. "Annoyingly tenacious. You'd keep coming long after she's forgotten you. And she will forget you. I'll force her to take necks until you're a distant memory."

Trying to enrage him. Vampires always sought to trigger the beast.

"Now that I've found the key to turning demons, I can turn her fully as well. A true vampire—a true killer. She was made for it."

Stir the beast. Why not give him what he wanted?

Ivo smirked, so confident. "The first neck she takes will be my own."

Lachlain cast his sword at the henchman like a dagger, nailing him through the neck. Then, with a mindless roar, Lachlain charged Ivo. As he'd known it would, Ivo's sword shot out for a killing blow. Lachlain struck it down with his fist, sending it plunging into his own thigh. He left it wedged there, pleased, and let the beast free. The sounds of cracking, tearing. . . . Through the haze, Lachlain saw Ivo's long, sadistic existence end with horror in his eyes.

Lachlain growled with satisfaction and dropped his body. He worked Ivo's sword free of his leg, and then his own sword from the remaining henchman's neck. "Video," he snarled.

The vampire clamped a hand to his neck, scrambling to a small computer in the adjoining chamber. When he handed up the video, Lachlain rewarded him with a quick death. Several more vampires had crowded at the opened door, but Lothaire, an enemy of old, was at the front and appeared to be blocking it, keeping them out. How long had he been there?

Lachlain could guess. Long enough to allow Lachlain to destroy Ivo. He asked Lothaire, "You know about her?"

A tight nod.

Lachlain narrowed his eyes. Lothaire couldn't take the throne, because he wasn't a blood heir. Lachlain knew of no one who could except for Kristoff—unless they went after Emma.

He bared his teeth at Lothaire. "Follow their fates if you follow their actions. I guard her ruthlessly."

Lothaire's lips subtly drew back from his fangs in answer.

No, Lothaire would never get Emma, so the Horde would surrender to the rebel king or descend into chaos.

Unless Kristoff had a sister.

Lachlain needed to kill them all, but needed to get back to Emma more.

He escaped into the sun, never so glad to see a cloudless sky.

Emma knew the cost.

She'd wakened, having dreamed of people pouring blood down her throat, but she couldn't hold it down. First came blood in glasses, and then everyone started shoving gashed wrists to her lips. But she drank directly from no one, unwilling to risk more memories.

Annika's voice was thrumming with worry. Myst tried to calm her. "Annika, we will think of something. Go speak to the Lykae downstairs. Maybe he knows something we don't."

Ten minutes later, Annika stormed into her room. Emma cracked open her eyes to see a man lurch in after her, hands shackled behind him. Following were Lucia and Regin, faces pensive, swords drawn.

The man was tall with a shadow of a beard. His eyes were a burnished gold, and he'd been frozen into his immortality with rakish laugh lines fanning out from them.

He looked so much like Lachlain that it pained her. Garreth.

Would he despise her for her involvement with his brother?

Annika pointed in Emma's direction. "Is this who Lachlain should take his vengeance out on? We've all suffered at the vampires' hands, yet that dog thinks to punish our Emma, who is nothing but innocent and kind." She uncovered Emma's leg. "Look at these gashes! They won't heal! What has he done to her? You will tell me or—"

"Christ," he murmured. "That's his . . . no, it canna be." He strode forward, but Regin yanked on his bonds. "Let me closer," he growled over his shoulder. "Closer, or you'll get no help from me." His voice grew deadly. "*Get her well.*"

"We've tried everything!"

"Why will she no' drink? Aye, Valkyrie, I hear your whispers from her room. I know what she is. What I doona know is how she is my brother's mate."

"Emma will never be a 'mate' to one of you!"

"It has been done," he grated. "I assure you."

Emma opened her eyes, needing to explain—

Annika struck him, sending him reeling back.

"He's marked her," Garreth bit out. "He'll be coming for her. I'm just surprised he's no' here already."

Annika raised her hand again, but Emma didn't want him hurt. "Annika, don't. . . ."

"Force blood down her throat," Garreth said.

"Think you we have not tried that? She can't keep it down."

"Try other blood, then. Take *mine.*"

"Why do you care?"

His voice was so strong, so like Lachlain's when he said, "Because that's my queen and I'll die for her."

Annika was shaking with emotion. "Never your queen," she hissed.

"Goddamn it, let her drink from me!"

"She *won't,*" Annika said, suddenly sounding like she was about to cry. That had happened only once before. Emma wanted to drink. She didn't want to die, but her fangs seemed to have grown small and useless. She feared Demestriu had poisoned her with his claws, and was so weak she could barely keep her eyes open.

Garreth said, "Let me talk to the vampire I scented in the house."

"He wouldn't know anything—"

"Let me talk to him!" he roared.

Annika told Lucia to go get Myst and Wroth. Seconds later, Emma heard Wroth's deeply accented voice, and her lids flickered open. Then, as if in slow motion, Garreth shook free of Regin and lunged for him. They caught each other by the throat.

"Heal her, vampire," Garreth bit out.

Low, deadly, all eerie calm, this Wroth simply murmured, "Don't do that again, Lykae."

He didn't use the if-then threat. As if he knew the mere idea of his displeasure would terrify others.

Garreth released the man. Seconds later, Wroth let go.

"Heal her."

"I don't know the old ways like some. For a price, I offer to contact Kristoff and ask this boon from him."

"I'll pay it—"

Annika interrupted, "But then Kristoff will know of her existence."

Garreth scoffed. "Surely the vampire's already told him?"

Myst said, "Wroth protects our interests," but Annika and Garreth clearly appeared doubtful.

Garreth turned to Annika. "If we worked together, the vampires would no' hand us our asses like the last Accession. We ally, and we keep her from them."

Wroth warned in a deadly tone, "Wait till I'm out of the room before you conspire." No consequence clause.

"But Kristoff has my blood and I killed Demestriu," Emma whispered.

Myst crossed to the bed and stroked her hair. "I know, darling. You've said this before."

Garreth asked Wroth, "What is your price?"

"I want my union with Myst recognized by all."

Silence.

Lightning flashed outside, and Annika bowed her head.

While Myst gaped at her sister, the vampire traced to just before her. He cupped his hand behind Myst's neck, and stared down into her eyes. Breathless, she gazed up at him as though with wonder, and then they were gone.

On the jet, Lachlain pawed at the DVD player.

Harmann had downloaded the video to this machine, and he'd explained how to use it again and again, but Lachlain's hands were shaking.

He couldn't imagine what she had gone through. Even the strongest Lykae never returned from Demestriu's lair, yet she'd *defeated* him—something no being that had ever lived had been able to accomplish.

Lachlain needed to see even as he dreaded it, needed to find out why she hadn't returned to him. To Kinevane. When he'd finally gotten far from Helvita and staggered back to Harmann, he'd had Harmann call Kinevane.

She wasn't there. She'd traced to . . . her real home.

The player finally started, the video loop beginning with her alone in the room, just before Demestriu traced inside.

As Lachlain watched their conversation, his heart sank to see Emma behaving as if Demestriu's comments didn't hurt her. She might even not realize they did, but Lachlain could see something fading in her eyes each time. Underneath all her swagger, she was still the same vulnerable Emmaline.

Demestriu looked as horrific and awesome as Lachlain remembered. And yet, when she'd admitted her mother had told them nothing about Demestriu, Lachlain could swear he'd looked—for the briefest moment—hurt.

"That's Lachlain's ring," Emma said at one point.

How did she know that?

Demestriu frowned, then glanced down at his hand. Moments passed before he said, "I suppose it is."

Lachlain had long imagined Demestriu continually staring at the ring, reveling in what he'd done, pleased to possess a constant reminder of Lachlain's torture.

Demestriu had hardly noticed it.

Then Lachlain heard the most horrifying revelation.

Emma had dreamed his memories. Of the fire. That's what had happened that night when she'd woken in such pain. Looking back, he could see she'd *felt* the agony he had.

He closed his eyes, appalled. He would rather have died than convey that horror to her.

Lachlain couldn't help but watch as events continued to unfold.

The fight made his muscles clench with tension, though he knew the outcome. But he had not known she'd been injured so grievously. Now his worry intensified, eating at him.

When Emma toed the pool of blood as she might the cold ocean, she flinched. She held the sword over her head, but it shook wildly and tears streamed down her cheeks. How he wished he could have taken that fear and pain for her.

Lachlain frowned when Demestriu's eyes changed and when the blood flowed as if he'd been lanced of a venom. He'd appeared . . . *relieved* to die.

Emma's beautiful face was drawn in an anguished expression as she knelt beside him, desperate not to kill him. Lachlain saw the exact moment she'd known that she would have to. Though it went against everything she was, she'd done it. All alone, his brave Emmaline had slain her own father, then had looked to be *sizing up Ivo* directly after. But luckily, she'd saved him for Lachlain.

Her final act—leaping into the sun . . .

He was awed by her courage, but knew the toll this would take on her. Knew the toll he himself had taken on her. Was he selfish to go after her?

What if he's my father?

Malevolent, filthy parasites.

Christ, no.

34

"I've come for Emma," Lachlain bellowed, standing in the shadow of Emma's home, Val Hall, which looked to be the face of hell.

Though the fog was cloying, lightning fired all around, sometimes corralled by the many copper rods planted all along the roof and the grounds, sometimes by the scorched oaks crowding the yard. Annika stepped out onto the porch, looking otherworldly in her rage, her eyes glittering green, then silver, and back. Wraiths flew about her hair, cackling.

At that moment, he couldn't decide whether this bayou shrine to insanity or Helvita was worse. Nïx waved happily from a window.

He fought not to reveal how weak he was becoming. Bowe had wrapped his wounds tight, but his limbs were still weakening. Lachlain had forbidden Bowe or anyone else in the clan to accompany him to Val Hall, fearing this would devolve into a war, but he still sensed them in the forest all around.

"I'm taking Emma from this place tonight."

Annika tilted her head as if to see him better. Emma did that, too. Emma had gotten it from this woman. "Never would I give my daughter to a dog."

No man had in-laws like these.

"Then trade me for my brother."

Garreth bellowed in Gaelic from somewhere inside, "Goddamn it, Lachlain, I just got *into* this house."

"Or take both of us. Just let me talk to her." He had to see if she was healing.

"The Accession is nigh, and you want us to imprison the Lykae king *and* his heir?"

Regin hurried to her side. She spoke in English, but with words he didn't understand, calling this a "slam dunk," admonishing Annika, "Just take it to the hoop, Shaq."

Annika's voice rang out. "She made her decision when she returned to her coven. When hurt and afraid and unthinking, she chose us. Not you, Lykae."

That pained him terribly, her choice. Not only had she decided to leave him, she'd decided to *stay* away from him. But what right did he have to her after what he'd made her suffer? He hid his pain. "Do I go in, or do we go to war?" *Just to see if she's healing.*

She looked past him, scanning the grounds, no doubt sensing their numbers. She tilted her head again, lifted her hand to the wraiths, and his path was cleared.

He limped into the darkened manor, seeing dozens of Valkyrie, curled up on chairs, hands on weapons, perched atop the stair railing. He fought not to gape at the sheer malice these fey beings exuded. For the hundredth time, he marveled that Emma had been raised among them.

They didn't restrain him. Did they know he wouldn't hurt them? Or did they want him to attack so they could slaughter him? He'd bet the latter.

Within two minutes of his entrance, he was shown to the cage in the damp half-basement that housed his brother

Garreth. He didn't resist even when the door clanged shut behind him.

Garreth stared at him as though seeing a ghost, then ran a hand over his face. "Do my eyes betray me?"

Lachlain's happiness at seeing his brother was overshadowed by worry. "No, it's me."

Garreth rushed to him, grin in place, and whaled slaps on his back. "Well, brother, what have you gotten us into now?"

"Aye, it's good to see you as well."

"I thought you were . . . When they said you'd taken Emma, I thought they were mad. Until I saw her, saw you'd marked her." He frowned. "Marked her hard, no?" He shook his head. "Ach, anyway, it's good to have you back. Under any circumstances. I've so many questions, but that can wait. You need news about her?"

At his nod, Garreth said, "She's injured, Lachlain. She has gashes down her side, and she could no' drink though she was . . . she was about to die in just the first couple of hours."

Lachlain flinched. Claws into his palms, he rasped, "What saved her?"

"An i.v." At Lachlain's frown, he explained, "They gave her blood through a tube that fed it straight to her veins. They think she's stabilized, but the gashes will no' heal. I suspect whatever got her had poisoned claws. Maybe a ghoul, but I doona know."

"I do." Lachlain ran his hand through his hair. "Demestriu did this to her. I saw it all."

"I doona understand—" Garreth broke off. He shot to his feet, then his entire frame grew still and tense. "Lucia?"

Lachlain glanced up, saw her descending the stairs. She tilted her head so her hair covered her face. The moment they saw she'd been crying, Garreth's face grew grave, his eyes riveted to the archer.

"She's no' better?" Garreth asked.

She shook her head.

Lachlain clutched the bars. "She heals when she drinks from me."

Garreth raised his eyebrows at that. "You let her . . . ?" To Lucia, he said, "Then let Lachlain go to her."

"Annika forbids it. He's not to go near her. Emma sees things that aren't there, mumbles nonsense as though she's gone mad. Annika puts the blame squarely on his shoulders."

She was right to. While Lachlain struggled with his guilt, Garreth asked, "What does she see?"

"Emma says that Demestriu was her father, and he put her in the fire, so she killed him."

"She—did."

Both of them swung their heads toward him.

What if he's my father?

"She did. She killed him."

Lucia shook her head. "Sweet Emma? Kill the most powerful and deadly vampire ever to live?"

"Aye. He hurt her. Do none of you believe her?"

Garreth gave him an incredulous expression. "Demestriu's finally dead? Because of that wee thing? She's as fragile as eggshell."

Lucia added, "Lachlain, when she finds a moth inside and tries to free it—well, if she accidentally dusts its wings, she's distraught for an entire night. I just don't see her killing this fiend on his home ground when Cara and Kaderin have failed to do so on a field of battle. And Furie, the strongest of us? If Demestriu could be killed by a Valkyrie, then surely she'd have done it."

"You doona know her as I do. No' anymore—"

"Then what does she mean when she says Furie is alive but shouldn't be?"

"She's been imprisoned by the Horde. Demestriu never expected her to live this long."

Lucia swayed, barely perceptibly. In a smaller voice, she asked, "And when she says Kristoff has her blood?"

"They're first cousins."

Her lips parted in surprise. *"Furie lives. . . ."* she murmured.

"If you doona believe me, there's a video of the entire fight. I left it with Bowen, a member of our clan."

Garreth stopped gaping at Lachlain and turned to Lucia. "Go get it. For Annika to see."

She raised her eyebrows. "You want me to go to the clan?"

Garreth said, "Tell them I sent you, and they will no' hurt you. I vow it."

Her chin went up. "I know they won't *succeed* in hurting me. But you're sending *me*, who'll be carrying a *bow*, among your people. They will not thank you for it."

Lachlain saw that his brother's eyes held much feeling for the archer, but Garreth still snapped, "I would do it myself. But I canna since I've been put in a cage after coming to *your* rescue."

She flushed as though with guilt, then finally said, "I will retrieve it and review it. Then give it to Annika, if it is as you say."

Lachlain strained against the bars. "Damn it, that will take too long. Can you no' just take my blood for her to drink?"

"Annika forbids it. I am . . . sorry."

When she left, Garreth continued to stare at the door. "Lucia will be quick about it."

"How long have you known she's yours?"

"A month now."

"I wondered why you were so eager to remain." Lachlain surveyed the cage, eyeing it for weaknesses. He'd escaped far worse to get to Emma—he wouldn't be stopped now. "You've no' told her?"

"Lucia's tricky. And I suspect she's a runner. Tell her something she does no' want to hear and she'll disappear. And she feels no love for me. She's the reason I'm here in the first place. She suffers agonizing pain when she misses her target—that's why she's so bloody good. Annika set a trap, baited it with Lucia missing and screaming in pain, and I ran headlong. I should have known there was no way she'd miss again. You've never seen a creature shoot as she—"

"I have a good idea," Lachlain said dryly, pulling his shirt aside to show him the healing wound on his shoulder.

Garreth clearly didn't know how to react to that. His brother shot by his mate.

"I harbor no anger toward her." Lachlain strained to stretch the bars apart, unnerved when they didn't budge. How had he gotten this weak? Yes, he was riddled with injuries, but he'd never found a cage that could hold him. Unless . . . "They've reinforced these?"

"Aye." Garreth rose and grasped the same bar Lachlain was struggling to bend. "These creatures ally with the witches. Annika told me nothing *physical* can bend these."

When they both couldn't budge the steel, Lachlain dropped his hands to pace, examining the cage for any alternative, desperate to get to her. He crossed to the one cement wall and pounded his fist against it. Too thick to dig through.

"I canna believe she shot you," Garreth grated. "When we get out of here, I'll—"

"No, I doona care. Especially since you seem to accept that my mate's a vampire."

He gave Lachlain an exasperated expression. "I would no' give a damn if she was a Fury, as long as you are content with her. And it's clear you are."

"Aye, but I have to get to her," Lachlain said, testing the cement floor.

"At least we're no' chained," Garreth offered. "When they open this door, we can attack."

Lachlain stabbed his fingers through his hair. "I'd prefer to be only chained. I'd take off my hands before I let Emma suffer any longer."

Garreth eyed him, and Lachlain knew he'd said the words without the slightest reservation.

"Trust me, Garreth, it is no' so bad as this feeling—"

Emma whimpered in pain, and he could hear the sound as clearly as if she'd shrieked. He growled in answering pain and lunged into the bars.

The bars were protected, the wall and floor solid cement. . . .

He slowly lifted his head, eyes focused on the ceiling. "I can dig through."

"Lachlain, I doona think that's wise. This house is centuries old and gets battered as you would no' believe."

"Doona care."

"You might care that all three stories are tongue-and-groove construction—one piece falls, it'll be like a domino effect. War, hurricanes, and constant lightning have made it unsound. I doona think Val Hall can take a Lykae biting through the first floor."

"Support it while I'm gone."

"Hold the floor? If I canna, you could be hurting both our mates. This place could come crashing down."

Lachlain slapped him on the shoulder. "Be sure that you doona drop it."

Time was running out. He let the beast have its way with the ceiling, slashing through the wood, digging with its claws, and pulled himself up into the cool house.

On his knees on the floor, Lachlain shook himself, struggling for control. Looking back down, he said, "You can handle this?"

"Just doona be too long," Garreth gritted out. "Oh, and Lachlain?" He was already straining. "Doona kill Wroth, a big black-haired vampire, if you see him about. He's the one who helped Emma with the idea of the blood straight to her veins. One of Kristoff's Forbearers. We owe him for Emma's life."

Lachlain snapped, "What's Kristoff's goddamned interest in her?"

Garreth shook his head. "No. I think this Wroth did it to have his union with Myst recognized."

A Valkyrie *unified* with a vampire?

"He seemed a lot saner than they usually do. Now, go!"

Lachlain leapt to his feet. He followed Emma's scent easily, moving through the expansive mansion, and stalked straight to her floor. A red-headed Valkyrie was just leaving Emma's room with a towering male. A vampire. Lachlain's first instinct was to attack him, but he stifled it. That had to be Wroth, the one who'd helped Emma, and her aunt Myst.

Wroth comforted Myst, brushing tears from her face. A

vampire comforting another? Suddenly Wroth's head jerked up; Lachlain flattened himself against the wall. Wroth scanned the area with narrowed eyes then clasped Myst to him to trace them away.

As soon as they'd disappeared, Lachlain raced to Emma's room. Inside, her bed was empty. Of course, she must be under it. He fell to his knees, jerked up the bedding. Not under it. When he glanced around, he saw Nïx standing in the adjoining sitting room with Emma in her arms.

"Nïx, bring her to me. I can heal her."

She stroked Emma's hair. "But your blood comes with a price. One so young as this dreams of wars she's never seen, feels injuries that would have killed her ten times over."

He shook his head, not wanting to believe.

"She dreams of fire." Nïx sighed. "Forever, forever fire."

Emma appeared frail, her skin and lips pale as snow. Her cheekbones stood out sharply. One look at her, and he was sweating with fear for her.

Nïx leaned down to rub her nose against Emma's. "Emma of the three. And you don't know it yet. Emma of the three hacked him in three. What do you have in your little hand? Darling girl. He's supposed to get *you* a ring." With effort, Nïx pried the ring from her hand and tossed it to him. He slipped it on without interest. Why the bloody hell wouldn't she give him Emma as easily?

"You gave her the Instinct. It shines like a star in her, radiating. She can see where you marked her as yours."

Impossible. . . .

"She will never lose it." Nïx petted her forehead. "She is all of us. Emma of the three."

"Nïx, what will make you give her to me?"

"What would you do for her?"

His brows drew together at the absurd question. "*Anything*," he rasped.

She studied him for long moments, then nodded firmly. "You have work to do, Lachlain. Give her new memories to fight the old."

He held out his hands for her, forgot to breathe . . . until Nïx finally handed her to him. He clutched Emma to his chest, but she didn't wake, and when he glanced up again, Nïx was gone.

Quickly, he crossed to the bed, laying her down. He cut his arm with his battered claws and placed it against her lips. Nothing.

He sat next to her and shook her. "Goddamn it, Emma, wake up." She didn't. Her lips parted, and he saw her fangs were dull and small.

He sliced his thumb and worked it between her lips, cupping her head with his other hand. Long moments passed. Then she grew very still, as though even her heart stopped.

She took, just barely. After a moment, she raised her hands to his chest, clutching him. He drew his finger from her, and when she latched on to his arm, he threw his head back, closing his eyes with relief.

Even as she drank, he pulled up her nightgown and the bandages beneath to check her leg and side. *Already healing*.

When she'd finished, she blinked open her eyes and threw her arms around his neck, weakly squeezing him.

"Why did you go, Emma? Was it because of what I said about Demestriu?"

"Had to go. Lachlain," she said, her voice faint, "he's my . . . he *was* my . . . *father*."

"I know. But that does no' explain why you would take that step."

She pulled back from him. "Nïx told me just before I left for Paris that I was on the verge of doing what I was born to do. I recognized it just as the vampire reached out his hand." She shivered. "I know it's hard to believe, but I-I killed Demestriu."

"I saw. I have the whole confrontation on tape. Lucia's going to get it from Bowe as we speak."

"How'd *you* get it?"

"Ivo had been taping Demestriu. And I took it from Ivo." At her frown, he added, "When you were in Demestriu's lair, I was already in the castle."

"You killed Ivo?" she asked in a hopeful tone.

"Oh, aye. With pleasure."

"Are you angry that you didn't get revenge on Demestriu?"

"I'm angry that you went alone. I understand it was your fate, but doona leave me like that again." He put his hand behind her head and pressed her to him. Her body had grown so warm and soft.

"How did you find Helvita?"

"I followed you. Emma, I'll always come for you."

"But how can you be right with me? Knowing who I am?"

He made her face him. "I *know* who you are. I saw everything that occurred, and we have no secrets between us now. And I want you so badly my mind canna comprehend it."

"But I can't understand this. I was his daughter."

"Seeing him with you eased some of my rage. I'd thought he gloated every day about what he'd done to me and for taking my father's life and his ring. He scarcely remembered these things, he was so twisted. And the kindness he showed you at the end . . . it meant much to me."

"But he took so much from you."

"Lass, he's given to me as well."

She gave him that shy look. "M-me?"

He nodded. "I dinna go mad after those years of hell, but I was just shy of it when I thought of losing you."

She whispered, "I saw it, Lachlain. That hell. I know what happened to you."

He dropped his forehead to hers. "I wish to God . . . I wish you had no'. That kills me inside, knowing I cursed you with that memory."

"No, I'm glad now that I have it."

"How can you say that?"

Her bottom lip trembled. "I would *never* want you to go through that alone."

He gripped her shoulders. Brows drawn, he rasped, "*My God, I love you.*"

She gasped. "I love you, too. I wanted to tell you—"

"If you felt the same, then why did you no' come back to Kinevane? To me?"

"Because it was day in Russia."

Welcome realization hit him. "So it would be day in Scotland."

"Exactly. It was only my second time ever to trace—the first was just before I went with the vampire—and I didn't trust myself to land perfectly in the sunproofed rooms. I knew it was just after midnight here."

"I wondered when you'd learned to trace." His tone low, he admitted, "I thought you'd chosen your aunts over me."

"No, I was trying to be smart, cold, logical. And besides, I've decided no one's going to force me to choose anyone over anyone." She wagged her finger at him. "Including you, Lachlain. Not again."

His lips curled. "You're going to keep me on a short chain, are you no'? Especially now that I know what happens when you get displeased with someone."

She play-punched his arm, but when her hand met the wet fabric of his coat, her eyes went wide. "You're hurt. Worse than I thought." She shot to her feet, but he eased her back down.

"Give it time. I'll heal, just as you're doing. Your leg's already better."

"But let me get a bandage for you." She looked him over. "Your hands? Your chest? Oh, Lachlain."

He wasn't ready for her to leave this room, especially not without him. "Doona worry." He kept her hand in his. "Now that I ken that you love me, I'll hold this over you and make you take care of me."

She fought a grin and lost.

"So what else do you see?" He coughed into his fist. "In my memories." This could get tricky.

"They're mostly connected to me," she said, clearly hedging.

Still tricky. Could she see him when he handled himself while imagining his mouth between her legs? "And . . . ?"

"I see things from the past. And I see you admiring my underwear." She blushed.

"Can you ken why this would make me uneasy?"

"It makes me so as well! I think I would die if I saw you with another woman."

"Are you *jealous*, lass?"

"Yes!" she cried, as if she couldn't believe the question. "While you've been running around growling 'mine,' I've been silently saying it right back at you."

This got better and better. "I think I like you jealous and

possessive. But I doona like what's available to you in my mind. What more have you seen?"

So she detailed memories of him on a campaign, of him with her in the hotel room, of him admiring her arse, the necklace. Nothing to embarrass him so far. "Have you seen me kill?"

"No."

"Have you seen me release into my own hand?"

Her eyes went wide. "No, but . . ."

"But what?" When she wouldn't tell him, he nipped her ear. "Tell me."

With her face buried in his chest, he barely heard her whisper, "I want to." Her admission sent a spike of heat through him.

"Do you, then?" His voice had gone husky. As she nodded against him, he realized that though he was injured—had been feeling damn near dead—she could stir him to life. "You've only to tell me what you want."

"But I *don't* want to see certain things. Like you . . . with another woman."

"Now, this I am no' concerned with. You take my memories, and none before you were memorable in the least."

"I don't know. . . ."

"I do. Every event you described was pivotal to my thinking of you. *I* remember all of them clearly, even over so much time." When she frowned, he explained, "I think you wake up too soon. That day by the stream, I grieved for no' having you, but afterward I swore to myself that nothing would stop me from finding you. I vowed that I would no' wait for you—I would seek you to the ends of the earth. And in the hotel when we were together, I promised myself I would do whatever it took to claim you, go to any lengths, even if they were no' honorable. I realized that night that you can make me craven for you."

"A-and the others?"

"The necklace? That entire journey home I slept with it in my hand, renewed in my belief that I'd see you wear it one day. And the night I stared at your arse—and you do have an arse I will be thinking of often—I joined you in the shower. When I took you under the water, you whispered in my ear that you dinna think you could live without me."

"I did?" she breathed.

"Oh, aye, and I thought that I'd give anything to hear it again. So rest easy on that score, love. I think this is like mind reading, and a lot of couples I know do that." He frowned. "Though those are usually reciprocal. Will you share things with me as though I had this talent? To keep no more secrets between us."

"No more secrets, Lachlain."

"And we set about getting past my . . . *our* memories?"

She nodded eagerly. "We will—"

"Emmaline!" Annika shrieked. Regin, behind her, rolled her eyes at the sight of them together. "Get away from him!"

Emma gasped, seeming embarrassed to be caught in bed with Lachlain. Then her expression turned defiant. "No."

"You can't mean this. We will discuss this when you're better." To Regin, she said, "Take him from here." Her voice was laced with disgust.

Emma tensed. "Don't touch him, Regin."

"Sorry, Em." She drew her sword and swept to the bed in a blur, her sword point under his chin before they could blink. He tensed, but with his injuries and Emma thrown over him, he couldn't react quickly enough.

"Put—the sword—down," Emma said.

"You're out of your head, kid. Why do you want to be with him when you have nightmares about him?"

Annika added, "You need to move away from this . . . this *Lykae*."

"I'm keeping"—her eyes flickered—"this Lykae."

"But the nightmares—"

"Are our business." When Regin pressed forward, Emma bit out, "I said *no*." She backhanded her with phenomenal speed.

Regin flew across the room. Lachlain shot up, head light, and threw Emma behind him. But instead of attacking as Lachlain expected, Regin wiggled her jaw and smiled brightly. "Sixty-five years I've been trying to teach you to move like that."

All of them were insane but for Emma.

Regin spoke to another Valkyrie on the wardrobe who'd come from nowhere and sat blowing bubbles with chewing gum. "Check her out. She didn't telegraph her punch. Finally, I can relax a little."

Annika clasped her hands. "Emma, please be reasonable."

Emma tilted her head at Annika. "What's going on here? The house should've been ruptured by your lightning."

Lachlain suspected Annika couldn't say a lot about this situation since she was now related by marriage to a full-blooded vampire. "Aye, Annika, why no' tell her why a Lykae does no' look so bad right now?"

When Emma frowned at him, he said, "She's agreed to recognize her sister's marriage to Wroth. I think she's figuring that anything is better than him."

Annika gave him a look of pure spite.

"You know what?" Emma said to Annika. "I can see that

you're going to accept this—unbelievable, but I can see it. And I'm going to keep my head down and not ask too many questions—"

"Christ! Garreth!" Lachlain shot to his feet, weak and stumbling. Dragging Emma to his side, half carrying her, he lurched out of the room and down the stairs. Regin and Annika followed, demanding to know what was happening.

Inside the half-basement, they found Wroth alongside Garreth, grappling to hold up the ceiling.

The vampire's voice was incongruously calm when he asked, "What kind of idiot would find this a worthy plan?"

In an astounded tone, Lachlain said to Emma, "Your family's adding in-laws like *him?*"

The vampire's gaze fell to Lachlain's hand clutching Emma's, and he raised an eyebrow. "Indeed."

35

"**M**ovie!!" someone shrieked, and to Lachlain's great unease, he heard the Valkyrie begin to stir throughout the manor.

Lachlain was exhausted from his injuries and from having to help hold up the house while a suitable Lore contractor was found who could stabilize the damage. He'd barely been able to stumble back up to Emma's bedroom so they could rebandage each other. He'd sunk into her bed, pulling her down with him with the crook of his arm, just minutes before, and had almost fallen asleep with her resting her head on his chest.

Now he stared, arm tightening around her, wishing he had a weapon, as they filed into Emma's room from all corners of the house.

Some had gotten popcorn, none of them eating it. They curled up on the windowsills, on top of the wardrobe, and one even hopped to the foot of the bed after a casual hiss at Lachlain's legs had prompted him to move them.

Lachlain found it disturbing that they were all so insouciant about this. Here a Lykae lay with the youngest member of their household in his arms, in their home. In her bed.

He waited for them to realize this at any moment and attack.

He was as weak as he'd ever been, and they surrounded him like a swarm. Garreth and Lucia were conspicuously absent. She'd returned with the video, but apparently had been so shaken by something that had occurred within the clan that she left directly after. Garreth had followed. Unbelievably, Lachlain was almost relieved when Wroth arrived in the room with Myst, but didn't hesitate to return the bastard's scowl.

Just before the video played on Emma's TV, she plugged in her old "outdated" iPod so she couldn't hear, then buried her face against his chest because of the "scary parts."

Unlike the others, Lachlain had no problem tearing himself away from the screen to think on all he'd learned, because he'd replayed this again and again. Lachlain had first viewed the video beginning with Demestriu's entrance, because Harmann had programmed it to start there. But Lachlain had actually been able to go back and see Demestriu in the hours and even days before Emma appeared. Lachlain had seen Demestriu staring out the window, dropping his forehead into his shaking hands, lashing out in madness—just as Lachlain had done.

Lachlain shook his head. He didn't know how to feel about everything—how to reconcile his past and his losses with what might have been a brief flare of pity. And Lachlain realized now, with Emma here, that he didn't have to know. Not yet. They'd figure it out together.

He turned from his thoughts and studied the Valkyrie's reactions as they watched. They laughed uproariously at the fact that Emma, a vampire, was spooked by the blood on the floor. During the fight, they tensed and leaned toward the TV, eyes wide when Emma shattered the window. "Ballsy," Regin muttered, and others nodded in response though none shifted their gazes from the screen. At one point, Nïx yawned and said, "I've already seen this part," but no one bothered to ask how. And when Demestriu told Emma he was proud, some cried, making lightning split the sky.

Proof that Furie was alive was met with cheers, and Lachlain didn't douse their happiness by saying that at this very moment, Furie was praying to great Freya to die.

When it was over, Emma pulled her earbuds out and peeked up from his chest. The Valkyrie merely nodded at him and Emma the Unlikely and filed out, with Nïx predicting that *The Demise of Demestriu* would outsell *One Goblin's Night in Paris* among the Lore.

As Regin exited, she summed up what seemed to be the attitude of the rest of the coven: "If Emma wants the overgrown Lykae bad enough to go drop Demestriu, then she ought to be able to keep him."

Annika alone remained.

"You don't have to decide right now, Emmaline. Just don't do something you're going to regret for the rest of your life."

Emma shook her head, dismayed to see Annika hurting, but resolved in this. "I kept thinking it was about my choice, but it's not. It's yours. You can choose to accept me with him. Or I leave." Lachlain drew her hand into his as though for support.

Annika clearly strove for a calm demeanor and her face was like marble, but lightning fired behind her, belying her efforts. She was torn about this.

"Annika, I'll always run to his arms." There was no defense against that, no argument to refute it—and they both knew it.

Finally, Annika, with her chin up and shoulders back, faced Lachlain. "We don't recognize *matehood*"—she spat the word—"or whatever you Lykae call it, as a bonding union. You will have to exchange vows. Mainly I'm concerned about the one where the Lykae vows he won't use this union to harm the covens in any way."

Lachlain grated, "The Lykae has a *name*. And if you'd like Emma to share it, nothing will please me better. I'll make that vow."

She faced Emmaline with one last pleading expression. When Emma shook her head slowly, Annika ordered, "Do not trace him here any more than is absolutely necessary."

As she strode from the room, she mumbled, "Coven's gone to hell on my watch."

Emma said, "Tracing! That's right. Now we can visit whenever we want. Coo-ell. Can we spend some weekends here? And Mardi Gras? And the Jazz Fest? Ooh, I want to watch you eat crawfish!"

With a pained expression, he said, "I suppose on occasion we could run through the bayou as easily as a forest."

Then her face fell. "But I don't know if I want you around all my gorgeous aunts."

He chuckled at her ridiculous statement, then winced when his wounds wouldn't cooperate. "Emma, you shame them. No, doona argue. I have eyes, I can see." He stroked his thumb over her cheek. "And I know none of them can howl at the moon half as good as my wee halfling."

"Cheeky werewolf!" she chided, leaning in to kiss his lips, but she was interrupted by a scream downstairs.

As they frowned at each other, Annika shrieked at someone unseen, *"What do you mean, we have a six-figure credit card bill?"*

36

Emma the Unlikely
Emma the King Killer
Emma of the Three

Her own page in the Book of Warriors!

Regin, Nïx, and Annika had taken her—and she'd insisted on taking Lachlain—into the war room, to the ornate, ancient pedestal with the light shining down upon it. They drew it out from under its Plexiglas case and opened it to *her* page.

Her likeness was painted there and below it, written in the old language, were her aliases and *One of Wóden's Cherished Warriors*. Warrior. War-ee-yur. This was so cool as to not be believed. With trembling fingers, Emma brushed the raised writing on the soft parchment.

Slayer of Demestriu, king of the vampire Horde, eldest and strongest of vampires. When she chose to battle him alone.

Emma raised her eyebrows at the implicit rebuke, and Annika lifted her chin.

Queen to Lachlain, king of the Lykae. Beloved daughter of Helen and all Valkyrie.

"Look at my resume!" Tears spilled over. "I look good on paper!"

Regin groaned. "Not the crying. That's so gross."

"And you left room for more!" She sniffled. Nïx handed her tissues she'd had the foresight to bring, and Emma brushed her face with them.

"Well, of course," Nïx said. "Even if you spend a lazy eternity doing nothing more than wallowing about with your wolf, we left room for your heroic, hell-raising kids."

Emma's face flushed, and she felt Lachlain draping a protective arm over her, squeezing her to his side. Chin up, he said, "We've decided no' to have bairns."

Nïx frowned. "Well, I'm not usually wrong about these things when I do see them, but if you both are so set on it, then never let her eat human food, especially not for back-to-back weeks on end, or she'll get knocked up faster than a rabbit after a Druid fertility ceremony!"

Emma said softly, "But I can't . . . I'm a vampire, and we can't have children."

Nïx and Annika both frowned. "Of course you can," Nïx said. "You just have to take different nourishment."

When Lachlain still looked unconvinced, Annika said, "Think about it—what do all humans do that not all in the Lore do? They eat of the earth and they spawn. The two are not unrelated."

Her heart thudding, Emma remembered Demestriu talking about Helen sharing meals with him just before she got pregnant. "And a Lykae with a . . . *valkire?*"

"Can you have little ankle-biters?" Nïx giggled. "Absolutely, and in the most literal sense. You know, you aren't the first time the different factions have had offspring together." She glanced around as if looking for someone in the manor, then waved it away. "Vampires who can walk in the sun, Lykae who can take sustenance from lightning. Valkyrie who run the forests at night with perfect joy." Nïx got an awed expression on her face. "And they're *strong*. Just look at you."

Emma glanced from Nïx to Annika. "Why didn't you tell me?"

Annika raised her palms, shaking her head. "I never imagined you thought about this at all, much less that you were under this misimpression."

To Lachlain, Nïx said, "When Emma yearns in her heart for children, it begins. She'll have to eat regular food for at least nine months."

Emma smacked her lips and grimaced, not relishing the thought of masticating.

"Doona hold your breath. I'm no' keen to share her."

"Very well. Until then"—Nïx paused to give him a lascivious grin—"honeymoon!"

Emma and Lachlain sat stunned.

Nïx waved an impatient hand. "All this would have come out during the three hour pre-joining counseling that you two are required to do."

That weekend after Emma and Lachlain's small, straightforward ceremony, and the raucous, bizarre party afterward, the members of the coven lounged in the TV room, sprawled over furniture, eyes glued to the television.

Lachlain and Emma sat among them, but he was restless, unable to watch the movie when Emma was making lazy circles on his palm with her fingertip.

Lachlain had invited only Bowe and Garreth to the festivities, though everyone in the clan hankered to meet the wee queen who'd felled Demestriu. But his kind liked to drink and rib and be boisterous, and he could just see the mad Valkyrie, who didn't drink—*anything*—reacting poorly. The preternatural versus the natural mixed with liquor.

But Lucia had "gone on walkabout," as the Valkyrie called it, or "fled," as Garreth more accurately termed it, and Lachlain had completely understood when Garreth had set out after her. Bowe had accepted, but after absently congratulating him that night, he'd spent an hour huddled in a corner with Nïx. Afterward, he'd been cryptic and preoccupied and had flown out early.

Casting looks that dared anyone to nay-say him, Wroth had audaciously shown up with a laughing Myst by his side. But the coven seemed to treat Wroth with the same indifference they showed Lachlain, who'd mostly been shrugged at as if he'd always been a fixture. Except for Annika—after she'd spotted Wroth, her chin hadn't been lifted quite so proudly, and Lachlain had heard her mumble, "Furie's going to kill me. . . ."

Lachlain shifted restlessly. He thought he was finally strong enough for them to leave tomorrow. He was physically ready to resume relations with his *wife*, and wasn't eager to do it under this roof.

He stood and offered his hand, and with a shy smile she slipped her hand in his. As they crossed in front of the screen, they barely dodged a volley of popcorn.

He didn't know where he was taking her, maybe out into the night fog. He just knew he wanted her, needed her, right then. She was too precious to him, too good to be true. When he was inside her, with his arms tight around her, he felt less like she'd slip away.

But they only made it to an empty hall before he pressed her against the wall, cupped her neck, and demanded once again, "You'll stay with me?"

"Always." Her hips arched up to him. "You love me?"

"Always, Emmaline," he grated against her lips. "Always. So damn much you make me mad with it."

When she moaned softly, he lifted her so she could wrap her legs around his waist. He knew he couldn't have her here, but the reasons why grew hazy with her breaths in his ear.

"I wish we were home," she whispered. "Together in our bed."

Home. Damn if she hadn't said *home*. *In our bed*. Had anything ever sounded so good? He pressed her harder into the wall, kissing her more deeply, with all the love he had in him, but suddenly they were falling, his balance somehow lost. He clenched her to him and twisted to take the impact on his back.

When he opened his eyes, they were tumbling into their bed.

Eyebrows raised, jaw slack, he released her and levered himself onto his elbows. "That was . . ." He exhaled a stunned breath. "That was a wild ride, lass. Will you no' warn me next time?"

She nodded solemnly, sitting up to straddle him, pulling her blouse over her head to bare her exquisite breasts for him. "Lachlain," she leaned down to whisper in his ear, brushing her nipples over his chest, making him shudder and clench her hips. "I'm about to give you a very . . . wild . . . ride."

Yet after everything that had occurred, his need for her was too strong, and he gave himself up to it, tossing her to her back and ripping her clothes from her. He made short work of his own, then covered her. When he pinned her arms over her head and thrust into her, she cried his name and writhed beneath him so sweetly. "I'll demand that ride tomorrow, love, but first you're going to see *wild* from a man who knows."

From the *Book of Lore*

The Lore

". . . and those sentient creatures that are not human shall be united in one strata, coexisting with, yet secret from, man's."

The Valkyrie

"When a maiden warrior screams for courage as she dies in battle, Wóden and Freya heed her call. The two gods give up lightning to strike her, rescuing her to their hall, and preserving her courage forever in the form of the maiden's immortal Valkyrie daughter."

- Valkyrie take sustenance from the electrical energy of the earth, sharing it in one collective power, and give it back with their emotions in the form of lightning.
- Possess preternatural strength and speed.
- Also called *Swan Maidens, Shield Maidens*.
- Enemies of the Horde.

The Vampire Horde

"In the first chaos of the Lore, a brotherhood of vampires dominated, by relying on their cold nature, worship of logic, and absence of mercy. They sprang from the harsh steppes of Dacia and migrated to Russia, though some say a secret enclave live in

Dacia still. Each vampire seeks his Bride, his eternal wife, the one who bloods him, or renders his body fully alive by giving him breath and making his heart beat."

- Have the ability to teleport, also known as *tracing*.
- Also called *The Daci*.
- Enemies of most factions in the Lore.

The Lykae Clan

"A proud, strapping warrior of the Keltoi People (or Hidden People, later known as Celts), was taken in his prime by a maddened wolf. The warrior rose from the dead, now an immortal, with the spirit of the beast latent within him. He displayed the beast's traits: the need for touch, an intense loyalty to its kind, a craving for the delights of the flesh. Sometimes the latent beast rises . . ."

- Also called *werewolves, war-wolds*.
- Enemies of the Horde.

The Forbearers

". . . his crown stolen, Kristoff, the rightful Horde king, stalked the battlefields of antiquity seeking the strongest, most valiant human warriors as they died, earning him the name The Grave-walker. He offered eternal life for eternal fealty to him and his growing army."

- An army of vampires consisting of turned humans, who do not drink blood directly from the flesh.
- Enemies of the Horde.

The Furiae

"If you do evil, beg for punishment—before they come . . ."

- Ruthless she-warriors bent on delivering justice to evil men when they escape it elsewhere.
- Led by Alecta the Unyielding One.
- Also called *Furies, Erinyes*.

The Wraiths

". . . their origin unknown, their presence chilling."

- Spectral, howling beings. Undefeatable, and, for the most part, uncontrollable.
- Also called *The Ancient Scourge*.

The Demonarchie

"The demons are as varied as the tribes of man . . ."

- A collection of demon dynasties.
- Some kingdoms ally with the Horde.

The House of Witches

". . . immortal possessors of magickal talents, practitioners of good and evil."

- Mystical mercenaries who sell their spells.

Ghouls

"Even immortals beware its bite . . ."

- A human turned savage monster, with glowing green skin, yellow eyes, and contagious bites and scratches.
- Their imperative is to increase their number by contagion.
- They're said to travel in *troops*.

The Accession

"And a time shall pass that all immortal beings in the Lore, from the strongest Valkyrie, vampire, and Lykae factions, to the phantoms, shifters, fairies, sirens . . . must fight and destroy each other." Occurs every five hundred years. Or right now. . . .

No Rest for the Wicked

Kresley Cole

Turn the page for a preview of
No Rest for the Wicked. . . .

No Rest for the Wicked

And none will hear the postman's knock /
Without a quickening of the heart. /
For who can bear to feel himself forgotten?

—W. H. Auden

one

For the second time in her life, Kaderin the Coldhearted hesitated to kill.

In the last instant of a silent, lethal swing, she stayed her sword an inch above the neck of her vampire prey—because she'd found him holding his head in his hands from grief.

She saw his big body tense, but he didn't trace away. He raised his face to gaze up at her with dark gray eyes—the color of a storm about to be unleashed. They were clear—not red—which meant the vampire had never drunk a being to death. He pled with those eyes, and she realized he hungered for death. He *wanted* the deathblow she'd come to his decrepit castle to deliver.

She'd stalked him soundlessly, primed for a battle with a vicious predator. Kaderin had been in Scotland with other Valkyrie when they'd received the call about a "vampire haunting a castle and terrorizing a hillside in Russia," and had gladly volunteered to destroy it. She was her Valkyrie coven's most prolific killer, her life given over to ridding the earth of leeches.

So why was she hesitating? Why was she even now easing her sword back to raise it before her? He would be merely one among thousands of her kills—his fangs collected and strung together with the others she'd taken.

The last time she'd stayed her sword had resulted in a

tragedy so great, her heart had been broken forever by it.

In a deep, gravelly voice, the vampire asked, "Why do you wait?" He seemed as startled by the sound of his own words as by her presence.

He must not have spoken out loud for years.

I don't know why. . . . Can't comprehend why . . .

The wind blew, making this high room in his darkened lair groan. Unseen gaps in the walls allowed a chill breeze in. As he stood, rising to his full, towering height, her shining blade caught the wavering light from a cluster of candles and reflected over him. His grave face was lean with harsh planes, and other females would consider it handsome. His black shirt was unbuttoned, displaying much of his chest and sculpted torso, and his pants were slung low at his narrow waist. The wind stirred his thick black hair and tugged at the tail of his shirt. *Very handsome. But then, sometimes the vampires I kill are.*

His gaze focused on the tip of her sword. Then as if the threat of her weapon was forgotten, he studied her face, his gaze lingering, it seemed, on each of her features. His blatant appreciation unsettled her, and she clutched the hilt of her sword tightly, something she never did. Honed to exquisite sharpness with her diamond file, her sword cut through bone and muscle with little effort. It swung perfectly from her loose wrist as though an extension of it—she'd never needed to hold it tightly.

Take his head. One less vampire. The species checked in the tiniest way.

Why did it want to die?

"What is your name?" His words were clipped like an aristocrat's, but held a Russian accent.

"Why do you want to know?"

"I would like to know the name of the woman who will deliver me from this."

"You assume I'll deliver your death blow?"

His lips curled at the corners, but it was a sad smile. "Will you not?"

Another tightening on the sword.

He leaned his towering frame against the crumbling wall. He truly wasn't going to raise a hand in defense. "Before you do, speak again, creature. Your voice is beautiful. As beautiful as your exquisite face."

She swallowed. "Why do you remain here in this castle . . . ?" She trailed off when he closed his eyes as though in bliss from hearing her voice. "The villagers live in terror of you."

That got him to open his eyes. They were full of pain. "I rightly own this place and so remain here. And I've never harmed them, other than frightening them." He turned away and murmured, "I wish that I did not frighten them."

"They say you live here alone."

He faced her and gave one sharp nod. She sensed he was embarrassed by this fact, as if he felt lacking that he didn't have a family here.

"How long?"

He hiked his broad shoulders, pretending a nonchalance she saw through. "A few centuries."

To live solitary for all that time? "The villagers have beseeched me to kill you," she said, as if she had to explain herself.

"Then I await at your leisure."

"Why not kill yourself, if that's what you want?"

"It's . . . complicated. But you save me from that end. I know you're a skilled warrior and will make this quick."

"How do you know what I am?"

"I used to be a warrior too, and your incredible sword speaks much."

The one thing she felt pride over—the one thing in her life she had left that she couldn't bear to lose—and he'd noted its beauty.

He lowered his voice. "Swing your blow. Know that no bad could come to you for killing one such as me. There is no reason to wait."

Frustration spiked in her. As if this was a matter of conscience. It wasn't. It couldn't be. She had no conscience. No feelings, no raw emotions. She was coldhearted—had been blessed after the tragedy to feel nothing. She didn't suffer from sorrow, from lust, from anger. Nothing got in the way of her killing. She was a perfect killer.

The eyes that had been pleading for an end, now narrowed. "Did you hear that? Are you alone?"

"I do not require help from others. Not for a single vampire," she said absently. Oddly, her attention had dipped to his body once more—to low on his torso, past his navel to the dusky trail of hair leading down. She had a flash image of her trailing the back of one of her claws along it, while his massive body shuddered in reaction.

Her thoughts were making her uneasy, making her want to wind her hair up into a knot and let the chill air cool her neck—

"Ah, angel, you seem to desire one thing from me that I'm unable to give you."

She jerked her gaze to his face. Caught ogling the prey! The indignity! *What is wrong with me?* She had no more sexual urges than the walking dead vampire before her. She shook herself, forcing herself to remember the last time she'd hesitated.

On a battlefield, an age ago, she had spared and released another of this ilk, a young vampire who had begged for his life.

Yet he had seemed to scorn her for her very mercy.

Without delay, the vampire had found her two full-blood sisters, fighting in the flatlands below them. Alerted by the shriek of another Valkyrie, Kaderin had sprinted, stumbling down a hill draped with bodies, living and dead. Just as she'd reached the flatlands, he'd cut her sisters down. The youngest, Dasha, had been caught off guard—because of Kaderin's panicked approach. The vampire had smiled when Kaderin dropped to her knees.

He'd dispatched her sisters with an efficiency Kaderin had emulated since that night. She'd like to say beginning with him, but she'd kept him alive for a time. . . .

So, why would she repeat the same mistake? She wouldn't. She would not forget a lesson she had paid so dearly to learn.

Squaring her shoulders, she steeled herself. *It's all in the follow-through.* Kaderin could see the swing, knew the angle she would take so that his head would remain on his neck until he fell. It was cleaner that way. Which was important. She'd packed her suitcase lightly.

As a young man, Sebastian Wroth had desired so many things from life, and having grown up wealthy among a large supportive family, he had expected them as his due. He'd wanted his own family, a home, laughter around a hearth, the luxury of giving a wife a surprise kiss behind her ear. . . . He'd been shamed to admit to this creature that he'd managed none of those things.

Half an hour ago, his only wants had been to kill his two older brothers and to die.

Now, Sebastian desired to gaze at this fascinating female just a little longer.

At first he'd thought her an angel come to set him free. She looked it. Her curling hair was so blond, it appeared almost white in the candlelight. Her eyes were fringed with thick black lashes and were dark like coffee, a striking contrast to her fair hair and wine-red lips. Her skin was flawless, light golden perfection, her features were delicate and finely wrought.

Fitting that hers would be the last face he looked upon while on this earth.

Yes, he'd thought her divine—until her avid gaze had strayed lower, and he'd realized she was very much flesh and blood. He'd cursed his useless, deadened body. He had no respiration, no heartbeat, no sexual ability. He could not take her, even though he thought . . . he thought this beauty might receive him.

The loss of sexual pleasure had never bothered him—until now. He lamented not being able to plunge into wetness, to watch her expression as she came beneath him. His eyes dropped to her slender neck, and then to her high, full breasts pressing against her dark blouse. He wished he could have kissed her breasts, run his face against them. . . .

"Why are you looking at me like this?" she asked in a baffled tone.

"Can I not admire you?" he asked, his voice sounding even more rough. "A dying man's last wish?"

"I know the ways a man looks at a woman." Her voice was so sensual, a voice from dreams. It seemed to rub him from the inside. "You're not merely *admiring* me."

No, he was thinking at that moment that he wanted to rip open her shirt, pin her shoulders to the ground, and lick her nipples till she came. Pin her shoulders *hard* and suckle her—

Suddenly, she gasped. "Your eyes are turning black."

But he scarcely heard her over the sudden explosion of sound. He swung his head around, his body tensing. *"What is happening?"*

She took a quick glance around her, eyes alert.

"You do not hear that?" Another explosion like that and this castle would collapse. He had to get her away. Even into the daylight outside. He *must* protect her—

Another explosion; he traced to just before her and her sword shot up, as fast as a blur. He snatched her wrist, but she struggled. Christ, she was strong, but he seemed to be more so than usual, more than he ever could have imagined. He pried the weapon from her wrist and tossed it to his bed on the floor. "Do not fight me. The roof is about to fall—"

"What are you talking about? What are you hearing?" She frowned, clearly listening for anything, then her eyes widened. "No, it can't be," she murmured as if in a daze. She stared at his chest in horror. "I am not a . . . *Bride*."

Bride. His jaw slackened. He remembered his brothers explaining that his body would come back alive when he found his Bride, his eternal wife. He'd always believed they'd lied to take away the bitter sting of all they'd robbed of him, including the death he'd craved.

Yet it was true. The sound he heard was his own heart beating for the first time since he'd been turned into a vampire. He nearly swayed when he inhaled deeply, breathing at last, after three hundred years.

His heartbeat grew stronger, faster, and his sudden erection shot tight and throbbing, pulsing with each beat of his heart. Pleasure seemed to course through his veins. He'd found his Bride—the one woman he was meant to be with for eternity—in this exquisite female?

And his body had woken for her.

But just as he was changing, so was she. He thought he saw silver flash in her glinting eyes. A tear dropped down her cheek. He couldn't stand to see her cry, felt like a knife was being plunged into his chest. He lay one palm on her slim shoulder, covering it. She flinched, but allowed the touch. He brushed her hair back and sucked in a ragged, unpracticed breath. Her ear was sharply pointed. His Bride was no human. He didn't know what she was, didn't care.

Brows drawn in confusion she patted the back of her hand against her cheek. She drew her hand down to see it was wet from a single tear. She stared in shock, first at the tear, and then at her sharply curling fingernails that were more like little claws.

"Please do not cry." He had a purpose now—to protect her, to care for her. "Tell me your name, Bride."

"Not a Bride to one of you. Never—"

"But you've made my heart beat," he rasped.

She hissed back, "You've made me *feel*." Waves of emotion seemed to flicker over her. The tears that had followed the first dried. Then she smiled, a heartrending curling of her lips. As quickly as it appeared, her smile faded. She shuddered violently, lowering her forehead to his chest from the force of it.

Just as his aching erection was becoming impossible to deny, she lifted her face, and her expression had changed once more. Her eyes grew intent on his face, and her tongue dabbed her plump bottom lip as she gazed at his mouth.

She was aroused. He didn't understand what was happening to her—nor to himself—

She laced her delicate arms around his neck, bringing their bodies together.

He groaned to feel her full breasts pressing against him. He'd suffered centuries without interaction with others, much less touch, and now he was feeling the most beautiful female, *his* Bride, in his arms. He feared he dreamed. His hands dropped to her tiny waist, squeezing, dragging her tightly against him. "Tell me your name."

As if in a trance, she said, "My name is Kaderin." Even the sound of her voice made his erection throb.

"Kaderin," he repeated, but the name didn't fit her. As he stared down into her eyes, he realized it was too cold, too formal for the fiery creature in his arms. "Katja," he rasped, brushing his thumb over her bottom lip. "*Katja*, I must kiss you."

At his words, her eyes went completely silver, and seemed unseeing. But her full red lips were glistening, beckoning him. He cupped the back of her head and drew her to him. He groaned when their lips touched; electricity seemed to prick and tease his skin. Nothing had ever felt so powerful, so *right*.

If it took becoming a vampire to have just this moment, he'd suffer it again.

"*More*," she moaned against his lips.

He clutched her tight in his arms, then somehow remembered himself and eased his hold.

Her claws bit into the back of his arms. "Don't hold back. I need more."

She needed more, needed *him* to give it to her. She was his. He wanted to roar with triumph. He had been despairing earlier, but no longer. The feel of her claws sinking deeper into him—as if she feared he would get away—was ecstasy. *She needs me*.

"Kiss me more, vampire. If you stop, I'll kill you."

He knew she meant this literally. So he did, tasting her tongue, teasing it, then claiming her mouth with a hot, wet kiss. He savored the feel of her slowly undulating her hips against him in time with each thrust of his tongue. He kissed her with all the passion long denied him, with all the hope that had been wrenched from him returning. He kissed this fiery creature until she panted and sagged against him.

He was losing control. Impulses came for him to do things to her body, wicked things, and he knew soon he would obey them. "I'll always give you more, until I die," he grated.

And now, for the first time in three hundred hellish years, Sebastian Wroth desperately wanted to live. . . .